VISIONS
NIG

VISIONS AND NIGHTMARES

RUTHLESS BOOK 3

D. J. Rintoul

For Thelma

All rights reserved. No part of this publication may be reproduced, stored in a retrieval system, or transmitted in any form or by any means electronic, mechanical, photocopying, recording, or otherwise without prior written permission from Podium Publishing.

This is a work of fiction. Names, characters, places, and incidents are either products of the author's imagination or used fictitiously. Any resemblance to actual events, locales, or persons, living, dead, or undead, is entirely coincidental.

Copyright © 2025 by Douglas James Rintoul

Cover design by Jack Nguyen

ISBN: 978-1-0394-6881-8

Published in 2025 by Podium Publishing
www.podiumentertainment.com

Podium

VISIONS AND NIGHTMARES

PROLOGUE

Claudius Galt wasn't sure, but he thought, as he caught his breath, that he might have soiled himself.

That's fine. Don't care right now. Even his thoughts were breathless.

He tried to suck air in as quietly as he could, though. He ignored the hot, wet pain radiating from the area on his back where the monster's claws had raked him. And he resisted the urge to peek out from the crevasse in the cave that he'd vanished into.

He'd only just barely managed to get out of sight of the dinosaur that was chasing him. If he poked his head out now, he thought he'd probably lose it.

Come on, man, he told himself. *Just stay calm. If you keep calm, you can wait this out—*

A clawing sound interrupted his train of thought. The unmistakable scrape of the Vorpal Velociraptor's talon against the stone of the cave chilled Claudius's blood.

No! God, please no! I just need a little more time. I'm so damn close. Please!

Claudius wasn't an especially religious man. He had gone to church when his parents had taken him as a boy. After he left home, he had stopped, just like most of his generation. He didn't exactly look down on religious people. He just wasn't part of their number. He still sort of passively believed in God, just in a completely noncommittal way.

But he'd found himself in the middle of an extended religious epiphany through the duration of Orientation.

Surely, this was the end of days foretold in the Book of Revelation. Since he and his family had arrived in this terrible place, they had been chased and harassed by a long line of monsters. From creatures that looked like giant insects to what Identify assured him were actual dinosaurs. These Vorpal Velociraptors seemed to be the final enemies in this place.

Either the Galts had been sent back in time to the prehistoric age, or God was bringing on the apocalypse, and He had judged them insufficiently faithful.

Per the timer that still ticked down in the corner of Claudius's vision, the ordeal was almost over. But if his siblings and father didn't make it, he felt in his gut that it would be because he personally had been faithless. Hadn't taken his beliefs seriously. Had barely spent any time on his knees in his whole adult life. He was only twenty-four, but still.

God knew.

His attention jumped back to his present predicament. He could hear the Vorpal Velociraptor stepping onto the ground just outside the crevasse. The clicking of the claws on the ground. The rustle of its feathers as it walked.

Claudius couldn't help himself: he whimpered, and he felt the warm trickle of urine roll down his thighs and down to his calves before seeping into his socks.

It seemed he hadn't vacated his bladder before after all.

The monster jammed its head into the crack where Claudius had hidden himself, and its eyes went wild with ferocious hunger. The yellow eyes locked onto his, and Claudius thought he was doomed. The beast snapped its jaws and stretched its neck, trying with all its might to reach its prey where Claudius shuddered and cringed with fear. But the monster's muscular body couldn't get very far into the crevasse.

The head stopped a foot away from Claudius's body. He knew it was too early to feel relieved, though. He'd had trouble cramming his body into the tight space at first too. It had taken determination, driven by fear, to force himself in; he'd suffered a claw strike to the back and witnessed the disembowelment of another human being to get that motivation.

And now, he was here, back literally pressed against a wall. He couldn't run; he could only trust in the inaccessibility of this place he'd chosen to hide.

God, please, please save me, he silently prayed, staring into the gaping maw. *I'll be Your most faithful servant forever.* But he remembered that God helped those who helped themselves. That was from the Bible, right? So, God might not show him any particular favor until he'd demonstrated that he was worthy in some way.

Undoubtedly, He was receiving similar entreaties from billions of people right now. Some of whom would have been better Christians than Claudius was.

I'll show I can help myself, Lord. I just have to survive a little longer, right?

There was only a short window of time left according to the countdown that had appeared at midnight when the ninetieth day began.

[00:01:48]

The Vorpal Velociraptor finally pulled back, and Claudius thought perhaps it had given up. Then it began clawing at the opening to the crevasse. To Claudius's shock, the long claws proved able to carve through stone fairly easily. They were apparently composed of something hard and sharp enough to slice rock like butter. Thick chunks of the stuff crumbled to the ground before his eyes.

In a few seconds, the monster was snapping at Claudius again, a few inches closer this time. When it became obvious it still couldn't reach him, the monster pulled back again to repeat its effort at widening the gap.

Claudius turned his head while he had a little breathing room. He looked deeper into the darkness that he'd forced himself into. He knew what he had to do now.

The one advantage he had—besides the fact that he was a being with a soul who fervently hoped that he might receive divine help, rather than a soulless monster—was that he was thin.

As the dinosaur cut itself a wider opening to attack through, Claudius wedged himself even deeper into the tight, dark hole.

He slid in past the point of discomfort. Beyond where the uneven stone began scraping and cutting into his skin. Until he felt it was more and more difficult for his lungs to expand, and the walls of the crevasse pressed into his ribs.

[00:00:28]

The Vorpal Velociraptor clawed and clawed, but it seemed unable to reach him in the limited time that remained.

Thank you, God! Thank you for sending me a hole so deep that this monster couldn't crawl into it after me.

Even as he watched the monster make its last efforts to shove its way in, his worries receded into the back of his mind. He had done it, as far as he was concerned. He had shown the lengths he would go to help himself. And surely God would reward him now.

Claudius spent the last moments of Orientation praying.

In a moment, which he blinked and just barely missed, he disappeared from the dark, cramped crevasse, inches away from the jaws of death. He reappeared in the mysterious white room he'd been in before his ordeal began.

"Oh, thank God!" Claudius exclaimed.

The clay figure that had explained the Orientation to him earlier stood in its same place in the room.

"Congratulations on surviving Orientation," it pronounced in a neutral voice. "Are you ready to take an inventory of the rewards you earned?"

"Yes, please," Claudius said. "No, wait! Could you please tell me if all my family survived the Orientation?"

"I apologize," the clay thing replied. "We cannot provide information about other participants, for privacy reasons. Now, about your rewards . . ."

In the end, Claudius just received a measly forty System Credits. He spent his meager winnings in the System Store to get a couple of Inferior Grade Health Potions. That was all he could afford. It hardly seemed worth the horrendous sacrifices he and those around him had made in the Orientation jungle.

But the point didn't seem to be to truly reward them. It was an ordeal. If Claudius was right, it was a test from God.

"Do you serve God?" Claudius asked. He had little hope that the clay person would give him a useful answer to any other question, but answering this one would seem like the least it could do.

"We do serve the gods, under the constraints imposed by—error! Error!" Those last two words came out with a strange staticky noise. Like interference on the radio. The figure slapped itself in the face twice, then returned to speaking as if nothing had happened. "I cannot answer that question with your level of clearance."

Did he say he served the gods? Good enough.

If there were gods, Claudius thought that his would be the biggest and strongest. He believed it almost as much as he desperately wanted and needed to believe it. His was the desperate faith of a child throwing himself on God's mercy.

Then Claudius was returned to Earth. He blinked and found himself on an Orlando street. Or what had once been an Orlando street. Because nowhere, as far as the eye could see, was there a traversable stretch of pavement.

The pavement and sidewalk were shattered, split by fissures and new hills and simple stretches of unpaved soil that he was certain hadn't been there before. In some places, he could see exposed piping that now led nowhere and carried nothing. Electrical lines lay dangerously across what remained of the streets where the power poles had toppled, though Claudius was all but certain the wires no longer carried power.

He had guesses as to what had happened. Claudius was no biblical scholar, but he thought he remembered something from the Book of Revelation about the Earth moving and lands shifting around.

For now, he focused on getting a grip on the physical reality confronting him.

What was left of the pavement was littered with broken glass and trash of all kinds, as well as heavily crowded with people. The mass of humans looked around with shoulders hunched like they expected to be attacked at any moment. Clearly, they had just returned from Orientation too.

The source of the glass was obvious. Everywhere Claudius looked, buildings had been moved or ruined. Almost all of them were further apart than they had been. Most of them were toppled. And the skyscrapers in particular had been utterly destroyed; most of them looked to have been knocked over like Jenga towers, their pieces scattered across the tabletop of the landscape.

Claudius kept one eye on the other people around him who had returned from Orientations of their own. He didn't recognize any of them from his Orientation, but that was unsurprising. The group that he and his family had joined to survive had figured out that they seemed to have been grouped by surname. A random collection of people on an Orlando street was unlikely to be largely comprised of people whose last names began with the letter *G*.

For now, the other people outside mostly eyed each other warily. They moved around slowly, cautiously. But he didn't expect that to hold.

Any moment now people would recognize the situation they were in. It was either the end of days or a natural disaster of some incomprehensible sort. Once these people grasped that, they would act like the dumb, panicky, dangerous animals that they always showed themselves to be in these emergency situations.

In hurricanes, in earthquakes, and sometimes even in the aftermaths of blackouts, people looted. They destroyed their own cities even when it wasn't a rational reaction to events. Claudius didn't want to get swept up in that.

Miraculously, as he turned to his right he saw that the building where he worked—where he had been working before the apocalypse hit, at least—was intact. Maybe it was because Orlando City Hall didn't stand quite so tall as some of the neighboring buildings. Even though one of the skyscrapers next to it had collapsed, and half of the fallen building now leaned dangerously into City Hall's south wall, the structure seemed stable.

It looked steady enough, at least, for Claudius to stick to the plan. He'd persuaded his father, Tiberius, and his brother and sister, Coriolanus and Julia, to meet at City Hall, where Claudius had worked security the last two years. It was a safe enough place to rendezvous, assuming that society wasn't devolving into wanton human-on-human violence just yet.

Safer than any of their workplaces now, certainly.

Tiberius was a lawyer who had been visiting Orange County Courthouse when the apocalypse scooped him up. Coriolanus and Julia both had office jobs that would have had them working in the skyscrapers that now littered the ground.

At least Claudius's old building was still standing. It was the only career success he could really boast relative to his siblings and his father.

He rushed up the steps, opened the front doors, walked around the metal detectors, and hopped the security barriers. No one to stop him. The lobby was deserted, as he'd expected.

If the System had said it was returning everyone to where they had been but dropped him outside, it stood to reason that the others in the lobby would also have ended up outside. Though there were only two others who'd been there that morning.

Emilia, the receptionist, and Oswaldo, the other security guy. When the

System spoke into all their heads, they'd called the building manager, who had warned everyone else who worked there not to come in that morning.

He hadn't seen Emilia or Oswaldo outside either, come to think of it.

They might both be dead now.

But Claudius didn't want to think about that. Not yet. And not while there was still hope that the cheery receptionist and the kind senior security guard would appear. There would be a time for mourning, but it wasn't now.

He walked over to the security station and made sure that his gun was there. He grabbed that, his uniform, his baton, and his walkie-talkie. You never knew what would come in handy in the end of days.

Then he went back to the front of the building and locked the big glass doors.

They didn't look like much, but they were supposed to be bulletproof. He would unlock them if and only if his family or someone he knew appeared out front. Emilia and Oswaldo had their own keys, and Claudius wasn't interested in dealing with the mob if he didn't have to.

While he stood at the doors, he took a last look at the slightly increased number of people on the ruined streets before he turned away.

Outside, people still weren't fighting, but Claudius saw some of them beginning to pick through the wreckage of the nearby stores, looking for something, anything of value, to take.

The looting would be in full swing soon enough, and it would be every man, woman, and child for themselves for the foreseeable future.

Claudius waited for his family with disciplined patience, trying to figure out if there was anything in City Hall that he could loot. It was the best distraction. The best way to keep himself from breaking down into sobs that wracked his whole body and despairing that he'd never see them again.

Don't think like that, he scolded himself. *They're all fine. Now, what should we take from here?*

It wasn't as if anyone else was going to ever use any of this stuff again if he didn't. Even most of the City Hall bigwigs were probably dead. Most of them would have keeled over from heart attacks if they had had to run half as much as Claudius had in the last ninety days.

Finally, he decided to break into the vending machines. He filled a couple of backpacks from the lost and found with junk food and sodas. Then he unplugged the vending machines. The building's emergency generator power was still functioning somehow despite whatever cataclysm had wrecked the city's infrastructure. Claudius didn't want to waste that power, even if it was going to go to waste anyway. Maybe someone would find some use for it.

After what felt like an interminable time, his family arrived—first his father, then his brother, and lastly the sister he'd been the most worried about. When they scolded her for taking the longest, she apologized and said she'd stopped to give a girl directions.

It felt surreal to think of Julia being a good Samaritan as anarchy erupted outside.

Where before people had looted tentatively, now they did it very openly. Some young punks had started lighting fires too. It was still a block or two away, but they could see the thick black smoke easily from where they stood in front of the glass doors. Wherever one fire started, another was sure to follow, unless someone came along to put it out and disperse the arsonists. People were good at following bad examples.

"I wish someone would come down here and restore order," Coriolanus said quietly, voicing what everyone else was thinking.

"I'm not sure if it will happen in our lifetime, son," Tiberius said in his usual stern, honest, gruff way.

"I have faith," Julia said, smiling sadly.

For a long time they all stared in silence as Orlando burned, until the sun went down, and the only light came from the fires.

CHAPTER ONE

Savior

Mina reached the bottom of the stairs.

The space around her was completely dark for a moment, and she turned her head automatically, looking, absurdly, for a light switch.

Then she felt a sudden whirlwind all around her, pulling at her clothes. Green flames sparked to life in the air above her head, then flew around the room lighting torches Mina hadn't seen in the darkness. As the torches lit, Mina was able to make out the shape of the room. It was a small chamber, lined with columns carved in the shapes of animals in a repeating pattern of three: one column in the shape of a dog's long body, one in the shape of a horse, and a third in the shape of a winding snake.

But her eye was drawn to a statue standing in the center of the room: a female figure with three bodies and heads, all connected from the back. The body closest to her held a stone torch in hand. She couldn't see if the other two bodies held objects in their hands, since the bodies further away from her were each facing a different direction.

So that no one can ever sneak up on her, Mina thought. Hecate was a goddess who could never be surprised. *Is that a metaphor for her role as a "gatekeeper"? Does it mean she can see the future maybe?*

The sound of music filled the silence. There were both voices and stringed instruments, though the song the voices constructed was a wordless wailing. Mina recognized the music only as vaguely Greek. An intense pressure made her heart race as the System's voice filled her ears.

[A goddess has descended to Orientation 0284722.]

The statue's eyes glowed green, and a female voice emanated from the area of the nearest head. It became apparent that the goddess had possessed the body of her statue, though it did not suddenly spring to life or move, aside from the eyes beginning to emanate light.

"**My dear child, it is such a pleasure to meet you at last.**" The voice felt ethereal and unreal, light but piercing, almost stabbing Mina in the heart. "**We have little time, yet knowing how way leads on to way, it is doubtful that we will ever cross paths again. We have much to accomplish together in this short span, you and I.**" The tone felt simultaneously intimate and formal, affectionate and melancholy.

"Goddess, the pleasure at our meeting is all mine," Mina said, bowing her head and curtsying awkwardly with her Mage's robes. She hoped her slightly stilted effort at formality would meet the Gatekeeper's expectations.

"**Be assured, you are not more pleased than I am, child. Much power has been expended so that this encounter could come to pass. My dear Charon traveled from another universe to participate and must return whence he came once our meeting is complete. I thought it necessary, to prevent the deaths of any humans who might be of value to you in the arena.**"

"I appreciate the effort you exerted on our behalf, goddess," Mina said. There were questions racing through her mind, but she didn't feel entirely safe asking any of them of a divine entity. Would she be smitten for impertinence?

Why hold the challenge at all if you were committed to making sure there were no consequences? Why are you so interested in me? What are you the goddess of, besides gates?

"**Congratulations on bringing your child across the threshold into this world,**" Hecate said. "**I had intended that you would complete this challenge before he crossed that boundary so that I could extend my blessing to the both of you, but fate is difficult to direct and often tragic. The strings of causality play themselves out according to many influences.**"

Mina nodded her head, pretending she understood. Were all deities this cryptic? And did they often fail to accomplish desired goals, as Hecate seemed to be saying she had?

It made Mina uneasy to think that gods and goddesses existed but were fallible. That wasn't the religion she'd grown up with. Even though her lapsed Orthodox Christian faith hadn't been much use to her in the pre-System times, she at least preferred the predictable world of a God who always had a plan, and bent all things toward it, over deities who could fail.

And what happens if two deities' goals are in conflict? Hecate seemed to be raising that possibility with her comment about the influences on the strings of causality.

"Thank you for your kind words," she made herself say. "Would it be too impertinent if I were to ask you questions, mighty and venerable goddess?"

Mina's cringing words almost made her wince. But she wanted to show nothing but humility in front of a being who Mina suspected could erase her existence or help her a great deal, as the mood took her.

"Please be at ease, child. I will satisfy your curiosity as best I can within our limited time."

Was it just Mina, or was Hecate putting a bit of emphasis on the word "limited"?

"Thank you, goddess." Mina smiled brightly. "You mentioned that you would have preferred that I complete the challenge while I was still pregnant so that you could bless me and my child. Is there something that prevents you from blessing both of us now?"

"Before, your two strands of fate were inextricably linked. Now, they run independently. Either may fray and fracture without destroying the other."

Mina swallowed. That felt like a negative prediction about either her or her child's future. She reminded herself that Hecate had framed it as a possibility, not a certainty.

"It is possible, of course, that James Jr. may earn his own blessings in the future, should that interest him," Hecate went on. "For the moment, it is you who has earned my blessing, and it brings me great joy to offer it."

And she did seem to speak the words with genuine pleasure.

[You have been offered the Title of Blessed One of Hecate. Accept? Y/N]

"Goddess, I am unworthy of this favor," Mina said, trying to stall while she parsed the meaning of becoming a Blessed One of Hecate.

Will I have to fight for Hecate in the event of a religious war? She already knew Cara's god had a Chosen One in their Orientation from the proctor's statement to that effect.

"You have richly earned it. But is there some other concern that troubles you, child?"

"There is," Mina admitted. "I am concerned that I may not live up to the obligations that accepting such a gift would incur. For instance, if my family or friends were to receive a blessing that was in some form of conflict with yours." Her voice trailed off lamely, but the goddess seemed to take her words in stride.

"Between the god who has blessed your husband and me, there is no conflict at present," Hecate said. "Nor do I anticipate that a future clash is likely during your lifetime. I would not expect you to betray your own family for the favor of your distant patroness."

There it was, then. James had already accepted a blessing, and it wasn't a god who Hecate hated. The goddess's reassurance was a relief. Not that she'd imagined for a moment that James could have died in his Orientation. *Of course he's already received a blessing. I always knew he was capable of great things. It's nice to hear that someone else recognized it.*

Then she processed what Hecate's statement meant for her present situation. *Given this information, if I turned her down, I would just be rejecting help and insulting her.*

She selected "Y."

A green light flickered around Mina's body, and the sound of the music from earlier began to play again, albeit much softer this time.

[**Required conditions met. Title obtained: Blessed One of Hecate!**]

[**Patron deity Hecate has granted additional Titles: Elementalist, Spellweaver, and Necromancer.**]

Mina felt somehow more solid. A pleasant but confusing sensation. Her body wasn't in any perceptible way heavier or more muscular than it had been. Her Mana reserves weren't any greater. But she felt *strong* in some indefinable way that she hadn't before.

That last Title feels slightly ominous . . .

"With that decision, we must move a little more quickly, dear child." Hecate's voice was soft but firm, pulling Mina back out of her head. "**We have burned through much of Charon's Mana, while he holds the space outside of here still. Once the challenge unfreezes, your Orientation will begin counting down to its end. When the timer for the end expires, you will be pulled away from this plane and back to your Earth.**"

"I understand, goddess. What should we do next?"

"**I am honored primarily as a goddess of magic,**" Hecate replied. "**We should discuss your future development in that sphere.**"

There followed a discussion in which Hecate attempted to quickly explain the basic elements of multiple different forms of magic and types of magic users. She covered the differences between Witches, Archmages, Sorceresses, Summoners, and Spiritualists.

Basically, Witches learned magic from books to replicate and innovate on uses of Mana developed by magic-wielders from ages past. Archmages were just like Mages, manipulating elemental magic, but operated on an ever-growing scale. Sorceresses relied on intuition and experimentation to achieve similar results to Witches; they were parallel types of magic users, with one emphasizing intuition and creativity and the other emphasizing book-learning and intelligence. Summoners brought forth entities from other realms to fight on their behalves. And Spiritualists harnessed the powers of spirits, as the name implied.

With the lecture done, Hecate dropped leaves from one of the hands of the statue. It was outside of Mina's field of view, but there was nowhere else the leaves could have been hidden. For the next part of her instruction, she told Mina to pick one of the leaves up.

"**Now, infuse the leaf with your Mana, without attempting to use a particular element,**" Hecate ordered.

Mina did as instructed, and the leaf suddenly burst into flames. She felt an instinctive urge to drop it, but the fire didn't seem to be burning her hands at all—only the leaf. So, Mina just stared, fascinated, until the leaf burnt to a crisp and the flames died out in her hands.

"Most impressive," Hecate cooed. **"This only makes your performance in the challenge all the more remarkable! To be so skillful at such a young age with the element of water when your most natural affinity is actually for fire is quite something, my child."**

Mina stood a little more proudly at the praise from this goddess of magic.

Hecate seemed to be about to say something else, when Mina felt the air shift slightly. It was barely perceptible, but it took her out of the moment and made her turn to see if someone had entered the room. There was no one.

[**Hidden victory conditions met! Orientation participant Mina Danailova has conquered the final challenge remaining within this Orientation! Due to above-normal performance, the remaining Orientation population is permitted to survive. Prepare to be returned to Earth.**]

[00:03:00]

[00:02:59]

[00:02:58]

"**It seems that Charon reached the limits of his body,**" Hecate said. She sounded neither displeased nor surprised.

"I hope you feel that the time you invested was worthwhile, goddess," Mina said, inclining her head respectfully again.

"**I only wish we could spend more,**" Hecate replied. **"The last thing I wanted to tell you about your magic is that you may wish to focus on developing your abilities with fire. If that is your most natural affinity, then it will always be a particular strength of yours, no matter how much else you learn."**

Mina hesitated, then decided to raise one final question.

"If you could give me any further advice, for the benefit of me and my family, what would you recommend I do going forward?" she asked.

"**A broad question,**" Hecate remarked. **"Just broad enough that I hope I may answer it usefully. Keep your family together. As a unified whole, you are strong. Isolated, even the strongest stick is easily broken. You will also want to seek out magical artifacts, regardless of which Class path you choose. Although your world is newly integrated into the System, there will be some ancient artifacts available, in part because monsters often possess unique, one-of-a-kind items. And one last thing. If you believe that your baby may one day be interested in following in your footsteps, I have a gift for you to pass on."**

She directed Mina's attention to an object the statue held in one of its pairs of hands. Tentatively, Mina reached up and took it. A small, ivory-white key. She wanted to Identify it, but she thought that doing so in front of the statue of Hecate would be blasphemous in some way.

Instead, she bowed her head, and the two women said their farewells.

Mina heard the vaguely Greek music playing again and saw the green flames go out, first in the torches that lined the room and then in the eyes of the goddess. Finally, she felt the pressure that Hecate's presence generated dissipate.

Then Mina turned and ran up the stairs, back out to the field. Her mind was still racing with the new knowledge she'd gained, and she worked to commit it to memory.

Finally, as she stepped out from the underground, Mina stopped focusing on her conversation with the goddess. She instantly received an alert.

[Required conditions met. Title obtained: Savior!]

I guess I really helped a lot of people, she thought, allowing herself a smile. *Maybe I changed the way this Orientation was meant to go for the better. What was it that the proctor said at the beginning? The expected survival rate was something less than fifty percent for this type of Orientation, right?*

She could see the crowd looking at her from the stands, and people were beginning to shout kind words. The people who had competed in the previous challenge before her were all revived and fully healed, and they were saying their piece too.

"Thank you!"

"You saved us!"

"You did it!"

Charon, sitting in his perch atop the stadium, looked down at the scene, seemingly rather pleased. Mina guessed that he had already explained to everyone else where Mina was and exactly what had happened. If he was like his mistress, he thought highly of her, for reasons she did not yet fully understand.

She shook her head. That didn't matter right now. Something to figure out later.

Mina glanced at the timer, ever-present in the corner of her vision.

[00:01:08]

Then she picked up speed and began running toward where Yulia and Leo waited, walking down from the stands to meet her with cautious smiles on their faces. She wanted to finish Orientation beside them.

I need to ask the proctor for my baby back, she thought.

Everything was finally safe. For now.

Soon they would be home. The Earth might not be safe anymore either, considering that the goddess had mentioned there would be monsters she could obtain magic items from. But she would face that with her husband.

Mina thought that she and James could accomplish just about anything together.

CHAPTER TWO

The Last Moment

James walked up to speak with the people he'd just saved from death—or worse. They greeted him with a cacophony of praise.

"Thank you for saving us!"

"That was amazing."

"You rescued us again."

"Thank you, James!"

The survivors were all happy to see him still standing, alive and apparently well, though several of them were unsurprisingly more preoccupied with healing their wounded than acknowledging their savior.

"Anyone else need healing?" James asked. "I still have some fuel in the tank."

Those who weren't already healing friends or loved ones looked around at each other and then shook their heads or responded with verbal noes.

A couple of Healers looked up from their charges only to say, "I got this," or, "No worries."

And no one actually looked critically injured. The few people who were in the midst of being healed weren't in danger of death. They were concussed or bleeding badly, but not badly enough to die while receiving magical healing as they were.

James had seen the sorts of injuries that it took to produce that result, back when he had fought the wolfpack. He remembered the dead woman's face, then forced it from his mind.

Maybe I could take a moment and actually heal my hand. The blackened, slightly smoky ruin of the left half of his left hand was still agonizingly painful.

But then James noticed Sierra, who was ominously silent. She looked up from where she sat, slumped against the trunk of the tree she'd been tied to, and gave him a weak nod and a very faint smile. Her face was drenched in sweat.

He looked down and realized that she was using Laying on Hands to regrow a severed hand.

Wow. She's surprisingly tough. I remember when we did that for Cliff, and he passed out from pain.

"Do you want help?" he asked.

"I—ah—got it," she breathed. "You've got problems of your own." She tilted her head at his maimed hand.

James glanced down at it again and winced.

"Just a scratch," he forced himself to say, smiling. It looked even worse than it felt. But he knew that the appearance was more reliable than his body's sense of pain. The hand reminded him of Camila's necrotic flesh when he first met her. The skin around his ring looked dead.

It might be better to cut it off and grow a whole new one, he thought.

And was it just his imagination, or had the affected area grown slightly? James's memory had improved a great deal, so he dragged up the image of his hand from a minute or so before, when he'd last examined it closely.

But no. When he compared the images, there didn't seem to be any difference. It must have just been a trick of the light or something up with his eyes for a moment.

James decided he'd talk to the Rodriguezes for the last few minutes of Orientation.

No, wait, why did I specifically check on Sierra before? He remembered now. *I needed her to use that Skill of hers on Damien and Luna!*

But she probably needed all the Mana she could spare for her arm.

She caught him glancing down at her again and cocked an eyebrow at him, as if to say, *What?*

"A couple of our people were infected with some kind of medical issue by the undead we just killed," he said in answer to her unspoken question. "I was hoping to get you to use your Skill on them. The one that removes foreign influences."

She started to rise to her feet, a little unsteadily, but he raised a hand to signal that she should stop.

"No. If we have to go, I'll carry you. You can't walk the distance in the condition you're in, and I can move much faster, anyway. Seems like time is a factor." He tilted his head to the lower left, to indicate where the timer should be in her field of vision.

She nodded, allowed herself to slump back down—and stopped healing her arm. It was just as he'd imagined. She was low on Mana, so she was conserving it in case the group needed her. *She's a much better team player than I figured.* But he really preferred not to let her sit there partially regenerated, with a stump for a hand, for longer than absolutely necessary.

He sent a telepathic message to his wolves. *How are Luna and Damien—that's the human I left with you—doing? I killed all of the enemies here, including the ones who infected them. Do they seem any better?*

A response came quickly.

Yes, my king. The smell of the corruption seems to have vanished from their bodies. Also, the Werewolf awakened when the System announcement came. He said, "I knew he could do it," before he passed out again. Both of them are healing well.

So, Sierra didn't need to save her Mana after all. And they didn't need to make a literal last-minute rush from the scene of battle to where Damien and Luna had fallen. He told Sierra as much, and then he thanked the wolfpack.

"You know, you're more responsible than I thought," she said. The words sounded begrudging, and James sensed a deeper respect underneath the surface of what she'd said. Perhaps the real meaning was something like, *You're not a half bad leader.* Then again, maybe that was just his preferred interpretation.

After that, she focused all her attention on finishing her regeneration.

James turned to the Rodriguezes and opened a discussion about plans for the future.

"So, what do you guys want to do when you get back to Earth?"

There was a flurry of answers, including a more than healthy amount of speculation about what condition they'd find the Earth in upon their return.

They only had time for a few snippets of conversation, though.

[00:00:53]

The timer was winding quickly through its last minute. As it drew close to the end, James used one final Skill—an ability that would, as Anansi had suggested, become his bread and butter. For now, he infused his dead skin cells with Mana to create a pair of Skin Cell Dust Devils. He pressed the creatures into the hands of Ramon Rodriguez and one of the members of Damien's group who had been kidnapped alongside them.

"They're basically walkie-talkies," he explained quickly. "They're connected to me telepathically. They'll help you find me back in the real—back on Earth."

The member of Damien's group, a young man with East Asian features, smiled and accepted the weird little ball of constantly shifting cells. Ramon shook his head in disbelief at the strange gift, but he also accepted the creature. Across the swamp, James's last remaining Skin Balloon was closing in on Moishe Rose. Hopefully, it would reach him and help him find James after Orientation.

There were other people who he wanted to help find him. Alan and Mitzi, of course. Damien. Hilda Rohm, in spite of her participation in the Moloch cult.

She had more than proven her worth. The trackers who had helped him catch up to the wolf king and his pack.

Really, he wanted everyone who'd played a part in this journey to come find him. James would keep them safe. Gradually, he hoped, he would make the world safe. But he wanted those who had helped him at the outset of his journey to reap their just rewards.

There were so many people who were deserving of his protection. His gratitude. His loyalty.

How many of them would be able to survive if they didn't find him on Earth? Anansi had indicated that any monsters that didn't die during Orientation would reappear on Earth. Some of James's weaker allies would surely be killed without his power shielding them.

But he could only reach a few. He wasn't sure exactly which tent Alan and Mitzi were in, while Moishe was outdoors, standing watch. With less than a minute to find a human to guide, he had been the one James's remaining Skin Balloon had seen.

At least the wolfpack shouldn't have any trouble. They would still be bonded to him telepathically, after all.

Nevertheless, it was a frustrating situation. James had saved these people's lives again and again. He hated the idea of them being ripped away from him and their loved ones just because he couldn't reach them in time. Each and every one of them was a valued asset. A valuable future resident of the country that James would build in the wreckage that this apocalypse would make of the once proud United States of America.

But that was a thought for the future.

James tore his attention away from his imagined losses for long enough to infuse Mana into his horribly scorched left little finger.

The blackened bit of flesh and bone began to spring to life even before James had separated it from his body, although he quickly rectified that. He bit through the knuckle connecting it to his hand. He was getting sloppy, not severing this body part before it sprang to life.

But these were his final moments in this place. He didn't have time to be precise.

He spat the finger out into the palm of his good hand. He ignored the blood slowly trickling out of the torn stump of his maimed hand. Instead of looking at that, he looked at the people he'd saved.

Without a word, he stuck out his hand, offering the severed finger to different people in turn. A couple of them appeared disturbed by its appearance, despite all that they'd seen.

But James thought that someone would have sense enough to want it.

Many of the people in Damien's group in particular hadn't come from the same general area when they were transported to Orientation. One person in that group having a way of reaching James didn't mean they all did.

First one person, then another shook their heads. A few looked disgusted, but most of them just looked around as if they thought someone else among them was more worthy.

Yet no one stepped forward.

James offered it to Sierra.

She responded with a quick shake of the head, and he realized he had expected that from her.

"Good luck," he mouthed. Despite her physical weakness, he thought she might do well making her own way in the world. Somehow or other. Despite her untrusting attitude, she was a good team player. The way she'd handled the last few minutes proved that wasn't just an act. She was a scrappy survivor type, he thought. With just enough empathy and care for others that the people around her would want to keep her alive too.

And most importantly, now, neither of them would have to worry about the other.

James sincerely wished her well.

He thought she smiled.

Then he turned away again, still holding the severed piece of his hand outstretched, still confident that someone would seize the lifeline no matter how grotesque it might look. And finally, a member of Damien's group eagerly pushed himself forward from among the others. He grasped the Scorched Flesh and Bone Golem, seizing it as if it were a winning lottery ticket. Which, in a very real sense, James thought it was.

He didn't know the name of the man who'd snatched the severed finger and barely remembered the face. It was an incredibly ordinary face. Almost instantly forgettable.

But not the man's eyes. In the moment when James's eyes met the man's, it felt a little bit as if he was locking gazes with a zealous religious believer. Someone who had been handed the bones of an extraordinary figure with the power to bless or preserve them, like a saint. Which, in a very real sense, James thought he probably was.

Then he blinked, and he was back in the pure white room he had visited before Orientation.

Time ran out, he thought. *Just when I'd done everything I could.*

"Hi, Sisco," James said, smiling like the cat that just ate the canary.

CHAPTER THREE

The White Room

"You returned," the System Homunculus said dully.

"Was there ever any doubt?" James replied. He was very pleased to be back. Not primarily because he got to see Sisco again.

Looking down at his hand, he confirmed what he'd felt on his arrival: it was fully healed.

"I suppose not," Sisco replied. He sounded distinctly unenthusiastic. When James had first appeared in the pure white room, he couldn't read the System Homunculus's emotions well, because its face was non-expressive and its voice nearly monotone. Now, however, he detected a richness of expression in the artificial life-form's tone of voice that had escaped him before. Between that and the creature's body language, a clear picture emerged.

There, there, Sisco, James thought. *There, there. I know you're not happy to see me again, but I'll be gone soon enough.*

"Congratulations on your success in Orientation," the homunculus said. "Are you ready to take an inventory of the rewards you earned?"

The words were just pro forma, James recognized. Sisco's mouth was already half-open, ready to list out the aforementioned rewards.

"Actually, I would like to go through Job Evolution first," James said. If his experience with Class Evolution and Race Evolution was any indicator, that would come with a significant power boost. And he didn't want to give the System Homunculus any chance to return him to Earth, to face who knew how many threats, before he'd done it.

Then he reminded himself of what he'd learned about the System Homunculi from his conversation with Mina. It seemed they had some control over how much time their guests got to spend in the white space, like DMV employees or other petty government bureaucrats. So, it was incumbent upon him to play nice. "Is that all right with you, though?" James added.

From his body language, Sisco looked a bit taken aback to be asked at all. "Do you actually care?" he finally said.

James manipulated his face into a sheepish, contrite expression. "Well, yeah, I do," he said. "Sorry for my inconsiderate behavior when we last met. I disregarded what your traditions were and just did my own thing."

"Well, these rewards aren't going to take too long," the homunculus said, "even though you received more than anyone else in your Orientation, and you're one of the top few hundred humans on Earth. You might as well figure out your next Job. Go ahead!"

It's weird. I feel like after having a bit of friction with him earlier, then making up with him now, I got at a bit more of Sisco's humanity—though that's probably the wrong word. But I have another little piece of what it is that makes him tick.

"All right," he said aloud. "I'm going for it!"

James called up the prompt that had appeared before him for Job Evolution before, and he selected "Y." As with the Class Evolution, a list of options populated. He found himself pleased with the contents.

[Strategos]
[Crimson King]
[Scheming King]
[Fisher King]
[Story King]

I like how many of them include the word "King." But I'll start with Strategos. Sounds Greek. He was actually fairly certain he'd heard the word before. If he had seen it in context, he was sure he'd know the definition.

[Strategos: An evolved Job. A civil and military leader who rules by consent of the governed. Proficient in persuasion, strategy, and all the competencies of battle. This Job receives experience when forces under the Strategos's command defeat an enemy, or the Strategos obtains another sentient lifeform's allegiance. With each level, gain +2 Agility, +2 Strength, +1 Stamina, +2 Dexterity, +3 Perception, +3 Will, +3 Intelligence, +6 Charisma.]

Very nice, he thought. Maybe a little unbalanced in favor of Charisma, but James was planning to emphasize getting others to do his fighting for him going forward. There was just one problem.

"Rules by consent of the governed," huh? Those words raised an instant flag.

Pre-System, James had probably believed in the value of a people's self-rule as much as anyone. But he'd been convinced from day one of the System's arrival that democracy was basically over. There were no elections in the apocalypse.

Not realistically. Who would count the votes? Why would the strongest people let the weakest have a real voice? A spirit of charity?

Now that James thought about it, he was pretty sure he remembered that there had been multiple strategoi in ancient Athens, and they had decided strategy by majority vote. *And what kind of garbage is that? Sounds like a really shitty command structure. No wonder they lost to Sparta in the end.* He also vaguely remembered something about the Athenians putting their less successful strategoi to death after at least one battle. *Nope.*

He put a mental asterisk by the option, to indicate that it was somewhat intriguing but unrealistic. Then he moved on.

[Crimson King: An evolved Job. A brutal autocratic leader who rules through fear, manipulation, and might. Proficient in intimidation, espionage, and slaughter. This Job receives experience when the Crimson King causes conflict and destruction, whether to enemies or to allies. With each level, gain +3 Agility, +4 Strength, +3 Stamina, +2 Dexterity, +2 Perception, +3 Will, +2 Intelligence, +3 Charisma, +2 Stealth.]

Well, that doesn't suit me at all! As much as I've been enjoying fighting, I certainly don't go out of my way to create conflict or cause destruction. In particular, the idea of getting experience from his own allies' suffering rubbed James the wrong way. *If anything, I've been a force for order in the world and unity among humanity ever since the nature of reality got flipped on its head. Next!*

[Spider King: An evolved Job. A plotting, scheming leader who rules by relying on wits over force and remaining one step ahead of political opponents. Proficient in deception and strategy, with a great capacity for coalition building. This Job receives experience when the Spider King successfully deceives others, obtains additional political influence, or forges a new alliance. With each level, gain +2 Dexterity, +4 Perception, +4 Will, +4 Intelligence, +6 Charisma, +4 Stealth.]

A complete emphasis on non-physical Stats, huh? It was an interesting and very different option, and it fit much more into the role that James imagined for himself in the new world that he expected to see when he returned to Earth.

So, that's a solid option. It had surprisingly little to do with spiders, considering the name. Given that James already had plenty of connections with spiders in his life, that was a point in its favor. He moved onto the next one.

[Fisher King: An evolved Job. A ruler with a profound connection to his territory and its peoples. Capable of exercising a deep influence over others and over the physical environment itself through means both physical and mystical. This Job receives experience when the Fisher King successfully expands or improves upon controlled territory and life-forms. With each level, gain +4 Will, +4 Perception, +4 Stamina, +4 Fortitude, +4 Charisma, +4 Stealth.]

James felt a gentle tug at his arm as he read that Job description. As if the Job were pulling him in. Then he realized the pull was literal. He looked down at the Soul Eater Orb that had transformed itself into an armband.

You have an opinion? James asked.

I like that one, the equipment replied immediately in its creepy voice. *Suits us.*

James suppressed a shudder. It was much more off putting to hear the voice of the Soul Eater in his head—now that his adrenaline was back to normal—than it had been earlier.

But he thought that Roscuro was correct. *It really does suit us. I can easily imagine a synergy with the Skills I got from the Soul Eater. And the Monster Generation Skill that Anansi was pushing me to use, for that matter. Expanding or improving upon controlled territory and life-forms gives experience, after all.*

Still, he would look at the last one. Maybe it would be the best, as Predator in Human Skin had been.

[Story King: An evolved Job. A ruler who controls followers through control of information and dissemination of ideas. Capable of exerting influence that cannot be contained by physical borders. A spiritual or philosophical ruler whose hold on others may outlive the Story King's own body. This Job receives experience when the Story King gains traction in another sentient life-form's mind or reaches a new audience. With each level, gain +3 Dexterity, +6 Perception, +4 Will, +5 Intelligence, +6 Charisma.]

"Hm." James was divided. This last Job seemed like exactly what Anansi would want for him, but he wasn't sure. It would certainly have suited Anansi himself. But was James really a philosopher king? *I'm not sure I'm that deep, honestly. And compared with sheer power, would a story or an ideology actually be enough to make people follow me? When the world is so dangerous?*

"Ahem," Hester said quietly from behind his ear.

James had forgotten she was there. Frankly, he was quite surprised that the System had brought her with him.

He looked away from his System screen and realized Sisco was also looking at him curiously. *Oh, they both want me to tell them what's going on!* So he explained what his Job options were, in detail, to both Hester and the homunculus.

Before long, Sisco was nodding along with interest. Then he and Hester began voicing their opinions.

"I have tended to see excellent results from humans who chose the Crimson King option," the homunculus offered.

James winced.

"I can understand why you might not like it, though," Sisco hastened to add. "Some Jobs are really not for everyone. All of the 'king' Job options are extremely powerful and exclusive, so they are all equally worthy of consideration."

James nodded. *He basically ruled out Strategos, then.*

"I know that Lord Anansi would be thrilled if you chose either Spider King or Story King," Hester said. She was standing on top of James's head and speaking openly rather than hiding, for a change. She seemed to be enjoying getting James's and Sisco's attention.

"Ah, but he isn't here," James said. "What do *you* think?"

"I think it's an intensely personal decision," she said after only a slight pause, "and I hope you won't pick either one. No, I don't *believe* you'll pick either of those, because you prefer to chart your own course. Naturally, I fully support your decision. Your independent streak is part of what my Lord admires, anyway. You won't want to lean too hard even into the abilities that you're developing at his recommendation."

"That is one consideration," James admitted. "I don't like the idea of being under anyone's thumb. Hester, you already know I like and trust Anansi and don't mean him any offense."

"Yes, I do, sir."

There seemed to be a "but" somewhere near the end of that sentence from the way she spoke, but James decided not to ask what she was thinking. If she wanted to share, she would.

"My Soul Eater Orb had an opinion," James said. "It wanted me to choose Fisher King."

"Not as reliant on Charisma as Strategos, Spider King, or Story King," Sisco observed. "Certainly not nearly as likely to stir the ire of others as Crimson King, for all that Job's positives. A well-balanced choice. Ideally suited to conquering and holding land, if that was something important to you."

So, this is the conversation I could have been having with him if I'd been nice last time, James thought. *Note to self: even when everyone starts to see me as someone important, it's important that I remember to be nice.*

"Is balance to be desired in a Job choice?" James asked.

"Well, you chose a Class focused on sheer aggression," the System Homunculus said. "If you wanted to double down on that, the best choice of Job would be Crimson King. If you wanted to go in the opposite direction, more diplomatic, you would choose Spider King or Story King. Strategos and Fisher King are the more balanced options that have synergies with your Class but are not opposed to it by nature."

"But you haven't steered him toward the Strategos Job at all," Hester observed. "Is there a reason why?"

Taking the words right out of my mouth, Hester, James thought.

"Any Job that appears at the first Evolution that lacks the 'king' or 'queen' modifier is simply inferior to the Jobs that have those modifiers," Sisco replied simply. "I cannot recommend choosing an inferior option."

That makes sense. Coincidentally, it also offers slightly fewer Stat points than the 'king' options, which each offer twenty-four points per level. The same as my Class.

"I think I've made my decision," James said. "Thank you both for your contributions."

The System Homunculus nodded. "Choose, then, and we can move on to the rewards."

James selected Fisher King, and his eyes widened as knowledge poured into his brain.

CHAPTER FOUR

The Fisher King, Part 1

James's knowledge of power seemed to expand in the moments after he took the Fisher King Job. How to get it, how to keep it, how to use it . . .

It was surprising to learn so much when he hadn't even chosen one of the Job options that emphasized manipulating sentient life-forms. Perhaps the knowledge that king-type Jobs gave was standardized.

But no. He felt more information trickling into his brain about land and his new relationship with it: how he could enhance it, make it flourish, and reshape it in a manner of his choosing. This had to be a fairly specialized package. He felt a rising excitement.

I hope no one else picked Fisher King, he thought. *The potential of this Job is insane. The description doesn't nearly do it justice.* His eyes crinkled as his lips curled into a greedy smile. *I could rule the whole world eventually!*

Even as knowledge filled his mind, System alerts popped up in front of him. James was extremely proficient in dividing his attention now, so he read the alerts while he pored over the new knowledge.

[You obtained the Job Fisher King!]

[Talent obtained: Fisher Land Management!]

[Talent obtained: Fisher Sentient Resources!]

[Talent obtained: Genius Loci!]

From the knowledge pouring into his head, James already knew what the Talents did. He read the descriptions anyway.

[**Fisher Sentient Resources: The Fisher King enjoys a special relationship with his people. They rise and fall with him, and they identify with him to** an increasing degree. The reciprocal relationships between the Fisher King, his people, and his land are the root of his influence in the world. Make your people into your power. Generates Skills Blessing of the Fisher King and Goodwill of the Fisher King.]

No one tell the gods that I can grant blessings of my own now, James thought. Though he was sure that *his* version of a blessing would be more limited in a variety of ways, it still felt subtly blasphemous and potentially heretical toward some faiths, which he liked. Most of the gods he'd crossed paths with were far from his favorite people. Barring Anansi, there hadn't been a single good god or goddess in his path. They ought to be taken down a peg or two.

He read the Skill description that came with the Talent.

[Blessing of the Fisher King: Touch a life-form with your power and join your fates together. Imbue it with power and benevolent wishes; if the life-form does not resist, these will guide and shape its fate. As long as the life-form remains loyal to the Fisher King, its fortunes rise and fall with those of the king.]

Holy shit. This might actually be better than the way a god blesses something . . .

He read the Goodwill of the Fisher King Skill too. It passively increased attachment and goodwill between the king, the residents of his land, and the land itself over time.

[Fisher Land Management: The Fisher King enjoys a special relationship with his land, which gives him unique advantages in developing his territory or simply operating out of it. The Fisher King is the land to a great degree. The two have a mutually reinforcing symbiotic relationship. Generates Skills Affinity of the Fisher King and Aura of the Fisher King.]

Affinity of the Fisher King was a Skill to passively transform ambient Mana in the king's territory. Essentially, the Mana in the air of James's territory would act as an additional Mana meter for him to draw from. Aura of the Fisher King was a Skill to help flora and fauna grow on his land and increase the effectiveness of efforts to improve the land, though it stated it was dependent on the king's own condition.

[Genius Loci: The Fisher King enjoys a one-of-a-kind relationship with his territory, which can foster unique developments in that land. When a place falls under the Fisher King's rule, it begins to adopt his own Intelligence and Will, acting as an independent extension of himself from the physical to the non-physical. Make your home a part of you. Generates Skills Intelligence of the Fisher King and Will of the Fisher King.]

Intelligence and Will of the Fisher King were perhaps the most interesting Skills and the ones he was most curious to see in practice. Essentially, the Fisher King's spirit became the spirit of the land. It would begin to act on its own, following the patterns of his Intelligence and Will.

Which sounded scary and cool.

"Are you ready for your rewards now?" Sisco asked.

James snapped back to the present. He had almost forgotten where he was, due to the intensity of his interest in his new powers. He focused back on the homunculus.

"Yep," James replied, although for once he felt that he'd been rewarded quite enough. He flashed a big smile, and he could see the System Homunculus trying to return the expression with his almost completely immobile face.

"Excellent. You achieved top marks across all categories and were in the top fraction of a percent among performers for humanity."

"For humanity?" James couldn't resist interjecting. "Do you mean for Earth?"

"No, the monsters are graded on a different scale," Sisco replied. "You're not directly comparable."

Oh. James felt a little uneasy at that. *Did every Orientation have something as deadly as you?* he transmitted to the Soul Eater.

I would hardly know, Roscuro replied. *I was sucked from my universe into your Orientation. In my world, we heard from our ancestors about such things as Orientation and the early days of the System. But its workings and existence were something we took for granted. The world had settled into a sort of equilibrium following the post-Orientation crises. Now I wish I had a clearer memory of history classes. I cannot help you with this one. Perhaps the homunculus knows.*

But James didn't want to ask Sisco directly. The System Homunculus was already talking again. Perhaps James could think of a way to make the subject arise naturally.

"As a result of your incredible performance, you earned forty thousand System Credits," Sisco said. "Naturally, they are redeemable through the System Store, which you will be able to access since you completed Orientation."

[Required conditions met. Skill unlocked: System Store Access!]

Neat.

"I'll make sure to check it out," James said.

"You should give it a look now," the homunculus suggested. "Just to see if it works for you," he added hastily.

He wants to see my reaction, James thought, amused.

"Sure thing," he said. "Do the top-performing monsters get access to the System Store too?"

"All sentient life-forms do," Sisco replied. "The non-sentient creatures would just waste their credits."

James nodded.

System Store Access.

A seemingly endless array of options appeared before his eyes.

There were Skills, Talents, Stat points, and equipment for sale.

The first option tree he found himself interested in was Skills. Stat points he could have for the very low effort of killing something. With all the slaughter he'd participated in, it was very natural to him now. And equipment that was for sale would undoubtedly be disappointing compared to what powerful monsters dropped.

Basic Elemental Magic: Fire for two hundred System Credits. Elemental Magic: Fire for two thousand System Credits. Basic Elemental Magic: Gravity for one thousand System Credits. Elemental Magic: Gravity for ten thousand System Credits. Time Magic for twenty thousand System Credits?!

Overpriced! was his immediate impression of the first few options he browsed. Then he reconsidered. *Maybe my standards are unreasonably high because I've been acquiring all the Skills I want so easily. And I'm also not used to there being a currency in relation to the Skills and loot I've been acquiring.*

James voiced his thoughts on the pricing out loud. "Is Elemental Magic: Gravity really supposed to be ten thousand System Credits?" he asked.

The System Homunculus let out a low sound. It took James a few seconds to realize that Sisco was chuckling. The laughing voice didn't sound like the homunculus's, though.

"Somehow, I knew you would be a bit cheap," said a thickly accented voice that reminded James of a young Joe Pesci.

"Vinny," James said quietly. One of the few entities he'd encountered toward whom he still felt cautious.

"You missed me, young man?" Vinny said, still speaking through Sisco's mouth like a demonic ventriloquist.

Something like that, James thought.

Aloud, he said, "Oh, of course. I would've loved having you nearby when that Soul Eater was shooting energy blasts at me, or maybe when the Flame Elemental was trying to melt me."

"Congratulations on surviving those ordeals. I hear adversity is character forming!"

"Thanks. My character is definitely changing as a result of all that's happened, I'll grant you. But I'm surprised you decided to take over from Sisco."

"I get it. You were having such a nice chat with him! Palling around with your new chum."

Well, yeah, actually, James thought.

"Forget that for now," Vinny said. "I have important announcements that Sisco wasn't privy to. Above his pay grade. I couldn't have you two finish your conversation and him return you to Earth without going over those. First, a gift!"

A small black stone popped into the air in front of James's face. As it dropped, he instinctively caught it. Then he held it up in front of his eyes. He detected a slight reddish tint to the blackened stone. And was the rock emitting the faintest amount of light? It certainly didn't look like any earthly stone.

"Thank you for the gift," James said, a bit uncertainly. "What is it?"

Wait, I could have just used Identify on it. Before he could bother, Vinny answered.

"Glad you asked. We were cleaning up the Orientation site, and we realized some knucklehead killed a Flame Elemental and didn't bother to retrieve the core."

"Guilty as charged," James said, giving Vinny a wry grin. *There were extenuating circumstances, a small matter of a lot of people who needed me to save them from a monster attack, but I doubt Vinny cares.*

"So, I brought you the prize that you fairly earned. You'll be able to sell it in the System Store and fetch a good price there if you want to, or you may want to find an Alchemist who can work the Flame Elemental Core into something for you. It's a potent product, after all. Elemental cores are valuable merchandise."

James filed that idea away for later and slipped the core into his satchel.

"There was the Flame Elemental Core, and what were the announcements?" he asked.

"The System administrators are pleased with how Earth's mightiest performed through Orientation. They've decided to organize a couple of events for the surviving sentient life-forms on Earth. A World Leaders' Summit for every person, whether human or monster, who has a 'Ruler' Title. And a fighting tournament for the world's strongest two hundred fighters, with excellent prizes for the top fighters."

James was wearing the Ring of Truth, and he recognized the hot, uncomfortable feeling it gave him as Vinny finished the first sentence. He was lying. The System administrators had not been "pleased with how Earth's mightiest performed," then. Maybe these two events they had decided to organize were regular features in every newly System-integrated universe.

Fortunately, the Ring of Truth had no reaction to the rest of what Vinny said. It was all strictly true beyond that first sentence.

Also, interesting that this divine ring could discern the truth or falsity of what Vinny said. Meaning that he wasn't a god himself; he was somewhere below them in the cosmic hierarchy. That wasn't surprising, but it was good to confirm.

"Those are very intriguing announcements," James said. "Are you going to give me more details? How many world leaders are attending the summit? And will the fighting tournament feature nonhumans too?"

"There will be more details," Vinny replied, "but not now. There will be a general announcement later, when we can set a date for the event. We're letting you and a few others know early only because you have Ruler Titles. There are only forty-five of you Rulers of human origin in the whole world. It's a very impressive achievement. I knew I was right to expect great things from you! And I can tell you that the fighting tournament will feature monsters too. Any creature of earthly origin is eligible."

James felt immediately worried about the phrasing Vinny had used in one of those sentences.

"Only forty-five Rulers of human origin?" he said. "How many nonhuman Rulers?"

How many creatures would there be, like the Soul Eater, preying on his fellow humans?

"Oh, hundreds," Vinny said, chuckling to himself. "I haven't taken an exact tally, but most humans didn't beat their Orientations' final bosses. There's still time, though. Maybe some of those crowns will be taken by humans in the period between now and the summit, right?"

"We are a resilient species," James said, smiling with teeth gritted.

He pictured a vast array of monsters occupying the Earth, looking for humans to eat, some of them as powerful as Roscuro had been. Some of them surely stronger.

He would see to it personally that some of those monsters didn't make it to the summit. Besides protecting his family, that would be his mission.

"Nice bling, by the way," Vinny said, looking pointedly at the Ring of the Sovereign on James's left hand.

"Thanks," James said.

"Make sure you put it to good use," Vinny added, seeming to emphasize every syllable.

James nodded slowly, slightly confused.

He looked down at the magical item that had once been his wedding band—and not for the first time, prayed to no god or goddess he could name that his wife would understand why he'd turned it into a magical object.

Then he finally read the description for the Skill he'd transferred into the band.

[Dominion: Seize control of territory with your aura. By pouring out your magical essence, imbue yourself into the soil, water, air, ambient Mana, and non-physical aspects of a region. This Skill may be ineffective where another entity's aura predominates. If two Dominions intersect, the conflict must be resolved by one withdrawing or defeating the other.]

If I understand that correctly, it intersects extraordinarily well with the Fisher King Skills, James thought. *If you didn't have this, how would you get territory? But if you didn't have those Skills, how would you get any benefit out of it?*

"You ready to go home now, kid?" Vinny asked, sounding satisfied. From the tone of his voice, James thought that Vinny had really wanted him to read that description.

But why? He wants to make sure I'll go out and take over some land? I was going to do that anyway. The proctor's intentions were still something of a mystery to him, but it bore thinking about. James didn't want to be a pawn in anyone's games, least of all those of the proctor whose face he'd never even seen.

He took a moment before he answered to read the other Skill he'd gotten from the Ruler of the Dark Waters Title.

[**Territorial Control: Observe anything occurring within your territory at your whim. Manipulate the physical and magical structure of your territory using imbued Mana and your conscious mind. This Skill consumes imbued Mana and is less efficient than other forms of magic.**]

Another Skill that has great synergy with Dominion. At least now he could see why someone who didn't have the Fisher King Job would want Dominion.

"Yes, I am," James said. "Um, will you say goodbye to Sisco for me? Or can I say farewell myself?"

"Fine, fine. Say your goodbyes. See you next time, James."

"Next time, Vinny," James echoed.

Then the homunculus was back to himself, blinking as if he was just waking up from a long nap. And was that a flicker of pain James detected in his eyes? It was so hard to read a face made of stone, but perhaps James finally knew why the homunculus had seemed annoyed at him in their previous encounter, after James had asked to speak to Vinny. Maybe it was actually painful for Sisco to be *possessed* in the way Vinny used, however briefly.

"Good luck, James," the homunculus said after a long moment of silence.

"Be well, Sisco," James said. He felt a little sorry for Sisco, but it couldn't dampen his mood. He was about to see his family again and return home.

Suddenly, he found he was no longer in the white room. He disappeared from that place and reappeared somewhere outdoors. He saw the clear blue sky, Mina, Yulia, and a tiny person who he'd never met before, but who he knew immediately.

Mina. Yulia. My son.

His face curled into an irresistible smile, and he looked into Mina's eyes.

And then they all began falling.

CHAPTER FIVE

Family Is Everything

One moment Mina was saying surprisingly warm farewells to the people from her Orientation, Yulia by her side, and exchanging contact details with people who wanted to try and find their way to her back on Earth.

The next moment she was in the white room where the System Homunculus had instructed her on how magic in the System worked. She was pleased enough with her rewards, although she couldn't help but think they would have been greater if she had managed to stop the Wendigos from carrying off or devouring a huge share of the population.

Two thousand System Credits. It sounded like it could be a lot at first, but it did not seem as if it would actually go very far. She looked through items in the System Store and finally bought an Alder Wood Wand for twelve hundred credits.

A few minutes later she found herself hovering ten feet in the air, staring James in the face. She could sense Yulia by her side, but for a moment, she only had eyes for her husband.

Time seemed to stop for a moment.

"James." The wind seemed to suck the syllable right out of her mouth as she began to fall. "James! No! The baby!" she screamed.

Baby James had been floating right alongside them, she realized as she dropped through the air. Then he was falling right with them. She clawed furiously at the air. But somehow, the System had transported him to a spot just out of her reach. Just out of her husband's reach. And out of Yulia's reach too.

So little James just fell.

Mina saw everything in a panicked haze. Yulia, trying to grab the baby, who was simply too far away. James, who Mina could tell was trying to activate multiple Skills at once. But he didn't seem to have anything that would let him freely move through the air.

He wasn't going to manage whatever he was trying in time, she realized.

She activated Quickened Spellcasting and Silent Spellcasting. A surge of power rose from her core and manifested in a small gust of wind. The wind pulled at the blanket the baby was wrapped in and began slowing his fall.

Mina let out a sigh of relief. She was still falling, but the wind she'd conjured would cushion all of their falls, the baby's especially.

And then the blanket began to unwrap.

She watched in stunned horror as the blanket that her wind was pulling at slowly unwound from around baby James. *No, please! Don't let my baby fall!* She tried desperately to guide and reshape the wind's movements, but they were falling so quickly, and it felt like the blanket, the baby, and the wind were moving too fast for her to adjust.

She heard a strange fleshy sound from where her husband was.

Then a dark shape flew by Mina's head in a flash. *What on Earth is that?*

She got a better look at the shape when it enveloped the baby.

It was an incredibly inflated disembodied human hand. The same skin tone as her husband. It was longer than little James, and as it landed on him, it latched onto the baby with two fingers, wrapping around his waist. It pinched the unwrapping blanket with two other fingers. With the wind still slowing the descent of the blanket, it turned into a sort of miniature parachute.

Oh, thank goodness. She turned and looked at adult James. His eyes were focused on the baby. His left hand ended in a stump now, though it wasn't bleeding as much as she would expect from such a recent and severe wound. He had a small black blade in his right hand. *Did he have to sacrifice his hand to make that thing?*

But even though there was a slight expression of pain on his face, his eyes were relieved.

Apparently, he doesn't feel pain the way he used to, she thought. She took her first really good look at her husband and noticed that he had grown bigger and taller than he had been. He was wearing some almost black armor that reminded her of an insect exoskeleton and a helmet that looked like it had definitely once been an insect's head. His face was much as it had been, but better defined. She realized that if she hadn't experienced him almost every day for over ten years, she might not have recognized him. He was barely the same person, physically.

This will take some getting used to. He was still very handsome, certainly, but quite different. There was a dangerous edge to his looks. An almost predatory cast to his features.

Then they landed. It felt like their time in the air had been extended somehow, but gravity was still functioning well enough.

Mina grabbed their baby out of the air, her whole body shaking. The severed hand creature leaped off of baby James and rushed back over to her husband, scuttling across the grass beneath their feet.

"It's so good to see you guys again," James said. He yanked off his helmet, stepped closer to them, and pulled Mina and Yulia into his embrace. Mina closed her eyes and inhaled the smell of James's skin. That, at least, hadn't changed. She felt safer than she had since they'd been separated.

They stayed like that for a minute or two, until Mina noticed droplets of water hitting the top of her head. She smiled. In the few seconds since they'd arrived, she hadn't consciously observed the weather, but the sky was clear and brilliantly blue.

When she pulled away, she caught James quickly wiping at his eyes with his remaining hand.

"Oh, um, my eyes are leaking a little," he said. "I think it might have drizzled a little, and, um, my severed hand was quite painful . . ."

"It's good to see you too," she said, and kissed him quickly on the lips.

Mina pressed close to him again, and James stopped talking and held her close for another few seconds.

When they separated this time, all three were crying and laughing.

"I was worried about you guys," James said, wiping away tears again with what Mina now noticed was a slowly *regrowing* hand. "Silly me, though. You both look great!"

"I am glad we all made it back alive," Yulia said with a small smile.

Mina noticed a flicker of concern on James's expression, and she frowned slightly. This was a discussion she wanted to have with James, but later.

"You look great too," she said, chuckling. "Though, you're dressed like a cosplayer or something. Um, there is someone you should meet. Someone you've already sort of met." She looked down at the severed hand, which stood on all five digits on the ground, looking like something from *The Addams Family*. "At least, part of you already met him." She held out the baby to him. "James Jr.!"

James smiled, and the tears welled up in his eyes again. Then he took the baby in his hand-and-a-half and stared him in the eyes for a few long seconds. Baby James was very quiet as he and his father met for the first time. Then James gave the baby a kiss on the forehead and pulled him into his arms, tight against his chest.

"I'm your daddy, little guy," he said quietly, whispering in his ear. Then he looked back up at Mina. "Sorry to have to tell you this, but he definitely takes after me. Looks just like his daddy."

"Well, like you *used to*, anyway," Mina said, raising an eyebrow. The words came out more pointed than she'd intended, but James just smiled.

"We've all been through a lot, haven't we?" he said, smiling down at Yulia.

Yulia smiled back. "I'm glad we all made it back home," she said softly. "I hardly believe it."

"Yeah," James said. "If your experience was anything like mine . . ."

He began to tell them the broad outline of what had happened to him, but Mina quickly interrupted.

"We should find some shelter before we start swapping stories," she said. "It's nice out now, but I think it's going to rain in an hour or so."

James and Yulia both looked at her strangely but said nothing.

Right, she thought. *Of course I'm the only one who knows that.*

"My new Class lets me predict the future in limited ways," she said quietly.

"Well, predicting the weather will be very useful in Florida," James said.

Yulia snorted quietly, and Mina smiled too. *We really are back*, she thought. *Everything's going to go back to normal. Thank the gods, everything's going to go back to normal.* Then she gave her head a little shake. *What am I saying, back to normal? Nothing is going back. There are gods now, for a start . . .*

"Let's look around, then," James said.

Mina turned away from her family and began taking in where they'd landed.

They had supposedly been transported back to the same spot they'd left from, but it became quickly obvious that either the System was inaccurate in its transportation methods, or the place they had left from had changed quite drastically in the weeks they'd been gone.

There were buildings around them, and they appeared to be the same in style as the blandly constructed apartment complex buildings they knew. But the structures were inexplicably further apart. Many of them had been destroyed. Some had collapsed completely or toppled onto their sides. The pavement between buildings, as well as the parking lot, had been mostly destroyed.

The ground everywhere they walked was spits of grass and large stretches of mud, with a lot more moisture than Mina remembered.

It was as if some monumental continental shift had occurred. Perhaps it had.

There were other people walking around in the strange landscape as well, but not nearly as many of them as Mina would have expected.

Some of their Orientations went very poorly, she thought. A cold chill went through her stomach. *That could have been any of us . . .* The System had claimed many victims since initiating Earth.

In the midst of searching visually for their old apartment, Mina couldn't help but look for the Indian family that had lived in the apartment beneath them. She hadn't known them, not really. Knowing your neighbors, or even talking to them at all, didn't seem to be fashionable or culturally accepted in America as it had been in Bulgaria during her childhood.

But the mother seemed so nice, she thought. Mina had *wanted* to know her.

She simply hadn't worked up the courage and energy to cross that intangible social boundary. So their main interaction had been smiling and waving when they passed each other. But when Mina saw the other woman playing with her young children, or watched the way she fussed over the little one, or heard her and her family's happy chatter through the thin apartment window when she passed outside, she would think, *When the baby's born, then I'll get to know them!*

Now that promise she'd made to herself might never be fulfilled. The apartment complex had lost many of its residents if the meager number walking around the courtyard was any indication.

Mina didn't talk to the wanderers. Some of them walked around purposefully as if they knew where they were going or what they were trying to do. A few looked traumatized and psychologically broken, as if what they had been through in recent weeks had been too much for their sanity.

Regardless, none of them approached Mina. For the moment, she decided she liked it that way. She was still processing the way the Earth had changed. She didn't need new social demands right now. They would probably need to make new connections later. It wasn't a necessity that she particularly relished.

James, Mina noticed, seemed very interested in observing everyone around them. He wasn't looking around so much to find their apartment as to take in the people who were wandering the grassy area. It wasn't any particular neighbor he was looking for, Mina felt certain. He'd shown even less interest in meeting them than she had back in the pre-System days.

Yulia was more focused than either of them, and it was she who finally found the building they used to live in. The second floor was mostly lying on its side, broken off from the top part of the building. The first floor, where their neighbors had lived, was exposed to the elements.

There was a sound of rustling in the wreckage. Mina realized that, given how long they'd been gone, it was possible that any number of wild animals might have settled in the ruins of their building. She instinctively stepped behind James.

"It's children," James said quietly.

She looked up at him questioningly for a moment.

How does he know? she wondered.

Then she heard one of them.

"Mama, is that you?" a little boy called. Mina couldn't see him, but now she understood how James must have known who was in the building. His senses were superhuman now. It wasn't just his appearance that had changed.

James turned to Mina and gently placed the baby, who seemed very comfortable and relaxed, in her arms. Then he took a couple of steps forward and leaped lightly over the half-demolished wall into the first-floor kitchen. Mina heard James walking around inside the apartment, then the distant sound of him speaking quietly, though she couldn't make the words out.

More rustling, as of movement. Then the front door unlocked and opened. It was James.

He had a child in each arm, which prompted a realization in the back of Mina's mind. *Oh. He regrew the hand he chopped off. In a matter of minutes. Without using any healing magic that I noticed.* This was her first indicator of how much more powerful than a normal mortal man James had become.

But the front of her mind focused on the children around him. All three of their neighbor's young ones.

Of the two cradled in his arms, one was a baby, a year or two old. The other was a couple of years older. And the oldest child, the six-year-old, stood behind him. James's expression was troubled.

"These kids managed to find their way back to their apartment," he said. As he stepped forward, Mina saw that the backdoor to the lower floor apartment, which had been a sliding glass door, was completely gone now. Just like the ceiling.

That explained how the children got back into their apartment. One fewer question that needed answering.

"I see," Mina said, not yet fully comprehending.

We must not be expecting them to come back, she realized after a moment. Otherwise, James would never pick up someone else's children. He set them down outside as she had that thought.

"I'll be right back," he said to the biggest one. "Don't go anywhere, okay? Especially not back inside the apartment right now. I'm not sure if the building is going to fall down."

The boy nodded solemnly.

James stepped in closer to Mina and Yulia.

"Sweet, could you watch the little ones for a moment?" Mina asked.

Yulia nodded and smiled brightly, then walked over to the children.

James waited a few seconds before he spoke. "What do you think about taking care of them?" he asked, his voice low. "Just until we figure out what we're going to do about all the orphans who are going to be running around. I don't think their parents are coming back if they aren't here already."

An open-ended commitment, Mina recognized. She was surprised. James had very easily accepted taking Yulia in when Mina and Yulia's mother got sick, but that was because, as he often put it, "Family is everything."

When it came to most other people outside that circle, though, James had only ever shown selective empathy. Back when he was a prosecutor, if someone was a victim of crime, he would seem to genuinely grieve their losses. Conversely, if the person in question was a criminal, James would usually tar them as "the scum of the Earth" in his mind, try to get them prison time unless there were obvious mitigating factors, and lose no sleep over it. Even though James had been a criminal himself in the past.

Mina was never bothered by this contradiction because James had always followed a simple pattern. If you were inside of his circle of love and trust, he was unfailingly good and kind to you. More than fair to people he cared about, he was generous.

He would never hurt her, but almost the whole rest of the world was fair game.

So, what was this? Volunteering to take care of a stranger's children instead of trying to pawn them off on someone else? Was his circle expanding?

It seemed to her as if James's whole outlook on other people had changed.

CHAPTER SIX

Small Miracles

"Mina?" James asked.

She realized she'd been staring at him, zoned out, for a few seconds as she focused.

"Oh, of course," she said. "They were our neighbors." The whole situation felt so strange that she could barely force the words out. "I hope they would've done the same for us."

"Okay. Good, then," he said, looking at her with slight concern.

"I'm okay," she whispered, smiling slightly. "We should talk to Yulia a bit. See what she thinks. She'd be doing a lot of babysitting, I think, with all these children around."

James nodded. "That makes sense."

Mina turned to where Yulia was sitting, playing patty cake with the toddler. She called to her, "Yulia, could you come here for a moment?"

Yulia excused herself with a few words to the little girl, who nodded and waved goodbye to her as she walked forward. *She's so good with little ones*, Mina thought proudly.

"We're thinking about letting the kids live with us," James explained quietly once Yulia was close.

She bobbed her head up and down energetically. "Of course! We can't just leave them outside."

Mina couldn't help smiling. She said it like it was so obvious. Put like that, it was obvious. There were no foster homes anymore, no government institutions or private charities of any kind to take care of children. They weren't doing something crazy. They were doing something human.

Caring for other humans.

"You know you're probably going to be doing a lot of babysitting?" Mina said. "All of us are probably going to be overwhelmed taking care of all these children."

Yulia was nodding.

"Soon, we'll organize and it won't be just the three of us," James said. "I mean, we'll figure out how to make it work, but I'm certain there must be other children in the area missing their families."

So, this isn't just a one-time act of charity, Mina thought. *He's thinking about plans for the future. Major plans.*

She nodded, and James said, "Let's let them know what we're doing, then."

They walked over to the children. James turned his attention to the older boy specifically. "You don't see your mom or dad anywhere around at all, do you, Abhi?"

Of course, James already asked the little boy for his name, Mina thought. She imagined a brief conversation inside of the ruined dwelling before James emerged with them, when he was trying to reassure the children that they were safe.

The little boy looked around at all the people walking in the former apartment area for a few seconds, his expression hopeful, before he shook his head. "That's right, sir," he said meekly.

"Okay. Do you know if you have any family around here besides your parents?"

"No, sir," Abhi replied.

So well-mannered, Mina thought. *Of course. Kids take after their parents.*

"The parents mostly kept to themselves," Mina added. *And I would've noticed if they had family coming around*, went unspoken.

Abhi looked sad, as if he was thinking about what might have happened to their parents.

"Well, if you'll have us, we'd like to watch out for you guys for a while," James said.

The little boy looked uncertain for a long moment.

Then Yulia spoke up. "I volunteer to babysit!" she said. She looked at Abhi. "We can play together."

Mina didn't need to look at Yulia to visualize her face as she spoke. She could hear the smile in Yulia's voice. Mina herself couldn't help thinking of those poor dead parents, but it was nice to imagine that the three of them might keep these children from any future harm.

Yulia's words seemed to make Abhi's mind up. He nodded, tentatively at first and then with a shy smile. Mina felt proud of her husband and her sister. In just the brief interactions they'd had, James and Yulia seemed to have won the little boy's confidence.

"All right, then," James said, nodding to himself. As he spoke, the first droplets of water began to fall onto Mina's arms.

"Um, I think we need to do something about shelter right now," Mina said.

"Right you are," James said almost absently. He put the children down gently on the ground. Then Mina saw a brown aura gathering around him.

Wait, did he become a Mage? That wasn't what we discussed.

Her next observation was that he clearly had a huge amount of Mana. It took a few minutes for him to gather what he needed from his core—perhaps she could help him learn Quickened Spellcasting—but the amount that he charged was very large, and he didn't look fatigued from the process of gathering it. Mina had occasionally experienced headaches from Mana overuse, so she knew running low came with some side effects.

Then he unleashed his power.

The ground in a large, open area in front of them rose in a single, sudden movement—a huge rectangle of dense soil, roughly the size of a medium-sized whale. She noticed he seemed to be guiding it with hand movements as well as thought. He tightened his fist, and the outer layer of soil visibly hardened into rock. Then he made some orchestra conductor hand gestures and window and door outlines appeared on the sides of the structure.

James's mental image of the building grew clearer as he continued guiding his Mana. It was clearly intended to constitute multiple separate dwellings.

As James was doing this, Mina and Yulia were just standing and staring, mouths slightly agape. Mina had used magic many times now. She'd practiced with it daily and honed her control of it until it was finely tuned. But neither sister had seen magic used this way before—the scale of it.

Yulia caught her eye, and they both shook their heads and smiled.

Mina recognized the inspiration for the building immediately once the shape was more defined. James had constructed a slightly smaller model of the apartment block they'd lived in.

Finally, he seemed to be finished. Yulia and the little boy started clapping, and Mina joined in after a moment. It seemed appropriate after the performance they'd just witnessed.

James beamed and took a little bow. He let out a long breath, as if he'd forgotten to breathe while he was working on the building. Then he walked up to one of the doors. He pulled on the handle. It opened, and Mina's jaw dropped slightly. Inside there was a staircase, and she could see that it led up to a wide living room.

He even structured it like our old apartment . . .

His technique was unrefined in her judgment—or at least inefficient. If she had his Mana reserves, she probably could have accomplished something similar with around half of the Mana she judged he'd used. But his earth magic was also incredibly powerful. If she had attempted to do what he'd done with her own power, she'd have run out of Mana early on and perhaps collapsed.

Quantity has a quality all its own. If he could do this much without running out of Mana, then with more precise control, he would be able to reshape the landscape around them. She resolved to show him what she'd learned as soon as she could.

"You guys should get out of the rain," James said. She saw that while she was thinking, he'd picked the smaller children back up and entered the new apartment. The biggest one, standing behind James, whistled.

"Wow," Abhi said, looking up and down the building. "Magic is amazing."

Yes, but no, not really, she thought. *James is amazing. I was blessed by a goddess of magic, and I know I couldn't do that.* How had he become so powerful? She couldn't imagine how hard he must have pushed himself.

But Mina just nodded, walked over to the little boy, and with the arm she wasn't using to hold her baby, she took his hand. Then they walked up the stairs.

Yulia ascended in front of them. Mina was numb, a thousand thoughts running through her mind. *How is he so powerful? What was his Orientation like? Is this building even stable?*

That last thought seemed especially pressing when it occurred to her, but it wasn't a deep enough doubt to make her run back outside into the rain that was rapidly turning into a signature Florida thunderstorm. And if her husband had screwed up the structural integrity of the apartment building, she was certain he'd sacrifice life and limb, if necessary, to keep their family safe. He'd already chopped off a whole hand and thrown it after their baby without hesitation.

The building didn't shake as they strode up the stairs, which did as much as anything could to convince her that it wasn't going to fall down, so she refocused on the less urgent questions. *What happened to James? How did he become this way?*

"I'm going to go outside for a few minutes," James said. He had placed the little kids on a sort of stone couch and was looking past Mina at the stairs.

"Sure," she said. *I need a minute anyway.*

He bustled out the front door.

For a long time, Mina just sat, tired, on the couch next to the children. She exerted a little bit of energy to introduce herself to Abhi and ask him the names of his younger siblings, and she introduced baby James, but it had been a long day, and her sleep had been interrupted the previous night. She found she wasn't up to much conversation.

"Sis," Yulia said quietly, coming back after looking around a bit.

"Yes?" Mina asked. She turned and saw her little sister smiling softly.

"We have a third bedroom now."

Mina snorted with a brief, choked laugh, then glanced at the children surrounding them. Then her lips curled in a small smile. "Well, I'm glad he didn't forget about our new guests."

Then she heard her husband's voice from outside. It was louder than he'd ever spoken before, and she wondered if it was some sort of magic or just a voice that employed super-Strength to increase its volume. It didn't matter either way. *He must be standing on the rooftop*, she thought.

"Former residents of Palm Breeze Apartments," he was proclaiming, "you can take shelter here. Some of you I've spoken with already. Others I will speak with tomorrow. When the storm is over, we can discuss how best to rebuild our community. This land is ours now, unless we let the monsters that live around here take it from us . . ."

"Oh, that makes sense," Mina said quietly, almost to herself. "We'll need a community to get through the days and weeks to come."

It was silly, she realized, that she'd even had a thought that things might return to normal.

"Mm-hmm," Yulia said. She was distracted, playing with the neighbor's baby, Mina realized. She had hardly noticed her older sister talking.

Mina got up and carried baby James to the master bedroom, closer to where James was talking. She wanted to hear him better.

James was delivering a bit of a speech, Mina observed. She had heard some people opening and closing apartment doors, but he continued on for the benefit of those still skeptical, standing out there in the pouring rain. Or maybe more for the benefit of the people who had already accepted his gracious offer of free housing. Letting them know what they were in for.

When she sat down on the stone simulacrum of a bed, James was talking about taking more of the land back from the monsters. Arguing that they needed to stand together and look out for each other. Promising to defend people.

Could he really deliver on that? The rest of the little speech had just been common sense, really. But was James strong enough to protect a community of people now?

Mina went back over her experiences of the new and improved James thus far.

Yes, she thought. He probably could deliver. She faintly recognized along with that thought that her husband's ambitions would expand to match his capabilities, but that was something they would address later. For now, she focused back in on what he was saying.

The flow of words had changed. His impromptu speech had continued, but he was clearly taking questions now.

There was a loud comment from one of the few people who were still outside. Mina distantly heard the word "rent" uttered in a disrespectful tone of voice.

"Rent?" James responded. "Don't worry about rent! We're living after the fall of our civilization. We should be glad we're alive. We don't need to talk about rent tonight. Just get out of the rain!"

There was a little mocking laughter, clearly at the rude commenter's expense.

Then the outside went quiet. A few more doors opened and shut.

Mina thought about going back into the common room. She still wanted to process everything that was happening. She'd spent hardly any time with her husband, and she mostly wanted to get his take on things.

He'd been busy performing small miracles since she first saw him, so she certainly didn't blame him for being occupied. But she felt very tired. Almost as tired as she'd been in the days just after she had given birth. If only this bed wasn't stone, she would sleep.

Suddenly, the window on the outside wall side of the room turned on an axis that Mina hadn't seen it spin on before. She braced herself for some sort of enemy, clutching her baby to her chest and backing toward the room's closet. Then James appeared, and the window swiveled shut again behind him. A cloak of brown Mana faded from around his body.

Oh, he modified the window so he could open and close it, she thought dully. She let out a long sigh. Then a yawn. *So sleepy.*

"Hey, sorry to keep you waiting here," he said. "Is everyone all right?" He looked at the baby as he spoke. He stepped down from the windowsill, dripping water all over the floor as he moved. He was soaking wet, she realized.

"No big deal, skapi," she said almost automatically. "I'm just really tired. Everyone was okay last I checked. No screaming since I came in here to listen to your speech." She yawned again.

"You'll need to invest some more points in Stamina when you get a few more levels," James said. "I don't know if you've noticed yet, but Earth's gravity has increased. I think that's probably why you're feeling tired so soon."

Her eyes widened and she stared, open-mouthed, at James. *That's impossible*, she wanted to say. But they'd seen more impossible things than that, she was sure. All that was required was an increase in the Earth's mass. *Could that be what explains the buildings being further apart? There was an asteroid crash or something, and that increased gravity and caused massive earthquakes?*

"You should probably just sleep for now," James said. "I'll try and make this more comfortable." He gestured at the bed. "Tomorrow, I'll get you something decent to sleep on, if I can. Usually, the rain helps with sleep." He smiled. "And I have something else that might help."

James pulled his Small Bag of Deceptive Dimensions out and opened it. A heap of furs fell onto the bed. She laid down, still holding the baby beside her, and arranged some of the furs until she was tolerably comfortable.

"That ought to do it," Mina said sleepily.

"I'll be right back," James said.

She wanted to tell him not to leave, but he was gone before she could get the words out. Her only consolation was that he returned with almost the same inhuman speed.

"Yulia and I put the others to bed, and I gave her some of my other furs to use," he said. "I think the kids are starting to be really comfortable here. Meaning more comfortable with us in general. Which is good. We'll have to figure out more permanent stuff later."

"That's great," Mina said a little impatiently, "and yes, we will. Tomorrow. Now lay down and go to sleep. You know I don't sleep as well without you."

Finally, he lay on the bed beside her, and she was able to go to sleep.

CHAPTER SEVEN

The Next Adventure

Mitzi stood in her kitchen, cocked her husband's service pistol, and listened.

The noises of movement outside seemed to be getting closer and closer. She responded by positioning herself further back in the kitchen and making certain that she had a clear line of sight on the front door to the house.

If Orientation had taught her anything, it was that she could not trust most of her fellow humans in a crisis situation. And her penetrating questions to the System Homunculus in the white room had validated her fears that humanity's crisis was far from over.

"I have a gun!" she shouted—or tried to. Her voice sounded quavery and weak from nerves. "I'm not afraid to use it." She began chanting quietly under her breath, gathering fire Mana. If a bullet didn't stop this intruder, she would throw something stronger.

The door burst open, and she instantly drew a bead on the intruder. A second later, she lowered the pistol and stopped chanting. She let out a breath, then shook her head.

"Jesus, you startled me!" Mitzi scolded. "You know, I was ready to shoot you!"

"Oh, is that what you were yelling?" Alan asked. "My hearing's not what it was."

He stood in the doorway. Her old, nearly bald, beautiful knight. She just shook her head again. *It's impossible for me to be mad at you*, she thought.

"Next level you get, you need to put some points into Perception!" she finally said.

Alan smiled. "I'm glad you were ready for anything," he said. He closed the distance between them and pulled her in for a long, passionate kiss. Electricity traveled through her whole body, all the way down to her toes. "You know, I thought I might never see you again."

Mitzi felt the raw passion in her husband's voice that had somehow never faded over the five decades of their relationship.

And she smiled, any tension between them now completely broken. "Why did you think that?" she asked softly. "The last thing we discussed before Orientation ended was that I would stay here and wait for you to come home."

She had appeared outside, strangely, but reentering the house had been as easy as remembering where she kept the spare key—inside a hollow rock in the front yard. Then it was simply a matter of waiting. She had been nervous, briefly, when she heard other people passing—and then again at his approach.

But she had never truly been in danger. Not the way she had sometimes been back in Orientation.

"You haven't seen what's happening out there, then," he said.

It wasn't spoken like a question, so she simply waited for him to say what he was getting at.

"It's pandemonium," Alan continued. "On my way here from the office, I saw people looting and fighting over food. Buildings burning. That's not to mention the damage the System did."

"What did the System do?" Mitzi was less interested in knowing the answer than in taking her husband's mind off of the human side of the problems outside, which she could tell was wearing at him.

"Oh, nothing much," he said, expression shifting to a slightly crazy smile. "Just moved the whole Earth around, it seems like." He explained the state of the buildings he'd seen. How some were just further apart than they used to be, but most were collapsed ruins. "We're lucky that the office was barely affected. Even the house"—he gestured around them—"is listing slightly to the left now."

"Listing, huh?" was all Mitzi could come up with. It was mildly shocking to think that she couldn't just pop down to the local Walmart if they needed supplies now. "I guess we're on our own as far as fixing things like that now," she said. "Basically back in the Stone Age."

"I'm just glad that the house is still up," Alan said, taking her hand. "Did you try getting hold of the kids yet?"

"You know, I couldn't think of it," she admitted. "I was too worried about you." She walked over to the landline phone and raised it to her ear. There was no dial tone, but she tried to dial their younger son's number anyway. *Nope.*

She shook her head wordlessly.

"I should've known," Alan said. "If the buildings have moved, power won't be on anywhere unless there's a generator. Phone lines are probably down too.

And my cell isn't working—I tried it on the way here—which means yours isn't working either."

A calm settled over Mitzi as her husband listed off problems. It was strange, but it restored a certain sense of normalcy to the situation. Even if it was only surface level.

"What do we do now, you think?" she asked. "Stay here and wait for the kids to show up?"

"That's one option," Alan said. "I told the folks from the office that I'd be back if it made sense for us, but I don't know if it does."

"We have the best chance of the kids finding us if we stay here." Mitzi stated the obvious, knowing that neither she nor her husband really wanted to just sit in place and wait.

"If they look for us," Alan said slowly, only meeting her eyes after he stared at the ground for a long moment.

Only Stephen, their youngest, had stayed local. Joe and Marcy were both out of state now. All three of their children had grown up and grown middle-aged, had lives and families of their own to worry about. Joe's daughter Sandra was engaged to be married now.

All three would certainly be more concerned about their own children than they would be with checking in on their aging parents.

"They probably assume we're dead already," Mitzi said, uttering the safer of the two unspoken thoughts they were both mulling. The other thought being that one or more of Alan and Mitzi's children might have died in Orientation. If that had happened, did they really want to know?

We can only learn so much and still endure in this life, Mitzi thought. *That's why people die of old age. They get too full of ugly truths and collapse under the weight of an accumulated lifetime's worth.*

"You're right." Alan nodded slowly. He looked relieved, Mitzi noted. She imagined the same look on her own face. This was a truth that they didn't necessarily want to know, even if they could. They couldn't learn it, though. Maybe that was just as well. "I'll at least leave a note, in case they come looking for us," Alan added.

Mitzi found herself nodding, then stopped herself. "Wait, where are we going, then?"

"We don't have any reason to stay here," Alan said. "We're still alive, despite everything. I want to believe it's for a reason. Maybe we'll be able to help restore some semblance of order in this messed up world. We have at least two options in terms of how we might do that. There's James, who clearly wants to gather a following around himself so he can try his version of rebuilding civilization. That seemed to be going well enough last time we checked. And we know he survived Orientation because the System said he was the one who ended it early. On the other hand, back at the office, Dean has the idea that we're going to fortify the old law building and turn it into a base from which we can reclaim the world. The one problem with that is that there's a pretty big pest problem in the area around it. I told him that I thought I knew exactly the right person to help solve that issue."

"James?" *All roads lead to James, it seems.* Whether within or outside of Orientation made no difference.

Alan nodded. "James and Dean are both big picture thinkers. Ambitious and energetic. Both of them would want to tackle these problems even if they didn't know the other existed. I figure if we can bring the two of them together, we're giving humanity a leg up on the monsters that are trying to take over the world already."

Mitzi nodded. It sounded like Alan had asked the System Homunculus much the same sorts of questions that she had. They both knew that the world was now crawling with monsters calling themselves rulers of various pieces of territory. Hopefully, they weren't in some monster's patch of land right now. But that wasn't something they could do anything about.

"How are we going to find him?" Mitzi asked. She thought her husband's vague plan was a pretty good start to the two of them making a positive difference in the world.

Alan's lips curled up in his usual charming smile. "It's not strictly appropriate, but I took a peek at James's personnel file before I left the fellows at the office. I looked at his address, and as it happens, I know the area."

"Then away we go," Mitzi said, returning the smile.

"Yep," Alan agreed.

"Onto the next great adventure," she said.

"You always make the best of things," he said.

"It's what we do."

The two of them spent half an hour making preparations. They packed their bags from Orientation with nonperishable foods—the perishable stuff from the refrigerator still vaguely resembled food, but overall, the interior of that appliance looked more like a biohazard zone than a storage area for edible items now. It overflowed with unnaturally blue, green, and gray discolored and moldy items.

They also packed flashlights, some old sleeping bags Alan found in the attic, and a couple of sharp kitchen knives. Mitzi checked to make sure there was nothing else she wanted to pack before she returned her bag to where she typically kept it, secured around her upper arm with a Velcro strap.

They each placed another knife on their belts, and Alan rested his service pistol in its hip holster. Alan went around making sure that all the doors and windows were secured, besides the front door that they were going to lock behind them. Mitzi spent those few minutes using their toilet one last time. She would miss her lavender-scented bathroom. She doubted that she and her husband would ever come back.

Then he wrote their children a note and placed it on the kitchen counter. It said where they were going, that they didn't expect to be back, and where the kids might find them. He weighed it down with a small paperweight, as if he was worried that the wind might somehow come into the house and blow the note away. Mitzi thought he felt guilty about just leaving a note there. Maybe he really believed that their children would show up looking for them and be disappointed.

She didn't think that any of the children would ever actually find the note, but she signed it too, with love. *You never know.*

Finally, they set out on their journey. Alan led the way as they ran for half an hour just off of once-busy streets, which were now cracked and broken shells of their former selves, littered with wrecked cars.

The couple kept to the grassy areas rather than to the streets. They tried to stick close to tree lines where they existed because the roads weren't completely empty or entirely silent. Occasionally, they would come across people, and when they did, they would hide.

Mitzi didn't like to be so suspicious of her fellow human beings, but she knew that Orientation had turned mundane, ordinary people into sun-worshiping murderers, people who made deals with monsters, and, occasionally, undead creatures. She and her husband were taking no chances.

They made good progress. Alan seemed to know where they were going, despite the many ways in which the landscape had changed since they left Earth. Then the sky became suddenly overcast. Mitzi and Alan exchanged a knowing look. Those dark gray clouds could only mean one thing in the Sunshine State.

"At least some things never change," Mitzi said.

The pair began looking for a building they could break into to stay warm and dry until the thunderstorm passed. Some things never changed, but there were some you could never see coming.

As the first droplets fell, the two of them spotted a gas station. They could see from the outside that the shelves had been ransacked, but the glass doors weren't shattered, so it seemed safe enough as a place to hole up and wait for the storm to pass.

Mitzi silently chanted as Alan walked in front of her, pistol drawn, into the abandoned gas station. She followed close behind him, looking out behind her in case an ambush was planned from that direction.

They were unmistakably vulnerable to danger now in this post-apocalyptic world, and she had never felt that more keenly than now.

Then she passed through the second set of glass doors, and they were inside the gas station.

"I'll check the aisles," Alan mouthed at her silently.

Mitzi nodded, then started slightly as someone—or *something*—moved at the edge of her vision.

She turned to face the mover, and her husband whirled alongside her.

Then she let out a sigh of relief for the second time that day.

"It's just you," she said. "I'm scared of my own shadow today."

CHAPTER EIGHT

Dominion

When the morning light hit her face, Mina felt better able to continue their conversation.

She also thought she noticed the possible increased gravity hitting her immediately. That and something else in the air. Not a smell or a taste. Nothing she could put her finger on easily. She decided to think about whatever it was later.

James was already awake. After they exchanged good mornings and kisses, she launched right into what they'd been talking about yesterday.

"So, you think the Earth increased in size?" Mina said. "Or the Earth's matter is denser?"

"I don't know for sure," James said. "But I can tell you that the distance between the buildings seems like a clue, the fact that they seem to have moved. And there are creatures under my control, flying creatures—you remember the severed hand creature from yesterday? Well, I have some balloon monsters made from my skin. Anyway, I have them scouting the skies. They're just supposed to give me the dimensions of the regions they're flying over. I just wanted the very basic lay of the land."

"Okay. What did your magical flying skin scouts tell you?" Mina couldn't help but find the image of monsters made of James's skin flying around grotesquely funny.

James smiled in response to her question. "They should have reached the beach by now on each side," he said. "But instead, they're still flying over land. It's a lot bigger than it was."

"Any other world-shattering revelations while I was asleep?" Mina asked.

"Yulia wanted to call your sister Elena and make sure she was okay, but her phone died while she was sleeping. Naturally, I wanted to check on my mom and Alice too. So, I took my phone out of my magic satchel—"

"You mean the Small Bag of Deceptive Dimensions?"

"If you like," he said with a shrug. "Anyway, cell service doesn't work anymore, just like before Orientation, so we'll have to make do with whatever technology we can make. I stuck my phone back in my *magic satchel*"—she stuck her tongue out; he smirked—"so that should save the battery." She wondered for a moment if her other sisters were okay, but James was already moving onto another subject, and she resolved to think about that later. "The first task once we start the day is going to be dealing with our neighbors. Then maybe we install some plumbing. That was the main thing about the structure of our building that I couldn't figure out when I copied it to make this. For right now, though, why don't we start by going over everything that happened in Orientation?"

Mina nodded. This would hopefully answer several questions she'd been wondering about. But she would let James take his time telling the story of his experience.

"I'll go first," she said. She launched into a thorough chronological retelling of Orientation as she and Yulia had experienced it.

The narrative was interrupted a few times. Occasionally, James reacted. He expressed his strong approval of how Mina handled the first challenge.

Next, the baby started fussing, and Mina realized that he wanted to be fed. Then Mina's stomach started rumbling, and James went up onto the roof of the building to build a fire and cook her some monster meat he had stored in his Small Bag of Deceptive Dimensions. The story paused at that point until James went around the apartment and made sure everyone was fed.

When they resumed, and she came to the challenges where she and Yulia had been separated, she made sure to say that for the full story, he'd have to talk to her.

Despite the interruptions, she gradually managed to get the whole story out.

When she reached the part where she had been shoved into a wall and had begun going into labor, James's face turned a bit scary. She couldn't help but smile. The man who'd done that was lucky Cara had killed him. If her husband had gotten to him, she could imagine James doing worse than just murdering them.

As she recounted the ensuing part where she gave birth, safely and without apparent complications, James relaxed again and put an arm around her and the baby.

"I'm glad that Cara girl was there to help you out and take care of those guys," he said. "When I meet her, I'll have to thank her."

Mina suppressed a look of sadness at that. She quickly moved on to the part of the story where she discovered Cara was a killer.

"Well, that's a surprise," James said. "Were you okay?"

She assured him that she was, or at least she would be, and she finished the story.

"Incredible," James said. He was smiling. "Yeah, you'll be all right. You're amazing. You did all that, solved a series of murders with literally no clues except the way the System works, and you became so proficient in magic that you got a blessing from a goddess of magic. I don't know how a little death could keep you down."

"It was more than just a little death," she said, but she was smiling even as she shook her head. How did he do this? He was making light of literal mass murder, but he could still make her smile. It felt almost as if they'd never been apart.

"Now it's your turn," she said. "What happened to you?"

James took a deep breath. It was time for him to share his half of the story.

So much to tell, he thought. *Mina was so concise, but I can tell that she really told me everything she could remember that might be important. I even feel like I have a sense for the people she met and how they connect to each other.*

He still didn't think of himself as much of a storyteller, despite having a blessing from Anansi. Back when he'd needed to go to a job every day, he would tell Mina things about it, but only when she asked. The bitter distaste of his job was part of the reason he was reluctant, but he also didn't feel the need to share as much verbally as she did. Eventually, since most of his stories were about how much he disliked his work or simply had no passion for it, she learned to stop asking. That kept them both in a better mood.

He realized, for the first time, that it was around the time when she'd figured that out that she first suggested they have a baby. He instantly wondered if the reason she'd come up with that was just to give him something happier to think about.

The idea of having kids was something they'd discussed before, but given when she broached it, he felt fairly certain that he was onto something about the timing.

So, as he began to recount his own experiences, he had a smile on his face.

It quickly faded as he remembered the story had begun with a bloodbath. But he tried to put a pleasant face on his journey even while leaving nothing important out in his retelling. Rather than emphasizing the horror of a pack of wolves tearing into the unprotected population on the first day, he tried to focus on how clever he was in seeing the attack coming and getting away. Even so, he expected some parts of the story to repulse her.

In particular, when he had eaten part of a human body and fed part of a human body to Tim in the forest, he imagined that Mina would react with horror. She hadn't seemed too bothered or even surprised when he mentioned fighting and killing the group that accompanied the Corpse Eater. But given her experience with Cara and her monsters, he thought actual cannibalism might be too horrifying for her to accept.

Before he realized it, his voice had trailed off. The room turned silent as he stared at her expectantly. It took her a moment to notice.

"Why did you stop the story?" she asked.

"I guess I wasn't sure what your reaction would be to everything," he said. *Especially those last bits, where I ate a piece of a human body and fed some to a teenager* . . . She seemed to be taking it all in calmly, but considering the circumstances of her own adventure, that was surprising.

"I'm relieved that you survived it all, skapi," she said. "And I'm glad that you're not a Wendigo. You acquired the Cannibalism Talent, you said, because the System judged you for the things you did years ago. I don't care that you ate human flesh—" She stopped herself and frowned. "Honestly, it is a little disgusting to think about. But it wasn't my flesh. It wasn't the body of anyone we care about. I won't judge you for doing it—or even for tricking that teenager into eating it too." Her face took on a slightly morbid smile. "It sounds like he almost victimized you, from the way you told the story." James nodded along. "Anyway, the last person in the world you need to worry about judging you is me. All I was hoping for from Orientation was that all three of us would survive. Even if you killed everyone else in your Orientation so that you could escape alive, I would just be happy that you made it out."

James let his body sag with relief. Mina was the only person whose judgment he truly valued. She accepted him. All was right with the world.

She sensed his tension and put an arm around him. They lay together quietly on the bed for a while, her hand stroking his hair softly, until she noticed something.

"Skapi, don't move," she said. "There's a spider on your head. I'll just—"

"No, wait," James said, half-rising. "That's actually Hester. She's a friend."

"Please don't crush me," Hester said in her tinny voice. That made both James and Mina smile. The little spider changed the mood in an instant.

"A pleasure to meet you," Hester added. "I'm a big fan! I guess it sounds weird to say I've heard a lot about you when I was sitting on James's ear the whole time you were explaining your story."

"A little bit weird, yes," Mina replied, giving James a rather uncomfortable stare.

He looked away and pretended not to notice it. *Okay, that was a mistake*, he thought. *I genuinely forget she's there sometimes, though!*

Fortunately, Hester resumed talking. After brief introductions, the mood had changed. Finally, he felt ready to resume the story.

When James recounted the events of the Spider Queen fight, Mina looked a bit sadder than he had expected. He could tell that she felt the Queen's loss of her children more deeply than she had felt any of the human deaths in the story thus far. Even though she kept silent, her face was an open book to him.

He arrived at the part with Anansi's descent, and she took on a knowing look. Based on her interactions with Hecate, he knew she had already heard about his Chosen One blessing.

But he still had more surprises to come. When he explained what happened with the Moloch cult, she looked as disturbed as she had been discussing the Wendigo threat. She took his hand when he explained his decision to kill the pregnant woman the cultists were tormenting; she could tell that this was the most difficult part of the story for him to relive.

In the later parts of the story, she smiled at his triumphs, both over the cult and against the remaining monsters of Orientation. She seemed especially intrigued when he mentioned that he now had control of a wolfpack, the leader of which had contacted him telepathically while he was telling the story.

"My conquering hero," she said, kissing him tenderly on the lips. "Somehow, I knew you would make everything right in the end. It was nice that your story had such a happy ending. Thank you for telling me."

James couldn't be sure, but he thought she was dwelling on the losses in her own Orientation as she said those last two sentences. He decided to distract her with the final revelation, the one last thing he'd been worried she would judge him for, though now that concern seemed silly.

"I received several power-ups for defeating the primary antagonist of the Orientation," he said. "One of them was a Skill that my body couldn't contain. It threatened to destroy me. The System said I needed to lose a Skill, or my 'vessel,' meaning my body, would shatter." He held up his left hand and showed her his ring finger. "So I used my Skill Transfer ability, and I moved the Skill into my ring."

She looked at it curiously, leaning in to take in the slight changes in his wedding ring's appearance. Then she looked back up at him and gave him her glowing smile. "Is it strange if I say that it sounds sweet?" she asked. "I know it was a desperation move, so you probably didn't have much time to think about it; you were about to die. It's just that I know this was the most natural place for you to put some important superpower, if you had to store it in any object that wasn't your body. Since I know you never take your ring off."

A few drops of liquid seemed to condense in James's eye for some reason, but Mina was looking down at the crown etched into the Ring of the Sovereign again, so he was able to quickly wipe them away with his other hand.

I must have been a really good guy in another life or something to deserve you, he thought.

He kissed her again, long and deep. They exchanged a look of shared understanding. Then he brought James Jr. over to Yulia and the other children to watch for a while, and he politely asked Hester to hang out on the ceiling in the living room. He even removed the Soul Eater Orb from where it sat attached to his bicep in the form of an arm band. He put that into his magic satchel.

He needed to spend some time truly alone with his wife.

Afterward, Mina ignored the thin sheen of sweat on her body and wrapped the wolf furs around herself. She curled up close to James, almost ready to sleep again until a thought occurred to her.

Not an urgent thought, perhaps, but it seemed important, given the context he'd given her earlier.

"What sort of Skill did you transfer into the ring, anyway?" she asked.

"It's called Dominion," he replied.

He explained what Dominion did, then added that he'd experienced Job Evolution after the final boss fight he mentioned. Then he went into how his new Skills from becoming the Fisher King complemented Dominion.

"I see," she said, still a bit sleepily. Though she couldn't completely grasp all of the interconnections between James's new Skills, it sounded to her like he would be able to exert complete control over land within some defined territory. "When are you going to try out the new Skill?" she asked.

"Oh, I already did," he replied. He seemed lively and energetic, as usual. She didn't know how, but in these moments in bed, it seemed almost as if energy left her body and drained into his. His face took on a slightly guilty look. "I tried it last night as you were falling asleep. It used up a lot of Mana, but I recharged overnight. I think it'll probably be a once daily thing for me. That way I can keep up a steady pace of expansion."

She pushed herself upright slightly to keep from falling asleep. "Well, this time you have to show me," she said. "Maybe I can learn it by looking at you, and we'll be twice as dangerous."

Mina did not bother to add, *Plus, I'm imagining that it looks cool!*

"There's probably not much to see," James said, but he half-smiled as he spoke the words.

He raised his left hand theatrically in the air, and he said the Skill name aloud, which she knew was completely unnecessary. **"Dominion."**

The ring glowed orange like it was being forged in fire. And a huge surge of dark-colored Mana enveloped his body in an instant and pulsed outward in all directions.

Mina sat up all the way, wolf furs forgotten as she looked at him in shock.

I didn't just see that. I felt *that*, she thought. *I felt it in my bones.* And she remembered. *I knew I felt something different when I woke up this morning. I thought there was something in the air. Now I know there was. His Mana. His energy. The power of Dominion.*

It was a heavy, thick aura that she felt slightly more intensely now than she had before. She'd never felt raw Mana from someone other than herself before; she'd only seen Mana used in magic. This was something else. When it hit her, it was like a wave of incredibly dense fog.

I knew he could change the environment, but to feel *that. It was so intense . . .*

Afterward, he breathed as if he'd just done some heavy exercise. And it did seem draining. Though the movement of Mana was almost too quick and sudden for her eyes to track—so quick that she still wasn't sure what color it was other than something dark—it was obvious to Mina that the quantity he'd used was substantially higher than whatever he'd expended to make the building they were in.

There was also something different to the quality of his voice as he spoke the Skill name. Although she couldn't pinpoint exactly why, the intensity of the sound made her feel as if she was back in Hecate's chamber beneath the stadium from the final challenge.

That was it. It felt a bit like a god was speaking.

Mina didn't voice that thought. She wondered if it was blasphemous, though she wasn't sure if she cared. From James's story, it didn't seem as if gods and goddesses were truly omnipresent or omniscient the way myths had often tried to depict them. Then again, there was no need to tempt fate. And she didn't want to say something like that unless she was certain.

"Well, impressed?" he asked once he'd caught his breath.

She nodded, uncertain of her voice. She was more than impressed. This power, she felt certain, would transform their lives.

She breathed in and out deeply, then finally tried to speak. "Wuddya—ahem, sorry. What do you plan to do with this power?"

CHAPTER NINE

The First Believer

Mina waited for James to answer her question.

She could think of many things that he might be able to do with the incredible powers he now possessed. She thought she knew where her husband's mind would go, but she wanted to hear what he would say.

James seemed hesitant. He turned away from her and walked over to the section of wall that he'd turned into a swiveling window, opened it up, and looked out, breathing in the fresh air. Then he turned, looked back at her, and smiled.

"I'm going to go out and conquer as much of the world as I can," he finally said.

Mina nodded and smiled. She was a little afraid of what the future would hold, but she had known that her husband would say something like that. He was still the same ambitious, unscrupulous man she'd fallen in love with and married. Despite her worries, she was also excited.

"Well, I believe in you," she said, blinking away the traces of sleep from her eyes. "I'll help you however I can."

She began pulling her clothes back on. Now was no time to nap. There was work to be done.

It seemed to her good and proper that her husband should be the ruler of as much of the world as he could lay his hands on.

In this situation, the governments of the world were certain to lose their holds on most, if not all, of the lands they had once controlled. Rulers could not hold a territory where the foundations of their power had been shattered.

Technology was a critical part of their control. Now their equipment, their buildings, and all symbols and semblance of their authority had been destroyed by the System.

Anarchy was sure to break out in regions without rulers—violence and disorder.

Then new leaders would emerge. Some form of order would take shape in the unsettled regions.

It was only rational to want to be in the ruling class. Anyone else would be subject to the rulers' whims.

If James had said he wanted to become a conqueror pre-System, she could and would have raised a million objections, all relating to difficulty. Who would let him take over any piece of land? How would he protect it and enforce his authority?

They were just one man and one woman, after all.

Following the System's arrival, things had been flipped on their head. James was one of the strongest people in the world, capable of defeating hundreds of enemies by himself, even able to weaponize the land itself. Any power disparities ran completely in their favor.

Now the question was: who could possibly stop him? And what if he didn't try to seize this moment? The immense power he had shown would inevitably draw danger toward them even if he wasn't ambitious. The monsters in this world had levels and a System just like humans. Surely they would seek out powerful enemies to destroy.

"What's your first step?" she asked.

"Get the people around here to accept me as the leader."

Mina nodded. "I don't think you'll have much trouble selling that. You're a very persuasive speaker."

"Really?" he asked, raising an eyebrow. "How would you write my speech? I think what I can actually promise is kind of limited, and these people are used to living in a democra—"

"Bah, don't worry about that," Mina said. "People will understand that reality is different now. You just need to convey how strong you are. Make sure they know that you have some plans, but don't promise too much. Above all, you need to boast about the things you've already done. Your story about Orientation would have won me over if I wasn't already on your side. Clearly, you're stronger than any of them will be. So, brag about your victories and basically tell them that if they join you, they'll be winners in this crazy new world, and if they go elsewhere, they'll end up being victims. 'Join the strong' is always a winning pitch."

She knew that this wouldn't be easy for James to frame in a palatable way, but he really was a persuasive person. He seemed to be even smoother with words since he had come back from Orientation—because of those new Skills, no doubt. And if there were items that were harder for people from a democratic society to swallow, maybe he shouldn't sugarcoat them. She was confident that there wouldn't be a better deal on offer anywhere.

"Well, I'll think about what you're advising," James said, smiling. "I'm glad we had this chat. It means a lot that you believe in me. You're really the only one whose opinion I actually value. Still more to talk about, but I'd better look at getting some food ready for all of us."

Mina nodded and returned to a relaxed posture. "Please and thank you," she said sweetly. "I still have some rations left from my Orientation."

"Whatever you have would probably be helpful," James replied. "In my Orientation, I only found meat to eat."

Mina didn't know how he prepared it without their kitchen appliances, but James left the bedroom, and half an hour later, he came back to announce that food was ready.

For the first time in weeks, James, Mina, and Yulia ate a meal together, along with James Jr., Abhi, and his siblings, Indira and Deepam.

The table conversation was delicate. Mina, James, and Yulia had an impromptu huddle before they called Abhi to the table. They agreed to avoid discussing what had happened to them in Orientation for fear of worrying Abhi about his parents. But James also felt it was imperative that they learn, as soon as they could, what had happened to children during Orientation.

"The kids here aren't the only ones in the complex who came back without their parents," James explained. "Yesterday, when I went out for a bit before the rain really started pouring, I searched the rest of the buildings. I found about a dozen children. Other people have agreed to look after them for the moment, but I think it's best that we figure out what sort of experience they all had, if we can."

Mina and Yulia spoke first. They thanked James for the meal, and Abhi chimed in as well.

"Thank you for breakfast," he said, smiling shyly.

"It's my pleasure to feed you all," James said.

Then there was some back and forth over the table about the condition of the buildings they had come back to, how everyone had slept, and changes that people wanted made to their current living space if they decided to stay there.

Abhi and Yulia, without being asked, took care of feeding Indira the toddler and Deepam the baby, respectively. James found himself impressed. Did Abhi do this when he was at home with his parents too, or did he just implicitly understand that he had more responsibility now? Naturally, James couldn't ask such a potentially painful question, but he thought he was going to like this kid.

Finally, James decided that the table had become comfortable enough for him to try gently broaching the subject of where the children had been. "So, Abhi, were you guys waiting in your apartment long before we came and found you?"

The little boy picked at his food quietly for a few seconds before he answered. "Not long, no."

"I guess you got back the same day as us, then."

Abhi nodded.

A series of gentle questions and answers followed before James felt confident in asking, "Do you know where you and your siblings were these last few weeks?"

The little boy shook his head silently and leaned down over his plate so his long bangs covered his eyes.

"I mean, I don't expect you to know exactly where you went, but could you describe the place?" James asked.

"Yes," Abhi said. Slowly, faltering and repeating himself, he told a story about being transported to a purely white room. This setting was familiar to James, Mina, and Yulia, and they gave each other looks as they listened to this part.

But there Abhi's story diverged from their own. He described the room being like a classroom. He was with other children his own age.

"We played games, answered questions, did puzzles—and they tested us." He spoke with a shiver in his voice.

James barely had to prompt him to provide further information. It was as if the boy had been eager to tell someone about his strange experience, but he hadn't thought the strangers around him would listen.

Children are used to adults not taking them seriously, James thought.

The picture that emerged was of a series of aptitude tests. Tests intended to establish the children's latent abilities in many areas: Mana manipulation, physical power and speed, intelligence, empathy, creative thinking, teamwork, problem-solving.

Most of them were disguised as games, pop quizzes, puzzles, story time—anything the System's agents could disguise as something fun. But for an adult, the description made it transparent. James thought that whoever controlled the System must have genuinely wanted this experience to be comfortable for the children.

But there was also something terrible and disturbing about it.

As Abhi said, horrified, his voice trembling, "Whenever someone didn't do well, if they messed up on too many of the tests, the grown-ups would ask the kid to go with them," a tear sprang to his eyes. "Then the grown-up would take them through a door, and we never saw them again."

James, Mina, and Yulia exchanged silent, disturbed looks.

"Okay," James said. "Okay, Abhi." He put an arm around the boy's shoulders and squeezed him. "You don't have to tell us any more unless you want to."

The little boy shook with sobs for the next few minutes before he was able to finish his meal. Then he asked to be excused, and James let him go.

"The things the children went through . . ." Mina murmured under her breath.

"What did they do with the babies?" Yulia asked quietly in obvious distress.

Mina looked, horrified, at James Jr. Of course, he was safe beside them, but what if they had decided to have their child a little earlier?

"Well, I wanted answers," James said to himself. "We already knew the System isn't exactly a benevolent force, but this is beyond anything I imagined."

Now his imagination extended further. What else would the System have done with these children? Ranked them and rewarded them accordingly, probably. He thought about the handful of countries in the world that still created child soldiers. How would the System have tested them? Would it have treated them as children or adults? What about their life histories? Was it possible that one day James would run into a violent, abused child with insane powers like his?

It was beginning to feel as if the System had set out to create the war of all against all that Hobbes had warned about in *Leviathan*.

"I hope Abhi will be all right," Yulia said quietly. Her tone wasn't reproachful, but James felt guilty all the same.

I needed that information, he thought. *It might allow me to anticipate future threats.*

But he felt he had crossed a line. He rose, leaving his meal half-finished, and went to find Abhi.

The boy was in the room that he shared with his siblings, sitting in bed with a book. James doubted he was old enough to read yet, but Abhi's eyes were glued to the pages, and James found himself smiling.

I've been there, he thought. *A whole new world is opening for you.*

He stepped into the room, and Abhi's head popped up immediately.

"Am I in trouble?" he asked, voice quavering.

What did the System do to you? James thought. *What did I do?*

"No," he said aloud. "I just remembered that all my books were in our apartment. I wanted to do some reading. What's that you have there?"

Abhi held the book up. "It's *The Little Engine That Could*," he said. He teared up a little. "My mom and dad used to read it to me."

Oh my gosh, I didn't know what I was doing, I don't know how to help these kids, James thought. Then he took a deep breath, and he made himself give his usual confident smile. His emotions were back under control.

"Do you know how to read yet?" he asked.

The little boy shook his head. "I know some of the letters, and I remember some of the words from the book, but I don't know how to read. Mom said I was learning fast."

"Would you like it if I read to you?" James asked.

Abhi nodded, and James spent the next fifteen minutes doing his best impression of an engine that thought it could.

Then they moved onto Babar the Elephant books, and after that, James made

Abhi actually laugh with stories that he had made up—twisted versions of "The Three Little Pigs" and "Goldilocks and the Three Bears." James had originally made his own funny variations on those stories to tell his sister when they were both children, but they turned out to be useful with strangers' children too.

Finally, Yulia came in to bring Abhi's siblings back. The little ones were apparently ready for a nap. Abhi decided to join them, and James was saved from pretending that he knew what he was doing in this area.

"Thanks for taking care of them," he said to Yulia.

She beamed with pride and then got back to putting the little ones down.

He got up to leave the room, and Mina stood in the doorway, looking bewitched with him.

"How long were you watching that?" he asked, faintly embarrassed.

"I knew you would be a good father," she said very quietly. Just for his ears.

"I'm starting to wonder," he said, smiling despite himself.

"It's also probably how you'll succeed as a conqueror," she added.

James raised an eyebrow.

"If you want people to accept your authority without elections to give it theoretical legitimacy, or a military to enforce it, you have to remember how you made that little boy feel just now." She drew closer and placed a hand on his chest. "The people you want to follow you have to feel that they have your love and protection. You have the advantage of being the sort of person people naturally trust and want to follow."

"So you say," James said. If his goal of conquering territory and reunifying the local society behind a common set of purposes was comparable to this matter of taking care of children, he was a complete novice.

"I'm serious," she said. "Get people here to accept that your authority and your protection are a package deal as explicitly as you can. They would probably follow you implicitly anyway, but to make this place safer for all of us, you need to be able to organize the community. That means that people have to agree to follow your orders, at least in some things."

James was about to reply when a knock came at the door.

He stood, looking at Mina and wondering who that could be, when the knock came again.

"I guess I should just be glad we had the time to ourselves that we did," James said finally. "I did promise to discuss the future of this community with people today. I guess some of them are taking me up on it."

Then the knock became a pounding.

With an annoyed expression spreading across his face, James descended the stairs.

CHAPTER TEN

The Landlord

In addition to minor familial drama, the morning brought with it its share of neighbor troubles.

When James reached the foot of the stairs, he recognized one of those who had sheltered in the building he had thrown up the previous day: an older man with gray hair and a close-cropped beard.

This was the one who was trying to bring up rent for some reason, James remembered. And now that he saw him again, there was some other memory stirring. Unfortunately, it was dim, from sometime before the period when James began to remember almost everything that happened to him in crisp detail. Before the System.

"I'm here to discuss rent," the man said, speaking hotly. "You said you would talk to people tomorrow. Well, now it's tomorrow. You aren't getting out of this, you hear?"

Wow. The way you're talking to me just reminds me that I haven't killed anyone or anything in front of any of these people. It was impossible for James to imagine anyone from the Rodriguez camp or Damien Rousseau's faction speaking to him so rudely. It was a little amusing.

"Sir, would you like to go someplace private to discuss whatever your problem is?" James asked in a calm, measured tone of voice—what he thought of sometimes as his customer service voice, for use both when he was serving customers and when he was talking to customer service.

There were several people walking around outside, though not many. It was still early in the day. James guessed the few people who were outside were thinking about feeding their loved ones. Not everyone who had completed Orientation would have acquired the same abundance of resources that James enjoyed.

James didn't want to have whatever this conversation was going to be in front of other people. He believed you should generally praise people in public and criticize them in private.

"No. No, I would not!" the old man said. "What I have to discuss concerns them too."

James noticed a few ears perk up as the people in the vicinity began to pay attention.

So, you have chosen the public humiliation route, James thought. *You're really leaving me no choice.*

"All right, then," he said lightly. "Have it your way. What's your name?"

The man appeared affronted that James didn't know who he was. "I'm John Carraway. The landlord. The person to whom you and all the other people living here were paying their rent. I want to know what you're going to do about this building you've erected on my land." He gestured at the structure James had put up.

"Oh, you used to own this land?" James asked. He thought he understood where this man was going. He wanted to parlay his old land ownership claim into some form of power or influence or even wealth in the new world. It was understandable, but he had no interest in being hamstrung. He'd have to cut this man off before he could get started.

"What do you mean 'used to'?" Carraway asked, raising his voice. "I still—"

"No, you don't," James said, cutting him off.

"I still have the deed!" The old man's tone was outraged.

"I don't care," James said with an almost careless ease. He made sure to project his voice so that everyone eavesdropping could hear him clearly. "I don't acknowledge your claim. You cannot defend it. There is no court to which you can appeal. Even when we do eventually create a court system, we do not live under the same system of laws under which you established your claim. This land is mine now by right of conquest."

"What?!"

"Sir," James said, sighing slightly. "I sympathize with you. You worked hard all your life to get a piece of land that was all your own. You improved it and built apartments on it, all so you could have a nest egg to live off of. Right?"

"That's right!"

"Well, sadly, the apartments you built are all gone. And based on the data I've gathered, the planet we're on is actually significantly larger than Earth used to be. There is no piece of land that can be reliably identified as your land. Where we are now is my land. I own it." He raised a hand to cut off the man, who was opening his mouth to interrupt. "I was a lawyer before this time, sir. There are several possible bases to claim property ownership. It's especially interesting, as right now there is new land that never existed before. In these cases, under Locke's theory of property rights, the original owner of property is the person who first mixes his labor with it. That was me." He gestured at the building behind them.

"The evidence is right behind me. I mixed my labor with this land. I have improved it. Unfortunately, whatever existed in the time before me has disappeared. Another basis for property ownership also favors me. I own this land by right of conquest. I have occupied it and can defend it against all comers." He raised his voice higher, to make it obvious that he wanted to be overheard. "If there's anyone who believes they can beat me in a fight and take this land from me, they're welcome to try. Whoever beats me will be the new owner."

The people who were gathered outside looked at each other like they were wondering if this was some sort of strange trap. They'd experienced enough of those in Orientation.

"It's not a trick," James said. "One time offer only. Anyone and everyone who wants to try and take me on right now, you can attempt it, and I promise I won't kill you for trying. I just want all of you to be satisfied that it's impossible for you. I am the owner of this land now, and you are all my tenants. For the moment, I have no intention of charging you rent—"

James stopped mid-sentence. A bold young man with bulging muscles had charged forward, armed with a thick bone club that looked like a piece of System-created equipment. He looked intent on taking James up on his proposal. His expression was intense; he was clearly prepared for violence.

As soon as he was within range to strike, James made a move that no one else could see. He lunged forward and struck his would-be attacker with a backhanded slap to the face. The man recoiled, stumbled backward, collapsed, and then lay unmoving on the ground.

Then James sat back down. Everyone stared at the unconscious man.

"He's still alive," James said after a moment. "Don't worry. I'm a man of my word. In any case, I can pledge that everyone who accepts me as the leader of this new land will be safe from harm while they stay here." He gave a very bare-bones explanation of the power of the Fisher King. It hadn't been his intention when he came downstairs to give a real speech, and there weren't enough people outside to justify it, anyway. But he hoped they would spread the word about what he could do—the safety that he could offer with his powers. "I know everything that enters or exits my territory," he finished. "And monsters will be scared off by my aura overhanging this land."

The former had only become true today, when James pumped out his second infusion of Mana with Dominion; it seemed his Fisher King powers took a lot of energy to become effective. And the latter wasn't a guarantee, but it was close enough to one. It would be even truer once the wolf pack arrived to patrol the borders.

"So, what, we'll be paying *you* rent, is that it?" the former landlord asked. He sounded despondent but resigned.

"No," James said. "At some point in the future we may need to institute taxes, but I'll try not to let things come to that. For now, I'd like to see us all try to serve the community according to our strengths. The System has given us a currency with System Credits. We can buy supplies we need with that. But mostly, I'd like to see us producing a civilization with the abilities we have. This isn't the last phase of your life that you were expecting. It's something more dynamic than that. You're not going to fade away into old age. You're going to be a part of the generation that rebuilds civilization after we got wiped out. Get excited!"

There were some murmurs of support from the people outside. These people needed more than this from him, James knew. They had suffered great losses in recent weeks. Many of them would have seen family members and friends die in Orientation. It would take time for them to form a community. And strong leadership would be key. But if he was going to make speeches, he wanted to do it when as many people as possible were present. Not waste it on a handful.

Great public speakers draw energy from crowds. And James decided at that moment that he wanted a crowd in front of him to hear him speak. He wanted that to help him kickstart the foundation of his new country and the reconstruction of the elements they would want to keep from the old.

"Three days," James said, before the people could disperse. "I'm going to take the next two days to make sure all of us can meet our basic survival needs—food, water, adequate shelter, plumbing. Then on the third day, we'll have an assembly to address our plans for the future. Anyone who thinks they can help with any of the survival stuff should come talk to me directly. And you all should pass on what I've said to your friends and family members, or any neighbor you run into."

People nodded. About half of them started to walk away, while three stayed back, huddling together in a discussion among themselves about what James had said. He didn't listen in too closely, because he was still dealing with the former landlord.

"What am I supposed to do?" Carraway whined quietly, his voice low. "This place was my whole retirement plan."

James looked at him with a degree of sympathy and tried to be kind in his response. "Look, no one's retirements are going to be working out as they had planned," he said. "You remember when Social Security started running low a decade ago?"

The old man nodded.

"Well, think about it," James said. "The Internet is still down for everyone on Earth as far as we know. Cell towers down, buildings demolished, monsters roaming the land. Is that money in people's bank accounts really going to do any good now? Or the land that they owned?"

"Well, no."

"So, you're just in the same boat as everyone else now," James said.

"It's just so unfair," Carraway said in a defeated tone.

"It is," James agreed. "People who worked hard should be rewarded for it. But fairness is a human concept. We can't expect the System that's running things now to follow our concept of fairness. Stick with me, though. I'll do my best to help you find the place where you fit in. I've often felt that our society dooms people to premature death by creating this idea of retirement. Hard-working people with years of wisdom and experience suddenly turning to inactivity, lying around on a beach or something and living off of their savings. That's not exactly healthy. Maybe it will ultimately benefit you that the old world ended. You might find a new source of purpose and energy in this new world. It's a primitive place with no electricity, but there's also endless opportunity. A blank slate."

James wasn't sure he entirely believed what he was saying about retirement, but he'd heard it before and thought it was plausible enough. Most importantly, he felt sure that it was what Carraway needed to hear. And the rest of his little pep talk was rehearsal for the larger speech he was planning to give his community in three days time.

Carraway seemed to take some solace in it. "I suppose you might be right," he said. The hard lines in his face relaxed a little. "I'll think about ways I can be of use in this new environment. Maybe it's like that Billy Joel song, 'Vienna.' You know it?"

"Um, vaguely," James said, shrugging. "Actually, probably not. I think I know maybe one song by him."

The old man shook his head. "The younger generation have no taste in music."

I'm not that young, James thought. But Carraway was walking away, and he seemed to have a little more energy about him now. James decided not to spoil the man's improved mood by indirectly calling him old.

"Hey, can we talk to you for just a minute?" James turned his head. One of the people from the huddled group of men was addressing him. He was wearing camouflage pants and a plain white T-shirt, and his dirty blond hair was cut in a mullet. The two men on either side of him were dressed more apocalypse-appropriate, in basic System gear. James instantly knew that they were a Heavy Warrior and a Light Warrior respectively. The former was an East Asian man with short hair and a small mustache, and the other man was Caucasian and had his dark hair in a ponytail.

"Sure, happy to talk," James said. "What are your names?"

"I'm Sam Masterson. These are my buddies Dave Matsumoto and Paul Mann." James immediately noted that they must have all been in Orientation together. "We were wondering if we might help with the survival stuff."

James smiled. *They're already treating me as the go-to guy. No objections so far. Excellent.* "Happy to have your help. I'm James Robard. What exactly were you thinking?"

"We thought maybe we could all go hunting," Sam said, returning James's smile.

CHAPTER ELEVEN

Blessing of the Fisher King

"Hunting, huh?" James said. "Well, it was on my to-do list already. Let's do it, absolutely."

In fact, identifying people he could employ to help keep the small community supplied with fresh food had been his top priority. *Way to make my life easy, guys!*

There was a part of him that wondered if these three gentlemen had anything more planned beyond hunting, but their whispered huddle conversation hadn't revealed it if so. It was just James's own dark instincts that made him suspicious.

"That's great!" Masterson said, high-fiving his two friends. "I knew you would be interested. How soon can you be ready?"

"Give me fifteen minutes," James said. "I'll just make sure everything is okay for my family, and then we can head out."

"Sounds good," said Masterson.

"Do you have a watch somewhere we can't see?" Matsumoto asked. "Paul here has a pretty good watch that's solar powered, but Sam and I have been having trouble finding a way to tell time. The phones are all dead."

"Oh, mine still has a little bit of charge," James said. This was a little bit of a lie by omission. His phone did still have some power left because he wasn't using it for anything, just keeping it in his magic satchel, which seemed to keep stored items in stasis until he needed them. But James wasn't using that to tell the time.

With Mind of the Predator, ordering part of his brain to count the seconds and let him know when fifteen minutes had passed was easy. But the details of his powers were on a need-to-know basis. All these gentlemen needed to know was that James's power was impressive and not to be trifled with. He would show them a taste of that during the hunt.

He turned and began walking up the stairs.

Mina was waiting for him at the top. "Well, what happened?" she asked.

He briefly went over it, and she nodded her approval. "I can't believe someone thought that they could use a property-rights claim for anything now. What was he trying to accomplish?" she asked.

"I think he was really hoping that I would agree to give him some sort of a free living, take care of him in lieu of paying him rent. He was talking about how this place was his whole retirement plan. I felt a little bad for him." Then he mentioned the hunting plan.

"That seems fine to me," she said. "I've realized I probably shouldn't be worrying about you as much as I used to."

He chuckled at that. "What, I'm not vulnerable enough now for you to worry about me?"

"You don't seem vulnerable to anything at all, as far as I know," she retorted. "Yesterday, I saw you chop off your own hand and turn it into a living thing, then grow a new one without using any visible magic. You know, I used to worry that you would get into an accident driving home from work. Now I think that even if that happened, only the cars would be damaged—and whoever the other driver was!"

James chuckled and shook his head.

You had some dark intuition about the intentions of those men downstairs, came Roscuro's voice in James's mind. *Are you sure you don't want to say anything to your wife about it?*

No, James replied. *I'm fairly certain I'm just being paranoid. If they did have bad intentions, those would only apply to me, anyway. Maybe they want to be in charge around here, so they planned to arrange a hunting accident or something.* Still, he didn't really like leaving his wife alone here. She was far from defenseless, especially with her new Class, but still . . .

"Have you thought about trying some sort of protection spell on this place?" James asked.

Her eyes softened. "You worried about me, skapi?" She planted a soft kiss on his cheek.

"Only whenever I can't see you," he said.

"Well, I'll try it," she said doubtfully. "My knowledge of spellcraft like that is very basic, though. Hecate mentioned Witch Classes need spell books to properly hone our Skills. I only learned a very small share of what's possible with the Class change."

What can I do to keep you safer? James thought. He remembered one of his Fisher King abilities.

"Mina, could you get on your knees for a minute?" James asked.

She arched an eyebrow. "Why exactly?"

James smiled mischievously. "So I can bless you," he said. "It's one of my Fisher King Skills. Whenever I want to use one of those powers, I get a mental picture of how it's supposed to work. When I use Blessing of the Fisher King, I'm supposed to be positioned above you."

"All right."

She bent and then sat down on the floor, legs folded in front of her.

"Is this good?" she asked.

"Yes, it's fine," he said.

Blessing of the Fisher King! Different options for blessings presented themselves to him. He sensed that the word combinations he was seeing were only a few of many possible; these were the ones that his subconscious mind had deemed most appropriate out of the available choices.

"As the flora and fauna of the Fisher King grow, so must you grow stronger, Mina Robard," he pronounced. **"As the beasts of the field and the birds of the air grow in their numbers, so will you be fruitful and multiply."**

James's body sagged slightly as he finished speaking, and his vision went slightly blurry. That had taken a lot out of him! He only dimly noticed that Mina was also showing a physical reaction. Her whole body shuddered.

After a few seconds of this, he sat down for a moment on the nearby sofa to catch his breath. He checked his Mana. He still had almost half of it. The blessing had used up more Stamina than anything else, though it had cost him a bit of Mana too. It felt as if he were speaking magic words, even though it was plain English.

Mina rose beside him. "That blessing is quite something," she said, her voice tremulous. "I feel different. You're going to need to only use that on people you really trust. It's quite a boost, I suspect."

James just smiled grimly and nodded. He didn't bother to mention that he was fairly certain there were blessing options that accounted for the Fisher King not fully trusting the recipient.

"I'm going to go now," he said. "It took a bit of a toll. I hope you feel comfortable holding down the fort?"

"I feel like I could tear down a fort," Mina said.

"Well, try not to do it while I'm gone," James said, giving her a grin. "I only just put the building up. I know it needs a lot of improvements, but I don't think starting from scratch is the answer."

She rolled her eyes and opened her mouth to respond.

"James," came Yulia's voice from the other side of the room, "could I ask you about something?" She looked worried.

He looked at Mina for a moment. She shrugged.

"I'm going to go and check on the little ones while you and Yulia talk," she said. She went into the children's room.

"What's up?" he asked after a long moment. "Did you want a blessing too?"

"No. Maybe. Not right now. It's about the kids," she said. "I'm so glad that you found them, but I was wondering if there might be others."

"There were," James said. "I went around last night and found over a dozen other children who used to live in these apartments. Fortunately, there were some responsible adults who agreed to look after them for now. We'll need to figure something more permanent out soon, but the situation is under control."

"That's great!" Yulia looked relieved, only for her face to turn downcast again.

"What's wrong now?" he asked.

"Well, I was just thinking. What about all the kids who weren't in the apartment complex? What's going to happen to them?"

James immediately sympathized with Yulia. *She's so compassionate*, he thought. *It's really something you can't teach. Who knows if I would've ever thought about the hundreds or maybe thousands of children around central Florida who are probably homeless tonight? It's a real tragedy . . .*

"You're right," he said. "I mean, I understand what you're thinking. I think there are some children who are going to be in real trouble these next few days."

Really, if no one finds them in the next forty-eight hours, a lot of them will die. James didn't want to say that, but he was certain it was true. And he was fairly certain he could do something to at least reduce the numbers. It would just use up more resources and energy that could be spent on improving his little community's odds of survival. Even if he was successful, any children he saved would become a future burden.

They're not your business, his dark inner voice said. *If you do nothing at all, they'll either be saved by other people or disappear. Do nothing. It's the best thing for you and your family. Objectively.*

"Is there anything we can do?" Yulia asked, searching his face for any sign of hope.

James suppressed a groan and made himself smile.

"Yeah. There is something we can do," James said. He checked his mental timer. *All good. I have another five minutes.* "Want to see something cool?"

She nodded.

James used Shed Skin twice and Monster Generation eight times, infusing moderate amounts of Mana into each creation. The monsters were each composed of one quarter of the total coverage of his skin, but each took on a semi-humanoid shape, with two limbs, a pair of wings, and a face.

There, now I've really done all that I can do, he thought, breathing heavily again. *If I make any more of those monsters, I won't have energy left to hunt with.* He was glad he had superior regeneration abilities. As long as he didn't do any heavy-duty magic, he would be back at a hundred percent by tomorrow. Though, his skin was incredibly tender right now as well. Losing so many layers in a row was far from fun.

"What *are* those?" Yulia looked slightly horrified.

"They're my pets!" James said proudly. "They can fly because they're my hollowed-out skins—lighter than me, with some of my strengths. I'm going to send them out to look for missing children. It should be more effective than searchers on the ground would be, so we'll know if there are kids anywhere for at least a few miles around in every direction. I'll keep them searching for as long as I can."

"That's, um, great," she said, looking a little nervous at the sight of the monsters.

"I know they're a little strange looking," James said. They looked, even to him, like some giant insect's discarded exoskeletons. Ominous and ugly. "But they're very useful and completely obedient to me. They require very little in terms of upkeep."

They just eat whatever's around, he thought, *assuming they aren't killed before they need to eat.* Not so different from him, really, now that he had the Omnivore Skill.

Yulia approached one of the monsters and took its hand.

"Thank you for helping us with our search," she said, shaking hands with it. The monster looked to James for a moment. He didn't give directions one way or another, though.

James had put a bit more of himself into these creatures than he usually did, giving them more independent intelligence and decision-making ability, as well as the ability to speak. That was part of why creating eight of them took so much out of him.

Even the mechanism of flight was different. Instead of being balloons like his first generation of flying monsters, these creatures would open the skin on their backs into a pair of wings and rapidly vibrate them to fly. This should allow for better precision and directional control, which could be important in a search and rescue mission. These creatures were so different that James had given them a new name: Skin Husks.

"You're welcome," the Skin Husk rasped after a few long uncomfortable seconds. Its voice sounded like autumn leaves crunching. Yulia looked like she was resisting taking a step back as she listened to it.

"We've got to get going, okay?" James said.

Yulia turned back to James and surprised him with a hug. "Good luck!" she said. As they separated, he saw there were tears at the corners of her eyes.

Right, he thought. *She manages to care so much even about people she's never met or heard anything about.* It was almost incomprehensible to him, but also sweet.

James sent the Skin Husks out through the window in the master bedroom, and then he descended the stairs.

Time to hunt—and decide if these guys are people I can trust or not.

CHAPTER TWELVE

The Haunted Forest, Part 1

"Are you ready for this hunt, old man?" Sam asked as they waited for Robard to come back outside.

"I don't know if any of us are," Dave replied drily. "Is that thing even loaded?" He gestured at Sam's rifle.

"You'd better believe it," Sam said. "I'm taking this completely seriously."

"Hm." Dave's tone was unconvinced.

"Not that I intend on using the gun if I don't have to," Sam added. "Limited rounds in this world now until we learn to make our own. At least in my gun. We can't all be like you."

Dave didn't even respond. Sam thought he was used to the older man's long silences by now, but today, the quiet unnerved him. They were about to go into danger. He wanted Dave to reassure him, not play mute.

He's just nervous, Sam thought. *What's taking Paul so long? Robard was the one who wanted time to prepare. If Paul doesn't get back here before he does, it'll make us look like we weren't ready.* It probably didn't matter, but he found himself wanting to make the best impression he could on Robard, this man who seemed to be taking it upon himself to lead the survivors in this area.

"You should relax, Sam," Dave said. "You don't want to make a bad impression." He said the words lightly, but as happened so often, he cut right to the core of what Sam was thinking about.

I guess I'm the nervous one, he thought. *Well, Dave did go to war. He has more experience with these types of situations than I do.* All three men knew what they meant when they had asked Robard to accompany them on a hunt. It was the chance to impress him, assess him in turn, and if he didn't measure up to the trio's expectations, deal with him accordingly.

If he's not fit to lead, we'll cut him down early so there's plenty of time to decide on a new leader. Sam naturally had the faint idea of putting himself forward in the back of his mind. Though Dave was older and more experienced in matters of violence, he and the more impressionable Paul had deferred to Sam's natural leadership throughout Orientation. The three of them had formed a de facto leadership group there.

It was strange to come back and see someone else assert command here, but they would at least give him a chance to show what he could do. If he was at least as good at fighting and leadership as Sam, they wouldn't kill him. The trio had only had to kill a couple of people back in Orientation, and that had been borderline self-defense.

None of them were truly comfortable with cold-blooded murder yet.

Paul emerged from one of the abandoned ruins. He waved merrily at his two companions, and Sam snorted to himself. Paul held up something in a wrapper as he approached. With his other hand, he was eating something that had come packaged in an identical wrapper. As Paul came closer, it became apparent that he was chewing a Clif Bar.

Of course he is, Sam thought. *Somehow, that bastard always manages to find food, but he never seems to gain any weight.*

"Hey, fellas," Paul said as he got within comfortable speaking range. "Look what I found!"

"Of course you did," Sam said, shaking his head. "Did you check your watch, man?"

At least we're all armed and ready, he thought. *We won't have any other delays. I've got my rifle and knives. Dave has his pistol. Paul has that stupid slingshot of his.*

"Sure did," Paul replied. "We have another minute."

"Ah. I guess it just *felt* like you were late, then," Sam said, slightly mollified.

"Thanks for getting some provisions, Paul," Dave said. "Did you pack up everything you found?"

Paul shook his head. "There were actually a lot of canned goods too. But it's a small community of people here. We're too far from the main road for people to wander over this way looking to loot. And it would be just my luck if that stuff belongs to someone still living in the building here." He gestured at the apartment building that Robard had erected. "I don't want to get a reputation for stealing things. We might as well wait for our dear leader to decide on the best way to proceed with those."

Sam nodded approvingly. "Putting our best feet forward, right, Dave?"

Dave gave him a nod back, his expression carefully blank.

I don't think Dave thinks this is a good idea at all, Sam assessed. Perhaps it wasn't. Dave's analyses of situations were usually very sharp.

Then Robard emerged from the front door of his apartment. A moment later, Paul's watch began beeping shrilly. It continued until he pressed a button on the side and turned it off.

Robard certainly had a knack for dramatic timing. *Did he sync timers with Paul when I wasn't looking or something?* Probably not. It was just luck that he appeared just before the timer finished.

"Well, are we all ready to go?" Robard asked.

"Born ready," Sam said.

"I'm ready too," Dave added.

"Lead the way," Paul said.

"I actually don't know where the game is," Robard admitted. "You see, when I used my powers on the area of land we're on now, most of the larger animals fled. The smaller ones mostly stayed put, but the big ones felt my aura as something hostile, and it scared them off. I could sense where they went while they were on my territory, but now I only know which direction they left in."

Sam nodded, secretly pleased. This would be his chance to show off. "I can track them if you can point me to where they were last," he said.

Robard nodded. "I'll take you to the place, and you can lead the way from there."

He guided the three men away from the cleared area around the buildings and into the line of trees that surrounded the apartment complex on three sides now.

"So, how long have you three known each other?" he asked.

"Just through Orientation," Sam replied. "We got pretty close there. You know how it is." *Assuming you made any friends in yours.*

Robard nodded. "Those bonds can be strong, I would expect. Some of the acquaintances I met in my Orientation are heading our way in the near future. Along with my pack of wolves. They should be here by tomorrow."

The other three stared at him. Sam felt certain he must have misheard. Either that, or Robard was trying to bluff them. Did he already know they were measuring him? If he was telling the truth somehow . . .

How do you get control over a pack of wolves?

"Here we are," James said after he'd led them for a half mile. "This is roughly the border of my territory. Small radius so far, but it's growing every day. This was the last place my powers detected the delicious creatures we're hunting."

He smiled to himself. He was pleased with how the men had reacted to his mention of the wolf pack. They didn't seem intimidated, but they were surprised. Good. He didn't want people he was hoping he could rely on for hunting to be easily scared. Hopefully, this was a preview of how everyone would react when he mentioned the wolf pack in the community meeting in a couple of days.

I guess Sam was the leader of the three of them back in Orientation, he assessed. *He's naturally more assertive and extroverted.*

"I guess it's my turn now," Sam said. "I'm using a Skill I got with my evolved Class." He said the words as if he was trying to boast, but James didn't give him any kind of reaction. Everyone would have a Class Evolution sometime in the next few weeks if they hadn't already. If they didn't, he wouldn't be doing his job as leader. "The Class is called the 'Lonely Hunter,'" Sam added.

James nodded at that. "Cool Class name," he said. "Show me what you've got."

Sam's eyes glowed slightly, then returned to their normal brown. He picked up a few tufts of hair from the ground. James had noticed them but hadn't expected any of the others to be able to pick up on them without his superhuman senses.

Guess I was wrong about that. Apparently, his Class is going to make him a very efficient hunter.

"Feral hogs," Sam said. "One of them scraped itself against this tree in the rush to get out of here." He looked at the ground as if he could see something that was invisible to James. Then his eyes moved up to James. His mouth moved in a brief expression of surprise that probably only James caught. "They really were running to get away from here."

James rubbed his hands together. "Good stuff. Where'd they go?"

I could probably track them myself, but I want to know what you can do.

Sam started walking in the path of broken twigs and shrubbery the hogs had left. The rest of them followed.

"I didn't think there were feral hogs in Florida," Paul said. "Thought they were more of a Texas thing."

"No," Sam said without looking back. "They're present in every county in Florida. Any local hunter worth his salt knows that."

"The way the System transforms animals, I wouldn't be surprised if these ones used to be some little piggies on a farm somewhere," James said. "I've never seen any this close to the apartments, anyway."

"What was your Orientation like, exactly, James?" Dave asked. "It seems like it may have been a little different from ours."

"We were in a forest, fighting monsters that had similar shapes to animals," James said. "How was it for you guys?"

Dave pursed his lips. "I suppose it wasn't that different," he said finally. "Most of our monsters didn't look much like Earth animals, though. There were Goblins, Hobgoblins, Bugbears, and Wargs. It felt wrong to eat most of the creatures, seeing as they had a humanoid shape." His eyes took on a dark look. "But we did what we had to do to survive."

James nodded grimly. "It wasn't so different from my Orientation. There was a monster in mine that could turn humans into the living dead. He was the final boss."

Sam turned back, a slightly startled look on his face. "Final boss?" he asked.

James nodded. "My understanding is that they tend to have a territory of their own. Like mine. Was there any place like that in your Orientation?"

Paul spoke up now. "There was. Most of our Orientation landscape was fields and caves, but there was this forest . . ." He left so much unspoken that James could feel that there was some aversion to that place still imprinted in the man's mind.

"No one explored that place, then?" he asked.

"We almost did," Sam said. "Not on purpose at first. The place had an ominous feeling about it, and we instinctively wanted to stay away. The Wargs prowled the outskirts of the forest, and they were the worst of the monsters we fought."

"But you almost explored?" James said. "Did you get any idea what kind of monster was there? It could end up being relevant. The monsters that survived Orientation all end up on Earth. They're likely to be in this same general geographic area."

Dave stopped walking and seemed to freeze completely. His eyes had a hollow look to them.

James threw a look at Sam. His intended meaning was, *Any idea what's up with him?*

Sam replied with a shrug and a look of helpless concern.

"Are you sure?" Dave asked finally.

"I heard it straight from the mouth of a god," James said. "And I trusted him when he told me."

"I don't even know where to start with the stuff you say," Sam muttered.

"We had a hard enough time with regular Orientation," Paul said. "To think we might still end up dealing with this boss monster. We barely got any distance into the forest when we tried to explore it."

"What happened to keep you from getting deeper?" James asked.

"Something tried to get Dave," Sam said gravely. His tone told James that he really wanted to drop the subject if possible.

But Dave spoke up then. "We don't really know if it was dangerous. I was just seeing things. Like a bad memory. I thought I saw someone I knew in there, but it was impossible."

"Why impossible?" James asked. Everyone looked uncomfortable, and James finally took the hint and dropped the subject.

The four men resumed the pursuit in silence.

"We're getting close, aren't we?" James asked after a while.

Sam looked surprised and then nodded. "You have a tracking Skill too?" he asked.

"Something like that," James said. "You guys get behind me. I'll launch the initial attack."

Sam opened his mouth, seemingly ready to object, but then Dave put a hand on his shoulder.

"That will be just fine, James," the older man said. "We look forward to seeing your stuff."

CHAPTER THIRTEEN

Hog Hunt

I *thought it was ill-advised from the start,* Dave tried to communicate to Sam with a look. *The idea of testing this man in this way. He's much more dangerous than he looks. So just let him lead the way. Don't try to show off.*

Sam gave an annoyed shrug as if to say, *Why didn't you say something sooner?*

But Dave couldn't answer that question. Not now, verbally, in front of Robard. Maybe one day, when the four of them were all close friends, they would be able to discuss these past misunderstandings and laugh about them. At present, it was possible Robard would turn out to be the sort of man who would kill them for questioning his authority. Dave sensed that Robard could do it, and in the right circumstances *would* do it, with little hesitation.

Dave had been trying to suss out what it was about James that gave him the heebie-jeebies for most of the hunt. Finally, he had fought his way through some mental blocks to a set of unfortunate memories that James reminded him of: recollections of Dave's service in the Sino-American War. That had ended a decade and a half ago, but the memories would last him a lifetime.

James moves like one of those special forces guys, Dave finally realized. Since the war ended, he'd never seen someone who moved so much like a predatory animal. Like his whole body was a deadly weapon and he knew how to use it.

The rest of the walk, unfortunately, Dave had been swimming in memories. Once he opened the floodgates, he couldn't easily close them again. His worst memories were of the men he'd killed and the good men he'd seen die at his side.

My father told me that the Chinese would hate me on sight, Dave remembered. His Japanese heritage would be obvious to them with one look at his face.

"When you see their looks of hate, it will be easier to pull the trigger," his father had promised.

But when he had actually been there, in the forests of China, things had been different. He had come upon two Chinese soldiers, and Dave had been quicker to aim his weapon than they. Both men had raised their hands over their heads in the universal gesture of surrender. Their eyes weren't hateful. They were surprised and afraid.

"You no American," one of them said in broken English. "Why you come here? We make no trouble with Japan."

And at first, Private Matsumoto had no answer to that. Not because he was Japanese, as they assumed—that was his father, not him—but because he didn't fully understand the causes of the war himself. He had enlisted because there was some incident in the South China Sea, and the two great powers of the world had declared war on each other as people had been anticipating for years. He was a patriotic American, and he would do his duty.

But like so many soldiers thrown into that meat grinder of a war, he'd been hastily trained. He certainly wasn't well versed in the nuances of the conflict. He couldn't explain, in any meaningful sense, why he was there.

Then one of the men made things easier for him. Seeing that his enemy seemed uncertain of what to do, the man lowered one hand and went for a pistol. Then the private's training kicked in. He quickly fired his weapon and executed both men.

That seemed to answer that.

In subsequent firefights, his finger felt more natural on the trigger. It got easier. Thank God, it got easier. Though that was probably bad in its own right.

One year and many engagements later, Corporal Matsumoto returned home and was honorably discharged. He even received the Army Commendation Medal, though he wasn't certain he deserved it.

But the images and the feelings never fully faded. Images of desecrated bodies, friendly and enemy alike. The constant feeling of being watched as he marched through a Chinese forest—borne out as true all too often, despite being dismissed by his commanding officers at first.

Then the System had appeared, and all those old memories resurfaced again. Now it felt like there might be a Chinese soldier around every blade of grass. Instead of soldiers, there were monsters. Creatures that didn't talk back were easier to kill, in some ways. But they also seemed to lack human fear.

The memories distracted him as he walked through the woods with his friends and Robard, who he hoped might be an ally in the future. He missed scraps of the conversation. Robard said something about wolves arriving tomorrow, which simply did not compute.

They pulled him back in when they started talking about the game they were hunting. Apparently, the beasts were feral hogs.

Dave segued the conversation into swapping Orientation stories. It seemed like a good topic for group bonding. Though, some of the memories were unfortunate. The strange spectral image of Dave's dead father being one of them.

And now they were creeping up on the feral hogs, which Sam—and possibly Robard?—had been able to track very precisely.

Dave used Identify on several of the creatures, as was his standard practice when they approached a group of enemy monsters.

[Short-Tusked Feral Hog, Lv. 12]
[Short-Tusked Feral Hog, Lv. 9]
[Short-Tusked Feral Hog, Lv. 13]

Not good. It looked like the average level was a little high, given the numbers. There were dozens of the monsters gathered in front of them, circled around a watering hole.

He locked eyes with Sam, who stood a foot behind James in the lead of the group.

"What?" Sam mouthed.

"The levels are too high," Dave mouthed back. "We should make a better plan."

Sam looked at Robard, and his face took on a stubborn cast. Then he shook his head.

Dave pressed a hand to his forehead. *Ugh. Macho bullshit motherfucker.* He loved that his friends Sam and Paul had never served in war. Sam's father was a military supplier, and Sam was employed by him in a mission-critical role in the company. Paul, like their new friend Robard, was too young to have served.

The fact of their non-service allowed them to move through the world with a lightness that Dave would never have. It was why Dave allowed Sam to lead the way through Orientation. Dave didn't want the responsibility; he already felt like he was carrying enough. It was more than fine to simply advise Sam, who would more often than not listen to good advice.

But sometimes, Dave felt an ugly wish. That Sam would have lost someone in the war. That he would have had to watch one of his friends bleed out before a medic could get to him. It was an atrocious thing to think, and he repented it every time. Especially after they actually did lose a few friends in Orientation.

Sam didn't seem to have learned much from the experience, though, if this moment was any indication. Refusing to back down just because Robard was willing to go forward was the decision of a child. A boy afraid to look like the lesser man.

We could all die if the monsters are coordinated in their counter to our attack, Dave thought, *because your ego is too big to back down from a challenge. Too big even to ask for a huddle to come up with a better plan—*

And then Robard struck.

He did something with his arm, a move too fast for Dave to see, and the closest beast went down. Then Robard's whole body blurred as he lunged forward, and it became difficult for Dave to track his movements. The only clue to where he had just been was the trail of destruction. Dead hogs fell where Robard had been, sometimes in pieces, sometimes gushing blood from a single vicious wound.

This wasn't a hunt. It was a massacre. It reminded Dave of one of the worst nights from his time in the war, when he and his team were sent up Elephant Trunk Hill—*no, damn it, focus! Any moment now, they'll kill him and turn on us*—

Then Dave saw the blurred figure zipping back to them as the hogs ran into each other in their confusion at the elusive attack.

He survived them. Somehow, he survived them. Wait, is he going to lead them back here?

Robard landed next to Sam. Dave was alarmed to observe he wasn't even breathless. He was smiling serenely through a spattering of blood.

"I'll let you guys get the next group," he said mildly. "I think I killed enough of them for the community to eat for a week at least. But, of course, we need to make our best efforts to secure all the supplies we can. The best information I've gathered is that our bags from Orientation seem to keep the meat fresh forever, so there's no downside to getting more."

Dave glanced over and saw the bodies of at least fifteen fallen creatures.

"So, you think we should kill all of them?" Sam asked. Dave turned back to his friend. He could see the pants-shitting expression on Sam's face as it dawned on him just how dangerous Robard was and how much he expected of them.

Robard tilted his head from side to side and then shrugged. "I don't know. There's a part of me that doesn't want to wreck a source of really good protein. And maybe we can breed these things. I would leave some of them alive, I think. Maybe kill a half dozen more, and we can try to capture the rest?"

Sam nodded. "Sure. Right. Just kill a half dozen. Sounds easy." He still looked gobsmacked as he spoke the words, but then a look that was almost confident returned to his face. "Come on, you guys," he said, looking to Dave and Paul. "We can do this."

Dave nodded slowly. Maybe they could. A few of the feral hogs were trying to run away. The rest were looking out for the next attack. Only a few had seen which way Robard went and looked in that direction, poised to attack.

If we just fight those ones, then we should be able to do it, Dave thought. *Our old tactics worked well enough against the Wargs. Why not hogs?* Of course, that had only been one or two Wargs, but now didn't seem to be the moment to doubt themselves. They had a new friend to bail them out if things got too rough.

"Usual strategy, then?" Paul asked.

Sam simply nodded, then drew his long hunting knives from their sheaths on his hips and waited for them. Paul loaded his sling with one of the small, hard stones he collected. Dave swallowed and drew his pistol. The one that the System had allowed him to upgrade to fire-Mana bullets.

Then he made an affirmative movement of the head aimed at Sam. They were as ready as they were going to be.

Without further thought, Sam charged in, long knives flashing in the air.

Sam wasn't as strong or as quick as Robard, clearly, but the Lonely Hunter Class excelled at solo combat with beasts. The way the other two had synergized with that was by supporting him with their ranged weapons while Sam got in close and drew the enemies' attention. While Paul and Dave pumped the enemies with rocks and Mana bullets, respectively, Sam butchered the beasts.

It helped when they had other frontline fighters around so Sam couldn't be overwhelmed and nothing could get past the front line. But he hadn't chosen to ask for Robard's help. Clearly, Sam wanted to prove something.

He stepped in front of the bushes that hid Robard and the other members of the party, and he took up a challenging posture. Dave had seen Sam go so far as to literally beat his chest to provoke a group of Goblins into aggression before, but this time just standing there was enough. Three hogs charged straight away.

Sam slashed at the center one's throat, and he managed to draw a fountain of blood with his first strike. But the huge monstrous thing was still alive, and it pushed him back with its body as its charge carried forward. Paul and Dave shot at the other beasts, aiming for their faces.

Dave killed one almost immediately. His Mana bullets were perfect for piercing natural defenses like the tough hog hides, and his headshot brought the hog careening to a dead stop. Paul was less successful. He landed a stone right in the eye of the other hog in the charge, which appeared to blind it without going deeper. The second stone scraped the hog's snout but didn't hit anything important.

And then the half-blind hog was flailing, charging blindly into trees, far from dead but not nearly as much of a threat as it had been now that its depth perception was ruined.

Dave focused on the other hog, which was bleeding heavily all over Sam but had smashed him up against a tree.

Damn it, Sam! This is why you should wear goddamn armor. Sam generally eschewed protective gear, claiming that it slowed him down and made him louder when he wanted to move silently while hunting. And there was truth in that.

Sam had been the most effective hunter in their Orientation. Even on the rare occasions when Dave had seen Sam's prey get the chance to fight back, he had tended to do well at dodging the projectiles or clumsy blows from Goblins and their kin. But Dave was fairly certain he knew the real reason Sam didn't like wearing armor.

Sam had been a recreational hunter in the pre-System days. Back then, he'd never needed to wear armor. Dave was more or less certain that when he was hunting, Sam sometimes felt as if things were back to normal. As if the world made sense again.

Wearing armor would only detract from the illusion that Sam was out in the woods, hunting and skinning animals with his pa, just pursuing his hobby with a surprising diversity of beasts. Sam was carrying his own emotional wounds. They were just more subtle than Dave's.

But now Dave wished Sam would just get over it. He was trying to fire shots at the hog that had Sam pinned but was just grazing its back. The body was too low to the ground for Dave to aim accurately without getting much closer.

Suddenly, the hog collapsed to the ground.

Dave saw Sam pull himself up from where he was on the ground. His shirt was drenched in blood. The white cotton would be dyed a dried-blood brown forever after this. But he raised his knives triumphantly in the air as if to say, *See me? I did it!*

And he had. He'd bled that hog out expertly with only a couple of cuts. Even if it was obvious that Sam had broken a couple of ribs waiting for it to die, he had managed to avoid getting gored on the hog's short tusks, which was probably where all his Strength had been applied while he was on the ground.

But as he was congratulating Sam in his mind, Dave noticed a real problem. Three more hogs were charging up now, replacing the ones that had just died. The one half-blind hog seemed to have spotted Sam as well. It, too, charged.

Sam stood his ground and took on a fighting pose. It was really the only thing to do.

Dave just poured more Mana into his gun. Sam wasn't going to die on his watch.

CHAPTER FOURTEEN

Bloody Work

Dave and Paul gave it the effort of their lives, covering for Sam.

They fired stone after stone, Mana bullet after Mana bullet, as the hogs closed the distance. Paul managed to blind the previously half-blind hog and shoot out the eye of another one of the creatures. Dave managed to shoot the nearest one to him dead with two bullets to the head.

He knew it wouldn't be enough. Sam slashed the closest surviving hog in the throat, and it began to bleed like the stuck pig that it was. But it also slammed into him like the last hog had. This time, Sam couldn't brace himself at all. Dave saw his body fly through the air and heard Sam's ribs cracking.

Then the half-blind hog and the bleeding hog converged on Sam's body with their full weight.

"Ahh!" Sam cried out in pain. Dave could hear the sounds of the hogs' tusks penetrating Sam's body, and as he fired his gun, tears streamed down his face. He thought his friend was a goner. He didn't know what else he could do.

"That's enough of that."

Robard's quiet, firm voice somehow carried over the sounds of carnage, the sounds of goring tusks and trampling hooves. He leaped into the space next to Sam, and both hogs seemed to become instantly aware of him as their primary threat. They turned to attack him—and this time, Dave actually saw what he did.

Or he thought he saw. What his eyes told him seemed impossible, even in a world of magic.

Robard swung his right arm, almost casually, and the hogs fell apart, as if some giant sword had dismembered them with a diagonal cut. Dave was so close that he could actually hear the sound of the wind. He stepped closer. Was that it? Was Robard some sort of powerful wind-based Mage? That might explain how he was so fast, as well as this insanely powerful attack.

"Don't get too close!" Robard barked.

Dave stepped back, startled at the sound. And he felt something like a sharp blade brush past him. He didn't need to touch his face to know that a thin cut had appeared on his cheek. After a long, quiet moment, a trickle of blood flowed from the delicate cut.

Jesus. What is he?

Dave turned his head to the tree nearest to where he'd been about to step. A deep gouge now marred the trunk.

If I'd been standing there . . . Dave pictured himself lying disemboweled on the ground, bleeding out. *And that was just the collateral damage. The real target was those hogs.* The creatures that now lay in bloody pieces on the ground.

A few of the other hogs looked interested in continuing the fight where their dead brethren had left off, but Dave felt a terrifying Mana emanate from Robard then. It felt like a wave of hot anger. The air seemed to become heavier and denser.

The remaining hogs ran away.

Robard's body glowed with the green aura of a Healer, confusing Dave further. *Does he have multiple powers? Whichever powers he wants? Is his Class Swiss Army Warrior or something?*

It didn't matter now. What mattered was that Robard was healing his friend. Dave's legs carried him forward without his conscious control now. He wanted to know if Sam was going to make it. As he pushed through the bushes, he could hear Robard muttering to himself.

"—pushed this way too far . . ."

His voice trailed off, and Dave immediately forgot that Robard had been saying anything. Where his hands were, the wounds were knitting back together, which was good. But Dave feared it would be too slow. Sam was bleeding so heavily now. His center of mass had multiple visible punctures, and it was hard to tell where the hogs' blood ended and Sam's began.

"Do you need a potion? Would that help?" Dave asked, wringing his hands helplessly.

Robard shrugged his shoulders without changing the position of his body, head, or hands at all.

"I'm healing him as fast as I can," he said. "I've seen worse. I believe he'll pull through, but I'm not in the business of offering promises and guarantees at times like this. If you want to make it a guaranteed thing, you could pour something in his mouth."

Dave reached into his Small Bag of Deceptive Dimensions and pulled out his last Health Potion, then advanced closer. But he saw then that the wounds were closing remarkably fast. Robard was able to shift his posture and place a hand on the less critical areas of the body that had also been gored. There were a couple of shallower holes in Sam's right bicep and left thigh.

"They really did a number on him," Robard said. "But your friend is going to pull through. Unless something else kills us." He looked up from his bloody work and offered Dave a grim smile.

"Right," Dave pronounced slowly.

"It's okay," Paul's voice sounded far away, but it pulled at Dave, yanking him back from the dark place his mind wanted to go.

"Can one of you carry him?" Robard asked. The last of the wounds were closing up under his hands, but Sam was very pale and remained unconscious. "That way I can keep a lookout for any other threats."

"Sure," Dave said. Something to do. Activity to occupy his hands so he didn't have to use his mind. *I almost lost my friend today.* The thought came uncontrollably, and he shoved it down into the same dark place where he buried his other regrets.

Robard lifted Sam up, and he and Paul placed him carefully on Dave's back.

Then Robard used a Skill on several of the hogs' bodies that were grouped together around them. The bodies began to glow, and parcels of meat and other gear separated themselves from the beasts and floated into Robard's bag.

He has some kind of group Loot Skill too? It would be exhausting to keep track of all this guy's powers . . .

"If the gear isn't anything special," Paul said, "could we just throw the rest of the body parts into the bags? The System isn't as efficient at using an animal carcass as a trained human can be, and Sam got the Job of Butcher in Orientation. I know he'll want to make himself useful when he wakes up, and carving up the meat is the best way I can imagine for him."

Robard seemed to consider this for longer than Dave would've expected. As if he had some reason why he wanted to keep using his Skill. After a long moment, though, he nodded.

"Be quick," he said. "There might be other things in these woods that aren't so easily intimidated by me."

Paul spent the next several minutes scrambling to gather all the bodies and pieces of bodies that he could find and throwing them into his bag.

Thank God those bags have expandable mouths, Dave thought. But as he thought that, his mind was on Sam. That was the big miracle today. And it wasn't God who was responsible.

Dave looked up at Robard, who was staring down at him with what Dave read as guilt on his face. *Why would he be guilty?* Dave questioned.

"I shouldn't have let things get that far," Robard said softly.

That's more responsibility than the man who sent us up Elephant Trunk Hill ever took, Dave thought. He knew he was being unfair to his command structure as he had the thought. But the aftermath of the Second Battle of Guilin had left him with scars both physical and mental, and it was hard to be fair in that context.

"You saved him," Dave replied quickly, firmly, brooking no disagreement. "I wish you had been there with us in our Orientation."

Robard nodded slowly. "I wish I could have been in several places at once already," he said. "My wife and sister-in-law were stuck on their own in a pretty violent place." He shook his head. "They still have a different last name," he added.

"I hope they came through all right," Dave said delicately.

"Somehow," Robard said, smiling thinly. "And we got some pretty good rewards out of the whole experience."

Dave wanted to ask him more about his Orientation, but suddenly Paul reappeared, breathless.

"I'm done, guys," he said.

"Excellent," Robard said. "Time to clear out of here, then."

"Can we head back via a more direct route?" Dave asked, looking at James. "I'm happy to carry him as far as we need to, but I'm afraid of what might happen if we run into another enemy right now."

"I understand," Robard replied. He looked around and sniffed the air as if monitoring for something Dave was unaware of. "We'll try it."

Robard led the way back. Instead of the winding trail they had followed to get there, he made a beeline for the borders of what he'd identified as his territory. As they followed after him, though, he began to slow down.

As they approached a small body of water, Paul took a few steps past Robard, eager to walk through it. Dave saw Paul's feet beginning to sink into the muddy ground.

"Stop," Robard said.

Dave had already stopped. He was standing behind Robard. Something felt dangerous about the area, though he couldn't put his finger on it.

Paul looked set to take another step forward, and Robard clapped a hand on his shoulder.

"Oh, I'm sorry. I didn't realize you meant me," Paul said, grinning sheepishly.

"Yeah," Robard replied drily. "You started to move into the lead. Whoever's advancing is usually going to be the one who needs to halt." He gestured at the water in front of them. "We need to stop moving in this direction."

"What? Why?" Paul asked.

"Do neither of you feel this?" Robard replied. He ran his hands through the air in front of him like it was water.

"No. What?" Paul said.

"I feel it," Dave said. Both Paul and Robard turned to face him.

Robard looked at his face and nodded. "Good that you're paying attention. What do you feel?"

"A pressure in the air. Something wrong. It reminded me a little of—" He cut himself off, looking sideways at Robard.

"It reminded you of the aura I emitted earlier," Robard finished for him.

Dave nodded.

"Yep. That's right," Robard said.

"Wait, what?" Paul asked. "What does it mean? Someone else like you here?"

"Some*thing* like me," Robard agreed. "It's not really as far away from our place as I expected. More pressing than the location, though, we should cut around this area. Step out of this thing's aura as soon as possible. It seems the hogs weren't just moving randomly. They were probably avoiding running into this thing's territory. I'd bet it's a predator. If we want to deal with it with confidence, we need to come back in force."

"Why would we want to deal with it?" Paul asked. "Shouldn't we just stick to your land when we're not hunting?"

"Because these things will be killing and eating each other—and humans like us—to get stronger. All the time. If we don't keep progressing ourselves, it'll be us on the menu. And this thing is probably our nearest actual predator. Something that would eventually invade my territory and try to challenge me to claim it."

"So, we've come back to a world at endless war?" Dave asked, exhausted. "Is that what you're telling us?"

"Seems like it," Robard said. "Until we make Hobbes's Leviathan."

Both men gave him confused looks, and Robard looked embarrassed.

"I just said something very nerdy," he said. "It means a force so strong that other powers within the reach of its territory can't easily challenge it. A strong government or power that forces people—and in this case, beasts—to behave themselves."

"And that's you?" Paul asked. Dave detected an undercurrent of excitement in Paul's voice, and he sighed to himself. "You're really that strong?"

"I'm almost certainly the strongest or at the least one of the top three strongest in North America right now. Out of the humans, anyway. I have no idea how I rank relative to the beasts. You've seen a bit of that power now, but far from all of it. You'd better hope I'm strong enough." His expression hardened. "Someone has to create order. Keep the peace." He took a last look at the body of water in front of them. It didn't seem that deep to Dave, but the way Robard examined it, Dave felt as if the man could see something in there that the two of them couldn't.

"Let's go, then," Dave suggested.

Robard nodded. They began withdrawing from the territory of the unseen predator. When they were out of it, Dave felt the difference. The air in the zone occupied by the monster was thicker, heavier, and more humid. Dave mentioned this to Robard.

"You have good senses," Robard said. "I think whatever lives in that territory might have similar Mana affinities to me. The air in my territory is similar except it isn't overtly hostile to humans." His eyes closed for a moment, then reopened. "Speaking of which, I think we have some guests back home."

"Guests?" Dave asked.

"Human or beast?" Paul said.

"Well, they're humanoid shaped, at least," Robard said. "I doubt anything would be stupid enough to invade my territory right now. None of the local monsters should think I'm an easy mark, and my aura is heavy in the air. But I can't be sure. I don't seem to have the same degree of sensory awareness about what's going on in my territory when I'm not actually there."

"Let's hurry, then," Dave said.

Robard led the way briskly through the remaining sections of woods. It was not difficult to keep up with him, but Dave and Paul gave him some space. They both felt confident in his protection.

Paul touched Dave's elbow once Robard was a certain distance ahead. "Well, I'm very impressed by him," Paul said. "Does he seem like the kind of guy you could follow?"

Dave had to resist the urge to roll his eyes. *Do you assume we're out of hearing range? We can still see him. I could probably hear this conversation if I was where he was.* But no use crying over spilled milk now.

Paul probably did think they were out of hearing range. While Dave had heavily invested in his Perception Stat, Paul had mainly focused on Strength and Agility. By the time he had realized that he wanted to focus on a ranged weapon, Paul was well behind Dave.

"I think he passed any test we might have thought to implement with flying colors," Dave finally said.

Then a sound came to him, carried on the wind. He immediately looked forward and saw Robard's mouth moving. He was muttering something quietly. It took a moment for Dave to parse what he was saying, from both the noise carried on the wind and some lip-reading.

"You passed my test too."

CHAPTER FIFTEEN

The Fisher King, Part 2

You have entered the territory of the Fisher King uninvited. Surrender to him or his representatives or prepare for battle.]

The words presented themselves like a System message, but they were accompanied by a terrible sense of pressure that made Alan want to stop walking and fall to his knees.

James, who the hell are you, deep down? You declared yourself a king? Alan was certain that this was the right place; he'd been checking addresses on the ruined buildings they passed when he could. This complex was off the main road, but it was in exactly the right spot to correspond to James's street address.

And the voice that he heard during the message was an automated-sounding version of James's voice.

Even if it hadn't been, how many people would have come through Orientation powerful enough to start dubbing themselves royalty? With System support to boot?

"Well, I think we're in the right place," Jeremiah Rotter said from behind Alan, chuckling nervously.

"Assuming that our guy is the 'Fisher King,' there's no question," Alan replied without looking. In truth, he had no doubt that Rotter was correct, but the man was getting on his nerves already, despite their short acquaintanceship. If he hadn't been in that gas station with Charlie Roebuck and Amalia Rosario, Alan would've tried to avoid him. But now they were stuck together, along with the others they'd encountered along the way.

On the road here, they'd run into a number of people who were clearly looking for some place to go. People who looked harmless enough. When they'd asked Alan, Mitzi, Rotter, or any of the party members where they were going, they had told the wanderers the truth. And more often than not, those lost people chose to follow them.

There seemed to be little point in rejecting them. How would Alan and Mitzi's little party have even forced them to stop following? Physical violence?

Mitzi had quietly suggested that there was safety in numbers, and Alan thought she had been proven right over the subsequent day. The roads were crowded with disreputable characters—people wearing a diverse array of armor, robes, and clothing obviously looted from stores, sometimes with price tags still on.

The law was no more.

If Alan and Mitzi had still been traveling alone, they would've had to retreat to the woods to avoid the possibility of being pulled into conflict. With their increasing throng of acquaintances, other people moved off the road to avoid bumping into them instead.

In that sense, I suppose James declaring himself a king makes sense, Alan thought. *If he's promising safety and order, I have no doubt he'll find his share of willing followers.* It felt a bit retrograde to bring back the concept of monarchy to these shores that had rebelled against it almost three centuries past. But then, Alan had to admit that it didn't feel much like they were in the modern world anymore.

He continued leading the group further into the Fisher King's territory, praying silently that it would actually be James who controlled this place. But forward progress was difficult. The unpleasant pressure in the air grew more intense with every step forward. It was as if James had chosen the defense mechanism of increased gravity for his land.

Perhaps he had. Alan couldn't remember if manipulating that fundamental force of physics was on the long list of James's powers.

Whatever the reason, a few yards into the Fisher King's space, Alan was pouring buckets of sweat down his forehead and back.

I don't think I can take any more of this, he thought. He and Mitzi exchanged worried looks. It wasn't clear they would make it far enough into James's territory to surrender to him even if they wanted to. *If I hadn't gotten so much stronger in Orientation than I was pre-System, I think my heart would have given out already.*

"Are we stopping here?" asked one of the followers, a young woman who was there with her father and brothers. She spoke through gritted teeth, but her voice was determined.

"I don't know if we can continue if the Fisher King doesn't want us to," said Rotter, who sounded as bad as Alan felt.

Then the pressure suddenly vanished like a mirage.

Alan's posture righted itself, and he threw his head back and sucked in a sweet gulp of air. Even his lungs, he realized dimly, had felt compressed under the increased gravity of this area. The Earth's gravity post-Orientation had already been bad enough, but with the additional pressure from the Fisher King's defenses, Alan thought it was possible that he might have suffocated.

Thank God, he thought. Then, his head still tilted back, he saw something flying through the air. It was too far away for him to get a really good look at it, but it was clearly looking at them. *Oh. That must be one of James's pets. I suppose they're putting out the welcome mat now.*

They proceeded further onto James's land, and the ruined buildings that Alan hadn't been able to see at all from the main road came into view, alongside a single very large crudely constructed building. The new structure was clearly modeled after the old ones, with the difference that it was clearly made from compressed earth that had come from the ground all around it. Alan thought he could guess who might be responsible for this.

"That's undeniably James's work," Rotter said aloud in a confident tone.

Quit talking about James as if you know him, Alan thought irritably. Then he felt a bit of inner conflict. Wasn't he just annoyed about James declaring himself a king? Maybe Rotter was more squarely on James's program than Alan himself was.

"He did construct your group a building at one point in Orientation, didn't he?" Mitzi asked indulgently.

Rotter nodded and began yammering to the whole group about how James had saved him and his Orientation group from certain death. This was not the first time he had told this story, but most of the group had not been present for the last occasion.

Alan sighed to himself and quietly led the way forward until they were standing directly in front of the new apartment building.

Then he looked around. There was no one outside and nothing to distinguish one door to this place from any other. It felt strange to go up to a random door and knock, but he didn't know the best way to find the single person he was looking for otherwise. Alan stood there, trying to think of a solution. Other members of the group began looking toward the woods, which surrounded the plot of land on all sides, bar the approach from the road.

Alan followed their gaze, and he saw James walking with two other figures.

Well, that solves the problem, he thought. But something strange presented itself as the figures approached. One of them was carrying an unconscious person on his back. *Someone's hurt.*

Alan began striding toward them, eager to lend his medical aid as needed.

"Good to see you, Alan!" James called as they got close to each other. "Sorry for the rough welcome earlier." The lack of urgency in his tone slowed Alan's pace.

I was wrong. No need for a Healer right now after all, he thought. It was a little frustrating to feel as useless as he sometimes did around James. And then he felt slightly guilty for resenting not being needed in this specific way.

"It was very impressive how the area sort of announced itself as your territory," Alan said, for want of a more interesting topic. "Makes this Fisher King position sound very official."

James tilted his head slightly to indicate confusion. Alan began to explain what had happened when he and those he'd brought with him had entered James's land. James listened with great interest, only pausing to give direction about the care of the incapacitated man—James indicated that the person had lost a lot of blood and should drink plenty of fluids and eat a sizable amount of the pork they had apparently acquired.

Then the others from Alan's group walked up and swarmed James.

"So, you're the Fisher King, then?"

"Is it true you created that whole building by yourself?"

"What, is construction, like, your hobby?"

"Can I stay here?"

"Can I live on your land? I can make myself very useful. I can . . ."

"I heard that you fought a giant three-headed wolf by yourself. Is that true, or is this fellow full of it?"

"One at a time, please, everyone," James said gently, smiling politely.

Alan began to feel a little bad. *I came all this way to ask James for a personal favor. Really, to make Dean's life easier. There's probably some solution to the monster problem around the office besides just getting James to help. And these people came here hoping he could save them from danger.* It was incredibly selfish even to think of asking James to walk away from this place for a while to try and fight Dean's enemies. What would happen to these people he was responsible for while he was gone?

As Alan had these thoughts, James was doing the work of a retail politician—making everyone around him feel important, giving them the sense that they knew the real James.

"I am the Fisher King, yes. I did create this building by myself, though I think I'm going to want some help with the next set of buildings. I'm not much of an architect. Whether you can stay is a great question. We haven't laid down rules yet, as such. The whole community is going to have an assembly soon, and then we're going to discuss the standards for who can stay. Oh, and yes, I did fight a three-headed wolf to the death by myself. The whole wolf pack is going to come stay here soon—no, don't look at me like that, they know not to attack humans unless I order them to. Just don't start anything with them."

He was direct, charming, and even a little bit funny.

These people will absolutely follow him, Alan thought. It made sense. James was the hero of Orientation, and he seemed to be an even bigger fish here, if that was possible.

[Any Mages who have earth magic, please come outside if you are

available. Your assistance is requested in constructing additional dwellings for new arrivals.]

Alan was slightly startled to hear James using the System-like announcement function that had threatened the new arrivals earlier as a public address system now. Then he snorted.

Of course he is. James hadn't known the land even had such a function before Alan told him about it, he was fairly certain. So, the Fisher King was testing his ability to control it. Alan thought that the function would be more useful now that James was consciously aware of it. For one thing, it sounded much more diplomatic in tone and style now. In addition, the slightly robotic sound to the voice was gone. Now it sounded like James speaking in a relaxed manner, his deep, calm voice gently caressing the ears.

Two Mages made themselves known to James, one from within the apartments and one who was already outside. And a woman emerged from another apartment, walked up behind James, and took his hand.

Oh, that's his wife, Alan realized. He had never met her, though he almost felt as if he had. James liked to talk about her quite a bit.

"Why don't you let me give construction directions, skapi?" she asked.

James smiled, a bigger and more unreserved smile than Alan remembered ever seeing from him before. "That sounds like a wonderful idea," he said. He briefly introduced Mina to everyone, and she walked away with the two Mages. Alan didn't hear the details of the conversation, though he did catch a few odd phrases. "Rammed earth" and "formwork" were among them.

Alan guessed the next set of buildings constructed were going to be a little more thoughtfully built than James's initial structure, which seemed all to the good.

He needs someone to make sure he thinks these things through.

For the next half an hour James continued schmoozing with the new arrivals and people who had been there for longer before Alan finally decided to seize a moment alone with him instead of waiting.

"James, could I have a word in private?" he asked.

"For you, Alan, we can have as many words as you like. I'll be back in a while, everyone. In the meantime, I hope people will try to make themselves comfortable. You may need to be ready to camp out. I know that Mina and the Mages who live here will do their utmost to construct lodgings for all of you as quickly as they can, but as they say, Rome wasn't built in a day. And anything worth having is worth waiting for."

Alan looked toward Mitzi, but she was engaged in conversation with some more residents of the Fisher Kingdom who had emerged from the makeshift apartment building.

Guess I'll go on my own, then. He felt inexplicably nervous.

But he followed James up into his family's apartment, still trying to decide exactly how he was going to say what he needed to say, to ask this man, who was clearly the leader of this rapidly expanding community, to abandon it for a while to go and help some other people, only one of whom he knew at all.

As they reached the top of the stairs, Alan saw a teenage girl. She looked like a miniature version of James's wife. *Oh, the little sister they adopted. He's mentioned her too. Julia, was it?*

"Did you find anything?" she asked James.

At first, Alan thought she was talking about the hunt James had just come back from when the newcomers arrived.

But James's expression became very serious as he answered. "My creatures found two so far. They're flying back with them. One of them is a bit hurt, which I hadn't thought of, so I'll make sure the next monsters I send out have healing abilities." He turned back to Alan. "By the way, Alan, this is Yulia, my little sister-in-law. Yulia, this is Alan. He was my neighbor at work, and he was in my Orientation. He's a Healer, like you."

"Nice to meet you," she said, shaking hands with him soberly. She seemed slightly uncomfortable, and she walked into another room immediately after introducing herself. But as the door closed, Alan heard the sound of children playing.

She probably just left because she's on babysitting duty, he thought. *I didn't realize they had other kids besides her.*

"What was that about?" Alan asked.

"We found some children in the ruins of the apartment complex. We're taking care of a few, and our neighbors are taking care of others. The new people are really a godsend in that regard, so to speak." He chuckled, and Alan smiled wryly. The gods were sending many things indeed. "Anyway, I'm sending my pet monsters out looking for other survivors. Yulia pointed out to me that with the way Orientation went, there were bound to be a lot of orphaned children."

Wow. They're really doing much more to rebuild civilization on a micro scale than Dean has even talked about doing. Even rescuing children. Well, I always knew James was the hero that we needed back in Orientation. Maybe he's the person the world needs.

"Actually, I'm really glad you and Mitzi are here in particular," James continued. "I know I'll need a lot of wisdom if I'm going to run this place. I really can't mess around if there are all these kids depending on me. I always thought of you as the wise counselor type—"

"We're not staying," Alan blurted out, only halfway cognizant of what he was saying.

Are you really sure you don't want to stay? he questioned himself. The answer, of course, was "No." He wasn't certain at all.

"Are you sure?" James asked, his expression showing surprise—and a bit of sadness? "No pressure on the two of you, of course. I know you have your own children to be thinking about. But if they're looking for a place to stay while we rebuild civilization, they're welcome here too. We have to stand together."

Alan didn't know quite what to say to that. If he said "No," he would just be giving James the impression that he was open to arguments. That he wanted to be persuaded. But that wasn't it. This was a decision that Alan and Mitzi needed to make for themselves. The facts would make their own arguments.

A brief but awkward silence ensued.

"Like I said," James resumed, "no pressure. Uh, what was it you wanted to take me aside for, anyway?"

"I feel terrible asking for this," Alan said, his mouth suddenly dry.

"Do it anyway," James said. "I never like to be constrained by what's reasonable."

"Dean back at the office has his own plans for rebuilding civilization," Alan said. "He wants to turn the office into a fortified base, but there are problems. Monsters in some difficult to reach places and a Dungeon inside part of the building."

"A Dungeon, huh? Is that a problem? It might be a decent place to train, depending on what kind it is." James seemed to be thinking aloud. "And most monsters are still easy enough to kill. If Dean and his crew can't do that themselves, how would they rebuild civilization? Would they even be able to outlast one monster attack? They're still going to be all over the place on Earth, you know?"

"I've been becoming gradually more aware of that," Alan said. "I hadn't realized before we set out. And I did have the idea that—well, I had thought that you would come back with us and stay there with your family. Maybe I could put you and Dean together and watch you rebuild the world as a team."

"Dean is the kind of guy I could imagine surviving the apocalypse," James mused. "I'm glad he at least made it through Orientation. Crazy that the firm office building survived too, honestly."

"At any rate, the idea that you would stay there seems very silly now. And I realize you have no reason to help Dean with his civilization-building project when you've taken on complex problems of your own already. You're building a community here, and it's bigger by far than what Dean had when I last saw him. I don't know what would become of this place if you left, and there are all these children—"

"I think this place will survive without me for a day," James said firmly. "I was gone for almost all of today hunting and people took care of themselves. There might not be any direct benefit to me or my people here, but since you're asking, I want to help if I can." He looked into Alan's eyes warmly. "As far as I'm concerned, you'll always be part of my team. Your problems are my problems. Your enemies are my enemies."

CHAPTER SIXTEEN

The King's Speech

After Alan had explained what he wanted, James issued another announcement with his public address system.

[**Attention, everyone who can hear this message. Tomorrow morning we will have our first public assembly to discuss future plans for this community, including residency requirements.**]

"This way, I'll be able to address the whole community as a group before I leave to help you and Dean out," James explained. "I was planning this talk for the day after tomorrow, but bumping up the timing seems appropriate."

The two of them exchanged small talk before Alan made an excuse to return to his wife. James was fairly certain that Alan felt guilty for even asking for his help. It had been written all over his face, and he didn't seem to be trying very hard to hide it.

I might still get him to stay here, James thought. *Alan and Mitzi could be valuable members of my community if I convince them that it's the best way for them to make a difference.* That shouldn't require any lying, since as far as James was concerned, it was objectively the truth.

More importantly, now was the time when he would make his case to the people living in his territory that they should accept his authority. Including his System-granted position of Fisher King.

He began his preparations for the next day.

The morning of the assembly, Alan watched James move about in mild awe.

He seemed to be in several places at once, communicating with as many people as he could and putting everyone at ease. More people had shown up that morning, seemingly just in time for the assembly. Though, it seemed this number—around a hundred adults in total, with an unknown but smaller number of children in tow—was within the parameters that James must have been calculating. Alan thought there was just enough space in the new in-progress housing to have everyone lodged by the time it was finished. Which, given the progress so far and knowing James, would be before he left with Alan.

The wolves were among the morning arrivals, and Damien Rousseau appeared with them. In front of all the onlookers, he walked up to James, addressed him as "King James," and pulled him into a hug.

The mood was triumphant. People who had not seen each other since Orientation confirmed that their friends and acquaintances were still alive. They were high-fiving each other, swapping congratulations, and competing for face time with "King James." And he somehow seemed to accommodate all of them.

Overnight, he and Mina had constructed a grand additional new building that they were calling the "community center." Mina was visibly tired, and her little sister hovered near her like a bodyguard, helping her politely make small talk and rebuff any longer conversations. The fact that Mina was carrying her baby around made people more understanding. James seemed as energetic as ever, flitting from person to person after he'd stayed in one spot just long enough to make an impact.

Alan found it mildly annoying that James made time to pay attention to Jeremiah Rotter, of all people, for a few minutes. James even showed Rotter something he had written on a paper he produced from his pocket. His speech for that day?

Why am I annoyed? Alan wondered. Was he a bit jealous? Yes, he probably was. Alan would have expected James to consult with *him* if he wanted a last-minute eye on his speech. They had known each other for years, after all.

What am I thinking, though? He was planning to leave and return to help Dean. Wasn't he? While Rotter would probably stick around and stay stuck onto James like a leech, if he could. It was only logical for James to invest time in cultivating people who were going to be around. But Alan's face still burned as he thought about the situation.

"Something the matter?" Mitzi asked quietly.

"Hm. What?" Alan was pulled back from his thoughts and only belatedly realized his wife had been looking at him with some concern.

"Are you okay?" she asked. "Your face—well, you look a little upset. What's wrong?"

"I think maybe my instinct about who to join might have been wrong," Alan said.

"We haven't made any final decisions about that yet, though, right?" Mitzi took his hand and squeezed it. "Relax. We can figure it out later."

Alan smiled. His wife was right. "As wise as you are beautiful," he murmured half to himself. He saw her lips turn up at the corners in his peripheral vision.

Then he very pointedly looked away from James. He took in the community center.

The results of James and Mina's late night construction efforts spoke for themselves. The new community center was a far more elegant building than either the first building James had thrown up or the two new residential structures the other Mages had begun building in collaboration with Mina. The founding couple had clearly thought that this might be the first of these buildings that would stand permanently.

In style, it reminded Alan of a church, though perhaps a church as Frank Lloyd Wright would have designed one rather than as most churches were actually designed. And for some reason, the building was an octagon shape. Other than that, it felt like a place where solemn matters were contemplated and discussed.

And so it was.

After some time had elapsed, James invited the crowd inside. The building was even more like a church than Alan had expected. There was a single large main room with a stage and a podium. Scores of stone chairs sat facing toward the stage.

At least they're sort of ergonomically designed, Alan thought. *If we hadn't brought our own blankets and gear, we wouldn't have slept at all last night.*

The crowd filed in, and the excited hum settled down to a dull roar.

Finally, James took the podium and began to speak. It was a serious speech, and Alan could tell preparation had gone into it. When James had found the time, he couldn't be certain.

"Thank you, everyone, for being here today. The fact that you're here on this land at all shows that you trust my leadership and protection"—a few enthusiastic people in the crowd whistled at this, until James raised a hand to silence them—"and the fact that you entered this building shows that you trust my wife's engineering skills." A louder general hoot went up. Mina smiled shyly from her seat behind and to the left of James on stage.

"There are several topics I've considered that we need to address. I will be unavailable tomorrow, so it needed to be today. First of all, I consider it my duty to update you on the state of this neighborhood where we're beginning to build our community. Several of us have scouted the neighboring territories. There are some small chunks of land that appear to be more or less unoccupied, or only occupied by wandering beasts. Unfortunately, if you move a little further out, you run into the territory of monsters that are comparable in power to me." A concerned murmur moved the crowd.

"For these reasons," James continued, "I recommend that we do not stray far from the borders of the Fisher Kingdom unless we go in force. Going somewhere with me counts as going in force"—there were some chuckles at that—"but the best thing is for me and a whole party of combat-capable people to go together. It is likely these neighbors will eventually become threats we will have to face. My territory expands slowly, day by day, as my aura reaches new patches of land. The territory of these rivals does the same. A clash is almost certainly inevitable, and that day requires us to prepare, build our numbers, and increase our individual strengths. We have, unfortunately, descended into a world where might makes right and neutral spaces will inevitably shrink and disappear.

"Related to this is the leadership structure. Some of you will have only heard secondhand that I am calling myself the Fisher King. That isn't entirely accurate." He smiled a bit sheepishly. "Well, I am calling myself that, but the System gave me the label first. And I did a lot to earn that name. I've killed somewhere in the high hundreds or low thousands of monsters—somewhere along the line I lost count. I defeated the final enemy of my own Orientation, a monster with the power to destroy human souls and turn the bodies of the fallen into his puppets. I drove more than one species of creature to extinction. Fought a three-headed wolf the size of an SUV until he admitted defeat and surrendered leadership of his pack to me. And I impressed a god enough that he courted me to become his Chosen One.

"That was the Spider God, Anansi," James continued. "He is a god of stories, and his representative is always with me, to chronicle my adventures." There was a tiny flicker of movement on James's head, which Alan guessed was the tiny spider trying to be seen. "Despite being favored by a god, my first loyalty has always been, and *will always be*, to you, my fellow humans. We live in a world that is constantly trying to kill us. This was true even before the System, with hurricanes, plagues, and everything wild that lived on the continent of Australia." There was a choked off bit of laughter from the audience.

"Well, now things are even worse. It's a fact that during these chaotic times, strong centralized leadership is needed. I firmly believe that in these circumstances, a chain of command dependent on multiple lines of authority, or any structure based on the old tried and true idea of checks and balances, will fail at the first test. People who completed Orientation, all of you know how long democracy lasted when the System arrived. Those who completed Orientation beside me know that there was no place safer than standing by my side. As this land is protected by my aura, and as I am likely to remain the strongest single person on this land, I will remain as the ruler of this area until and unless I am violently deposed.

"I won't expect anyone to stay who can't accept that. If you find me too intolerable, you are welcome to leave, with our well wishes and a reasonable quantity of food, in search of a more democratic society. Those who remain have a right to know what to expect from my leadership. First, in exchange for accepting me as leader, you should understand that I will always be prepared to risk my life for any of yours unless my family is in jeopardy at the same time. I will work hard to keep you safe." Alan looked around, and he found people were nodding along. *Of course. They were already prepared to accept something like this as soon as they decided to stay on land controlled by someone called the Fisher King.* They were just lucky that James happened to also mean what he said—as far as Alan could tell.

"My family, for those of you who haven't already met them, includes my wife, Mina, her sister Yulia, and my son, James Jr." The two women briefly stood up from behind James. "We are also taking care of our neighbor's children until their family returns." Alan saw that those three children were in the front row. Someone was watching them for James and his family. *I'd guess that phrasing was about sparing the little boy's feelings?* But James was on to the next topic already.

"Second, I will expect effort from you all. Survival itself will require the best from all of us. My understanding of my powers is that they will help us more successfully work the land, but there will be farming required. Continuing construction of buildings. Salvaging materials from the civilization the System just wrecked. We'll honor the fallen—and we'll try to move forward, try to recreate some of the technology we had before the collapse. But the bottom line is, there is no room to be idle. I know in my bones that you all understand what I mean. You're all survivors. We've all been through a great deal. The struggle isn't over. Make yourselves useful in some way to this community. If you don't know how you can best do that, come and see me. We'll discuss how your knowledge and capabilities fit in. I don't expect people to automatically know what to do, but we'll discover the way together bit by bit.

"Third, we are an extremely diverse group of people, and I expect more of us to arrive each day. We won't even all be human in this community. Some of you have already seen my pack of wolves. They arrived this morning, and although they are not inside with us, they are aware of the rules we are discussing. In order for us to work together and be able to trust each other to some degree, we have to have a common set of ideals that we pledge ourselves to, much like the United States when the country was formed. I think that we need to all—including me—pledge that we are going to stand for these common values, and that can be the foundation for us to build something new. For that reason, I want to introduce a loyalty pledge for everyone who wants to live here. We will all swear to uphold some common values." He took out a piece of paper from within his pocket and read it aloud with his hand over his heart.

"I pledge allegiance to the Fisher Kingdom and to the ideals for which it stands: protection of the innocent, justice for all, and the promise to reconquer the Earth for humanity and our allied species. Only our sacrifices honor the fallen. Only victory can bring peace. Only we can win back the world." Alan found the citizenship pledge a bit cartoonishly idealistic and slightly jingoistic—but then again, had the Pledge of Allegiance and the old national anthem been any different? And people had treated both with such solemnity. Looking at the faces of the crowd, he couldn't see anyone laughing or smiling. They took this invented oath as seriously as they took the person who had written it.

"Anyone who wants to remain on this land, the only formal requirement is that you must make the citizenship pledge. The informal requirements are the obvious things: don't hurt other people; don't take their stuff; and do your best to pull your own weight. There are so many other things I want to talk about. The ongoing effort to rescue more children who were orphaned in the midst of this crisis—we will need more people to take in children and, if trends continue, possibly a larger scale solution. That assumes children continue being found. Also, after the meeting, I will take volunteers to search the old buildings and look for salvageable goods and materials. At least one person with construction experience is needed to help figure out if any of the buildings are salvageable. We already have at least one hunting party, of course—my friends who went hunting with me yesterday know who they are! And we will need to figure out the matter of farming as well as of forming a militia to defend us.

"But I intend for these meetings to be held regularly. It would be unreasonable for us to hammer out every problem today. For now, I want to open the floor for your thoughts. Another promise I can make is that I will remain open to people's opinions before making important decisions—unless the decisions are urgently needed for our survival. So, who wants to be heard?"

Hands began to shoot up.

James called on the fastest one first.

Alan saw who the eager beaver was in his peripheral vision, and he rolled his eyes. It was Rotter.

He tried to speak, but Alan couldn't hear what he was saying.

"The acoustics in this building work best if you're on the stage," James said. "Why don't you come and stand up here at the podium?"

CHAPTER SEVENTEEN

Loyalty Oath

Rotter began to speak from behind the podium.

"My name is Jeremiah Rotter, and I am one of those who experienced Orientation beside this man," he began, gesturing toward James. Some loud whooping came from the crowd. "Yes, that's right! It was amazing. If anything, he understated all the crazy shit he did!" There was laughter. James kept his expression neutral, though he found Rotter's words slightly embarrassing. "Seriously. He didn't mention the time he saved us from a pack of coyotes, for one thing. But I have a problem with something he said." A slightly nervous hush fell over the crowd. James raised an eyebrow.

"It's the wording of this loyalty oath. The citizenship pledge doesn't mention James personally once!" James returned his expression to a careful blank. He thought he knew what was going to happen next. "So, I'm going to rewrite part of it for myself. I pledge allegiance to the Fisher *King* and to the ideals for which *he* stands: protection of the innocent, justice for all, and the promise to reconquer the Earth for humanity and our allied species. Only our sacrifices honor the fallen. Only victory can bring peace. Only we can win back the world. May all the gods bless the Fisher King!"

Rotter stepped down to raucous applause. James tried not to smile. He felt Mina's eyes on him, and he knew what she was wondering. *Did you arrange this?*

It had been Mina's idea to make everyone swear allegiance to the country rather than to James personally. That was a real stroke of genius, James thought, because they didn't all know him yet. He couldn't reasonably make everything about himself. And no one could have any reasonable objection to pledging allegiance to the place. This place, and the community it would harbor, was meant to protect and maintain their lives, after all.

James wouldn't even accept a religious exemption to this requirement, he had decided, because there were so many gods in this new world. The idea that some god could have a superior loyalty claim to the place that was directly keeping each and every citizen alive was unacceptable to him.

Loyalty to the person versus loyalty to the place wasn't so different.

But James had considered whether it was possible that he could secure a promise of the former by asking for an oath about the latter.

He didn't want to force the issue, but just in case, he had showed the citizenship oath to Rotter in advance. Just to get the brownnoser's opinion on the wording.

"It doesn't mention you directly," he'd observed immediately.

"Oh. No, it doesn't," James had replied with false humility.

So the answer was no, he hadn't arranged this. But he had hoped and suspected that it would happen semi-organically.

James didn't comment on Rotter's answer. He walked up to the podium and called for more public comment.

"Yes, you. Then you. And third will be you."

Then he returned to his seat beside Mina and Yulia, and he took baby James into his arms. The next few speakers should take a while, he thought.

Dave Matsumoto took the stage next.

"I'm Dave Matsumoto," he said. "I haven't known James Robard long, though we've apparently lived in the same apartment complex for years. But yesterday I learned the most important things about him. He's strong. Impossibly strong. Incomparable to what I expected from a human. And he will throw himself into danger to defend us. Hell, just to feed us."

Matsumoto mentioned his military service, he compared the war he had fought in to the circumstances they now found themselves in, and he joined Rotter in taking the citizenship oath to James personally.

Then Amalia Rosario, who had been one of the scouts for James's group back in Orientation, spoke. Similar to Matsumoto, she mentioned her military service, though more briefly. She said that she knew James was the best person for the job, and she compared him to Teddy Roosevelt, which he found flattering.

"There are always three possible options in any given situation," she concluded. "There's doing the right thing, doing the wrong thing, and worst of all, doing nothing. I think James will do the right thing most of the time, but more importantly, I know from personal experience that when you're in danger, he'll never do nothing." She likewise opted to take the loyalty oath to James specifically.

Did I save her at some point? James wondered. He was almost certain he hadn't. There were others in the wolf pack fight who had brushed closely with death, but she must be referencing the fact that he had brought the whole battle to an end by killing the Wolf King. There was a slow glow of pride spreading over his face even as he questioned whether he deserved so much praise.

But most importantly, he felt Mina and Yulia looking at him with pride. That was exhilarating. That made it real.

Damien got up next. He told the story of how James had fought the Alpha Desert Coyote to save him and his group, even though it was invisible and incredibly fierce. James found the account slightly exaggerated, but he also knew Damien had been semiconscious or completely knocked out for the whole incident. He must have heard what happened from someone else in his group. Rotter? Then Damien moved on to the fight with the wolf pack, which was presented in full dramatic detail. And he concluded by taking the loyalty oath to James personally.

He really could have gotten a blessing from a god of storytelling too, James thought.

Then he rose and called on a few more people, and the pattern repeated.

Avery Daniels stood up from the crowd this time. She had apparently accompanied Alan and Mitzi from somewhere down the road. James was pleasantly surprised that she was still alive. It had been a long time since he had seen her, when she drove him home on the first day of the apocalypse.

"I have had the good fortune to experience the impressive qualities of both King James and his queen," she began. James looked over at Mina, who mouthed the words, "Last name."

Oh. She was in Mina's Orientation. It will be good to hear someone from there praising her as well, especially since I intend for Mina to be in charge whenever I'm gone.

Avery explained how James had served the community as a prosecutor. She had only been in court a couple of times, and James was impressed with how much she seemed to have observed. Specifically, it was surprising how much she remembered of what he had done in dealing with other defendants. *She must have been horribly nervous back then. She was trying to gauge how I would treat her by how I treated everyone else.* Those observations wouldn't have been very useful, most likely. No two cases were alike, and the prosecutor's office trained its attorneys to deal with specific circumstances very differently based on a number of factors.

Then she started talking about Mina. "Our new queen defeated the final challenge of our Orientation; she faced a monster that was far beyond her level in order to save the entire rest of the population of our group. Thanks to her, the deaths in our Orientation were, um, kept to a reasonable level . . ." Avery's face took on an obviously troubled expression. It was clear that some of the death and destruction she'd witnessed was still affecting her.

But after a few seconds, she continued, "All of this was after Mina solved the mystery of what—and who—the monsters were that were killing and eating a few of us every night. She chased the Wendigos away, or—I don't really know—at least persuaded them to leave or something."

I really need to ask Mina some more questions about the Wendigos, James thought. *They sounded horrifying when she mentioned them, and they basically vanished from the scene. Unless there are some additional details to the story, they're still out there. And I think she would've mentioned a Wendigo xenocide.*

Avery turned and looked at Mina, and James saw tears in Avery's eyes. "I want you to know that I'm so glad that I can be here where you and your husband are. You're such kind and good people and"—her voice broke down into sobs for a moment—"I know that I'm only here thanks to you! So many of us are—" She swallowed whatever she was about to say, sobbing again. Then she wiped away tears and snot with the sleeve of her blouse until James approached softly and gave her a handkerchief.

"Thank you," she said, smiling slightly.

He smiled back at her, trying to keep the guilt from showing on his face. For a moment, he felt like a little bit of a fraud. As he sat back down, he reminded himself that everything anyone had said about him was because of something he'd actually done. He had risked life and limb over and over, and apparently so had Mina. He knew it from her story of Orientation, of course, and he had also spoken some with Yulia about her experience. But it was quite another thing to hear testimonials from the beneficiaries.

He turned to Mina as he had this thought and whispered, "You make quite an impression, my queen."

She shook her head gently at him but couldn't keep herself from smiling. "I'm afraid I'm starting to resemble you," she whispered finally.

After Avery had wiped away her tears, she made the same pledge as everyone else, voice quavering as she spoke. James was surprised that she didn't add "and queen" to the oath, but he figured she just didn't want to be different. It was obvious to him that Mina had impacted Avery more than he had. She approached the royal couple to return his handkerchief, which she had at least neatly folded, before she returned to the audience.

Then the next speaker came and stood on stage.

As the morning wore on, every single person who got up, without fail, had something nice to say about James. Even the ones who James only vaguely remembered or didn't think he knew at all. Some of the latter spoke in vague terms or only mentioned things James had done since returning to Earth. Every speaker concluded by reciting the citizenship pledge as a loyalty oath to James personally. The ritual of it had clearly developed a certain momentum.

As the various speakers got up to praise him, the same or similar notifications played in front of James's face several times.

[Sufficient experience accrued. Fisher King leveled up!]
[...]

He couldn't easily block them out. Far from focusing on some specific objective, he was glorying in every aspect of this moment. The feelings of power over, and admiration from, the crowd. The way he had orchestrated this whole small-scale revolution in people's sensibilities and what they expected from a government. The looks on people's faces. His wife's hand, held tightly in the palm of his own.

I'm so lucky, he thought. *I'm remarkably fortunate. Once upon a time, I would've said I was blessed. Now that I have a literal blessing from a god, it feels weirdly less appropriate. Even though I consecrated this ground to Anansi, his connection to what's happened is tenuous at best. Most of what's happened I couldn't credit to Anansi even if I wanted to.* It was hard to put into words exactly what imaginary force he wanted to praise for his present circumstances instead.

But there was so much to be thankful for.

His beautiful family, still intact and now enlarged, somehow all together in this world that had been torn apart. Somehow, he felt certain that his mother and sister had survived too, even though the System, if its initial announcements had been borne out, had purportedly killed half of all the humans on Earth. And James had gone from a mediocre lawyer bored with his work to a king acknowledged by a whole fledgling community of people as their leader.

It feels like fate, he decided. *Like some cosmic force of destiny put its thumb on the scales for me. Maybe there's some cosmic force for order out there that really appreciates that I rejected Apophis.* It was hard to imagine that he and his family deserved all the credit for this themselves, after all. It just seemed like too much. *My cup runneth over, as the Bible says.*

After some time had passed and another speaker returned to her seat, James took the podium again. "I'm sure there are more of you who would like to speak today. The reception has been truly humbling. But there are a couple of friends here who helped guide some of our new residents to the Fisher Kingdom, and I don't believe these two friends of ours are staying. I'd like to escort them to where they're going, and I am hopeful that I can do that and be back by tomorrow morning at the latest. I believe it's about midday now, so we need to wrap things up. I'd like it if we could make these meetings a weekly occurrence with optional attendance. One thing that's become clear is that I would really enjoy hearing more of people's stories about their Orientation experiences and about their lives before the System. There have been a lot of great stories today, and I think it would be nice to end future meetings with a story. They don't have to be about me"—this drew a chuckle from the crowd—"or even my wife! For now, would everyone who hasn't already taken the pledge please stand and recite it if you're willing to? Then we will adjourn."

The crowd obediently rose as a body to their feet. Even several of those who had already pledged their allegiance stood, James noted. Only Alan, Mitzi, and a very few others remained seated. Of those, one of them was sitting in a wheelchair and placed his hand on his heart for the pledge. Two others had already come up and sworn their loyalty. James only counted two people who seemed uncomfortable with the idea, who he imagined would be leaving shortly.

"I pledge allegiance to the Fisher King and to the ideals for which he stands: protection of the innocent, justice for all, and the promise to reconquer the Earth for humanity and our allied species. Only our sacrifices honor the fallen. Only victory can bring peace. Only we can win back the world." Though the sound of individual voices in the gallery had been muted before, the combined voice of the mass of people swearing loyalty to James in sync had a powerful resonance now. Each syllable seemed to echo through his body. The words already spoken bounced off of the walls and echoed so that the sounds wrapped around each other and embraced James like a warm coat.

It really was humbling.

Mina walked up beside James, the baby clutched close in her left arm, and the picture felt more complete. Then Yulia appeared on Mina's left as well, and the picture became fully complete.

If I live to be a thousand years old, I'll never forget today. It really can't get much better than this.

CHAPTER EIGHTEEN

Departures

After the meeting finished, Mitzi and Alan watched James and his family from a distance as they spoke to their new subjects.

James found ways to make everyone who approached him feel important for at least a moment or two. Mitzi could tell by the way their faces lit up. He also seemed to be giving out responsibilities, based on how serious some people looked as they nodded in response to his words.

It was clear that James had become more comfortable with being in command over time. Still, there was definitely something else on his mind. Even as he stood there, talking to everyone with his baby held against his shoulder with one hand, she detected a trace of melancholy in his expression.

But Mitzi was most concerned about how Alan felt after witnessing James's first assembly.

"So, do you want to stay here?" she whispered. "It's okay if you do. I'm comfortable enough here. We'll get by just fine, and I have no doubt we'll make ourselves useful."

"I—I don't know." Her husband's face looked conflicted. "I am tempted. I had resolved to go back to the office unless something kept me away. James even agreed to go with us, so in my mind, that settles that. But after—well, I don't know."

I know, Mitzi thought. *I know where we're going to land on this.*

"There's no hurry to get to an answer," she whispered, smiling softly.

"Why are you whispering, anyway?" he whispered back.

"I feel like he could hear anything we're saying if he wanted to," she replied in a not quite whisper, "but if he wants to hear a whisper, I imagine it takes more concentration than listening to normal speaking voices. Especially if there are a bunch of people standing all around him, all competing for his attention."

Alan turned his back toward James before he spoke again. *That's smart*, she thought. *That makes it impossible to read his lips.*

"Do you think he listens in on all the conversations in his territory?" Alan whispered. "That would be a gross invasion of privacy. That sort of thing is part of where my doubts come from. Can we really trust James with the authority that these people are imbuing him with?"

"I think our old government was working to do much the same thing," Mitzi whispered, "on national security grounds. I wouldn't be surprised if it occurred to him. Hopefully, he won't take that idea seriously. Then again, maybe that's part of the good work you and I can do here. He takes our advice seriously; we've seen it already. The world has changed. James has decided to found a kingdom, and the System gave him powers to support that, I guess. But we can guide him. Keep him following his better instincts." She realized that she was selling a bit.

"I didn't intend to persuade you either way," she hastened to add. "I'm still figuring out how I feel too." *Though, there is an undeniable excitement in the idea of helping found a new country*, went unspoken. "Well, I am leaning one way, but you know him better than I do, even after Orientation. You know what he's like in normal times. What his temperament is. We're not always going to be facing emergencies. I want you to be the one to make this call. Do you trust him? Do you want to stay here?"

Alan looked back at James, his gaze steady, for a few long seconds before he replied.

James spent what felt like a long time fielding questions from his new citizens.

It wasn't actually very long as tracked by the movement of the sun through the sky, which he kept a distant eye on because he was hoping to reach Dean's camp before the end of the day. But it felt like forever.

Maybe I shouldn't have chosen the Politician route, he thought as he finally politely excused himself from the gathering. He looked at his son in his arms. *This is who's important. I have to make sure I never neglect my family while I'm dealing with them.* He was a bit sad at the idea of leaving James Jr. for any length of time, which was why he was spending all this time holding him. Mina would have him to herself for the next twenty-four hours. James needed to get in some time with the son he'd only just met.

On the bright side, Mina had given him a long list of items to pick up if he could. Some of them, like diapers, were things he would have needed to get regardless of whether he went to help Dean. So at least he could tell himself that he wasn't de-prioritizing his family to assist a bunch of strangers and one of his old bosses.

"Are you feeling all right, skapi?" Mina asked as they reached the top of their apartment stairs. "You look like you're thinking about something unpleasant."

"I'm just sad to leave you guys for any length of time," he said. "I hope you'll all be all right."

"We have plenty of people here to protect us," Mina said. "People who are loyal to you personally now. The people you care about will be important to many of them too."

"We survived a pretty dangerous place with less help before," Yulia said quietly. She was standing a few feet back, close to the children. James heard her quietly tell Abhi, "Take the little ones to the room."

"You made sure to tell your new subjects to mind me while you're gone," Mina said. "That will help. Since that was one of the last things you said while we were outside, I don't think they'll forget it. They only just swore their loyalty. As long as you come back soon, we'll be okay." She stood on tiptoes to kiss his cheek. "So just get back here as soon as you can, all right?" James caught the hint of sadness in her voice, though. They had just been reunited and already he was leaving.

"I'll always come back," he said fiercely, looking back and forth between Mina, Yulia, and the departing young children. Abhi had begun shepherding his siblings, one holding his hand, one in his arms, but he stood listening in the space between the stairs and their room. Halfway between staying and going. "Anytime I have to go anywhere. Don't believe I'm dead unless you see a body."

Mina, Yulia, and James shared a laugh at that.

"I know it," Mina replied, giving his bicep a quick squeeze. "Let's go put Junior down. He's been trying to go to sleep since halfway through your speech but couldn't with all the people talking."

She has a really good read on the baby, he thought. *I was wondering what all the wriggling was about.*

"I'll go watch the kids," Yulia volunteered. She moved toward Abhi, and he reluctantly continued walking toward the children's room.

"Our baby is very quiet," James observed, staring down at Junior in the crook of his arm and following Mina into the bedroom.

"He is," she agreed. "He's a strangely calm boy. I can't help wondering if it's the influence of this System. I know he was inside my womb during Orientation, so he didn't go through what the other children did. Still, I wouldn't put it past them to interfere with him in some way. And you know I had to let the proctor look after him a few times . . ." Her voice trailed off into a silence pregnant with worry.

James nuzzled the baby's stomach and was rewarded with little happy noises. And Mina's anxious expression shifted to a smile.

"There's no point in thinking about the System's plans for the children right now," he finally said. "We know it tried to at least give us what we needed for a shot at survival. I think we can assume it's trying to do something similar for the kids. And there are potentially much more immediate threats."

"I guess so," she said. There was a short pause. "Did you have something specific in mind?"

"There is that Cara woman. In my conversation with Anansi, he mentioned only three big threats to look out for in our two Orientations. I destroyed two of them, but the third was in your Orientation. I think he meant her."

"So, you're wondering if you need to destroy her," she finished. "Have you tried following up with Anansi to find out if she's still a threat?"

"I haven't. I don't know how that would change, though. Someone as power hungry as she is only becomes more dangerous over time, though. I would know."

Mina bit her lip. Her body language radiated conflict in James's eyes. *She wants to protect her.*

"There's more than one way to neutralize a threat," she finally said.

"Can you be sure she'll never be a problem in the future?" he asked.

"No, but by that standard, you'd have to kill everyone in the world."

He snorted. If anyone else had said that, he'd have disregarded their opinion, but he trusted Mina's judgment. It had been invariably good through the years he had known her.

"Let's assume you're right about her," he said. "Can she keep a muzzle on her creatures?"

Mina swallowed. "She did during the last days of my Orientation—no, that's not true. She funneled their wrath in specific directions. But the Wendigos' hunger is endless. It's inevitable that we'll face her unless she leaves the region completely."

James nodded. "I'll order my flying creatures to keep an eye out for her kind. Any telltale signs they should be looking out for?"

She considered it for a moment. "Just unseasonably cold weather."

"So, anything below eighty, then."

He smiled. She returned the expression, but hollowly. He could tell she was a bit troubled at the thought of that future conflict. *When I destroy the Wendigos, I'll make sure she's not there.*

"Is there anything you need from me?" he asked. "Besides the items you already mentioned." Mina started to shake her head. "Anything for the family, then?"

She thought for a moment. "I know we spent some quality time with Yulia last night. She seems to be adapting well to being back on Earth. Maybe having the kids around helps her. Gives her something to focus on other than how her life has changed. But I think you need to have a few words with Abhi before you go. He won't say anything—he's hardly talked so far, which is understandable given what he's been through—but I think he's bothered by you leaving. Maybe scared of you not coming back. He's just old enough to understand some of what's going on, but not much of it. I think he's becoming attached to you on an instinctual level, even though he's still waiting for his parents to come home. Whatever you do, don't leave without saying goodbye. He'll probably have nightmares."

"That makes sense," James said slowly. "I am the one who found them. I don't want to make the world feel more unstable than it already does." *Maybe I'm already doing that just by leaving right now,* he thought. He frowned.

"Yes, there's that," Mina said. "And you're strong. Steady. You make everyone around you feel more secure. I would become attached to you myself if I wasn't already!" She chuckled a little as she spoke those last words.

He smiled. "Thank you. And I'll talk to him."

They kissed.

When James entered the children's room, all eyes turned to him immediately—Yulia, Abhi, Indira, and even little Deepam. It made James feel slightly self-conscious, but at least they were happy to see him.

"I hope I'm not interrupting anything," he said.

"We're playing!" Abhi said, smiling. He held a transforming robot action figure in one hand. James saw that Yulia held one too. The kids and Yulia were all sitting on the floor.

That's sweet.

"Did you come to join us?" Yulia asked, raising an eyebrow.

"No." James chuckled a little. "I would love to, but I was actually just getting ready to go with our friends Alan and Mitzi. I wanted to say goodbye to you and Abhi."

Abhi's smile dried up like a raisin. "You're going?" he asked. "Will you be back?"

James closed the distance between them in a few short strides. It wasn't a very large room. He'd already thought, when he was putting the children to bed with Yulia the other night, that it ought to be enlarged. *I'll put in some windows too, more windows all over the apartment.* That would be his last order of business before he left: narrow slit windows that children couldn't fall through. For now, he sat down so that he was almost at eye height with Abhi.

"I will," James said. "I'll be back tomorrow or probably the day after tomorrow—"

"What if you're not?" Abhi interrupted. "What if you aren't back by tomorrow?"

He really is anxious about this.

"I'll be back by the day after tomorrow," James said. "If not, I'll be back the day after that. But you don't need to worry. I'm very tough. I built this whole place by myself, remember? I just wanted to make sure you guys are going to be okay while I'm gone. You can help me out by listening to Mina and Yulia and taking care of the little ones. You're going to be the man of the house for a little while, right?"

Abhi seemed to think about that carefully for a long moment. "All right," he said. He still didn't look happy, so James pulled out his trump card.

"I also made this." He took a small spider out of his pocket and held it out. It wasn't a real spider, but a crude sculpture made of James's hair mixed with clay he'd pulled from the soil. It wasn't much to look at, in his assessment. *I'll never be an artist.*

"What's that?" Abhi said. He didn't extend his hand to accept the spider, but he looked transfixed by its strange appearance all the same. The spider walked slowly, clumsily, back and forth across the surface of James's hand as it moved for the first time. The movements had a slightly crunchy sound as the clay shifted around to make its legs move a bit better. Finally, it began to get its footing and straightened up its posture.

"It's a monster that I made," James said.

"Hello, human!" The clay spider opened its disproportionately large mouth and spoke, and Abhi jumped six inches off the ground.

"Wow," Yulia said quietly. "That's such a cool Skill."

"Thanks," James said, smiling as he looked back and forth between her and Abhi. It wasn't his best work, but it was nice.

"What's it for?" Abhi asked, grinning like he hadn't been scared a moment ago.

"This little guy is for you," James said. "He's a Clay Spider. Think of him like a pet that can talk. He doesn't need to be taken for walks, but this spider can play with you when Yulia is busy. If you need me, you can tell the spider, and I'll know."

"That's so cool," Abhi said quietly. "Can I name him?"

"Of course you can!" James said.

Abhi extended his hand, and the spider jumped onto it. Abhi jumped a little again despite himself, but the spider managed to hang on.

James struggled not to laugh. "You two will get used to each other," he said. "By the time I'm back, you'll be good friends."

Abhi suddenly rushed forward and wrapped his arms around James. "Thank you," he said, holding James tightly around the neck and shoulders.

"You're welcome," he said, a little unsure of how to feel as he returned the hug. There was an odd sentimentality swirling in his heart. *It feels a little like I'm this kid's dad now. I guess I probably need to get used to it. Unless some relatives suddenly appear, we're responsible now.*

Then Yulia was hugging them both too. "Travel safely," she said. "I know you'll be home soon." James felt the tears on her cheeks.

"I will," James said. "I'll be back very soon. I know you'll be fine while I'm gone. Thanks for taking such good care of the kids."

"It's fun," she said, and he could hear that she was smiling.

"I decided to name my new friend Peter," said Abhi quietly, "after Spider-Man."

James smiled and shook his head. "That's a great name," he said.

This trip had better be worth it, he thought. *I'd better accomplish some meaningful stuff. It feels rotten leaving them all like this.*

Before he left the apartment, he went from room to room and created those small narrow windows he'd imagined. Hopefully, this would make things just a bit more comfortable for them while he was gone.

"I'll try and make sure we get some glass or screens for those soon," Mina said as she watched him.

"We're making this place a little better all the time," James said.

They said their final goodbyes, and he descended the stairs.

"Ready to leave, Your Majesty?" Mitzi asked as James emerged from the apartment.

"Absolutely," he replied. "Your chariot awaits." He gestured to the sky, and Mitzi's eyes went wide as she saw two large creatures shaped like balloons that appeared to be made of human skin. *James's skin, by the looks of them.*

"I don't think I could ever get used to seeing those," Alan said quietly.

"You took the words right from my mouth," Mitzi said.

But they both allowed the Skin Balloons to grab hold of them. Each of the monsters extended long tendrils that they wrapped around their passengers' bodies. Mitzi found their grip surprisingly comfortable. Like being wrapped up in fairly plush backpack straps.

"These are made of your skin, right?" she couldn't help asking James. When she turned to face him, she saw that a third similar creature was attached to him. She wasn't sure where it had come from.

"That's right," he said. "I read once that the skin is the single largest human organ. That makes it very useful if you need to make something like balloons."

She swallowed. "Right." *Why did I even ask?*

"So, why don't you guys tell me about the trip here?" he asked. "We have a bit of a long flight ahead of us."

CHAPTER NINETEEN

Diaper Run

Alan and Mitzi recounted the journey from their home to the Fisher Kingdom as James's creations flew all three of them forward. It was a clever trick, Alan thought, to keep them talking.

That way, they couldn't take as much time to be bothered by the fact that James had them flying what seemed to be a couple of thousand feet in the air. It wasn't high enough to make breathing difficult, and the turbulence was less than on many plane fights. The creatures, being living things, were able to move gently and surf the wind rather than resisting changing air currents violently. Even the grip of James's monsters felt more secure than a seat belt. Still, Alan studiously avoided looking down.

Once the story of their journey to the Fisher Kingdom was done, Alan and Mitzi took turns finding other things to talk about. She informed James in more detail about what they'd observed of the condition of the Earth. Alan discussed the state of the area around the law firm building, where they were going. Mitzi asked about James's new family situation, which got him talking about Yulia's idea to find any and all lost children in the area.

And they both assisted James with navigation as needed, since every landmark had moved around as the Earth shifted. The Rogets found many ways to distract themselves from the flight. James himself didn't seem to mind either the sensations of flying or the conversation.

Eventually, he asked them if they minded the idea of a pit stop.

"Not at all," Mitzi said.

Alan nodded his head in agreement. He was fairly certain that Mitzi wanted a restroom break but had been hoping someone else would bring it up first. It was her body language that gave it away to him. And now they happened to be flying over a shopping center that had a few intact buildings.

Most of what they'd passed in the hours they had been flying were the ruins of buildings destroyed in the System's transformation of Earth. Some of the other buildings had been ruined by what Alan suspected must have been human causes—fire, vandalism, and so forth. Only perhaps one in four buildings from the pre-System era remained standing, so seeing a largely intact shopping center felt like a piece of incredible luck.

As they descended, he muttered, "I bet there are even functioning toilets."

Mitzi gave him a raised eyebrow look that confirmed his theory.

"So, why did you pick this area to stop?" Alan asked, deliberately turning away from her to look at James. "I can't imagine you're just tired."

"Two reasons," he replied. "First, Mina asked me to stop at the store. I have a list of items to get." James chuckled a bit, apparently at the thought of making a shopping trip in the midst of the apocalypse. He shook his head and lapsed into silence.

"And the other reason?" Mitzi finally asked as their feet touched down on the cracked and broken asphalt of the nearly empty parking lot. Only a few scattered abandoned cars remained in the big empty space.

"Ever since I became a Ruler, I can sort of sense the territory of other Rulers," James said after a short silence. "I don't want to worry you guys, but if we enter another Ruler's territory, there's a good chance we'll get challenged to a fight. Or more likely, we'll just be attacked. The monster that rules that territory will assume we want a fight."

"Monster?" Alan asked. "Aren't some of the Rulers human?" *Like you?*

"Almost all of the Rulers are monsters," James said. "The proctor told me very few humans won their Orientations outright like I did. And we also have no way of distinguishing a human's territory from a monster's. A lot of them are also expanding their territory, just like me."

Alan's expression turned to one of horror.

"So, the monsters are taking over the world," he said.

Mitzi placed a hand on his arm, and Alan reminded himself to take deep breaths. Surely things weren't all that bad.

But James was nodding. "We're in a race against time with the monsters at this point, yes. If we lose, then it's a monster's world."

"Are you sure it was wise to set us down here at all?" Alan asked. His head whipped around nervously, looking to see whether monsters would creep out from under any nearby cover.

"Yes," James replied confidently. "This territory is sort of sandwiched between two monsters' territories. Neither one of them has reached it with their auras yet.

In a few days, both of them might get here at the same time, and then it could become a zone of conflict—"

"Why would they fight each other?" Mitzi interjected. "Do the monsters have their own internal rivalries?"

James explained that there had been a rivalry between the Wolf King and the final boss monster back in their Orientation. "There's no reason that different species should get along," he finished. "They're all competing for the same scarce resources. Food and territory are limited."

"Well, I hope they all kill each other off," Alan said bitterly. "Why the hell did the System bring them here?! The System claims to be benevolent. Why did it introduce monsters into the world?"

James looked away for a moment as if listening to a sound from somewhere else. Finally, he turned back to Alan and Mitzi.

"The System doesn't create most of them," James said. "The stronger ones already existed. It just decides where they go. Apparently, there is a higher purpose to this that we just can't see yet. I know it's hard to accept that answer, but it's the best I've been given."

Alan felt like arguing, but Mitzi put a hand on his shoulder, and he forced himself to calm down. It was just quite a heavy thing to know that the world where he had grown up, formed his family, learned his profession, and ultimately grown old was now no more and perhaps would never reappear.

"I'm going to clear that building," James said, pointing at the store. "I sense there is some life inside, though I can't tell if it's humans or just lower-level monsters. Either way, it shouldn't take me long to render the building safe."

"Do you want backup?" Mitzi asked.

"No, but thanks," James said. "I want to go in and look around first. If I need help, I'll yell as loudly as I can. But if it's something that's below the level of a Ruler, I should be able to take it out on my own."

"Are there any monsters in that building over there?" Alan asked. He pointed at a hamburger joint that stood thirty feet away from the store.

"Nope," James said. "Nothing with Mana inside. No signs of life that I can discern."

"We'll forage for supplies if we don't hear from you, then. I don't imagine any of their meat is still good, but sometimes these places use fresh potatoes. Depending on how long we were actually gone, those might be decent to eat. Or possibly to plant."

Most importantly, it's an intact building that's bound to have a restroom.

James nodded absently; he was staring at the store as if it was a puzzle to be solved.

Alan and Mitzi walked off toward the restaurant, leaving him to his thoughts.

* * *

What is with that place? James wondered. *I sense Mana. A sort of life force. But I can't tell where in the building it might be coming from. Is the whole building a monster?* It didn't seem possible. And if the building was a monster, it must be incredibly weak for its life signs to be so hard to read even while he stood right in front of it.

"Sorry I couldn't give you a better answer about the monsters, sir," Hester said. She sounded guilty. "I could tell your friends weren't satisfied with it."

"Well, we would all like to understand what's going on better, Hester," James said, "but no one thinks it's your fault that we can't. Now that Alan and Mitzi aren't in immediate danger, they just really want answers. Anansi really can't share more, huh?"

"Lord Anansi says you could have used one of your questions to get the big picture information back when you were with him in person. He thinks you were wiser to spend them on more immediately useful intelligence, though. The purposes of the System and the monsters will become clear with time anyway."

"I suppose," James said. "I hope you enjoyed finally getting some public recognition back at the assembly, by the way."

"It was very satisfying, sir. Thank you again. I was especially glad that there were some children in the audience who could clearly see me. Children always make up the most imaginative stories and embellish them with crazy details that adults would never come up with. People are going to think of me as some kind of wise, magical spider who gives amazing advice and helps you perform your miracles!" There was an obvious tone of pride in her voice. She added, almost as an afterthought, "Lord Anansi also appreciated that you consecrated the building as a temple to him. I know he wouldn't have asked, but I could tell that the fact that you came up with it meant something to him."

"I know he's had my back so far," James said mildly. "I try to always honor my debts. And I expected that a lot of stories were going to be told there. It seemed fitting."

He began walking toward the sliding glass doors of the grocery store. He wasn't going to figure out the mystery of this place by just standing outside staring at it.

To his surprise, the doors opened automatically to let him in. James stood outside with a raised eyebrow. *There's still power to these things during the apocalypse? How?* Now that he looked for them, he saw the building also still had some lights on, though not all of them. Maybe it was on some form of emergency power. *A generator somewhere? Maybe we can use it . . .*

It still wasn't entirely clear to him how much time had passed on Earth while he and the others were in Orientation. Even the smartphones didn't know the correct dates and times. The phones disagreed with each other, as he, Mina, and Yulia had found. They reflected how long each person had spent in Orientation.

James's Orientation had lasted until a later date in that separate space, so his phone thought it was weeks ahead of theirs as well as a different time of day. Mina's phone was some minutes ahead of Yulia's, apparently thanks to a period when a monster had stopped time so that Mina could commune with her patron goddess.

Okay. Maybe a generator could be working. I guess I'll investigate. He walked into the building and immediately paused.

[Dungeon entered! You have arrived in Dungeon: Carol's Retail!]

The doors suddenly shut behind him, moving with uncharacteristic speed.

Shit, he thought. *I don't have time for this!*

"Oh dear," Hester said quietly. "So that's what the life energy you sensed was."

"Dungeons give off their own life energy too, huh?" he asked, looking around and waiting for a threat to emerge. But nothing seemed to move.

"Sometimes Dungeons are just the plaything of a god or a creation of the System," Hester said. "But a Dungeon can also arise as a living thing. A form of monster."

"Good to know," James said. "And there was no way of recognizing it from the outside?"

"I'm afraid not. I don't even have your senses. I couldn't tell that there was life inside the building."

"Do you know how to kill it?"

"If you beat the Dungeon, you should have the option of destroying the core," Hester said without hesitation.

"Just perfect." He shook his head. "I guess I'd better speed run this thing."

He finally darted forward and moved beyond the area with the shopping carts near the front of the store. And he saw a blinking light as he passed.

He turned his head and got a better look at it: a blinking red light set into an electronic sensor. *Motion detectors? The Dungeon is using human technology?*

But he didn't have much time to consider that strange fact for very long.

Motion appeared in his peripheral vision. James turned his head and realized he'd spotted movement in one of the large spherical mirror domes scattered around on the ceiling. From one of the back doors, a line of humanoid figures was approaching. As they moved, a bank of fog pushed forward alongside them.

Still, James's superhuman senses could clearly make out the movements of the monsters even through the thick clouds of water vapor.

They were slow and clumsy, their bodies moving with painful-looking shambling movements. *Zombies*, he thought. *Looks like a dozen. I thought I'd seen enough of them in the Dead Marsh.*

James walked over to the aisle where the Zombies were emerging, and he slashed forward with his arm. *Air Strike!*

A blade of wind surged forward and bisected the entire line of zombies and dissipated the fog in an instant, so James clearly saw the arms, legs, and partially rotted internal organs as they went flying. Thankfully, the congealed blood in the bodies meant the liquid part of the mess wasn't as bad as it could have been. Eerily, the wriggling corpses dragged themselves forward, continuing to try to find their intended prey. Whole halves of human bodies with strange sunken faces and white eyes stared in James's general direction.

Well, that's pretty gross, he thought. *And creepy as hell. They even seem more resilient than Roscuro's zombies were.* If this place had enough of their kind, that could be a problem.

He moved to the next aisle over so he could go around the assortment of moving body parts.

As he reached the end of that aisle, another half-dozen zombies emerged from the doorway. A sign above the door frame blinked on and off; "Exit," it read.

"I'll take that as a sign that this is the right way to go," James said quietly.

"Seems reasonable," Hester said. "Unless there's another exit you can see."

"I mean, I could *make* an exit," James said. "Unless this place is indestructible or something. But there's no reason to destroy the building if I don't have to. I'm not in a desperate situation, and there are supplies here. If I was trying to run away, I would just smash the automatic doors so I could come back later with reinforcements."

Roscuro, would you please assume a more useful form? James thought at his ego weapon. *Any weapon would be nice right now. I don't want to just chop these things up into pieces and have them go flying into the hallway ahead. They'd be crawling around on the floor, trying to bite my ankles. But I also don't want to touch them bare-handed and get zombie juice on me.*

So, I do the dirty work, came Roscuro's deep voice in response. *Very well, Master.* The black bracelet form that the Soul Eater Orb had assumed changed. It shapeshifted first into shadows, then into a dagger that placed itself in James's hand.

You couldn't be a longer weapon? James asked as he planted the tip in the closest monster's eye.

Roscuro dematerialized again so that James didn't have to pull the blade out of the defeated zombie. He repeated the killing blow over and over on the remaining creatures before casting Mass Pillage to harvest them for Stat points.

I need souls to develop my power, Master, Roscuro pleaded. *Otherwise, my flexibility as a weapon is limited. Human souls, spider souls, wolf souls, it doesn't really matter. I'm happy to feed on the souls of your enemies. But using me against soulless enemies like these creatures is a waste of my particular gifts. They're not even real dead people!*

Um, I'll take that under advisement, James sent back. He would have said yes if Roscuro hadn't specifically begun by mentioning how happy he would be to consume human, spider, or wolf souls. That was far from the way to win his heart.

Wait, did you say they're not even real dead people?

Correct, Roscuro replied. *These do not behave like zombies. It is as if someone made up a monster based on some old legends.*

Well, they're very real looking! James thought back.

He walked through the doorway with the Exit sign hanging above it and found himself facing a long hallway. Another line of zombies began emerging from a darkened doorway at the end of the hall.

Is that all this Dungeon can do? he wondered. *Anyone could overcome this place with the basic level of training that Orientation provided.*

He quickly killed his way to the end of the hallway, and he found himself in front of the darkened doorway.

The wooden sign above the door read Employee Lounge.

James looked into the room and immediately saw the only light source: a glowing purple orb. It appeared to be a gem as large as a watermelon, sitting on what looked like an ordinary break room table.

He walked toward it.

As he entered the room, alerts popped up.

[Congratulations! You have cleared Dungeon: Carol's Retail!]

[First human to clear Dungeon: Carol's Retail!]

[You gained 500 exp!]

He dismissed them with his mind.

"Stay back, human!" said a loud female voice that seemed to be coming from the orb. It sounded like a human voice but with a rough vocal quality. "Don't get any closer! You have successfully cleared the Dungeon, and you won a free shopping trip—so, um, please, don't destroy me!" With those last few words, the facade broke down.

James looked down into the glowing purple orb.

"Why shouldn't I?" he asked. "Didn't you just try to kill me?"

"Please don't!" the voice said. "I didn't—I wasn't—I'm sorry! I just figured that's what Dungeons are supposed to do."

"You don't sound like you really know what you're doing," James observed.

"That's because—well, I don't." The voice sounded softer now. A little sad. Pathetic, if James was being honest.

"How could that possibly happen?" he asked. "An intelligent Dungeon that doesn't know what it's doing."

"I achieved Race Evolution," the voice admitted. "A total fluke. I was a Rogue, and I had survived by making traps for things to fall into. I found it really scary getting through Orientation. So, I decided to accept the option to become a Dungeon Core!"

"I see," James said, not really understanding. "So, how does this work for you?"

"Well, I accept challenges, and then I provide access to prizes if people win. If they lose, I get their stuff. And either way, I get experience."

"Huh. That sounds like a convenient situation, actually. How did you get the supplies you have out in the Dungeon? Were they things that were left after the System showed up?"

"Mostly no," she said. "The food here was all rotten, but the System gave me credits, and I have access to a lot of special items as a Dungeon Core, so I spent about half on monsters and half on prizes! Mostly food. Which is funny, since I don't need to eat now." There was a distinct enthusiasm to her voice now, despite the fact that her life was still in James's hands.

"Do you have baby products in this place?" James asked.

"Some," she said.

"And you can restock the items you have here?" he said.

"Absolutely."

She's an invaluable resource, then.

"Would you be willing to promise not to kill any humans I send inside here?" he asked.

"If that's what you want, I'm happy to do that in exchange for you letting me live. Just have them tell me that you sent them. If that's all right?"

She's not lying . . . James thought it over for a few seconds.

"I think I'm going to let you live, then," he said finally, "and use your space as a training location for some of my people. What do you think of that idea?"

"Hey, man, I get to live, and I even get more Experience? Sounds like a big win!"

"Good, then. I'll send someone in to let you know what to expect in a week or two. My name is James, by the way. Also called the Fisher King. I'll have them say that King James sent them."

I'll have to conquer the surrounding territories to get this place, but having a slowly growing benevolent Dungeon inside my territory seems like it might be really useful for training the lower-level people. And possibly some of the really young wolves.

"A week or two? So, you're just going to leave, then?" she asked. She sounded slightly disappointed.

"Not yet," James said. "First, I'm going shopping."

"You can do that," Carol said. "I mean, of course you can do that. It's your prize! But I'm thinking, um, what if you took me with you?"

James was already turning to walk away when she said those last words. He turned back and stared at the Dungeon Core.

"What?" she asked. "Do I have something on my face?"

He shook his head and groaned slightly. "Your sense of humor is almost as bad as mine. What do you mean, take you with me?"

"I mean, I'm not stuck here. I can rebuild the Dungeon wherever my body is. And that's this orb. I just—well, it sounded like you might be going pretty far away, and, uh, I couldn't help wondering if you were ever actually going to get around to coming back. It *is* a little lonely here. You're the first human I've had the chance to talk to in days . . ."

It was an easy decision for James.

"All right. Go ahead and hop inside my bag. You're coming with me."

Without legs, Carol did not have the ability to hop, as it turned out, but James managed to pick her up and store her in his magic satchel with no trouble.

CHAPTER TWENTY

Arrival

After James completed his shopping trip and placed Dungeon Core Carol carefully in his bag, he met back up with Alan and Mitzi. Alan reported that they had collected all the potatoes in sight in their bags, and then the trio resumed their voyage.

The flight was largely uneventful, though there was a surprising moment when they had to take a detour to stay away from what appeared to be an epically large and dangerous thunderstorm. The surprising and disturbing part was that James sensed a massive and powerful life force at the center of the largest cloud.

In other words, that was no naturally occurring storm. It was simply a marker of the outer boundary of a Ruler's territory.

I suppose I'll eventually have to deal with whatever that is myself, he thought. He did not look forward to the idea of fighting some kind of monstrous thunderbird inside of a thunderstorm. James sent a silent instruction to his other flying monsters not to worry about looking for Wendigos after all. He would have to assume that the whole world was hostile and threatening from now on. The Wendigos were just the tip of a very large iceberg. Seeking them out would just be making trouble for himself for no good reason. It wouldn't make his world particularly secure to eliminate their kind. *Better to start with my neighbors.*

James was beginning to regret agreeing to help clear out whatever monster infestation Dean and the surviving population near the firm were dealing with. *I have plenty of my own problems, given the number of growing monster territories in this area.* He estimated he still had at least a few days before the nearest one could reach the edges of his own territory, but those were days that would have ideally been spent preparing.

I can rely on Mina, he thought. He sent a message to the monster he'd left behind with Abhi, and he ordered it to ask Abhi to present it to Mina. Then James put the Fisher Kingdom at the back of his mind. They were arriving.

The trip had taken longer than James had hoped. His creatures were still slower than he'd have liked. But at least they'd made it while the sun was still out. He estimated sunset would be there in an hour or two, but there was enough time to get the lay of the land.

As they approached, James saw the old law firm building separated from the main road by a big fissure. Surprisingly, it was still just as intact as Alan had conveyed, despite both the movement of the Earth generally and the existence of that big gaping crack in the ground specifically.

I guess it's a relief seeing another building still standing, James thought, *but man, I do not miss this place*. It was surreal to think that just a couple of months ago, he had been employed full time in this place, managing files and reporting to partners. *Bleh!*

There were also figures walking around outside working, he thought. Dean had assembled more people than just those who had worked in the building previously. There were eighteen figures walking around outside, including two men in prisoners' uniforms. One wore an orange uniform, and the other was dressed in deep red.

A serious criminal, James thought. *Dean has to know what that color means, right?* The man in orange was no angel either. James thought he recognized him from his days as a prosecutor. *Arrested for breaking his wife's jaw, I think?* Domestic violence offenders had always been the lowest of the low in his eyes, a position that was universal in the State Attorney's Office where he had worked.

But the other man's uniform indicated a serious threat to public safety. A particularly violent murderer. Serial killer. Terrorist. Serial rapist. There were a variety of horrendous crimes that could earn the red jumpsuit, but inevitably something vile and dangerous. If James had run into someone in a uniform like that just out wandering the Earth, he would have considered whether to avoid him or simply kill him.

But now I'll be helping him, he thought. Or at least the man would be among those he would be aiding if he assisted Dean. James tried to reserve his judgments for now. The System onset would have changed everyone's lives. Some people had changed for the worse—the images of Officer Ross and Cliff came to mind—but others would undoubtedly have changed for the better.

I remember Mina and I used to talk about when Yulia would finally grow up. She's so nice and accommodating that we thought she might fall in with the wrong crowd, like their sister Yelena. Now look at her.

Everything he'd heard about Mina and Yulia's Orientation told him that Yulia had really come into her own. She wasn't someone they needed to worry about in the same way as before, and probably never would be again. She was growing into a strong adult.

Alan and Mitzi had been rather heroic in Orientation.

Damien had gone from an ordinary man to a Werewolf who took on the responsibility of protecting a group of people until James had showed up to relieve him of that burden.

Some people had been criminals going into Orientation. James knew Rostov had been convicted for murder, and he had ended up being the worst human in James's Orientation.

But there were a couple of Moloch cult members who James felt had redeemed themselves in the end by fighting Flame Elemental Rostov alongside him. So anything was possible.

Then he remembered that he didn't have to think about this by himself. Maybe Alan knew something.

"Hey, guys," James said, speaking up just loud enough to be heard over the wind, which was louder at their height in the air.

"What's up, James?" Mitzi asked.

"Do either of you know the people down there?" he asked. "I'm wondering about the men in prison garb in particular. That red uniform usually means a really dangerous inmate."

Alan looked down, frowned, and shook his head. "I think I recognize some people from the building, but not those two. They must be, uh, people Dean invited," he said hesitantly, brow furrowing with the beginnings of worry.

"Hopefully, Dean knew what he was doing," Mitzi said. "There is a woman I recognize down there." She pointed at a woman in Mage's robes. "I've been volunteering at the library since I retired, and she's a librarian at the local branch back that way." Mitzi pointed a thumb in the vague space behind them.

"Guess she found the group too," James said. "Probably good for her chances of survival."

"Yes," Alan agreed. "One thing Dean has to his credit: he's organized. You know he's been imagining the end of the world for years. Some of these people are probably from his community."

Still kind of a small group, though, James thought. *No way they could survive out here like this. Not with these numbers and no Ruler present to scare away potential invaders.* He didn't feel the aura of a Ruler, at least, though James knew it was possible to conceal the power to some degree. He'd been containing his own power within himself as they flew this way, to avoid provoking any fights.

"What do you suppose they're moving down there?" Mitzi asked, pointing.

James looked at the ground again and saw the prisoners hefting what appeared to be some form of heavy equipment toward the fissure.

"Looks kind of like military hardware," James said.

"It is," Alan said, squinting. "Now that you mention it, I recognize what they're moving. They have some canisters of—no . . . No, they wouldn't have let these guys get it off base. How did they manage it?" He trailed off into a troubled silence.

James tried to let him work things out, but as they drew closer, he felt the need for an answer more pressingly.

"Alan, what is it they have exactly?" he asked, barely controlling his tone. But the urgency must have come through.

"Chemical weapons," Alan said, speaking quickly and quietly. "Some kind of gas. What kind, I don't know. I recognize what the canisters look like from the Persian Gulf. But I don't know what the army was storing in their Orlando base. I just know they got a lot of funding for new projects way back in the war with China. That was when they put up the new base. I guess they were storing some of this stuff there." He shrugged helplessly.

"Good enough," James said. "Now I at least have an idea of what we're walking into."

He ordered the Skin Balloons to release their hold on him and slowly lower Alan and Mitzi nearby.

Then James dropped the thirty feet or so that had separated him from the Earth. He landed just a few feet to the side of the former prisoners. As he touched down, he felt the distant presence of a Ruler somewhere below ground. But his mind was immediately pulled back to the surface.

Both of the men put the canisters they were holding down and turned to face him, their guards visibly raised. They looked bigger up close.

I wonder what their Orientation was like. He was betting on violent.

"Hello, there!" James called, raising a hand and waving casually. "I hear you guys have a monster problem?"

The convicts visibly relaxed a bit and looked at each other before either of them spoke. James used that moment to Identify both men.

[Viktor Cremieux, Lv. 8]

[Olivar Cruz, Lv. 9]

Neither of them has been through Race Evolution. They're just naturally this size. Viktor was the one in the red jumpsuit, while Olivar sported the less stylish but also less concerning orange.

"Who are you?" Viktor asked gruffly, clearly not the brightest bulb.

You could've just used Identify, James thought. *I have a False Impression up, but it has my real name on it.*

"My name is—"

"James!" Dean Crocetti's voice cut through the background noise and interrupted James's self-introduction. He turned and saw the law partner rushing toward him from the firm building.

"Well, I guess we have a friend in common," James said, turning to the convicts with a small smile. Neither of their expressions showed anything but suspicion as they looked back at him. But that was fine. He didn't care if he won them over. The reverse was what mattered.

Alan and Mitzi landed beside James just as Dean reached them.

"Guys," he said breathlessly, "so good to see you made it back here! James, you're looking, uh, large."

"Race Evolution," James said. "Once you get your Race to level ten, you get some new options for how you want your body to function."

He Identified Dean as well.

[Dean Crocetti, Lv. 10]

Huh.

"Oh, I just got there myself," Dean said, answering James's unspoken question. "I've been too busy to go into Race Evolution, though. Someone else in my Orientation did it, and I realized it took about an hour for him."

"Busy doing what?" James asked.

He could see in his peripheral vision that Alan and Mitzi were looking uncomfortably in the direction of the canisters of gas the convicts stood beside.

"Just trying to solve problems, man, same as always," Dean said, a smile playing over his lips. "You probably know how it is, with the power grid down and the gas and water disconnected. But before we can deal with any of that, we have more immediate problems. Right now, we're playing whack-a-mole."

James was slightly startled by the sound of Cruz beginning to laugh off to the side. He turned his head and saw Cremieux affixing Cruz with a disapproving look.

"Whack-a-mole, huh?" James asked, turning back to Dean.

"Would you explain the situation, Dean?" Alan asked. "What's the nature of the problem? I know there are monsters, but when I left, we didn't know what kind." He lowered his voice. "Who exactly are these guys? And, um, why do they have military-use canisters of gas?"

"We're right fucking here," Cremieux said loudly, taking an aggressive step forward. "Anything you want to know about us, you can ask us yourself."

Alan took a step back. Cremieux's face took on the satisfied look of a bully whose victim was ready to hand over his lunch money.

And James released some of the aura he was holding in.

Cremieux's expression changed. Beads of sweat formed on his forehead.

"What are you—" He looked at James. Then Cremieux stepped backward several paces until he stood behind the canisters. James reined his aura in a bit.

"Sorry about that, guys," Dean said awkwardly, casting a disapproving glance in Cremieux's direction. "Vik, these are my friends from work. Alan, one of my partners, and James, one of our associates." He looked at Mitzi. "I assume you are the famous Mitzi I've heard so much about?"

"Guilty as charged," she said, trying to put on a winning smile but landing more on the side of obvious discomfort. "Though, I don't know what I might have done to get famous."

"You can't spend time around a guy like Alan and not know about his wife!" Dean said. "Anyway, these two gentlemen are Viktor and Olivar. Got to know them a bit in Orientation. They both have a bit of a temper"—he threw them a look that seemed to carry an emotion somewhere between impatience and indulgence—"but they saved my ass more than once in Orientation. They're good guys. Solid. Brave."

Brave when they know they can win, James thought. Olivar was definitely the man he'd seen in court for smashing his wife's jaw. And Viktor had just demonstrated he wasn't any more patient than Olivar.

"Hopefully, we can all get along," James said, not bothering to hide the deep suspicion with which he regarded the two convicts.

"I believe we can," Dean said, not giving either former prisoner the chance to respond. "In fact, I would say it's more like we have to. We need to work together if we're going to rebuild the world." He was clearly warming to his subject.

James gave him the thinnest of nods, to convey, *Yes, go on.*

Dean turned to Alan. "When you left, Alan, I had an inkling about what the monsters in that deep hole might be," he began.

James's Ring of Truth began throbbing on his finger for the first time. He realized this was its way of indicating deception. Since he had owned it, no one had outrightly lied to him. At most, he had felt a twinge from the ring when someone told him a half-truth. Dean was lying about something.

CHAPTER TWENTY-ONE

Negotiation

"After you were gone, we used a rope to lower someone down into the pit to investigate. Our unfortunate volunteer barely survived, though I believe he'll be as good as new soon since we got him some prompt healing. When he regained consciousness, he described the creatures that had attacked him. Those descriptions fit with what I had been, uh, concerned about. I remembered a monster from my Orientation, and our volunteer's report fit them to a tee."

James listened closely to the explanation, and the Ring of Truth didn't give him any further indications of deception. He guessed that the only thing Dean had been lying about was that he'd had "an inkling" about what sort of monster he was dealing with.

He must have actually known what kind of monster it was right away. And, what, he lied about it? Pretended he wasn't sure? Hoped against hope that he was wrong? In the end, he sent someone down into that pit who got hurt . . .

James looked at the faces of the convicts who were still standing nearby. They had been nodding and looked satisfied with Dean's recounting of the story. *How would these two men—these* violent *men—behave if they knew Dean was lying about not knowing what kind of monster was inside that space?* And that question, of course, assumed that this was the only important thing Dean was lying about. *This place is a powder keg that could explode any time. Why bring such unstable people in?*

"So, what sort of monster are we dealing with, then?" James asked, not wanting to waste time. "I can already sort of feel its presence."

"You can *feel* it?" Viktor asked, sneering.

"Yeah, like you were just feeling me, Viktor," James replied scornfully, releasing some aura for a moment to drive the point home.

"Okay, guys," Dean said, stepping forward so he stood almost in between Viktor and James. "Let's please try not being at each other's throats for a bit."

I could literally rip his throat out at any moment if I wanted to. Viktor needs to know he can't behave aggressively in front of me.

James simply stood silently, eyebrows slightly raised, waiting for Dean to answer his question. The tension in the air seemed to ebb slightly as a few seconds passed without any eruption of violence.

"The monsters we're dealing with are Mole People," Dean said finally, his expression grave.

James waited for the punchline. When it didn't come, and he realized Dean was serious and telling the truth, he said, "Really? Mole People? Like in some cheesy old science fiction movie?"

"They're a serious threat," Dean said. "We encountered them in Orientation." His eyes seemed to fill with fear as he began recounting the story. "It was me and the Crespo brothers. We were in a field where there was supposed to be a nest of monsters according to our group's scout. The scout thought they looked edible if we could manage to kill them. Probably a good source of meat." He scowled at the memory. "But we couldn't find anything. The scout had a long-distance communication Skill, so we were talking to her through that. She insisted that the monster was some sort of giant rodent, and where you see a rodent, there's almost never just one. She thought they might be some kind of burrowing type, so one of the Crespos started digging." Dean put a hand to his face and started massaging the areas under both eyes, moving his fingers inward until they reached the bridge of his nose. It took him a few seconds before he was willing to continue.

"Mike Crespo had dug about a foot into the ground when a *claw* burst out of the ground and pulled him thigh deep into a hole. Mike was screaming and hollering, and we were standing there staring at each other trying to figure out what to do. He starts yelling, 'Help me, help me! It's trying to pull me under!' So, me and his brother Javier each take an arm, and we start pulling. We get the leg about an inch out of the ground, and this horrible *force* yanks on the other end and pulls it right back in. The creature pulls even harder, clearly trying to get as much of Mike's body underground as it can. At a certain point, Mike's voice gets loud and shrill, and we start to see the blood pour out of the section of his leg that's planted in the ground. He tells us, 'Leave me, save yourselves.'"

James's Ring of Truth detected deception again here.

"So, we start running." *Another lie.*

"But Javier was too slow." This also registered as untrue.

"I managed to escape that field with my life, but as I turned back, I saw this big quasi-humanoid *thing* covered in fur. It was half out of the ground, grabbing onto Javier with claws as long as this." He gestured at his left hand. "It made this horrible squeaking sound, and then another one popped up next to it and grabbed Javier with its claws. I saw them pull him down, deep underground somewhere, where I wouldn't be able to hear him scream." He shuddered. "During those last moments when they were yanking him under, I managed to use Identify, so I figured out they were Mole People. We tried to avoid them the rest of Orientation, but they were one of the primary monsters. Their territory seemed to span roughly a third of the space. The rest of it was less hospitable, if you can believe that. So, we kept occasionally losing people for a while. Once we spotted a Mole Person in the act of taking a team member, we started spending a lot of time in the trees. But it was difficult. They made it a nightmare."

Well, at least he doesn't seem to be exaggerating the nature of the perceived threat. The Ring of Truth isn't giving me anything.

"Were the two of you there for this?" Mitzi asked the two convicts.

Viktor just gave her a sullen look before he caught James glaring back at him. Then Viktor turned his face to gaze elsewhere.

"We were," Olivar said solemnly. "Well, we weren't there for the first encounter, but later, when the monsters snatched a teenager, we had already joined. We witnessed that."

"So, you were planning to gas them?" Alan asked. "I saw you had some canisters of some kind of gas there." He bent down to look slightly closer at the canisters. James had already glanced at them but didn't have the chemistry knowledge required to interpret the labels.

"What is it, exactly?" James asked.

"Nerve gas," Alan said. "The System is translating the text for me, but I can still recognize that the characters are Mandarin. Looks like weapons confiscated from the People's Republic of China after the war."

"Yes," Dean acknowledged. "I asked our friends here to get their hands on whatever they could. Based on our volunteer's testimony, there's more than one or two of those monsters down there. It's not safe to go down there and fight them in close quarters—"

"So you're going to gas the area?" Alan interjected. "That stuff could kill a lot more than just your Mole People!"

"Well, what's the alternative?" Dean replied calmly. "The building"—he gestured to the firm's office building—"is perfect as a base. We just have to clear out some pests. We can't have them making fissures like this. But we have to clear all of them out. Gas is the only way to be sure."

"If the wind takes it, that stuff could kill everyone you have here," Alan said.

"Our friend at the base assured us that we'll be safe as long as we wear the masks he provided." Dean held up a dark-colored gas mask.

"What if the creatures realize what you're doing and decide to come up for a fight?" Mitzi asked. "It sounds like you don't believe your group would win a straight fight with them."

"I'm told that the gas is odorless and colorless. They have no way of realizing what's going on. They're just dumb animals, but they're too tough to fight head-to-head." Dean was trying to sound calm, but James could detect that he was a bit frustrated with the conversation. Still, James had his own serious reservations about this idea.

"Are you sure?" James asked.

"Am I sure about what?" Dean asked, sighing.

"Are you sure that they're just dumb animals?" James asked. "In my Orientation, I drove a species to extinction only to discover when I was fighting the last one that it could talk. And they had been attacking us in part because they perceived us as invading their territory. It was an avoidable fight, and I regret that it happened. I don't exactly disapprove of the idea of using chemical weapons here. If you're right, they're just like pests that live in the walls of your house and gassing them is the appropriate solution. I hate to ask this, because you obviously had a traumatic experience in Orientation with these things. But have you ever tried talking to them?"

Dean just stared at James, slightly flabbergasted, for a moment.

"No," he finally admitted. "I haven't tried that. Do you think it's possible?"

"Why don't we step inside the firm for a bit and discuss strategy?" James suggested.

"That seems fine," Dean said.

Viktor spat on the ground, obviously annoyed at the delay. "We will remain out here, in case one of your pet monsters"—he pointed at James—"decides to take a bite out of someone outside."

"Then it's just the four of us," James said, giving a small smile. *I don't care what you think, dumbass. You're the dumb muscle Dean decided to put up with in a moment of weakness.*

James, Dean, Alan, and Mitzi walked across the broken parking lot pavement and entered the firm building. It was remarkably intact, James noted. Dean had been right that it was a sturdy structure. It even apparently had a Dungeon somewhere inside, though James was less interested in that now that he'd found Carol. But still . . .

As the doors closed behind them, Dean began talking. "So, what couldn't you say in front of our new allies?"

James and the others took seats on the chairs in the lobby before he responded.

"For starters, why are those two thugs here at all?" James asked. "They're both violent criminals. Do you even know what they did to end up in those jumpsuits?"

Dean's face colored. "They're two of the strongest warriors I met in Orientation," he said after a long pause. "We're lucky they agreed to join us."

"Is it lucky?" James asked. "People don't necessarily turn over a new leaf just because circumstances change. If they're among the strongest people you've met, that just makes the lack of basic anger management skills even more of a problem. How will you restrain them?"

"Well—" Dean looked uncomfortable. "That's a bridge we'll cross if we come to it. So far, they've both been doing well. I've never seen them strike another human in anger. And what would you propose, anyway?"

"Come with me," James replied instantly. "Alan and Mitzi can tell you because they've already seen it, but I've carved out my own territory. Much safer than being here."

"So, you're not staying, then," Dean said, clearly disappointed. "I can tell you're strong. I don't know how strong. But you can hardly defend any land by yourself—"

"He's not, uh, alone, Dean," Alan cut in. "He actually seems to have a lot more people in his Fisher Kingdom than you have here."

"What? Wait, you declared yourself a king?" Dean looked at Alan and snorted a little. "Are we back to monarchy?"

"It's not a joke, Dean," Mitzi said, sighing.

The humor on Dean's face dried up, and his tone became slightly hostile. "So, I'm in the presence of royalty now."

I could be with my wife, my baby, and the kids right now, but no—I decided to come and help this guy. I don't need this.

"Well, clearly you have this situation under control, Dean," James said. "You're building yourself a community that includes violent felons, you're about to use up your deadliest weapons to solve a pest problem—and possibly contaminate your own living space—and there's no one in your whole group who's actually strong enough to maintain order, let alone to defend it when the real threats show up."

"Spare me the holier-than-thou attitude, *Your Majesty*," Dean spat. "We're a self-governing community. We don't *need* your kind of order here. And what do you mean about real threats?"

I suspect that in the long run, much of the world is going to get *my kind of order, whether they need it or not. Dean doesn't get it yet, but the circumstances now make dictatorships almost inevitable. Monarchy lasted for millennia because people could be convinced that the royals were meaningfully different from them, because of magic blood. Fast forward to now, when I'm so genuinely different from the people in this little crew that I could slaughter all of Dean's people without using up most of my Mana. I would never do that, but there is some extent to which might makes right.*

"I mean that we live in a monstrous world now, Dean. There are probably as many monsters in the world now as there are people. No, probably a lot more. And there are thousands of particularly territorial ones, which the System calls

Rulers. Including several whose territory isn't far from this area. That's part of why I suggested leaving the Mole People alive. If you can negotiate with them, they might be willing to coexist in peace. They could stand and fight with you against other species that could invade the territory."

James wanted to add, *If they don't fight alongside you, and I wipe them out, I doubt you'll last a week here*, but Dean was already shaking his head.

"No." He spoke through gritted teeth. The next words were something between a whisper and a groan. "I can't—I can't let them get away with all that they've done. The people they've killed." He shook his head and locked eyes with James. "Alan claimed you're some great monster exterminator. Do it or don't do it. But if you're not going to help, then just stay out of the way."

James sighed and stood. *Fuck it.*

CHAPTER TWENTY-TWO

Underground

James turned and began walking toward the front doors.

"Well—hey, wait! Are—are you going to do it or what?" Dean's voice came through the air behind him.

I'm so profoundly disappointed in you, Dean. James didn't bother answering the question. His answer would be obvious soon enough.

As he reached the door, James heard Alan's voice. "Let me speak to him. The two of you are talking past each other. You could try to understand his point of view, you know."

Then he heard the sounds of Alan's shuffling old-man footsteps following behind him.

James moved through the door and held it open for Alan. Mitzi was back there saying something else to Dean, but James focused all his attention on Alan for now.

"I thought that went well," Alan said sarcastically.

James couldn't help smiling. "I'm glad the end of the world hasn't meant the end of your sense of humor."

"You have to admit he has something of a point, James."

"About?"

"These monsters attacked him and his allies without any warning that we're aware of," Alan said. "Why would he be willing to believe they're trustworthy partners to form an alliance with? And—" He hesitated.

"And you think my governance structure is less than ideal," James finished.

"Potentially," Alan said. "I'm not as sour on it as Dean. I've seen you lead."

James looked Alan in the eyes. "It's a form of government for a harsher, more unpredictable time. We can't have checks and balances in the world we're experiencing right now. We have to make instant decisions. There can't be any question of second-guessing me when we're in the middle of a conflict. And you know how stupid people can be when they're in groups. The ancient Athenians elected their generals and they would try to remove them at the first sign of trouble. That's probably why they lost to Sparta. The madness of crowds is practically a cliché. People need a strong source of authority." He looked off to the side.

"I admit there is an element of personal ambition at work here. More than a little bit. But we're all compromising one way or another. You might think that Dean has beautiful ideals, even though he's decided that it's okay to have violent criminals in charge of his munitions and that another possibly intelligent species shouldn't be negotiated with, despite the fact that the world is now populated with powerful nonhuman species. You might reasonably agree with him that we should be democratically governed. I used to think that before the world turned upside down. But setting all that aside, he isn't strong. Not strong enough. He's not even seeing things clearly. That man tries to be a hard-nosed realist, but he's delusional right now. Or he just doesn't believe the truth I'm trying to show him.

"You know me, Alan. I'm not as idealistic as Dean, maybe, but I will always defend my own. And I have the power to back that up. The day is coming, and I suspect coming soon, when this place is going to get overrun by monsters, captured by someone stronger, or Dean gets shivved in the back and replaced by someone more ruthless than he is. What happens to his ideals then? He's going to die or take orders, maybe from monsters, maybe from some contemptible people we haven't even met yet." James met Alan's eyes again. "I'm not trying to sell you on myself as a leader. I *am* the leader in the Fisher Kingdom. That's a fact. You know that I listen to advice when I'm acting as a leader—" He stopped himself. "Damn it. Okay, I am selling myself a bit, I guess." He chuckled a little before he started talking again. "My bottom line is, I don't want to be wondering what's happened to you and Mitzi. I hope you'll decide to come back with me and not stay here with Dean in his 'Gangsta's Paradise.' You don't have to answer now. Please discuss it with her and let me know what you two have decided when I come out of the pit."

"So, you're actually going in?" Alan asked, raising an eyebrow.

James gave a bittersweet smile. "Well, I promised you I would, didn't I?"

He began walking toward the fissure. He sensed rather than saw as the figure of Alan trailed along after him, with Dean and Mitzi walking further behind.

It's a shame that Dean fellow isn't joining you, Roscuro's voice commented in James's mind. *Clearly not close to your level, but he would be one of the stronger members of your kingdom.*

I know, James replied. *But what are you going to do? Pride is a killer.*

"That was quite dramatic," Hester said quietly. "Another great speech, sir. You missed your calling as a priest."

"Thanks—I think," James replied, quietly laughing to himself.

He reached the fissure and looked down into the inky darkness. It reminded him of a fall from a cliff he'd taken not too long ago. Even though he felt almost invincible now, there was a tiny splinter of doubt in his mind. The environment would be on his enemies' side. There was another Ruler down there. He hadn't faced one other than Roscuro before—and he knew the Soul Eater had genuinely possessed the power to put him down for good.

Quit worrying, Master, the Soul Eater's voice pronounced reassuringly. *I can't sense anything in there as dangerous as you. Certainly nothing as crazy as you are. If nothing else, just make sure you use me to kill a decent number of these Mole People. With their souls inside me, I'll have enough power to protect you in the event of a landslide.*

For a moment, I was almost reassured, James thought to himself. *But Roscuro just wants to eat souls.*

He looked around and saw that a number of Dean's people had gathered around the hole and were staring at James. It was the perfect chance to give them all the same information he'd given Dean.

"All right, Dean," James said, loud enough for his voice to carry. "I'm going to do you a favor and solve your monster problem, since I already came all this way."

"Thank y—"

James cut Dean off and continued talking even louder. "There will undoubtedly be more creatures on the way once these things are gone, though. This place won't ever really be settled or safe until it's part of a Ruler's territory." He cast a quick look around at the assembled faces, and he saw many of them, including Dean, looked worried. "I'll talk more when I'm back from exterminating the Mole People," he added.

Then James leaped in. As he fell, he drew his Ego Spidersword from his magic satchel and ordered Roscuro to transform into the longest dagger he could—which wasn't very long, but James hoped to make the weapon a lot stronger over the course of the next several fights. James was already wearing the Royal Exoarmor and Solar Helm, though the latter would be of limited use here.

As he fell, he felt the Ruler's aura getting stronger the further down he dropped—but not as strong, he was fairly certain, as his own. Roscuro was right. James should be able to win this if he played it smart.

He wondered if it would be possible to capture the Ruler alive.

As he had that thought, James heard skittering in the darkness. Then he could make out a shape rushing through a tunnel toward him. It managed to leap onto James before he fell out of reach. Then he was locked in combat with his first Mole Man.

The creature was shrouded in darkness almost up to the moment that it made physical contact, but James had a solid second to get a good look at it before it could attempt its first attack. He wanted to know what he was dealing with.

The figure that had attacked him was exactly what the phrase "Mole People" would have led him to expect: a six-foot-tall mammalian monster covered in fur, with big sharp teeth and claws, and no eyes that James could see.

It really is just a simple animal, he thought. *Maybe I gave Dean too little credit for deciding that he just hated these things and that negotiation wasn't worthwhile. These things might be just like the Desert Centipedes.*

Before he could give it any further thought, the monster hissed and tried to bite him. And James focused on killing the thing.

Fortunately, James's Predator in Human Skin Class and his overpowered Stats were made for close combat. As the monster attempted to sink its teeth into the Exoarmor—they glanced off like plastic trying to cut through metal—James threw a single punch. He heard and felt the snap of bone and the ripping of meat—and then a ding.

[You killed Menacing Mole Man, Lv. 11! You gained 110 exp!]

Well, that was super easy, James thought. *I barely felt any resistance to my fist.*

Could I please kill the next few, Master? Roscuro asked gently.

Yeah, I'll let you go ahead and do that, James replied. As he sent the message, he caught hold of a wall to stop himself from falling.

And he Pillaged the Mole Man's body for Stat points. *Waste not, want not!*

"Can you see what you're doing?" Hester asked as the mole meat and fur floated into James's bag. "I heard the sound of you killing something, and I saw a glowing body just now, but while you were fighting, I couldn't see my foot in front of my eyes!"

"It's a little dark, but I can still see," James replied. "I do have a trick for this situation, though."

Hand of Glory!

Sparks of light emanated from his left hand, scattering to all sides within a large radius around James. Rather than falling with gravity, the lights hovered in midair, scattered at varying elevations slightly above, just below, and roughly at James's height.

For the first time, James took in the small canyon-like space he'd leaped into. He could see how the walls were pitted with oval-shaped tunnel openings that looked to have been dug with claws and teeth alone. They appeared to lead in all directions, and they appeared at different elevations as well. The sight reminded James of the game Whack-a-Mole, and it raised the question of whether monsters might pop out of any hole at any given moment.

How many creatures live in this place? James thought.

So many souls to eat . . . Roscuro observed at almost the same moment.

Well, I'm happy for you, then.

"I can see now!" Hester called out excitedly.

The effect of the sparks was limited to only those whom James allowed to see it. Otherwise, he wouldn't have used them, just in case there were non-mole enemies down there that might be drawn to light sources. James was fairly certain that he could fight blind with near complete effectiveness by relying on his other senses.

But he enjoyed Hester's reactions a great deal.

"Oh my gosh, how did they make this place?" she gushed. "Didn't they get back here at the same time as you?"

"Well, I've put up a small apartment complex since I got back, and I only had a few people helping me," James said. "The Mole People might have hundreds of workers in their number from the way this place looks."

You'll have an accurate picture after you've slain the Ruler, Roscuro suggested. *Once you flood this place with your aura.*

That would imply I want to keep this underground realm as part of the Fisher Kingdom, wouldn't it? James replied. *Is there anything down here worth the effort?*

The residual aura fades if you don't reinforce it after a few days, Roscuro told him. *I have no way of knowing what's in the midst of all these tunnels. There may be some sort of treasure that the Mole People are interested in harvesting. I would just think of it as a useful way of scouting the area so you don't leave any stragglers behind. You're aiming to commit a xenocide here, right, Master?*

Against my better judgment, probably, James sent. *Definitely, if I can't talk to them and negotiate in any way. If there's an army of intelligent creatures down here, I'd rather not kill them all off. If only the boss is intelligent, though, it might be unavoidable.*

Then there were sounds of movement that came from several directions and cut off any further frivolous exchanges. James saw the gleam of reflected lights on bared fangs in several tunnels.

"Oh dear," Hester murmured. James didn't need to turn his head to recognize that there were Mole People coming from behind him too. That was fine by him. More than fine.

They don't appear to have numbers that would be hard to handle so far. And the one that attacked me earlier couldn't pierce my armor with its fangs, so it's not looking good for the moles. James mentally prepared for what he was about to do.

He sent a message to Roscuro. *Hey, if I can't negotiate, I think I'm going to just smash these things apart with my fists. How about you turn into a shape like brass knuckles?* He provided an accompanying mental image.

As you wish, Master. There was no mistaking the bloodlust in Roscuro's tone.

"I come in peace," James said loudly and clearly "I am here to negotiate. Can you take me to your leader?"

Then the Mole People, moving almost as one body, leaped toward him.

CHAPTER TWENTY-THREE

Into the Labyrinth

"So, we need to make up our minds," Mitzi summed up.

"I would say so," Alan agreed.

"I still think we made the right decision back at the Fisher Kingdom," she said gently. Lowering her voice, she added, "I also think I agree with James about the, uh, former criminals. I really thought that man was going to attack you before, and I wouldn't have been able to use my magic quickly enough to do anything about it."

He squeezed her hand. "Neither James nor Dean would have let that happen," he replied quietly, "but I would prefer that you not have to worry. I don't know if Dean realizes the challenge he seems to have taken on here."

"Just the opposite," Mitzi said, her tone slightly bitter. "He's buried his head in the sand."

Alan looked at her for a moment, apparently taken a little off-balance. She realized her sudden vehemence had surprised him.

"He's bringing his family here," she said in a lower voice. "When you followed James out, I asked Dean whether he really believed in this place. Whether he really thought they could rebuild civilization from here, without someone more powerful supporting it. And he said he's bringing his wife and kids out to this place. They're already on the way. Once they have the office building secured, he wants to move them in—after the Mole People are exterminated, and he has some Mages shore the building up. He thinks it's the safest place."

Alan turned his head to look around at the surrounding area. There was no one near them. A few minutes before, the whole group had been staring down into the fissure to watch James. They had seen him kill a large number of Mole People, seemingly with just his bare hands. Then he'd vanished into the darkness, either dropping deeper into the crevasse or disappearing into some side tunnel that the group couldn't see.

Either way, the result was that the crowd's excitement gradually waned until they dispersed to carry out the tasks they had been working at before James's activity had drawn their attention. Now they were doing various chores. Pitching tents. Cooking. Laundry. The mundane realities of daily life in a post-collapse world.

"I think that's absolutely insane," Alan said finally, quietly, as if he still thought someone might be watching them or trying to listen in. "At the least, it's criminally overconfident. They're on the way? Already? He really said that?"

Mitzi nodded.

Alan shook his head in frustration. "He was just about to fill the fissure with some noxious gas. Even assuming he has gas masks for everyone, assuming they work, and assuming that the chemical is somehow lethal to the monsters but not to humans who happen to take their gas mask off for a minute, that's unspeakably reckless."

"I know it's not something you would do," Mitzi agreed, placing a hand on her husband's arm.

"You know, it's not something James would do either," Alan said. "Call him an egomaniac for deciding to establish a monarchy, but his tendency is at least to keep other people away from danger. If even one of those creatures survives, they're right here, and they'll be mad as hell! You would send for your family *after* you secure the base, not before."

I guess we're decided, then, she thought. Mitzi agreed with Alan. But she decided to play devil's advocate for a moment—they needed to be certain about this. "Maybe Dean was very confident it was going to be a complete slaughter. They might have other military weaponry here besides gas."

Alan gazed down at the pit for a moment before he looked back at her. "Well, I think it's going to be a bloodbath down there now."

From just the right angle, James's hands would have looked to a hypothetical spectator like they were encased in a pair of dark red gloves, stretching from fingertips almost to the elbows. The substance shimmered in the dim light like satin.

It was only when one saw the blood dripping from his black knuckle dusters that it became obvious that he wore no gloves over his armor—just remnants of the enemies he and the Soul Eater had splattered. Mole Men and Mole Women. None were spared.

That's what happens when you try to attack first and ask questions later, he thought. *I didn't especially want to kill any of those creatures, but I suppose they were incapable of understanding that I wanted to talk.*

And somehow nothing was left of any of them, though James had not used Pillage. They had disappeared at each vicious killing blow.

"Roscuro, what happened to the bodies?" James asked. He brushed his hands off on the walls as best he could and ordered the Ego Spidersword back into the magic satchel for the moment. The fights thus far had been so easy that the sword the Wood Spider Queen had become was not a contributor. James suspected he was about to go into tighter quarters where a levitating sword might actually get in the way.

Well, Master, if I absorb their souls, they disintegrate, the Soul Eater replied. *The same thing would have happened to you if I had hit you with Soul Magic during our fight. The soul and the body are a union. One cannot continue to exist in this plane without the other. That is what makes Soul Magic particularly deadly.*

"Well, these creatures disintegrated before I could use Pillage on them," James replied.

Oh. Yes. Honestly, I had not considered that issue. Roscuro sounded slightly uncomfortable.

So, this place is mainly going to benefit him *unless I just stop using Roscuro as a weapon*, James thought. *At least I'm gaining experience, but these things are so weak I haven't gotten a single level yet. If I don't get to gather meat or Stats from anything I use Roscuro to kill, this expedition really just benefits the Soul Eater and Dean.*

"How much is this actually helping you?" James asked.

Roscuro transformed by way of answer. The form he took now was that of a short sword. Before, the largest weapon he could make was a dagger. The difference was just a couple of inches, but it was something, at least.

"Fine, we keep going this way for now. But if we kill the boss down here, you don't get to absorb him, got it?"

Of course! Roscuro sent.

"How exactly are you going to find the boss, sir?" Hester chimed in.

James took a couple of deep breaths. Ambient aura in, ambient aura out.

"I can feel the Ruler's aura. Just like I was able to avoid them by sensing auras outside, I can move closer to where the Ruler is by feeling where the power is thickest." He looked down. "This thing is somewhere down there. These little pockmarks on the walls are just distractions, or maybe they're where the minions live. But if I want to be able to have a one-on-one with the leader, I need to go down."

I don't really want to, he thought. He could see the bottom of the hole from here, so it wasn't insanely deep. But he felt a little uncomfortable continuing further underground into an environment controlled by his enemy.

And Florida soil is notoriously prone to sinkholes. I wonder what the odds are of this place collapsing at any given time. Then again—James tapped the earthen wall he was clinging to with the hand he wasn't using to hold himself up. The touch confirmed the surface was solid stone.

Okay, so I'm already in bedrock. The walls probably won't just accidentally fall in on themselves. I don't know if this Ruler can collapse its own lair. If its power is as strong as I think mine is, I imagine it could. But it probably wouldn't do that and crush all its own minions just to get at me. So, I should at least make it to where the monster is. Then I either have to negotiate or get close enough that it can't collapse the structure without being crushed along with me. Well, here goes nothing.

James released his grip on the wall and plunged further into the depths of the pit.

He hit bottom, and his knees bent slightly to better take the landing. As he got his bearings, he felt the temperature had risen slightly, and the aura of the Ruler had intensified. He found himself in a relatively small underground space, perhaps ten feet across and thirty feet long. Before him, the sparks of light that had fallen with James revealed a honeycomb of further holes. Some of them led further down, some led up, and some led sideways.

"Roscuro, turn back into the knuckles," James said. "With short blades on the ends this time, please." He was about to enter one of these confined spaces. Best to have a closer range weapon than a short sword. Roscuro began changing his shape, and James considered his next move. *Should I enter a tunnel going up, down, or sideways?*

He knew he was closer to the Ruler now, but he didn't know if that meant it was above or on the same level as him. It couldn't be above—no matter how much James would like to move up closer to the surface. *So, I'll have to descend further just to be sure whether this thing is above me or on the same level right now. At least, I think that's the best way to get a better idea of the location. Great. Hopefully, the place doesn't go too deep.*

He looked up and saw the sky had diminished to a slender sliver of blue. He tried not to think about how far down he was. He had never thought much about how small and suffocating underground spaces could be. Back when he was just a normal human, he had never spent time in caves or thought about exploring sinkholes. Leave that for crazy people. Or so he had thought.

Now that he had signed up to be a spelunker, he wasn't altogether convinced he was comfortable with this. He was already further underground than he had been in his entire life. The space he was in did not exactly feel confined, but the tunnels probably would be. Or they could be a never-ending labyrinth of tunnels that looped back in on themselves until he could never find his way out again. And the Ruler might very well be able to close the entrances after he entered. A discomfiting thought.

Worst of all, James could imagine a scenario where an intense enough fight with the Ruler would collapse the area they were in, crushing James in an instant, or worse, leaving him alive but trapped. Buried alive. Doomed to slow death by suffocation.

In the latter scenario, perhaps he could survive using earth elemental magic, but would it be enough? Trapped under tons of stone and earth?

I don't think I'm tough enough to survive a cave-in here, anyway.

But he had given his word that he would get to the root of this problem. As far as James was concerned, a leader was only as good as the value of his word, so he said "Goodbye" to the natural sunlight in his mind. He set aside his trepidation and took a deep breath.

Into the labyrinth I go . . .

And he stepped into the nearest downward-facing hole. Like the other openings he'd seen above, it was obviously carved by bestial claws, rather than human machines, for the use of those same monsters. Were the claw marks even bigger on these holes? No, probably just his imagination . . .

Since this wasn't carved for human use, there were no steps, only a moderately steep incline. Like a playground slide.

As James began slowly, carefully moving down the tunnel, he felt the pressure from the Ruler's aura steadily increasing. *Great. So this thing is probably below me somewhere.* He would have to continue his descent into the bowels of the Earth at least a bit further.

The floating sparks from Hand of Glory provided plenty of light by spreading to all corners of the tunnel within reach of James's body. And the space had been dug to be large enough for the monstrous Mole People to move freely in. Large enough for several walking side by side, actually. Perhaps it was so that some larger version of their kind would be able to move freely too. After all, moles tended to crawl on all fours. This hole was large enough to accommodate James walking upright. Ever since Race Evolution, he was a bit over six feet. And the holes were wider than they were tall, so the tunnel was easily large enough for some kind of mega mole. He tried not to think about what was waiting for him ahead, in the deep unfathomable darkness. In the places where his light could not yet reach.

Master, do you sense an enemy somewhere ahead? Roscuro asked. *I cannot detect anything, but your pulse is elevated.*

"No," James whispered fiercely. "Everything is *just fine*. There's nothing ahead that I can see. Just endless tunnel!"

"Sir, do you think you could use earth elemental magic and make this trip easier?" Hester asked.

James resisted the urge to snap at Hester. *Really, if I could do that, do you think I wouldn't have tried it already?* It wasn't her fault that he was uncomfortably far underground.

Why do I even feel this tension? he thought. *I'm not even a normal human anymore. I'm as close to a superhero as has ever existed in the real world. Maybe even on the way to immortality. Am I really nervous about just being in some dark underground place?*

Then again, this might be the most helpless he had ever been since the System appeared. He could be killed at any moment if this Ruler decided to cause a cave-in. He had thought about putting on the Shapechanger's Cloak to become invisible, but considering that it didn't keep him from making sounds as he moved, he had no reason to believe it would hide his presence from the Ruler.

"The enemy's aura permeates this place," James explained, trying to disguise his agitated mood. "It's just like when I fought Roscuro and my water elemental magic didn't really work in his swamp. It was because his aura was everywhere. Unfortunately, I would just be wasting energy trying to manipulate the stone that's here."

"Darn," Hester murmured.

"I appreciate the thought, though," James said. "Always open to your suggestions. Maybe—"

Just then, there was the sound of movement somewhere in the tunnel ahead of him—several pairs of moving feet, James thought.

"What were you about to say, sir?" Hester asked.

"Can't talk, Hester," he whispered. "There's something moving down there now."

Shapes began to materialize in the darkness.

James opened his magic satchel and ordered the Ego Spidersword out. Then he assumed a fighting stance as he waited for the creatures to move close enough for him to strike.

CHAPTER TWENTY-FOUR

The Goblin Battle, Part 1

As the shapes of the approaching enemies became clear, James raised an eyebrow. The image that presented itself before his eyes only created further questions.

Four Mole People moved forward—and seated on their backs were hunched figures, dressed in ragged clothing. The figures were like overgrown children, somewhere between the size of a grown adult human and an adolescent. Their yellow-green skin sprouted unruly tufts of gray hair all over. Each of the humanoid creatures clutched a rusty-looking pike in its misshapen hands. On their heads they wore peculiar goggles with crystalline lenses.

Identify.
[Goblin Knight, Lv. 17 (Male)]
[Goblin Knight, Lv. 15 (Male)]
[Goblin Knight, Lv. 18 (Female)]
[Goblin Captain, Lv. 19 (Male)]
[Mole Man, Lv. 13]
[Mole Woman, Lv. 14]
[Mole Man, Lv. 17]
[Mole Woman, Lv. 16]

What the fuck is going on? Dean hadn't mentioned anything about Goblins. Had he not known? If so, where did they come from? When did they appear?

No. Figure it out later.

"I come in peace!" James proclaimed loudly. "Take me to your leader."

"Oh, take you to our leader we will!" cackled the first Goblin Knight in a voice that fell somewhere between a frog croaking and trying to sing. "You can come in pieces!"

"Kill him for the King!" agreed the Goblin Captain. "He looks weak!"

At that taunt, all four of the vile creatures dug their heels into their mounts—James noticed at that moment that the Goblin Knights wore makeshift shoes with spurs—and the Mole People charged.

This feels cruel, he thought as he easily dodged the tips of their weapons. *I expected to find a monstrous Mole King or Queen somewhere, but it looks like the Goblins have enslaved the Mole People or something.*

He punched the first Goblin Knight, the one who had spoken the taunt, with such force that his head turned to paste in one strike.

Oops. I need to take at least one of these things alive. The body began disintegrating before his eyes. The Mole Man that had been under the Goblin Knight tried to claw James, so he kicked it on the side of the head. The creature slumped to the ground, instantly unconscious.

Better, James thought. *I used more control that time. I don't want to kill all of them until I know what's going on. Especially not the Mole People. They might not be in control of their own actions.*

He barely dodged another pike thrust and grabbed the next pike that followed after it. The Goblin Knights had wheeled around on their mounts for another charge, but their weapons were too unwieldy for the tight tunnels. It was easy enough for James to yank a pike out of one of their hands, and he used the butt of it for a sideways swing that knocked two of them off of their Mole People. The third mounted figure, the Goblin Captain, managed to lean back on his mount and avoid the blow.

The two Goblin Knights that had been forced to dismount drew daggers from their sides and rushed at James alongside their mounts.

Forcing them off of the Mole People might actually have made both the Goblins and the Mole People more dangerous, James thought as the Goblin Captain tried once more, again unsuccessfully, to impale James with his pike. *Those weapons clearly weren't made for this environment. They're way too damn long for these tunnels! So where did the Goblins come from if not here?*

James grabbed the closest Goblin Knight to him, the female, and tossed her headfirst down the long slide of the tunnel. A sound of distant screaming echoed for several seconds as she fell a long distance. Then he kicked her mount under the chin for another knockout blow.

The next Goblin Knight and his Mole Man mount both slashed ineffectually at James's armor. He saw that the dagger the Goblin Knight used and the Mole Man's claws both left scratches but did little actual damage to the Royal Exoarmor.

"This is a real bad matchup for you guys," James said, looking down at the scratches. "I just wanted information and to talk to whoever's in charge. Do you really want to die over that?"

"You will be doing the dying!" the Goblin Knight insisted as he inflicted a particularly deep scratch on the surface of James's armor.

I tried. Stubborn bastards.

James gave the creature an open-handed slap to the face, and he flopped to the ground, unconscious. The Mole Man tried another slash, aimed at the chest of his armor, and James punched him in the torso. The monster instantly collapsed, clutching his chest.

James dodged another pike thrust from the Goblin Captain, still on his Mole Woman mount, and delivered a quick and decisive chop to the back of the injured Mole Man's head. He went down.

Then there was just James and the last remaining Goblin and Mole Person pair, squaring off.

"I want answers," James said. It was obvious that the Goblin Captain and Mole Woman were not a threat. He wanted to give them one more chance to behave rationally so he wouldn't have to beat the answers out of the next Goblins he encountered.

"Find them in the afterl—" The Goblin Captain's face went slack in mid-taunt. His head dipped down as if he was falling asleep. Then it sprang back up.

What the hell happened to him?

The Goblin Captain's eyes were hidden behind those strange crystalline goggles, but his face had a strange cast to it now.

"What was it you wanted to know?" asked a voice that seemed much deeper than the Goblin Captain's.

"Who—how—" James stopped and took a deep breath. "Why are there Goblin Knights mounted on Mole People here? Who put them together? For what purpose? Who's in charge?"

"Such silly questions, human," the unnatural voice said. "The Goblin King is in control down here. He defeated the Mole King and subjugated the rest of them to his will. Naturally, he needed creatures for his Goblin Knights to ride."

James heard, rather than saw, sudden movement close to him. He spun and lashed out with his foot before he could even see what the movement was. He struck a solid living thing, and it slammed into the tunnel wall. He looked to see what it was he'd hit, and he saw the Goblin Captain. His kick had caved in the creature's right set of ribs, and a trickle of blood oozed from his mouth.

What the hell? James turned his head to look at where the Goblin Captain had been before, but the image he had been looking at had vanished. *How?*

It looks as if he caught us in a sort of illusion, Master, Roscuro commented. *It seems these Goblins are tricky creatures.*

"I'm familiar with this style of fighting," James said. It was how he had decided to approach fights when he thought he might be outmatched. It was how he'd beaten the Soul Eater. Illusions and trickery were powerful weapons.

I thought these Goblin Knights seemed weak for their levels. But if their usual fighting method is to rely on trickery and illusions, I need to be very careful. I can't afford to just keep taking on squads like this one; he'll try to slowly bleed me and wear me down. I'll eventually be surrounded by a whole army, if this Goblin King has any sense. Which he probably did.

It's time to fight dirty.

James grabbed the Goblin Captain's goggles and ripped them roughly off his face.

He leaned in close to make the most direct eye contact he could in the darkness. *Compulsion!*

"Take me directly to the Goblin King," he hissed. "Use the safest possible route. I don't want to pass by any Goblins that I don't need to."

We're not going to play it the way this Ruler wants to.

He released the Goblin Captain from under his foot. James knew he would win the battle of Wills, so he let the creature's body slump to the ground.

But as he looked at the Goblin Captain, expecting the inner conflict to begin at any moment—or perhaps for the creature to simply fold to his Will in an instant like a house of cards facing a stiff breeze—the creature's eyes rolled back in his head. He began foaming at the mouth and then lay still.

James received a notification.

[You killed Goblin Captain, Lv. 19! You gained 800 exp!]

Huh?

"Are you serious?" James said.

What happened? Roscuro asked.

"I tried to mind control this creature and he died."

"I guess his mind wasn't very strong?" Hester said.

"That's not a result I've ever experienced before, though, Hester."

It seemed as if his mind was already being controlled, Roscuro suggested. *By that Goblin King.*

Yes, and? James replied. *Does that make it dangerous for me to use Compulsion?*

For weaker minded creatures, I believe it can cause brain damage. Sometimes fatal damage.

"I can't believe I killed this thing just by trying to use it to find the Goblin King," James said.

I think there are more coming if you would like to try again, the Soul Eater observed.

James could hear them as well: a slow crunching movement of clawed feet climbing uphill from further down in the tunnel. They were further away than the first crew of Goblin Knights and Mole People had been when James had sensed them; he was paying more attention now. But they would undoubtedly be here in a minute or two, if he wanted to fight them.

No, I'm not going to waste my time beating up any more of these stupid Goblins if I don't have to, he replied.

"What are you going to do now, sir?" Hester asked.

My question exactly, Roscuro sent.

"I'm going to bypass the shrimp and go straight to the leader."

James began Silent Spellcasting, gathering non-elemental Mana around his body. As he worked, he could hear the Goblin Knights and their mounts moving toward him up the tunnel. That didn't add much pressure, since he was confident he could kill them all without breaking a sweat. But he was trying to avoid casualties here as much as he could.

Since I'm leaving this place behind as quickly as I can . . . He used Mass Pillage on the Goblins he had actually killed, harvesting them for Stats as well as a few odd items: their Goblin Meat, Weak Goblin Daggers, Crude Crystalline Goggles, and Rust-Coated Pikes.

It was interesting that the Goblins did not drop any useful items made from their bodies. It seemed that they really had no natural weapons at their disposal, unlike other monster species. Their hands had long, almost claw-like nails, but those weren't fit to be used as weapons.

James tried on the Crude Crystalline Goggles and almost blinded himself—it turned out that they were devices that, through a combination of magic and optics, sharpened vision and made dark areas significantly brighter. With James's Hand of Glory still active, it was almost as if he stared directly into the sun for a moment until he removed them.

These things are like primitive little engineers, aren't they? This increased his desire to avoid killing more of the creatures than he needed to in order to resolve this situation.

"In terms of the way they fight and survive, they might be more like humans than any other monster species I've ever encountered," James murmured.

"How so?" Hester asked.

"Instead of fighting with teeth and claws and magical energy attacks, they mostly use cobbled-together items that they probably invented. They have some magic, but they're basically relying on their wits. It's a very human quality."

"Well, Lord Anansi did always say that was the greatest strength humans have," Hester replied. "And also their most dangerous trait. They never stop tinkering. Never stop inventing. Even if they're tinkering with the things that keep them alive."

James wondered if that was meant to be passed on as some sort of a warning from Anansi. Perhaps a little oblique, but that was Anansi. He liked to be indirect much of the time, even when it inconvenienced his Chosen One. Like when he declined to describe the nature of the threat in Mina's Orientation. Or when he tested James's willingness to run from a challenge rather than fight it directly by making him think Anansi's sons might eat him.

Anansi had indicated that the System required this circuitous approach to certain kinds of divine information and aid, but James wouldn't be surprised if the Spider God also preferred for things to be this way. He was also a Trickster God, after all.

Those were probably fun moments for him. Definitely the bit with his sons. He would probably think that was good, clean f—

Are you almost done casting? Roscuro asked urgently. *They are almost upon us!*

"I know it," James said, responding to both Hester and Roscuro. "Hold onto your seat, Hester!"

The non-elemental Mana took the form of a ball shape wrapping around James's body.

"Are we about to hit some—"

James leaped down into the darkness.

"Woooo!" Hester screamed in her tinny voice. It wasn't a bad scream, James imagined. More of a roller-coaster ride scream.

As the invisible Mana ball containing James and Hester struck a surface within the tunnel, it bounced but continued spiraling downward. The tube-like structure only became steeper as they moved further down, it seemed. James imagined he would probably want to use a Skin Balloon to float back out of this place, or it would be a long and steep climb.

But that was a problem for later. For now, he used Full Body Control to keep his organs from being too jumbled by the uncontrolled descent. Otherwise, he was certain the insane turbulence would have made him vomit.

As they dropped further down, James's ball struck and bounced off of several lumps in the surface of the tunnel. He recognized by the sounds of pain and alarm that these were more Goblin Knights and that the sudden impacts knocked some of them out. He didn't try to slow down. The goal right now was as few casualties as possible until he at least got in front of the leader.

After all, these creatures might be mine sometime soon. The Goblin King had probably thought something similar at some point, James was dimly aware. But James was different. He had never exploited the creatures he controlled in such a degrading way as turning them into mere mounts for his minions.

The non-elemental Mana ball kept going despite all obstacles until it finally came to the end of the tunnel. James burst out into a vast underground cave; the open area was the size of a football stadium.

And what looked to be a thousand Goblin heads or more turned to face in his direction.

CHAPTER TWENTY-FIVE

The Goblin Battle, Part 2

Well, there are a lot more of these things than I was expecting, James thought. *My quality definitely beats theirs. Who was it that said quantity has a quality all its own, though?*

His non-elemental Mana ball bounced off the ground, and he used the opportunity to survey the battlefield from above. The sight was not reassuring.

Though the Goblins weren't organized in any particular fashion, he definitely counted in the high hundreds of heads. Probably over a thousand.

I don't think xenocide is a viable option here anymore. I didn't want *to do it. Now I'm pretty sure I* can't. *Not unless they let me stop and take a break in the middle.*

Some looked to have been mining shiny rocks from the walls when he came in. Others had been cooking, cleaning, playing some form of sport with a red ball, and one small group of Goblins were operating a little smithy that had a primitive stone chimney that led somewhere outside of this chamber. At one end of the chamber was a small lake, and several Goblins sat around it fishing. The chores and joys and habits of everyday life.

These things really are like us, he couldn't help thinking.

A large number of Goblins were wrangling or playing with or otherwise training Mole People—like humans with horses. There seemed to be a few hundred of the mole people amongst the Goblins, standing or laying or walking around docilely. An area of the cavern was fenced off like a petting zoo with young Mole People and young Goblins playing together affectionately.

Most of the space was more threatening than that, though.

Some Goblins, usually on the periphery of the cavern, were armed and prepared for battle. A small share of these were mounted on Mole People—more Goblin Knights.

And, of course, most of the Goblins, whether apparently civilian or military, had now paused in their activities and turned to look at James. Their gazes were not quite friendly; cold, scrunched up eyes were filled with suspicion. In many eyes James saw fear.

Those he viewed as part of the warrior caste—those who were armed—appeared particularly afraid of him. The civilian Goblins seemed more confused and wary. They didn't know what to expect, he assessed. The quasi-military types looked at James like a nightmare they had never expected to see in real life.

And in the back of the vast underground chamber, he sensed an aura. Through the thick tangle of Goblin bodies James couldn't directly see the owner of the energy he felt. Or perhaps the owner of the power could conceal himself in the crowd. These Goblins were undeniably tricky.

The Mana ball bounced twice on the stone floor before James was satisfied that he had done as much reconnaissance as would do him any good.

Then he ordered it to change shape to fit his body around his armor so that he could land properly.

How are we doing this, Master? Roscuro asked.

As nonlethally as possible, James replied. *Do you have some experience with Goblins?*

I seem to recall they existed in my universe too, the Soul Eater sent.

Well, how would you deal with them? James asked.

As Goblin King Duncan looked over the crowd's reaction to the human's arrival, he swallowed nervously.

Three months ago, he had been just an ordinary Goblin. Fortunately for him, the non-Goblin population of his Orientation, humans and monsters alike, had been incompetent. Now, by cunning, violence, and leadership, he had ascended to the pinnacle of his Race in this universe. The leader of all his kind.

Now a human had arrived with a fearsome aura. Duncan had some difficult decisions to make.

How can I get rid of him? How do I protect my people? I hoped the knights might send him packing, but that was obviously ridiculous. At least without more of them. Maybe if they all swarm him now, in this place with enough space to properly use their weapons . . .

He also considered how he could save himself. *My aura failed to scare him off, so that trick is out . . .* This human was perhaps not susceptible to mental attacks. *No, the illusion worked on him back in the tunnel.*

That settled it.

Duncan used his power as the Goblin King to speak into the minds of his subjects.

All civilian Goblins, take the children and the Mole People that are not fully combat trained and retreat from the main cavern into the side tunnels. A battle is about to commence. All adult Goblins, protect your families and my queen.

Duncan paused, thinking about what to say next. The Goblins were already moving with his orders.

The Goblin Queen stepped forward to stand next to her husband.

"What will you do, beloved?" she asked. Theirs had been a whirlwind courtship. Neither of them had expected to live this long. Every creature had some intuitive idea of its own rank, even if they occasionally challenged enemies out of their leagues. And Goblins knew they were at the bottom of the hierarchy. If Kobolds were the dirt, then Goblins might well be the worms beneath the dirt, though the Goblin King would never admit that openly.

It was a miracle they had lasted this long—Duncan and Sarah's miracle.

"Sarah." He squeezed her dainty, yellow-green hand. "I think I must—" He sucked in a breath. "I think I must stay behind and support the troops' morale. You know their powers are most effective when they fight near me."

"In the thick of danger? The rest of us need morale too, you know." She attempted to keep her tone playful, but Duncan could hear the worry in her tone.

You are a soft magic user. How will you survive in the thick of this clash? She had to be wondering something like that. And until he spoke, Duncan was uncertain as to what he was doing. He had run away from more than his share of fights in the past. It was his illusions that had allowed him to best the Mole King in this place, not his Strength or Agility.

He smiled thinly. "Go, Sarah. Support the others' morale while I guide our warriors."

She placed a hand on his shoulder and swallowed.

"Remember what the Goblins were like without your leadership, Duncan. You can't die here, damn it!" As she finished speaking, Sarah choked up slightly. Her grip on his shoulder tightened like a vice.

But Duncan did not need the reminder. He remembered everything about the environment he and his queen had been born into: chaos, brother eating brother, cousin killing cousin over half-rotten scraps of food. No better, at first, when the System had transported them to this universe. They remained feeble creatures, weak willed and slow-witted. Their default survival strategy morphed from killing and stealing food from each other into ganging up on humans and trying, usually unsuccessfully, to defeat them in combat. Until Duncan showed them a better way. Duncan and Sarah, who had been born with just a few more wits than the average Goblin.

Now my brothers and sisters are even armed, Duncan thought. *Not with rocks* and sticks, but with real weapons. They are not the best quality of weapons, but we have had to improvise our craftsmanship and steal. We earned every piece of equipment we have with grit and violence.

Duncan blinked and realized his mind had wandered for a moment. His queen was walking away. His eyes returned to the front lines. The human had stopped bouncing now. He stood at the front of the cavern, still far away from Duncan and Sarah. The man didn't seem to have spotted the Goblin King and Queen.

They were behind a veil of illusion that kept them invisible to everyone in the chamber. Duncan had triggered it when this human shot out of one of the tunnels. But even so, the Goblin King did not feel safe. Did not feel that his love was safe.

Leave her out of this, he half-prayed. *Let her survive, even if my head ends up on this man's wall. Sarah and our unborn child.*

He knew their lives might become worthless to the other Goblins if something happened to him. It was not as if the Goblins had some long-established and honored history of respecting lines of succession. But he could not afford to think of that now.

Warriors, hear me! Follow my instructions and we will emerge triumphant. The knights must strike the enemy first. This single warrior is highly dangerous. Form up in rows of five and hit him hard! Carry your charges through even if your pikes do no damage to him. Do not be afraid. Use all your power and crush him beneath the claws of your mounts.

Duncan had been trying to teach himself tactics ever since he received the Lesser Blessing of Loki. The Dungeon where he received his blessing held a multitude of books, but Duncan had only been permitted to take one book with him from the unrestricted section of the library. His interest in tactics had pleased the god, he had thought. But it was only now that it became urgent.

Infantry will follow on after cavalry have disoriented and damaged the enemy. Rush in with spear points from as many directions as you can so that he cannot dodge and turn him into a pincushion!

Everyone was moving as he sent the instructions, following his orders. Trusting in his leadership. That had been hard-earned. Those with natural Strength became leaders far more easily. The power of the mind was compelling, but it required more effort to achieve the same result.

He thought a moment more before he added a motivational line.

This is the champion the humans have sent to exterminate us. One of their strongest fighters. The walking symbol of their desperation. If we can best him, this land is ours!

With that, the first of the knights, Daven, let loose a loud battle cry.

"For the king!"

The front row of knights who stood alongside him all echoed his call. Then they added a war whoop of their own.

"*Raaahhhh!*"

Thank you, Daven, Duncan thought. His older sibling was a better Goblin than Duncan deserved to have for a brother.

Daven led the charge toward the armored human.

Though Duncan had little confidence that any of his warriors could actually defeat this fighter, he felt a stirring of something in his heart as he saw them formed into lines and ready to rock the human's world. Even if the human had great power, he was only one man.

What can one human do, anyway? Duncan and his Goblins had managed to outsmart and outfight the humans in his Orientation, even though there had been hundreds upon hundreds of them.

His eyes returned to where the human stood, and he saw the man was glowing. Duncan recognized the blue-with-sparkles shimmer of illusion Mana around his body. It was the same form of magic he specialized in, after all.

The human seemed to ignore the charging knights and continued pulling Mana from within his body even as the Goblins drew near him.

The first wave of warriors struck the human—or should have. Daven, who rode in the lead closest to their opponent, smashed the tip of his pike into the center of the enemy's armor. But it did not seem to even reach the human's body. Duncan blinked to clear his eyes, thinking he must have missed something. Daven's body was thrown from the back of his Mole Person mount, and he slammed heavily into a wall.

The other charging warriors were slightly luckier. Two of them missed the human—not quite as well trained as Daven—while the others seemed only to graze the area around his body. Duncan now dimly saw there was something there.

An invisible shield had appeared on both sides in between the tips of the pikes and the enemy's body. He immediately started thinking about how this battle would be affected by that, and how he should use his own powers to support the remaining waves of knights.

But Duncan's mind was slightly distracted by the continuing growth of the aura around the man. *He must be preparing an unusually complex illusion*, Duncan thought. And more importantly, *He has so much damn Mana! Are there others out there like him? Why was our Race cursed to stand at the bottom of the universe's hierarchy?*

All of a sudden, the huge swell of Mana dispersed as if it had never existed.

Where did it all go? What is the illusion going to be?

The one thing Duncan felt fairly certain about was that the human had not targeted him. Nothing in his field of vision had altered at all in the moment since the Mana had disappeared. And even if the enemy had wanted to target the Goblin King, Illusion Magic required designating an area of effect. But Duncan had hidden his location behind a curtain of illusions of his own—along with hiding the side tunnels where the civilian Goblins were now lurking.

With time, the human would surely be able to suss out the locations of both Duncan and his vulnerable civilians. But before he could do that, more waves of cavalry would hit him until his magic shield was drained of energy, and then Duncan's cavalry and infantry would poke him full of holes.

The second line of Goblin Knights began charging the human as Duncan had this thought.

This time the human moved. Now that he was no longer busy casting, he was pouring his whole attention into the fight. This time he only blocked a couple of the pikes with his magic defense. A third one missed. But he stopped the other two of them with his hands and tipped them straight up with a whip-like flick of his wrist. The two riders holding the pikes lost their position on their respective Mole People's backs and flew through the air toward the human.

Duncan sucked in a deep breath as he saw the human's foot make contact with the first Goblin Knight's body. The enemy's kick struck the Goblin right in the seat of his pants—and kept going until the enemy's foot emerged where the Goblin's shoulder had been. The Goblin Knight fell to the floor in two uneven twitching piles of flesh and bone, joined together by a thick tangle of blood-soaked entrails.

The other Goblin Knight landed near the human and had a moment to gain his footing before the human could turn his attention to him.

This Goblin, seeing what had happened to his squadmate, tried to run. With a single punch, the human tore his head from his shoulders, and a small geyser of blood gushed out as the body tumbled to the side.

Duncan put his hands on his knees and stared at the floor, trying desperately not to vomit.

No one could see him, but if he let himself throw up, he thought he would lose all composure and command of the situation.

Have to remain calm. Have to analyze what he has done. How he is doing this. More than just prodigious Strength and Agility were involved, that was certain. Though, those were undeniably there too.

It must be the illusions, Duncan thought desperately. That was the only thing that made sense. The human must have thrown off the knights' coordination slightly and made it easier to grab their pikes out of the air without risk to himself. *Well, two can play the illusion game.*

Duncan began focusing his power. He only had to manifest his intention to use Illusion Magic in this space. This was his Dominion. He had tried to infect the human with fear earlier, then attempted to fool him with an illusion when Duncan had fought the man through the Goblin Captain's body. Neither had properly succeeded.

But this time it will work, Duncan told himself. *It has to work—or it will mean extinction for us.*

CHAPTER TWENTY-SIX

The Goblin Battle, Part 3

As the next group of Goblin Knights prepared to charge, Duncan used his power to cast a low energy, but highly effective, illusion on the human.

This was a trick he had played on more than a dozen humans at once before, and that was before the System crowned him the Goblin King. Even if this warrior had some sort of anti-magic power, Duncan hoped it would get through somehow.

It should give the impression that he was facing twenty times the number of Goblins as were actually there. The illusion would be far from convincing, of course, but making the warrior believe he was outnumbered was far from the point. No one who knew how Illusion Magic worked would be fooled so easily.

Rather, Duncan's intent was to make it impossible for the human to determine which of the Goblin Knights he was seeing were the real ones and which were fake.

Though the Goblin King stood far away, he thought he detected a flicker of surprise on the man's face. As the group of knights charged, they shouted an array of fierce battle cries.

"Fear us, human!"

"Your kind shall run from us!"

"This is our land now!"

Then, as they drew close, Duncan saw the human swing his arm like a blade. *What is he doing? They are too far away for—*

Duncan felt the pressure of the wind even from far behind every other Goblin in the fight. He wanted to shout a warning, even as he knew it was far too late.

As the five Goblin Knights' heads tumbled from their shoulders, the words died on his lips.

"No," he whispered instead. *With such a wide-ranging attack, he does not even need to see to aim. The only chance now is to overwhelm with numbers.* The old strategy. The only technique the Goblins had known to employ before Duncan had taken charge and showed them how to use basic tactics, deception, and traps.

The fight was going to turn into a melee. An ugly, bloody brawl. Most of the Goblins involved would probably have to die to bring the human down, but Duncan saw no other choice.

This is all my fault, he thought. *The limitations of my planning are really showing now. I never imagined someone would manage to descend so deep underground without being torn limb from limb by the Mole People or killed by the Goblin Knights. I thought I could at least whittle him down slowly as he traveled down that damn tunnel, but he bypassed any obstacles I placed in his way.*

The Goblin King shook his head. *Stop thinking like this. The troops need you.*

He sent a command to all of the Goblin fighters he had left. *The strategy is not working as planned. We must revert to our backup plan. All able-bodied infantry, attack the human at once. Cavalry will wait to see if the warrior gets back up after he is crushed under the weight of hundreds of Goblin bodies.*

Duncan tried to project confidence in his voice, but he feared that his own desperate fears might come through. Still, the Goblins began to move with his orders. They had enough courage to make up for his deficiency.

The Goblin infantry charged forward toward the human and leaped upon him with daggers drawn. Duncan saw the human buried under a pile of yellow-green figures that were barely armed and dressed, let alone armored. Then Goblins began screaming and falling away. Duncan saw their bodies gushing great gouts of blood before they were covered by more Goblins rushing in to attack. The figure of the human was barely visible for a moment, hacking away with some sort of short-bladed weapon. Then he was covered in Goblin flesh again.

Please let this be the end of him, Duncan prayed. *Please . . .*

More Goblin bodies piled on top of the stack that covered the human. Each new warrior added to the heap struggled to find a gap, a place to stick his or her dagger in and hopefully wound the human. They all did their utmost.

As he looked on helplessly, Duncan reflected that he had witnessed a change in his people over the course of their Orientation. There was a much greater community spirit, a willingness to sacrifice for the sake of the group, and an accompanying courage. It had not been transmitted all the way from the bottom of their ranks to the Goblin King himself, perhaps, but it was nevertheless quite real.

We have evolved as a species, he thought. Not in the System's sense, in the way that he had evolved successively from a Lesser Goblin to a Goblin and finally a Greater Goblin. No, in a sort of moral sense? It was not an idea he understood well yet. Something ineffable.

Maybe the difference is that we no longer feel like just a bunch of losers, he thought. *In Orientation, we became winners for the first time. It was hard. I would never say it was easy. But there is something about coming out on top. Something that changes your spirit for the better. After you get used to being kicked around all your life, you stop expecting anything good, if you ever did. I know that was how the generations before us were. I was lucky to be born when I was.*

As he had these thoughts, Duncan's eyes widened. He had been staring at the pile of Goblins crawling all over where the human was. They had all been frantically stabbing into the space where their target stood, attacking any perceived gap they could find, even where that risked hitting fellow Goblins.

But it wasn't their frantic movements that raised the Goblin King's alarm. The Goblins looked almost frozen for a moment, in fact. Some of them had stopped moving, and others were starting to push themselves away. Then Duncan spotted something odd. The top of the pile was smoking gently.

Then it smoked much more intensely.

A few Goblins managed to push themselves away from the smoking column, but most of them simply fell away and collapsed to the ground, their bodies blackened. The human's body stood, unbent, apparently as strong as ever, covered in flames from head to toe.

His magic is powerful, Duncan thought. The human strode forward suddenly and began stomping on the Goblins that had managed to get away from him. Everything he touched burned, except his own body and his armor.

Avoid him until he runs out of Mana for that flame attack, Duncan sent to all of the remaining warriors. There were still a number of them. Perhaps around three quarters of what Duncan had started with if one counted the injured as well as those who had not yet participated in the battle. Still, even if most had not participated yet, that did not mean their morale was unaffected.

After the human's display of killing prowess, they were all more than happy to do their best to keep away from him.

And fortunately, he did not waste much Stamina in chasing them; he just lumbered after the slower Goblins. Perhaps he was tiring.

As soon as the flames die down, charge in again! Duncan sent. *A row of Goblin Knights first. Then, infantry, rush in quickly while he's off balance.*

This was the whittling down process the Goblin King had envisioned, albeit at a greater cost to Goblin lives than he had hoped or imagined. But if the greater community was to succeed—even survive—they had to at least be able to defeat a single powerful human sent to kill them.

The flames gradually died down, and the Goblins resumed their assault. A half dozen mounted on Mole People prepared to charge. Daven had regained consciousness and sat on his Mole Man, ready to lead the way.

"For the King!" he shouted once more.

Thank the gods for you, Daven, Duncan thought. *If not for you, I have no idea how I could get away with commanding from an invisible position like this.*

Then the Goblin Knights rode into close quarters with the human, the infantry following close behind. Duncan turned to look at the enemy, and his stomach flipped. The human was rushing to meet them, a sword in one hand and a long dagger in the other. He wore a grim smile.

The next minute was a tornado of carnage the likes of which the Goblin King had never seen before. The human leaped and twirled between targets—*so much for him being tired*, Duncan had time to think—and wherever he landed, death followed. His two blades always found targets, while the Goblins always seemed to be following a step behind the human's grim dance. Putting him into another melee situation seemed to have been the worst thing Duncan could have done. Perhaps if the human had been forced to fight the Goblins two or three at a time, he would gradually have been worn down.

Perhaps. But that hypothetical was as useless as the reality before Duncan was painful.

The reality of Goblins screaming as a single man shredded them with his blades, the cavalry feebly trying to pivot and chase after him, the eyes of other Goblins beginning to fill with fear.

The reality was incredibly ugly.

The sight of his troops dying by the dozen almost paralyzed the Goblin King. Then the man turned toward Daven, and he stuck his dagger through the center of Daven's chest.

No . . .

Daven's eyes widened, and his mouth pursed in a small O shape. His face contorted with pain and fear. His right hand released his pike, and his left reached up to clutch at the wound in his chest. Before it made the full journey to the gushing wound, Daven tumbled from his mount's back and fell out of sight.

Tears welled up in Duncan's eyes.

It was futile, he thought. *Futile. I killed my brother. I sent him to his death. All for nothing!*

He stared at the enemy warrior, unable to look away. The human was covered in blood and gore, with no visible wounds or damage to his armor that Duncan could see. He did not seem to have spilled a single drop of his own blood thus far. *I cannot even tell if he is getting tired.* He just looked angrier.

Oh gods . . . Please let it stop. Loki, what do I do? How can we stand up to him?

As he had this thought, the Goblin soldiers began to break and run at the human's approach. All it took was a couple of warriors too afraid to stand up to him to ignite a panic. Most of the rest of the troops began running for the tunnels where the civilians hid. Only the most ferocious warriors stayed out in the open where the human was.

We Goblins always end this way, Duncan thought bitterly. *Brutish, short-sighted, and cowardly. Our true nature is finally coming out.*

As the human advanced toward the next nearest group of remaining soldiers, Duncan began altering the illusion he presented to hide the escape routes the fleeing Goblins were taking—and to make himself visible. Or a version of himself, anyway.

The image he wanted the human to see was roughly two feet taller than the real Goblin King, significantly more muscular than him, and carrying a large, mean-looking metal club studded all over with spikes.

The real Goblin King was just under five feet tall, well muscled compared to a human of his height, and carried a long dirk.

This would be his last gambit.

Everyone else should get away from the human. I will handle him as best I can. If I should fail, then beg for your lives. In the event that he is not inclined to spare you—as Duncan felt certain the human would not be—*then try to flee with the children or die defending them.*

They seemed insufficient as last words, but the Goblin King knew that he was probably about to join his brother in the next life.

Duncan cleared his throat and then distorted his voice into the most intimidating, gravelly noise that he could make.

"Human! Now you face me, the Goblin King! Prepare yourself."

Duncan puppeteered the illusory Goblin King in a charge straight at the warrior, while his real body took a slightly more oblique route. It was just possible that if he engaged the human in a duel with his fake body, there would be a moment when he could attack with his real weapon. The dirk was long, sharp, and narrow—perfect to fit into a gap in the human's armor or slit his throat.

I just need to make an opportunity.

Duncan was so focused on placing his body at a good angle to the enemy and maneuvering the fake Goblin King around that he missed a key detail.

The human warrior had closed his eyes. Duncan only noticed when he was a few feet away from the human, ordering the illusory Goblin King to swing his club at the man's head.

What—who would close his eyes in the middle of a fight?

Then the human lunged at him—at Duncan, the real one, not the false body. Suddenly, his hands were tightening around Duncan's throat, and all hope seemed lost.

"Surrender, Goblin King," the man's voice pronounced. "Swear that you and all who follow you will obey me and my heirs until your dying day. Otherwise, I must continue my terrible task."

CHAPTER TWENTY-SEVEN

Hallucination

James stared into the space where he imagined the Goblin King's eyes were.

He still couldn't see the figure, but since he held the Goblin King's throat in his hand, he had a pretty good idea of where to look for eye contact.

It was fortunate that his senses were superhuman. Even if the Goblin King could create a convincing false version of himself, James could still feel the vibrations of the real figure's footsteps on the ground, could still sense the real Goblin King's aura, and he could smell the sweat that ran down the Goblin King's body in warm, sticky rivulets.

With his eyes shut, James could essentially ignore the illusion. Then he had the real opponent's location pegged in an instant.

"I swear it," the Goblin King said, his voice almost a croak as he spoke through his compressed throat. "You have our unconditional surrender. Please spare my people. I understand that my life is probably forfeit. I only ask that you allow me to give my brother's body an honorable burial. The Goblin Race will serve you well, I promise you."

He saw his brother die. That's—wow. Shit. Did I overdo it? If someone had done that to James, he doubted he could get past it. He only had his sister, no brothers, but he couldn't imagine the sheer rage that would possess him if something happened to Alice. An abstract tornado of fury. But the idea didn't feel real. Thankfully, it was only imagination. At least for now. He still didn't know what had happened to her . . .

"Very good," James said, trying to keep his tone neutral for now. "Dispel your illusions, and I will dispel mine."

The Goblin King hesitated, then spoke. "Yes, as you say. I did pledge my unconditional surrender."

James heard him swallow. Then the air shimmered, and the Goblin King's face came into view. His eyes were just where James had imagined, but they weren't locked into the staring contest that James had envisioned when he tried to anticipate where the Goblin's body would be. Instead, the Goblin King's gaze was fixed on the ground, clearly concerned with trying not to agitate the deadly human who had him by the throat. The figure would have been small for a human, but he probably would have looked down on most of the Goblins who James had fought.

More than just the Goblin King came into view. Dozens of small tunnels appeared where James had only seen solid stone walls before.

Excellent illusions, he thought. He looked closer and saw the civilian Goblins again—and behind them, frightened children trying to avoid James's line of sight. James frowned. *I have to reassure them.*

He dissolved his own veil of illusion. The Goblin King's face lit up instantly.

"How is it possible?" he murmured. His eyes returned to James's face, and his look transformed into one of awe. "You spared them? Was it all a hallucination? Some sort of masterful illusion?"

James nodded. "I think I avoided killing any of them," he said. "I tried, at least."

He put the Goblin King down, and the little person stared up into James's face with unmistakable gratitude.

"I will serve you forever," the Goblin said. "You will never have cause to doubt my loyalty. All my descendants and I are yours. Thank you for sparing us!"

No deception detected, James noted. *Cross "Acquire Goblin army" off my bucket list, then.*

[Sufficient experience accrued. Blame Avoidance leveled up!]
[Sufficient experience accrued. Blame Avoidance leveled up!]
[Sufficient experience accrued. Blame Avoidance leveled up!]
[Sufficient experience accrued. Blame Avoidance leveled up!]

I don't even know how that happened. Then James saw the other Goblins watching the interaction between him and the King, and he understood. *They were all very upset at me for killing their kinfolk, and I completely dodged that bullet once they realized I just knocked them out. I really hope I didn't actually kill any of them.* He thought of the Goblin Knights who had died up in the tunnels with slight regret.

[Goblin King Duncan, Lv. 24, has surrendered. You gained 1200 exp!]
[You have successfully obtained the surrender of a Ruler. Usurper Title has been activated.]

Huh?

[Title Obtained: Ruler of the Low Places!]

[Existing Ruler Title detected!]

[Merging abilities of Ruler of the Low Places into Ruler of the Dark Waters Title.]

[Required conditions met. Skill unlocked: Command Structure!]

Well, I have no argument with that . . .

[Sufficient Experience accrued. Fisher King leveled up!]

[Sufficient Experience accrued. Fisher King leveled up!]

[Sufficient Experience accrued. Fisher King leveled up!]

[Sufficient Experience accrued. Fisher King leveled up!]

Fisher King? Not Predator in Human Skin, after all this fighting? Well, since I didn't kill any of them—

So, it worked out well, Master? Roscuro's voice cut into his thoughts.

Extremely well, actually, James replied slightly reluctantly.

As expected. Fear is the way to master these creatures. Roscuro's voice rang with satisfaction.

I suppose so. James was not quite happy with the looks of fear on the little Goblin children's faces, but the Goblin King had not negotiated with him while possessing the Goblin Captain's body and had hidden from him with illusions when James arrived in the Goblins' cavern. So, he had handled this as nonviolently as he could, aside from just leaving the Goblins and Mole People alone; that seemed like a bad plan in itself.

I did the best I could, and I'm being appropriately rewarded. A thousand new comrades in my struggle to rebuild the world. If they would follow his rules, James had no issue accepting Goblins, Mole People, or any other monsters. They just had to understand that humans were friends to be protected rather than prey or enemies to be fought—unless instructed otherwise.

Goblins really aren't so different from humans, he thought. *Mole People either, probably. There is a tendency to behave badly when left alone; the purpose of government was to stop that. In the absence of the previous government, the only thing I can do is create an image so fearsome that they don't dare defy the rules I lay out.*

The civilian Goblins began to slowly emerge from their hiding places and gather around to get a better look at their new Ruler. The Mole People did the same.

Even some of the unconscious Goblins were beginning to wake up. *Good*, James thought. *I won't have to repeat myself. So many of the Goblins who are awake are paying attention to me. I imagine even the ones who are unconscious will hear what I've said repeated by others later.*

"Your Majesty, by what name are we to call our new Ruler?" Another taller-than-average Goblin was speaking. Most of her physical attributes looked similar to the male Goblins, but by her voice and her face James could tell that she was female.

Out of the corner of his eye, James caught movement. He turned and saw that Goblin King Duncan was moving toward the female Goblin while looking nervously back and forth between her and James.

Is he afraid that I'll have some kind of a bad reaction to a regular Goblin speaking to me or something? Or maybe that Goblin female is his partner and he's just being protective because there are any number of ways this interaction could turn sour.

James smiled reassuringly and introduced himself.

"I am called the Fisher King. My name is . . ."

"James! James is coming back up!" Alan's voice rang through the air with obvious excitement.

Mitzi smiled in turn. "I'm glad he survived. Not that we thought it would go any other way, right? I recall you used the word 'bloodbath' to describe what would happen."

"Well, I didn't say whose blood," Alan replied, "but I'm glad it was our guy who came out on top."

"No doubts, then?" Mitzi asked.

"No doubts," Alan said.

James floated into the light as everyone else outside gathered around the chasm in the ground. His Skin Balloon floated alongside two others, which carried two different figures: a short but muscular humanoid creature with yellow-green skin, who wore a slightly dinged up tin circlet around his head, and a tall, well-muscled creature with long claws and a thick coat of black fur. The latter creature did not have eyes that Alan could see. Both gave him the creeps.

So, he didn't wipe them all out, he thought. It was hard to be certain whether that was a good or a bad thing.

"Holy crap!" Dean's voice floated over from close to the firm building, where Dean had withdrawn to wait out the extermination effort. He sounded intensely distressed. "What the fuck, man?! You brought the monsters up here?"

"It's your lucky day, Dean!" James announced loudly. "I'm taking them off your hands."

"You what?" Dean was almost yelling. "These are dangerous monsters. You should have let me gas them! They'll kill you in your sleep."

James just shook his head, then turned his focus to everyone else who was gathering at what they felt was a safe distance from the monsters next to James. There were more monsters, Alan noted, slowly climbing up the chasm walls: more of those Mole People and, on their backs, more of the strange yellow-green figures that had apparently also been living under the firm building.

Identify. Alan was at least going to understand what they were dealing with in these yellow-green people.

[Goblin Overlord Duncan, Lv. 24]

He aimed a second Identify at the Mole Person.

[Mole Lord Magnar, Lv. 20]

These are strong monsters, James, he thought. *I hope you know what you're doing.*

"Meet my new friends," James said, turning to the gathered people, most of whom were on the opposite side of the fissure relative to Dean. He continued to project his voice so he could be heard by all. "They are the leaders of two species of creatures: the Goblins and the Mole People, respectively. Both of them wish to live in peace with humans. They and their people have agreed to follow the same laws as we do. They will be accompanying me back to the Fisher Kingdom. Both of them will serve as councilors to me as representatives of their species, alongside select humans. We will be leaving here, so there is nothing for any of you to fear from the Mole People or the Goblins."

Alan heard some barely distinct murmurs from his sides. People saying things like, "I didn't even know we had anything to fear from *Goblins* in the first place," and, "Easy for him to say. They're following him *for now.*"

There was a slight but real atmosphere of apprehension. The others gathered here were still not comfortable about sharing their world with monsters. Or perhaps they weren't certain of how they felt.

Alan had seen and heard some strange things in the last several weeks: monsters eating people, humans sacrificing other humans to an occult god, but also, a whole pack of monstrous wolves following and obeying James. The man had also left the wolves behind in his Fisher Kingdom as protection for his family. He had an absolute faith in the strength of his control over these creatures that Alan found compelling in its own right.

James continued addressing the crowd. "I am also open to bringing others."

Someone in the crowd barked out a short laugh, but James seemed to ignore it.

"The monsters in the neighboring areas will find this place eventually," he said. "The goblin standing next to me was previously a Ruler. That's a kind of high-level life-form. Now that he has surrendered to me, his aura will dissipate from this area. That means another creature or person with the power of a Ruler can come in and take its place. I've removed the potential for you to be attacked by the Goblins or the Mole People, but there will be other threats from less agreeable species of sentient life. Or other humans who aren't as friendly as I am. This place won't ever really be settled or safe until it's part of a Ruler's territory."

"Why can't you make it your territory?" a woman's voice asked.

"I could temporarily do that, but my aura signature would fade over time. There's really no point in doing it now. The former Ruler of the Goblins' aura is still here. And I won't come back to this place just to periodically sprinkle my aura. It's too far away from where I live. It would become a full-time job, and I have to save my power to use in my own actual territory."

There were murmurs of concern from within the crowd.

"Which is why I am happy to take people to the Fisher Kingdom if they want to go now. With some limitations, I will accept almost anyone."

"Not us, then." Viktor's voice was recognizable even from the opposite end of the chasm relative to Alan. He wasn't even visible from this angle, hidden behind other people. Alan found himself glad of the distance between them. The convict spoke in a resentful tone.

"For you and your colleague," James said, looking toward where Viktor must be, "I would want to have a separate conversation and discuss things privately. I'm not discounting any possibility right now." *Settle down.* That was what Alan read in James's voice. A note of warning.

Alan suspected that James would accept just about anyone into the Fisher Kingdom who was willing to take his loyalty oath—but he doubted that would be the only condition for these two men. *He probably has some sort of monster he could attach to them that would kill them if they disobeyed him or something.* Arguably, a perfect way to deal with criminals. The prison system was never an ideal method.

But Viktor was shaking his head, anyway. "I don't need to go with you. I have people here. We'll defend ourselves, thank you."

"A very respectable position," James replied, shrugging. The monsters were coming up out of the pit now, so he raised his voice again to be heard over the sounds of their scrabbling up the stone and dirt. "Does anyone else want to come with me?"

Even as people backed away from where the creatures were emerging from, hands went up. Around half of them, by Alan's count.

He looked at Dean. The man was clearly devastated. His community was already being ripped apart. Only the worst elements would remain—though Alan saw Olivar, the other convict, was raising his hand to go with James.

Well, at least he didn't seem as bad as the other fellow. Hopefully, James actually has a plan for this "separate conversation" he mentioned.

Alan approached Dean. This might be the last time the two men saw each other, but Alan didn't want that. He was afraid of what would happen to Dean if they left him behind. Even though James had conspicuously turned his back to Dean during his pitch, Alan felt certain he would not object to bringing Dean into the Fisher Kingdom.

"Dean, are you going to go with us?" Alan asked.

"What, so you guys are leaving with him too?" Dean sounded affronted.

"He's right," Alan said. "About everything he said. Nothing was untrue. We've been on this adventure with him. All throughout the trip here, we avoided areas that were coming under the control of monsters of every stripe. This isn't made up. I think if you stay here—well, I think you might die. Now is no time to be proud."

"No, it's apparently the time to bend the knee to tyranny," Dean replied. He raised a hand to stop Alan from disputing. "I know, I know. He's not a tyrant, right? He just gave himself the authority of a tyrant, the regal title, and is going around telling everyone what to do as part of an elaborate role-playing game you're all in on."

Alan sighed. Dean wasn't completely wrong. "I don't think he's going down that road," he said softly, "but if he does, it's the job of the people around him to head him off and lead him in a different direction. Or, if necessary, stop him. What makes a man a tyrant? Is it just that he wants other people to call him king? I've come away from your little community with the distinct impression that everyone here understands that you're the leader here yourself. How are you so different?"

Dean sputtered. "D-democracy! People have chosen to work with me. I don't have any titles either. No one has to kneel and bow—"

"No one has bowed before James in my presence either," Alan said. "Maybe that's because, just like you, he knows how far to push this and doesn't press any further. People have dignity, and he doesn't trample on that. He doesn't actually think he has magic blood. Are you really going to stay here, with your numbers reduced and monsters surrounding you, out of pride?"

"Don't call it pride," Dean said. "It's independence. We'll manage. You watch. He'll become a tyrant even if you don't think he is one already. And we'll be here. Free."

How can you think that about him? You knew him before all this. Alan knew he had his own doubts about James as a monarch, but Dean's feelings seemed to go beyond rational doubt. Suddenly, it became clear that no argument could persuade him.

"I hope you're right," Alan said. He extended his hand, and after a long pause, Dean shook it.

"I am," Dean said. His voice was almost friendly again. "After you get tired of King James, maybe you'll come and join us."

I hope you and your family survive this somehow, Alan thought as he turned and walked back toward Mitzi and the others. *Pride is a hell of a thing to die for.*

CHAPTER TWENTY-EIGHT

Meanwhile, Back at the Ranch

"James will be back home early tomorrow, then?" Mina confirmed.

"Correct," the Artificial Spider said.

"He had better be," she muttered. "James is not going to leave me stuck with all this Fisher Kingdom business. He said he wanted to be a conqueror. That means he runs things, not his poor wife. I already have the baby . . ."

A knock came at the door.

"The next group is here." Yulia's soft voice carried through the wall. She lowered it. "Should I tell them that you need some time to rest—I mean, I can make up an excuse . . ."

"No, don't do that," Mina said firmly. "I have to be able to conduct the business of the Fisher Kingdom in James's absence. These people have to develop confidence in me. That won't happen if I'm ineffective the first time he's gone for a couple of days."

A pause. "So, he won't be back today, then?" Yulia asked.

Mina smiled. "You miss him too?"

"Things are a lot easier when we're all together," Yulia replied. "Abhi's asking about him too. He likes being told that James will be back soon every hour or so. Preferably by a human rather than a spider monster."

That made Mina frown. The little boy was in a delicate place, with who-knew-what fate having befallen his family. Probably something horrible. Abhi seemed to have latched onto James, but he wasn't here.

"Well, send in the next group," Mina said. "One challenge at a time. We'll spend some time with Abhi later."

Thank goodness for Yulia, she thought. Not only had she handled dealing with the Child Rescue Commission on Mina's behalf, but Yulia was also screening all the other people who wanted to see Mina and sorting them in order of priority.

In her gentle way, she could ask people to wait without them becoming offended or acting self-important—even when the individuals seemed like the self-important type. Mina could hear some of the interactions through the wall. *This could have been so much worse without her.*

The next party to enter their living room—no, now it was an audience chamber—was the Salvage Commission. Mina dealt with them as quickly as she could. The chair of the commission, Taylor Bunting, explained that the whole crew had spent the day going through ruins, and they had experienced lots of success. Mina tried to mirror her enthusiasm and not show how weary she was of dealing with people today—while also moving the conversation toward what the Salvage Commission needed as quickly as she could.

They wanted to know what to do with all the usable items and equipment they were finding in the old apartment buildings. Mina gently encouraged them to take items that would be immediately useful and put them to use. As for the other supplies—the furniture, carpeting, clothing, and anything else that had somehow been spared from water damage in the time they had been away—Mina assigned them a space in the community warehouse that the Construction Commission was working on. If they had extra time in the day that wasn't spent collecting additional salvage, they could begin an inventory. She resolved that she herself would pay the storage area a visit later and see if the Robard household needed anything.

Departments of government were proliferating, it seemed. Everyone to whom James had given an assignment was taking it as seriously as if it were the only task on which the whole new country's survival depended.

Almost all of them had come for some clarification on their instructions, and Mina couldn't just tell them that there was no greater specificity to be had—that James was operating on intuition and had no larger plan.

The second that idea gained any currency, people would start to doubt this place. As Mina had needed to remind herself several times today alone, she was a part of founding and running a real nation. If it collapsed for any reason, people would probably die.

If I had thought about that, I might not have let you go even for a couple of days, Mina thought. *Not so soon after you started this place, at least.*

Yulia knocked at the door again.

"Who goes there?" Mina called, smiling.

"It's a man named Jeremiah Rotter," Yulia replied, her voice guarded.

"Hm." Mina resisted the urge to tell her to send him away. *I don't have the energy for this right now . . .*

She and James had already discussed him after they had spoken about the Wendigo threat and before James had gone to say goodbye to the children.

"Why do you think that man decided to volunteer an oath of loyalty to you personally?" Mina had asked. "There's no apparent benefit in it for him, and it changed the nature of the citizenship pledge completely."

She did not particularly mind the citizenship pledge becoming an oath of loyalty, but she was skeptical of Rotter's motives. What did he expect to gain from this? Surely he would expect some form of favor from James later on. She did not like the idea of giving a stranger a blank check that he might try to cash in at some future date.

"He saw a slight oddity in the way the oath was formulated, and he made his own judgment as to what he wanted to say." James had shrugged. He wore a mischievous expression. He was clearly still in an elevated mood. "Why would it trouble me if someone decided to advocate for our interests, entirely on his own? With luck, I may acquire more such advocates."

This, Mina suspected, was the most dangerous part of her husband's nature. His willingness to embrace convenient solutions to problems, even when they might cause problems down the line. Or when they were wrong.

Since they had been together, she had seen this quality of his recede further and further beneath the surface of his personality. He had worked hard to become a better version of himself. But a tiger could not fully change its stripes.

Her response came more forcefully than she'd intended.

"Be careful about that! Before the System, people like that ran things in many countries. People who lived on trading favors and accumulating power. This man is undoubtedly cut from the same cloth. He will think you owe him something."

James scowled. "Then he'll be wrong. I saved the man's life. I think he's still repaying that."

"You've saved a lot of people's lives, skapi. But this man leaves a bad taste in the mouth."

"That's all the better. He leaves a bad impression on more than just you, I'm sure. But his character is so obviously different from mine that it can't stick to me. People like that have their uses. And I'll keep him carefully insulated from any real power."

That was the unsatisfactory ending of the conversation.

Now Jeremiah Rotter slid into the chair opposite Mina, and she tried to forget her previous judgment of him.

She looked into his narrow eyes. *No, I can't forget who*—what—*he is.* She saw a snake sitting across from her, trying to look like it was smiling.

"You wanted to meet with me to get further direction on what my husband asked you to do?" she asked. For the life of her, she could not now remember what responsibility James had entrusted to this man.

"No, it's more that I wanted to give you a progress report, Mrs. Robard. Uh, Your Majesty."

You can't win me over with cheap words, she thought.

"The King asked me to take a census," Rotter added.

That was it! I remember now. I thought it was a meaningless little task to keep Rotter busy. He really thinks we need a progress report?

"I see," she said in her most carefully neutral tone. "How is that going?"

"Naturally, it's an expansive task, with more people coming every day. There were already plenty yesterday, but it feels like today we opened the floodgates."

Mina nodded. She had been dealing with those issues all day: planning additional housing, meeting and greeting new people, and figuring out food for an extra hundred occupants. The fun part was that some of these people were very nice. The Rodriguezes were going to be fast friends of hers, she could tell. They brought a warm family atmosphere with them.

Camila Rodriguez had said some very flattering things about James. The older woman had somehow persuaded Mina to invite her over for dinner without ever asking, despite the fact that it had already been a long day by that point; she was just too *nice*. A part of Mina wanted to crawl into a hole and disappear until James came back. The other part was ready to enjoy Camila's tamales as soon as the day was over. It would save Mina from cooking for the family tonight. If things turned out well, maybe this would become a regular tradition.

But she had to get through this conversation and whoever else was left before she could relax at all.

"Do you need me to ask people to help you or something?" she asked. She was prepared to refuse if he was going to request support. This was the least urgent task she could imagine anyone doing right now.

"Oh no, I'm making great progress. Unless there's a daily wave of immigration that's bigger than today going forward, I should have some pretty good data for you and your husband very soon. The task was almost too easy, in fact. I thought that, in order to add value, I should do more than just find out who's here. So, in addition to taking down people's names, I also got the new arrivals to agree to take the loyalty oath a couple of days from now, in the morning. A minor scheduling matter, but I wanted to save you and your husband the trouble."

Mina wanted to find some fault with what Rotter was saying—that he had overstepped his bounds or something. But considering how annoying she had found it to interact with so many people today, it genuinely felt as if he was doing them a favor.

"They're happy to sign up, just like that?" she said a little suspiciously.

"Well, most of these people are here because they interacted with the Fisher King in the past. They know how he operates, so they're happy to sign on."

He smiled with what seemed genuine pleasure. "Your husband really inspires loyalty."

"Indeed. You were in the same Orientation, so you must know some of these people as well." She continued trying to deduce Rotter's motivations.

"I do," he acknowledged. "It was an easy enough matter to try to mention the loyalty oath when I was around other people who had already taken it. That makes people much more willing to consider it. And the residents here don't want to be the only ones who signed on. They're also happy to proselytize." He stopped and looked her steadily in the eyes for a few seconds. It seemed abrupt to Mina.

"Were you going to report further on your progress?" she asked finally.

"I don't have much more to say," he said. "Only—you don't seem to like me much, Your Majesty. Maybe I'm mistaken, but I feel a wave of distrust coming off of you. If you'd like, I can try to keep my distance in future."

Mina thought for a few seconds before she responded carefully.

"I think you are an ambitious man who has attached himself to my husband. I have no way of knowing your motives or loyalties other than that you are trying to make yourself useful. But I have to be careful. I have to protect his interests because there aren't many people whose goals are exactly aligned with his."

Rotter nodded. "You're a wise woman. It's true that I've attached myself to your husband. I admit it. I'm pretty shameless, honestly. But there's one point you're wrong about. I'm not particularly ambitious for myself. I can see the way this world is moving. I was ready to follow anyone strong in Orientation. Your husband could probably verify that. Back then, I just wanted to survive." He smiled. "Like I said, shameless! You can't have any values when you're dead. Now, though—now, I see your husband is building his own kingdom, his own country. I see that he wants to be a great man who changes the world. And I just want to help. I have a selfish motive. But it's not as bad as you might imagine. First and foremost, I desperately—I can't stress this enough—I desperately want to survive. I want to live a long life and die of old age in comfort. Second thing, I want to be close to greatness.

"Throughout history, whenever there's a person like this, there are other people he carries with him. People who go around supervising the construction of the imperial monuments or enforcing the draft or teaching imperial propaganda. Just doing the nitty gritty work of the empire. The important quality that I bring is that I have no ambitions at all. I know I'm not a guy anyone would follow, not even if I was an usher in a theater! Maybe I don't have the chin for it. Maybe it's my personality." That was the first and only time his smile faltered in the exchange. And the best indicator for Mina that Rotter was admitting something real. Something a little uncomfortable for him.

"Anyway, being up front leading a movement can be dangerous," he continued. "If I'm being honest, I wouldn't want power of any kind if it meant being in danger. I'm a complete coward. So, all I'm saying is, I want your husband to feel free to use me. Send me anywhere you want, ask me to do anything—just please don't put my life in danger, and I'll always strive to exceed expectations. Because I want to be one of those guys the two of you carry along with you on your way up."

Mina wished James was in the room with them right now. His ability to detect lies would have come in handy. But she thought that Rotter actually was telling the truth. Probably.

If so, he was someone they would actually be able to make good use of—until and unless he found a more promising "great man" to follow. She would watch him carefully.

They exchanged some further pleasantries, but the conversation was essentially over. Mina promised to pass on his good wishes to James, and Rotter left.

Yulia stepped into the room after he was gone.

"Last guest for the day," she said. The air about her was obviously different, Mina observed. "Then we can have dinner with the Rodriguezes!"

"Sounds great, sweet. You may have to do most of the talking at dinner, though." Mina felt like taking a nap on the spot. And baby James was beginning to stir beside her. Mina picked him up and began preparing to breastfeed, removing her bra, unbuttoning her blouse, and covering her left side and the baby with a blanket.

"Has he been asleep through these last couple of meetings?" Yulia asked.

"Asleep? This boy? Never! He's just absorbing Mama's political skills," Mina replied. "If you look carefully, you can see how closely he's observing. He's a little prince, after all. They have to learn these things early."

Baby James's eyes looked back and forth between his mother and aunt, and though Mina doubted he understood any of what was happening, there was an obvious intelligence in that gaze.

"Uh-huh. Well, there's someone from the hunters who wants to see you," Yulia said quietly. "He seems nice. Was the last guy okay?"

"I think James can make good use of him," Mina said ambivalently. She wasn't sure what to make of Rotter just now. "Please send in the next person, but tell him I'm breastfeeding. If that bothers him, he should come back tomorrow. *Then he can deal with James instead.*"

Yulia went back out, and a minute passed. Then a familiar figure stepped in.

He gave one of the most convincing endorsements of James as leader, Mina thought.

Dave Matsumoto smiled but looked slightly uncomfortable. "May I sit?" he asked.

"Oh, of course," Mina said. *I suppose since we're technically a monarchy, people expect some ceremony or something. Not something we have time for right now, even if we were so inclined.* And she suspected that people who founded monarchies were probably a lot less ceremonial than the royals whose weddings people had watched on television pre-System.

Matsumoto folded himself into the chair opposite Mina and looked her carefully in the eyes.

"How is the hunting going?" she asked after a moment.

"Ah. Well, it's going fine, I suppose," Matsumoto said. "I wanted to discuss the hunters' *other* duty."

Mina's expression tensed. "There's something dangerous out there, then?"

Matsumoto reached into his Small Bag of Deceptive Dimensions and produced a large rolled-up sheet of paper.

He unfurled it on the table between them. Mina saw that it was a map.

"Someone made a map of the Fisher Kingdom already?" she asked. That was impressive, although she knew it would be out of date soon with James expanding the territory.

Matsumoto nodded. "A member of the team. Amalia. It seems we are well balanced for both killing and scouting." He spoke without noticeable pride. Very matter of fact. "Here and here." He pointed to two X marks on two different edges of the map.

Mina looked to the corner and found the compass rose.

"I see," she said. "Threats to the south and the northeast."

Dave nodded. "We stumbled on one of them when we were hunting with your husband, actually, but given that one of my friends was injured, we didn't stop to investigate. Now we've gathered more information. It's not good news. And the other one—" He sighed. "The other one is even worse. At least if my read on the situation is correct."

"Tell me all about it."

Dinner would have to wait.

CHAPTER TWENTY-NINE

Home at Last

James led his new followers across the vast landscape that separated the old law office building from the Fisher Kingdom. He led them through the latter part of the day and after the darkness faded into night.

Unlike the trip to the firm office, which had been relaxed, almost like a hot air balloon ride, James wanted this one to be quick. He was a little apprehensive about the growth of the territories he remembered traveling near. He couldn't help worrying that something might poke its head into *his* territory and threaten his family or his people.

"I really hope that things work out for Dean," he said quietly. "I know it probably didn't look that way . . ."

"Because you led a lot of his people away," Alan finished.

"Yeah," James agreed.

"I'm certainly glad we decided to go with you," Mitzi said, half-shrugging. Her mobility was slightly limited by the Skin Balloon that gripped her around the arms and torso.

"We're all adults here," Alan agreed. "I was a little surprised you decided to let him come along." He tilted his head to indicate Olivar, who rode on the back of a Mole Person. Most of the small band of humans James had brought with him were doing the same now that it was dark outside. "But probably a good decision." The last sentence ended on a slight upward inflection, so James recognized there was some question in Alan's mind. Some uncertainty that needed clearing up.

"I questioned him about what he was in prison for," James said. "I have ways of knowing when people are lying, and he was honest. It was domestic violence, which isn't great. But it was what I expected. I recognized the guy from when I was a prosecutor. His wife finally left him and testified against him in court, so that's how the office got a conviction. Anyway, he promised he's learned to keep his temper in check. He was telling the truth, to the best of his knowledge. And I decided that I can't just exclude anyone who admits they've been a criminal in the past. Maybe if he was a serial killer or something, but not for any crime less than murder. I have to be pragmatic."

Alan nodded slowly. "I suppose that's for the best." He did not sound entirely comfortable with the decision.

Mitzi was looking down at the man with pursed lips, as if wishing she could look inside Olivar's brain and read his future plans.

James moved the conversation onto other matters.

"You two spent more time with our new guests than I did. Learn anything interesting about them?" he asked.

There was a general exchange about the new potential Fisher Kingdom citizens, followed by some back and forth about the possible survival of James, Alan, and Mitzi's family members. Then another subject change when it became obvious to James that Alan and Mitzi still hadn't fully resolved how they felt about that.

Finally, they settled on talking about future plans for the country they were traveling home to. Alan was interested in discussing a legal system for the new nation, while Mitzi was more absorbed in figuring out how they would build a sense of community. James speculated on how much Mina would have organized the Kingdom while he was gone. Alan guessed that she would probably have focused mainly on physical infrastructure as an engineer, while Mitzi thought Mina would have tried to work mainly in areas where James had not done much before he left.

The discussion carried on for over an hour before it gradually lapsed into a general silence, punctuated only by occasional remarks. They went from pragmatic to idealistic, from excitement at the idea of building a new nation to fear because the world they were living in had never been more dangerous. The Fisher Kingdom seemed like a subject the three of them would never fully exhaust, and James was glad to observe both Alan and Mitzi seemed invested.

The journey back from the law office was quicker than the journey there and largely uneventful. Even though it should have been more difficult to navigate through the dark, the Mole People did not need vision to navigate, and the Goblins had those strange goggles that magnified the usefulness of ambient light. James enjoyed an intuitive sense of which way his own territory was, and he also employed his ability to sense foreign, potentially hostile, auras to guide his new allies. None of the nonhumans complained about needing to stop, and the small number of humans benefited from Mole People willingly carrying them on their backs.

So, the journey continued well into the night until the final moment when the primitive structures of the Fisher Kingdom came into view. All of the travelers seemed to spring to life at that point. Even the people who were half-asleep sitting on Mole People's backs rose to their feet and almost sprinted the rest of the way.

"Try to move quietly!" James stage whispered to the eager people below him. "It's pretty late."

If he was to go by how late it felt, the time was a little after midnight. But it was worthwhile to get back a little earlier than he'd told Mina to expect.

Much better early than late.

Then a blue screen appeared in front of James's face. By the staggering and tripping of several people below him, James guessed they saw the screen in their fields of vision too.

[Congratulations once more to all of Earth's inhabitants, old and new! Congratulations on surviving the first great threat to this world's life-forms.]

Shit. What do they have in mind for us now?

[We firmly believe that all of you who survived are deserving of your success. Do not take this as a matter of luck but as the well-deserved verdict of fate. All who survived the System's initiation have been baptized by fire.]

Yes, yes, get to it . . .

[This announcement is to give everyone hearing it time to prepare for the next great System-sponsored events.]

Oh. I think I know what the System is telling us about, actually. They gave me advance warning.

[In five months and twenty-three days, as reckoned by your method of measuring time, those with a Ruler Title will be permitted to attend the upcoming World Leaders' Summit. Though attendance is optional, this will be an opportunity to meet with fellow Rulers, make agreements, forge alliances, engage in cultural exchange, and assess the state of the international community. There will also be complimentary room and board.]

James wanted to figure out what the System's angle was in having an event like this. It seemed to be a genuinely helpful idea with the potential to assist humanity in restoring a semblance of normalcy. But in his experience with the System so far, it always seemed to have its own plans; normalcy wasn't a part of them.

[The summit will be held in a neutral location in which the use of aggressive magic, mental manipulation abilities, and physical violence are neither permitted nor possible. Each Ruler will be permitted to bring along up to five guests, who must be in physical contact with the sponsoring Ruler at the moment of transportation.]

So, I'll take Mina, maybe Alan and Mitzi, and who else? The former Goblin King, so my new followers don't feel left out? Someone from the Rodriguez family? Mina had informed him that they had arrived while he was gone.

[Following the conclusion of the World Leaders' Summit, the Rulers and their guests will proceed to the Victors' Tournament, a fighting competition for those the System deems to be among the strongest two hundred life-forms on Earth. Those Rulers and guests who are not participating will be treated as honored spectators of the battles.]

That's a nice way to sweeten the sting of not being included among the world's strongest warriors. He thought there was a good chance that any Rulers who were not in the Victors' Tournament would be taken less seriously than the others. *Then again, there might be some Rulers who are Healers.*

[Those who remain behind in each Ruler's territory will be provided viewing devices so that they may also observe. Those who place well in the Victors' Tournament will win spectacular prizes!]

Of course they will. Otherwise, why would they fight?

[Take the remaining time to make your careful preparations for both events. Those who are not currently Rulers or ranked within the world's strongest life-forms still have five months and twenty days before the System locks the participant lists.]

Nothing singling me out this time, James noted. *I can't tell if that's a good or a bad thing. Did they stop expecting great things from me? Or maybe they feel that I've already lived up to their expectations. Either of those could work. Is it possible there's someone else out there who the System expects more from now?*

James imagined the System sending a personalized message to some other person. Perhaps someone on the other side of the world. Alternatively, someone just a few counties away. Maybe even a monster.

You're destined for great things, Soul Eater Roscuro! he thought to himself. *And hell, maybe the System really did say something like that to him.* Roscuro was a rather special kind of monster. A former human warrior transformed into a creature involuntarily by a witch's magic.

On some level, James knew that there was "always someone better," as the common saying went. But the idea that there might be someone out there who was above him in the new world's hierarchy in the System's view did not sit well with him.

Ultimately, he just shook his head and ordered his Skin Balloon to drop him off outside of his apartment. They were so close to home now that it only took a few seconds to glide the rest of the way. He was far less interested in spending more time picking apart the meaning of the System's announcement than in reuniting with the people most important to him.

As he landed, he heard a rustle of movement from inside, then the unmistakable sound of someone rushing down the stairs. Then Mina was in his arms.

"You aren't leaving me alone here again!" she whispered fiercely in his ear.

"Wasn't planning to," he replied breathlessly. The smell of his wife's hair filled his nostrils, and he sighed. He was really home again. "I don't want to leave again."

"That's good. You have lots of decisions to make, and you're not pushing any more of them off on m—" Mina stopped mid-sentence, and James pulled back from her. She was staring behind him.

He looked back and saw the horde of Goblins and Mole People. The small number of humans who had followed him here were almost completely lost in the visual spectacle of the army of creatures.

"I made some new friends," James said quietly. "They'll be your friends too."

"You had mentioned new friends," Mina said, "and I remember your message mentioned that many of them were not human. But you never gave me an idea of how many. These are hundreds. Perhaps over a thousand. How will we house them? Feed them?"

"They're not children," James replied gently. "They can mostly fend for themselves. I'm mostly concerned with just making sure we keep the peace between our kind and them. Ideally, we'll get along well and both respect each other's space."

"And how much space will they need?" Mina asked, arching an eyebrow.

From among the horde, two Goblins stepped forward and approached the ruling couple. James recognized them instantly: Duncan and his wife, the former Goblin King and Queen, now Overlord and Lady.

Mina stopped talking and watched them approach. Then she began frantically whispering in James's ear. "What are they expecting? Who are they? What do I need to know?"

"Former king and queen coming to pay their respects," James replied succinctly. "They're eager to make a good impression on you. Nothing to stress about."

Then the Goblins were within earshot, so neither of them said anything for a few seconds. James and Mina separated slightly so that Duncan and Sarah would know they could approach without interrupting a tender moment.

The two Goblins got close to James and Mina, and both fell to their knees.

"Um." Mina was instantly at a loss as to what to say.

For a moment, James wondered if he would need to lead the interaction to keep things from turning awkward. Then the Goblins started talking.

"Thank you very much for your hospitality, Your Majesty," Duncan said. "Your husband, the King, has told us much about your warmth and kindness. We will work until our fingers bleed to contribute to your kingdom."

James had to keep his facial expression under control. He had barely said anything about Mina when he was discussing the Goblins' future with Duncan earlier—at least, hardly anything compared with how much he might have said when speaking with someone he knew better.

"Consider us your humble servants," Sarah added. The former Goblin Queen produced a bouquet of flowers from within her magic satchel and presented them to Mina. "For Your Majesty."

Mina took them but looked slightly uncomfortable. "Please, please get up," she said awkwardly. "You were royalty before. I would rather not make you kneel, especially not when the other goblins are watching. And we should see about getting you all someplace to sleep." She helped Sarah to her feet, and James reached down and did the same for Duncan.

"We really don't need much," Duncan said. "We like dark, quiet places. His Majesty could tell you that we were living underground when he found us. The Mole People will undoubtedly want to burrow and create a new underground warren. Unless you have something else in mind, we would be happy to simply bed down with them."

"That seems reasonable to me," James said, nodding.

"Once we are settled, we look forward to showing off our prowess as creators of useful objects," Duncan said, directing the remark to Mina. "I understand that you are an inventor."

"Engineer," James corrected. *I think that's one of three things I said about Mina.*

Mole Lord Magnar interrupted the conversation at that point. He approached on all fours, touched his front knees to the ground, and began introducing himself in his thick, deep voice.

"I am the leader of the Mole People appointed by His Majesty," Magnar said. "We will strive to be worthy of the King's faith in us. Thank you for accepting us into the Fisher Kingdom. We pledge our undying loyalty to the King and Queen. Long may they reign!"

"Hear, hear!" Duncan echoed.

Sarah seemed to have read the situation and recognized that Mina was uncomfortable being the center of so much attention. She remained quiet and simply smiled up at the queen.

Finally, the leaders of the newly allied Races separated, and James sent them some telepathic orders about where they could burrow and where they could safely sleep while they rested during the construction process. There wasn't enough housing for over a thousand new residents, but the community center had enough room for the short goblins to squeeze together if they slept in shifts.

The next order of business would be announcing to everyone else that they had some new citizens. That ought to wait for the morning, though, he thought.

The System's agents might be comfortable with making proclamations while people were sleeping, but James knew it would not be received well if he started waking his citizens up in the middle of the night just to make introductions.

"They know they only have to kiss up to you, right?" Mina asked quietly once she and James were in the apartment again.

"Oh no," he said. "I'm pretty sure I told them that you're the most important person in the kingdom. Or did I say most important to me?" He shrugged. "Details, right?"

"Details." Mina tried to twist her face into a scowl, but she was still too happy to see him to manage it.

"Did anything interesting happen while I was gone?" James asked. "I know you worked hard. Hopefully, other people missed me too, though I'm guessing everyone's asleep."

Mina nodded.

"Maybe I should specify: anything I need to know about before we go to bed?" he asked.

Mina frowned. "Unfortunately, yes," she said. "We have two neighbors we might need to go to war with."

CHAPTER THIRTY

Preparations for Battle, Part 1

"When you say, 'two neighbors we might need to go to war with,' I guess the first thing I should ask is 'why?'" James said. "But honestly, what I really want to know is whether they're human or monster."

"Still not fighting humans," Mina said, smiling thinly. "Is that surprising? You mentioned there are hardly any human Rulers anyway."

"But hundreds of monster Rulers," he replied. "Which means our kind is going to work overtime to try and even out those numbers. One thing I know about people is that we rebel against constraints. I think that might be why the System scheduled this World Leaders' Summit so far away. It's plenty of time for some Rulers to lose their Titles. We humans would rather die in large numbers than be subjugated by some creature of another species. Most of the time we'd prefer death to being subjects of other humans. So, I suspect we'll be fighting against other humans before you know it."

"I was starting to worry we'd never get the opportunity," she said drily. "Sometimes I think you want it to happen."

James shook his head. "It's an eventuality, but it's going to be a massive morale crisis whenever it happens. People here will not want to fight other humans. Thanks to us they have food and shelter and don't have to fear wild monsters. That's good, but the net result is that we're barely separate from the civilization they're all used to. It's going to be very psychologically hard on them."

"I imagine that's true. I doubt you're the only one here who's killed other people, though, skapi." She placed a gentle hand on his shoulder. "You'll get volunteers if you need them. People appreciate you. They know you wouldn't put them in danger for no reason."

James allowed a smile to slowly steal over his face. "Thank you, my love. That's enough hypotheticals for one night. Let's talk about the wars we're actually in for right now. We can get some sleep after that."

"Okay." She took a map from her bag and unrolled it on their living room tabletop. There were two X marks at two different edges of the map.

"Oh, someone made a map of our territory," he said, nodding appreciatively.

"Yes," Mina replied. "Someone named Amalia. I think from your Orientation?"

James nodded and half-shrugged.

Mina continued, pointing at the X to the south. "Here, the hunters found a territory that seems to belong to a bunch of alligators. It abuts our border, and it looks like the alligators are expanding their territory everywhere that your power doesn't reach. So"—she traced a line from the X up and down the side of the map—"the swamp that they control is expanding everywhere along this line, but not crossing the line."

"That sounds dangerous, but it sounds like they haven't entered our land. We're just worried about them expanding right next to us."

"That's right. We don't know if it's just a matter of time before they try to come in or if they will continue to respect the border. The concern is that since the monsters are extra-large alligators, a single creature entering could become dangerous very quickly."

James nodded. "Alligators sound pretty nasty to deal with. Do we have any idea of their numbers?"

"The hunters said there only seemed to be a handful when they looked, but we know that alligators are pretty good at hiding, especially when they're waiting for prey."

"That's true. But if there were too many of them, and they were big ones, there would be a limit to how well they could hide. They also take a couple of months to reproduce, assuming these things are like pre-System alligators, so this might not be something we need to deal with right away. There's time to figure out if we can negotiate—or if they're willing to just live in peace."

Mina stared at him for a long moment, before she finally asked, "Why do you know that?"

Why do I know what?

"Oh. The alligator reproduction timeline?"

"Yes!"

"We live in Florida."

She shook her head, seemingly smiling despite herself. "Yes," she said finally. "Yes, we do. And we're about to try to establish a peaceful coexistence with the alligator people. Of course. All perfectly normal."

"So, the other X?" he asked.

"That's more immediately concerning. Dave Matsumoto thinks that something is replicating a setting from his Orientation: a scary place where he saw things he wasn't comfortable describing."

"What kind of ecosystem is it?" James asked.

"Just a forest. The ecosystem isn't the problem, though. The issue is that people who get near that part of the border report *seeing things*, just like Matsumoto in his Orientation. Two of the hunters got close to the forest, thinking they should explore that area, and they saw apparitions of some sort. I spoke with a couple of guys who were with the Orlando Public Works Department before the System, and they made a barrier with wooden stakes and caution tape so that people wouldn't get near the forest until you were back. One of them saw *something* in the forest too. He kept saying a name, but it wasn't anyone we know, and he didn't want to talk about it. No one has been able to stand being near the border with that place for the length of time it would take to erect a more permanent barrier. The public works people who didn't see anything said that the place gave them an 'evil feeling' after just a few minutes."

Sounds like something I want to take a look at, James thought instinctively. But he tempered the impulse.

"I think we'll probably have no choice but to do something about that," he said. "Tell me, has anyone gone in there?"

Mina bit her lip. "Not that I know of," she said after a long pause. "But our people only started paying attention to that area once it was obvious there was something wrong there. We have a lot of people showing up here all the time"—she smiled bittersweetly—"and your monsters rescued around a hundred children while you were gone. I don't know if you knew that."

James smiled. "I sort of dimly realized what was happening, and sometimes I check. But they aren't constantly reporting in. Those ones are pretty independent. I didn't have a count on how many kids, but that's really good to hear."

"Your good deed for the century," Mina replied. "Your good deed that people will be talking about for decades. If anyone ever doubts your goodness, this is the thing that your defenders should bring up."

"You're sweet." James thought that this would not be anywhere near an adequate defense if he gave people cause to doubt him. "How did this come up again?"

"You were asking about people slipping through the border with the creepy forest, and I was just thinking that it would be easy for one of our new arrivals to wander over there without us noticing."

"Good point," he said. "Maybe I should do something right now. Not go charging in, but just put up a real fortification there."

Mina nodded. "I think so. Before you do, there was one more thing." She visibly hesitated.

"What is it?"

"Only one of the witnesses heard it. Amalia Rosario. The same person who made our map. When she stood near the border, she thought she could make out the distant sound of screaming. Don't go in after that sound if you hear it, skapi. If you do, I'll chase after you. And if something happens to both of us . . ."

James finally nodded his assent to her grim demand. He knew what would happen if both he and Mina disappeared. Their children would be orphaned, and their country would dissolve. The children would probably die, and hundreds—no, now thousands—of citizens would be left adrift and defenseless. *They would probably get eaten by the alligators or possessed by demons or whatever lives in that forest.*

His mind returned to the accounts of the forest Mina had relayed. *The distant sound of screaming. What the hell kind of neighbor do we have?*

With the discussion concluded for the evening, James began moving to secure the Fisher Kingdom against the new threats.

First, he used Dominion to refresh his aura print over the whole area—and spread it into areas that his new neighbors' auras had not yet touched. There was no sense in losing ground to them, after all. And he was relieved that the potential invaders had not actually pushed any of their respective auras into his territory. If they had tried, his aura—his hold over the land—had apparently held firm.

Then he walked out to the border with the eerie forest. Mina insisted on going with him, over his objections, but he at least persuaded her to stand twenty feet behind so that any magical effect that struck him would probably not be able to reach her.

He took a look at the stakes wrapped in caution tape that lined the area in a makeshift fence of flimsy wood and plastic.

Really, the former public works fellows did a good job, he thought. It was completely inadequate to keep a determined person from getting in or out of the creepy forest. But given the time constraints and materials they'd had to work with, James was pleased. *Everyone is making themselves useful, finding ways to contribute. The community is almost self-organized, the way Mina's telling the story.*

He imagined he would find out just how much direction the community actually needed tomorrow, when the brunt of the responsibility would fall on his shoulders rather than Mina's.

James began focusing his mind on the problem of erecting an earthen wall in the space just behind the stakes. Rather than using the Mana imbued into the land, he gathered most of what was left in his body.

As he was preparing to raise his wall, though, he looked across the caution tape fence, and he saw into the forest.

What James saw seemed impossible. It sent a shudder through him, and he barely kept his focus on spellcasting. *Now I understand what left our hunters and public works people so shaken.*

At the sight of that abominable image, James resolved to make the wall several feet higher and a few feet longer. It would consume almost all the Mana he had left after the last day of nonstop activity and the use of Dominion, but it seemed necessary. He wanted to not only keep people from inadvertently crossing over into that evil place, but also prevent them from accidentally *looking* over the border.

What people see when they look across that border is just as dangerous as anything offensive the Ruler of that territory could conjure up. He tried to imagine fighting with the apparition that had just appeared lurking before his eyes, and it seemed impossible; he would focus on what he had seen, not any enemy placed in front of him.

He very deliberately looked away from the forest as he finished charging his Mana.

Finally, he poured his power into the earth and built a mighty wall almost twice his own height.

There, he thought, panting slightly. *Now let them try to screw with us.* Assuming that Mina was out of range where she stood, he calculated that no one within range of the forest's power would actually be able to see into it now.

Unless the forest expands its border. Which it surely would.

He could tell already that this was going to be a difficult problem. Perhaps a deadly problem.

Could he lead troops into a place like this forest? If he did, would any of them come out again?

He couldn't confidently say that he knew the answer.

My own visual distractions made the goblin fight so much easier. I can't imagine things would be different here when the shoe is on the other foot.

He walked back toward Mina.

"You saw something too, didn't you, skapi?" she asked softly, staring him in the face.

"I did," James said, frowning.

She took his hand, and they walked back to the apartment in silence.

While Mina made up the bed, James prepared to shower for the first time in over a month. That was the big change to their apartment while he had been gone. Mina had come up with the idea of having plumbers come and work in conjunction with Mages to install drainpipes in as many apartments as they could. That way if people just used magic to conjure water, they could bathe like civilized humans, without having to look for a river or something.

As someone who had only washed with conjured water for weeks and who'd had to bathe outside whenever he wanted to clean off, James thoroughly approved.

"Hester, Roscuro, do either of you know anything about dealing with ghosts?" James asked. The water was running over his body now, warm and inviting, but he still felt a chill.

"Not much, sir," Hester said.

Is that what you saw? Roscuro asked.

Did you not see it? James replied.

No, Roscuro replied. *Which I suspect means it was not real.*

"I need to talk to Dave Matsumoto in the morning," James said aloud. "I want to know what or who other people see when they look into that forest."

CHAPTER THIRTY-ONE

Fisher Kingdom Business

In the morning, James got up early and made his family a hearty breakfast.

He used a frying pan that someone had recovered from one of the old apartments, flames that he could generate from his own body and control at will, and ingredients he'd found in Carol's Retail. It really was a brave new world.

That was the best way James could think of to tell his closest people that he was home again. Ideally, they would all associate the times when he was at home with the sound and smell of his cooking, happy memories of him reading aloud and playing with the children, and other similar scenes of domestic bliss. He had a bad feeling that he wasn't going to be as present as he would prefer.

The new neighbors brought it home to him. There would always be more enemies to fight.

At least everyone seemed happy to see him. Yulia looked relieved, which James guessed was in part because she and Mina had suffered through quite an annoying series of meetings and bureaucratic tasks while he was gone. Abhi ran up to James and embraced him silently but fiercely. And even baby James seemed to be in high spirits, gurgling and wiggling energetically at the sight of his father's face.

After breakfast, James announced his return to the Fisher Kingdom using his powers.

[Greetings to all residents of the Fisher Kingdom! I am back within our territory, and on my return journey I was accompanied by a small group of humans as well as roughly one thousand Goblins and two hundred Mole People. If you see giant fur-covered creatures that look a bit like a bear or humanoid figures with yellow-green skin, please do not be alarmed. These are friends who are eager to live and work alongside us to build our new nation. You may not see them very often, as both Races primarily dwell underground. Please treat them with the same courtesy that you would extend to members of your own Race, whether you are a human, a wolf, or some other life-form. The Goblins and Mole People are instructed to do the same.]

People reacted to James's announcement all across the territory. Some were simply glad he was back. Their body language reflected relaxation or mild euphoria at the thought that they were a bit safer than they had been before. Others were immediately worried about his decision to welcome so many new nonhuman immigrants into the country. Their frantic movements conveyed a sense of urgency as the most concerned paced back and forth.

James felt their movements all through his territory as he reached out with his aura to gauge the state of things. He was primarily focused on the land rather than the people right now, but in observing the condition of the territory, he couldn't help but get a general sense of people's activities and, by extension, their feelings.

This is a powerful ability that I'll have to be careful in using.

Not much about the land itself had changed since he'd left besides Mina beginning construction on a few new buildings.

There had been a bit of tunneling, which James was fairly certain was the work of Mole People burrowing where he had authorized them to dig.

Elsewhere, there were some changes to the surface, including some new seeds planted. Someone was preparing to farm a certain section of land. James had authorized the formation of an Agriculture Commission before he left. It seemed they were already hard at work.

And there were a hundred or so new people, which was the most interesting development to him.

James resolved to meet as many of the new residents as he could and begin familiarizing them with his style of leadership. He walked toward the stairs leading out of the apartment.

Then there was a knock at the door.

James was going to answer it, but Yulia rushed out of her room and marched downstairs with an air of such certainty that he just let her go ahead of him. He was left standing upstairs alone for a moment.

What's going on? he thought. *Yulia's answering the door now? What happened while I was gone? Well, if it's another complaint like the landlord's, she can go ahead and get it. Maybe they'll be nice to her.*

James heard the door open, and then heard her greeting what sounded like more than a few people.

She called up to him, "Citizens here to see the Fisher King!"

"All right," James said, just loud enough for Yulia to hear a floor below him. "I guess there are a few things to discuss." He had given a fair number of them tasks to work on while he was gone, after all. "Please have them form a line, then send them up. First come, first served."

Then he wondered if he'd said something wrong or unintentionally funny. Even from where he stood at the top of the stairs, he could see Yulia's mischievous smile as she stood in the shadows by the door.

From then until lunchtime he had hardly a minute alone.

First, there were a couple of people who wanted to express how enthusiastic they were about the new citizens—which James quickly realized was code for, *We need reassurance that the Mole People and Goblins aren't going to kill us and eat our children, please!*

He provided that as best he could and then announced to the whole Kingdom that there would be a meet and greet with the leaders of the Goblins and Mole People in the next few days, and that any questions about the new residents should wait until then.

Next, a group of engineers and plumbers showed up. Mina had apparently authorized them to begin planning the construction of a large sewer system for the Kingdom. The names of the Sewer Commission members were Jeremy Zucker, Steve Hsu, and Angelina Zuccarini.

Steve was their "sewer historian." He was weirdly excited to explain the historical models they were referring to in making their plans. The London sewer system was apparently a great historical example.

Once James felt he had sufficiently attempted to express his enthusiasm for the project, he gently pushed them to get to why they'd come to see him this morning.

"Oh, we heard your announcement, sir," said Zuccarini. "We wanted to check in with you about the underground locations we're allowed to consider for the sewer. Since your, uh, new subjects will reside largely underground."

"Ah." That made a lot of sense. "Well, let me just connect you with the parties directly concerned. They can probably help you with construction anyway."

He reached out to Magnar and Duncan with telepathy, and once he confirmed they were both available, he sent the Sewer Commission out to meet them. James would have preferred to make introductions himself, but he was confident enough in Duncan's social graces, and he also didn't feel that he could just leave right now. There were more meetings to attend . . .

"Ready for the next group!" James called.

A moment later, he heard another small party climbing up the stairs.

This group was comprised of three men in robes. Two of them wore glasses, and all moved with the hunched postures common to those who were perpetually at a computer desk or staring down into a phone. For humans who had survived the System apocalypse, they looked remarkably physically weak. James automatically labeled them as geeks in his head. He spent the next twenty minutes trying unsuccessfully to put that judgment aside.

The lead geek, Christian Zito, spent most of that time explaining, in highly technical terms that they apparently had not figured out how to dumb down, some information about wires, cables, radio waves, satellites, and the size of the Earth. It gradually dawned on him that the Geek Squad was trying to explain something about the Internet. After that, the explanations seemed to flow more easily.

Eventually, James raised a hand to signal that they should pause.

"Hold on, please. Gentlemen, I have to be the first to admit that I am not a very technical person by nature, nor was I particularly good with pre-System technology. So, I need to try and summarize the gist of what you're saying before we get any further into the weeds on this topic. You're talking about the Internet, right?"

A tentative nod.

"What does the Internet have to do with the challenge of surviving in this semi-wild environment?" James asked, raising an eyebrow.

The three men visibly deflated.

"Not much," admitted Darryl Brush.

"But it means a lot for people's quality of life," Christian said. "If we could get the Internet up and working again—"

"Guys, I don't want to put a damper on anyone's spirits," James said. "I want the Internet back." He was not entirely sure that he did, but that seemed the civilized tack to take. "But we don't even have electricity and running water right now. We have to prioritize. If you come up with a way to get the electricity back on, I'll devote some resources to trying to turn the Internet back on."

Hopefully, they won't bring this up again until years from now, he thought, *when people won't miss the Internet so much anymore.*

"That's a very reasonable decision, sir," said Mateo Rivera. He had spoken less than the other two during the conversation, but James noticed that both Darryl and Christian looked as though they considered the matter closed once Mateo had spoken.

A natural leader, then?

"If the three of you are interested in tackling these broader civilizational priorities, though, I am very interested in restoring power and getting a semblance of modernity back. Maybe you can be the founding members of the Electricity Commission. If you come up with a plan for electricity, we can move on that very soon." James looked from man to man but made sure to make slightly longer eye contact with Mateo.

The three looked at each other, and then Christian spoke up.

"We'll talk about it and see if we can come up with something," he said.

"We won't let you down, sir," Mateo said, throwing side-eye at Christian. "Thank you for giving us this responsibility."

When they were gone, James shook his head. *Getting the Internet back on?* he thought. *That's so insanely ambitious that I have to hand it to them. Mainly Mateo, I guess. But the idea's a fantasy. What's next? A delegation from the Lollipop Guild?*

By the time of his next meeting, with the Agriculture Commission, James was starting to think seriously about what kind of governing structures he might put in place to minimize the number of meetings he had to attend.

People need to understand they have the authority to make decisions about things. If I put you on a commission, the commission should make decisions in the area it has responsibility for unless they're really big decisions that require more input. And if you want to try a moonshot project, maybe you need to go and do your best at it yourself. A meeting to figure out if we can get the Internet working again isn't a good use of my time. I can't be everywhere at once, unfortunately. And I'm really more interested in figuring out what the laws should be, directing foreign affairs, and protecting this land than anything as specific as which crops we should grow.

James made eye contact with the leader of the Agriculture Commission, an older gentleman named Harry Luntz, who had been a farmer pre-System. Luntz had just finished giving the group's report on their farming recommendations and activities thus far.

"May I be frank with you all?" James asked.

The members of the commission looked back and forth at each other and finally nodded in a disjointed agreement.

"I know very little about agriculture," James said, smiling sheepishly. "I know that farms are where the food comes from, and I feel ignorant on this subject. I am, however, absolutely thrilled that there are actions we can take to have our own food grown and ready for the end of the year. Given that spectacular possibility, I'm happy to take all of your recommendations. Let me know what you need from me, and I'm happy to assist however I can."

I didn't even know you could plant crops this late in summer, let alone that they could grow so quickly. But I guess farms were always just something I drove past.

Fortunately, the commission looked relieved at his admission of ignorance.

"We are eager to take your help, Your Majesty," Luntz said. He and James set a time to meet later that day, before they planted their crops. He did have tasks that he needed James's power to accomplish—or at least to accomplish quickly. The Fisher King's land would naturally be much more responsive to his Will and his Mana than to anyone else's efforts to manipulate the soil. Apparently, the farmers had learned that the hard way.

And maybe I can bless the seeds, James thought. That would be a contribution that only he could make.

The Agriculture Commission seemed to be in high spirits when they left James. The Fisher King himself was getting tired of dealing with administrative matters.

James finally got something done that was among his own priorities when Hester reminded him that he was traveling with Carol the Dungeon Core, who probably ought to be planted somewhere so she could start doing her work of rebuilding her Dungeon. He asked Mina to take the next meeting for him. It was the Building Commission, whose work he knew she would be invested in.

Mina smiled.

"I'll help you out," she said. "I know meetings are a pain. But could you make time for one extra meeting later? Yulia would really like to talk to you about the Child Rescue Commission. I know that's not at the top of your mind right now, for good reasons."

"Oh, it's not a problem," he said. "It would be nice to deal with a human situation instead of sewage and agriculture, honestly."

Then James put on his Shapechanger's Cloak.

Invisibility.

And he was escaping through the bedroom window, unseen, looking for the perfect spot to stick a Dungeon Core.

He removed Carol from his magic satchel midway through the search so that she could help him figure out the best place.

"Not there," she said of the wall between the Fisher Kingdom and the forest. "I don't want to be too close to your border with that creepy place."

She was much more interested in the community center, but James vetoed that idea. "We're going to be in and out of there all the time. I know you probably want more social activity, but I think this would probably be a little too much."

Finally, they settled on a building that was still under construction.

"I can actually finish filling out the structure that's there with my powers," Carol told James.

"That's great," he said. "And it can still perform its function as a warehouse." The latter was phrased almost as a question.

Carol quickly reassured him that yes, the items people were storing and planning to store would still be safe inside her Dungeon. So, James put her down and began thinking about how he would word his next announcement.

We now have a Dungeon in the territory, located where we were building a warehouse. Please don't be alarmed . . .

INTERLUDE

The Great White Nowhere

Cara Dahlhaus twisted her cold, hard lips into a vicious smile as she set eyes upon the frosty track.

The bitter winds that beat down on the frozen plains left her gray-blue skin unharmed, but the increasing chill did not go unnoticed. It was one of the signs that Cara was following.

And now she had another.

She bent down to more closely examine the bits of frost sticking out of the ground. Atop the snow-covered ground, sticking up like a ring of stalagmites, a circle of icicles in the shape of a hoof stood out.

Cara rose and cast her eyes forward four feet, eight feet, then ten feet. Sure enough, at ten feet she saw another frosty hoofprint.

This thing was really running, she thought. *Moving at high speed.*

She imagined it was fleeing from her. The notion was not implausible. She and the Wendigos that followed her had chased this creature across a huge chunk of the landmass that was once Canada. They had only gotten close once, and she had gotten a good look at it then before it dashed off, riding the winds like one of Santa's pets.

A freakishly gigantic white deer, crowned with a forest of golden antlers.

Identify labeled it as the Great White Hart, level thirty-two, which was worrying. But Malsumis had reassured her. Through his messenger, a rabid bison, the malevolent god had explained that the Great White Hart had abandoned its greatest strengths, its herd and its territory, in order to run from her more quickly.

"Just kill this single creature and you become a Ruler," the bison had wheezed with Malsumis's strange, eerie voice. "Easy work. You have killed so many others with far more potent powers. Remember the Shadow Mage?"

It was at least true that the only power Cara had witnessed the creature display proficiently was the ability to run away.

Still, is this really the easiest Ruler for me to kill? Cara did not feel confident that Malsumis was motivated by her best interests. She looked out for herself at all times, but she had felt forced to place her trust in the god's counsel more than once already. First, when he had persuaded her to become a Wendigo. Second, when he had explained that she would only be able to survive as a monster if she created others of her kind. Third, when he had told her how Wendigos navigated internal conflicts.

Now this. She was stuck in the middle of the Great White Nowhere, following the advice of a possessed bison that had deteriorated over the course of the journey west until it could no longer walk. The dead body of the bison had been ripped to shreds by Cara's fellow monsters at that point, and the last sound out of its mouth had been Malsumis's creepy wheezing laughter.

"Well, where to next, eh?"

Cara turned her head, though even before she did, she knew who the speaker was.

"We follow the tracks, Letitia," she replied, imbuing her voice with a special layer of frost that was reserved for this specific woman. The only Wendigo who had dared to challenge her leadership since the return to Earth. Also, the only one to ever contend with her and live.

Cara pointed down at the icicles she had just been examining as she spoke, as if Letitia were blind.

"Very good, then. More blood at the end of this trail?"

Cara frowned. *She's losing too much of her humanity. Like her brains are leaking out. Why did you want me to spare her, Malsumis? For what purpose? She would have served me far better as an example than as* this.

But it seemed to amuse the god to test his Chosen One in new and inventive ways now that she was back on Earth. He had promised power but never that it would be without cost.

One cost of the Wendigo Transformation that Cara had observed was that the longer one remained in the monstrous form, the more it sapped the underlying human's basic Intelligence. You could counteract that by Pillaging more bodies and absorbing Stat points, but it was a crapshoot where those Stat points landed.

Cara had been spending as much time in her human form as she could, whenever she was not moving at the Wendigos' superhuman speed or fighting. So, of course, Malsumis had sent them to this horrid frozen place, where only the Wendigo shape kept them from dying of exposure.

"Don't you remember, Letitia?" Cara asked. "You literally just ate."

She gestured at the smoke several hundred miles behind them. It had still been morning when they had hit Edmonton, and now it was almost night, but still, Letitia had enjoyed a banquet there. It ought to have sated even her Endless Hunger for a little longer.

Letitia's face took on a blank expression. Then she looked back at the column of smoke from the still-burning city, and her lips curled into a twisted smile. "Oh, yes. That was fun. Those people were delicious. Their blood tasted as sweet as maple syrup! When do we hit the next settlement?"

Cara resisted the urge to yell at her and instead returned her expression to the icy smile she had donned when she first saw the Great White Hart's tracks. *Our stay in Edmonton was a bit of a waste of time, but it did increase our numbers. No matter what I think of the hart's tendency to run from us, having cannon fodder to throw at him can only help me. Underestimating a Ruler could be fatal.* That last thought had been Malsumis's warning, even as he had instructed that she must pursue and defeat a Ruler to reach her full potential and secure her leadership position among the Wendigos.

"We continue forward, in search of larger prey," she replied, pointing in the direction the tracks led. "That way."

Then she sent a telepathic message to the whole group.

All, we have the tracks of our prey. You know how fast the beast is, so follow close behind me. We won't let it escape again.

Cara resumed tracking the monster. She only had the very occasional hoofprint to follow, so she was mainly trying to catch its scent on the wind and looking for small bits of fur left behind on trees as it raced by.

Looking for scraps of white fur in a winter wonderland, she thought. *It gives searching for a needle in a haystack a good name!*

But somehow, each time she was almost ready to give up, she would find some renewed sign of the creature's continued life, some visual indicator that she was on the right track: a tree scraped by the hart's antler, a scrap of white fur caught under a small stone but moving slightly with the intense winds, a series of branches that had clearly been trampled under the foot of the leaping, gliding creature.

And the latest: a tiny chunk of gleaming golden antler that must have broken off on contact with a large rock formation that seemed to loom up out of nowhere in the midst of the snow.

Cara picked up the chunk of golden antler and found it surprisingly heavy.

"Why is the weather like this?" a voice said from her side.

"We're chasing a monster that rides on the wind, Matt," Cara replied. "Why should we be surprised it's a bit windy? We've been moving north. And it's fucking Canada."

"It wasn't this bad on the way here," he replied. "Was it? It's still late summer."

Cara shrugged. "I've never been to Alberta before. I don't know what it's supposed to be like."

"Would you come back?" Matt asked.

She flashed him a hideous but genuinely amused smile. "I'd love to. Anytime. The food's great."

They shared an evil laugh. Then Cara directed her attention to their environment.

Although it was Matt who called her attention to it, Cara had also noticed the weather. Malsumis had informed her that once she became a Ruler, she would be able to manipulate the environment around her within a certain territory, so she assumed that the Great White Hart was exercising that power, although she declined to tell Matt this information. More information for the other Wendigos would only lead to one of them wanting to take the killing blow against the hart.

If one of the other Wendigos killed the hart, Cara would certainly lose her position of leadership. She would not let that happen. *I will never be powerless again.* It was her only principle.

So, she marched forward through the snow and banished all doubts to the back of her mind.

Several hours later, the terrain had become rockier. The Wendigos were nearing a mountain. The signs of the hart's presence were fewer and fewer, and the weather had continued to grow worse. Snow was falling in fast-flowing waves, faster than the Wendigos could produce themselves. But they still had a coherent trail to follow, with all the hart's clues moving in one direction.

The Wendigos followed the trail for another hour, and it ended with a scrap of fur lodged between two stones at the base of the mountain.

We'll need to scale that, Cara thought. Then she sent an order to that effect.

The Wendigos were nearly tireless. Even so, with the snow beating down more, the winds howling more harshly, and the air growing thinner with each step they took, their pace of ascent gradually slowed to a crawl. Their inexorable forward movement continued, but at an incredibly drawn-out speed. Cara could not criticize them. She knew that any human climber would have given up on this place already.

My creatures are superior to any human, she thought with pride. *That's why this world will fall to us.*

The climb continued for monotonous hours as the ground receded into the distant background, but no Wendigos gave up or even questioned the directive to advance.

Finally, as Cara stepped over a large jutting rock, she saw it: a white-furred four-legged figure.

Everyone be as quiet as you can! she sent to the whole group instantly. *We're very close.*

Then she heard the sounds of movement from somewhere ahead of the hart: multiple life-forms crunching the snow with their footsteps.

There was a moment of confusion for Cara. *I thought he left behind all his kind. Are there more hidden up here? Did he arrange to meet them?*

Then she saw a heavy rock flying through the air, thrown from somewhere further up the mountain. It was clearly aimed at the Great White Hart, but the creature nimbly sidestepped it. The rock tumbled through the air, now moving straight toward Cara. She smacked it away with the side of her arm, but the strength of the throw surprised her. It was enough to leave her skin a bit numb—something the cold weather alone could never do to a Wendigo.

Cara looked up and saw at least a dozen humanoid figures covered in white fur. They were approaching slowly but ominously. Most of them appeared to be staring at the hart, but a few were looking at her. They didn't have a single trace of fear in their body language.

Identify. She aimed at the closest monster.

[Ancient Mountain Sasquatch, Lv. 20]

Shit. He's a big one. But they were all around the same size. The Sasquatches were even larger than the average Wendigo. Probably stronger too.

She looked to the hart, and it turned and gazed right back at her. Its face was non-expressive, but she could swear there was a smug look in its eyes. Maybe it was the way the creature tilted its head. As if to say, *Oh, were you expecting it would just be me up here?*

Then the creature leaped into the air and began almost gliding away from the mountain using its strange ability to run on the wind.

Cara saw the Sasquatches throw heavy rocks and icicle spears at the hart. The creatures seemed to form the spears out of thin air, which suggested they might be a legitimate threat. But the hart was far more agile than the projectiles, and it drew further away by the second.

The environment wasn't changing with the beast's departure either, Cara realized.

Was that because it had changed the weather here and had no wish to change it back? Or was there just another Ruler somewhere on this mountain? A Ruler of these creatures? She began to have a very bad feeling about things.

She started to climb back down from her position and sent telepathic messages to the rest of the Wendigos to do the same. *Flee! The creature has led us into a trap!*

There were objections.

We want meat.

Let us fight these monsters.

We came here for blood.

Cara didn't bother arguing. The more sensible of her allies had already begun climbing down alongside her, though their progress was as slow as the climb up had been.

When the hart had flown completely out of the monsters' range, the situation changed. All attention turned to the Wendigos.

Cara felt the change in the atmosphere when the attention of the monsters shifted. The air around the Wendigos somehow grew even colder and the wind pounded even more harshly, though that could not harm them. Much more important were the projectiles.

The Wendigos that had been the most eager to fight were the first to be struck. Most of the blows, Cara saw when she bothered to look, were nonlethal—just Wendigos getting knocked on their asses.

A few of them were potentially deadlier. One ice spear drew very near to hitting a Wendigo in the heart, though ice alone would probably not destroy a Wendigo's heart. And a couple of Wendigos struck in the head with heavy rocks fell to the ground and then didn't move again.

Cara was well aware that her monsters were still mortal. They could be killed, though she did not think a blow to the head would be enough to do it. But the Wendigos couldn't afford to remain immobile while the Sasquatches advanced either. The monsters were moving briskly down the mountain, pursuing their fleeing enemy with the advantages of the high ground and their superior knowledge of the terrain. Their steps were sure-footed, like a mountain goat's.

Whenever a Wendigo tried to throw rocks back at the attackers, the Sasquatch would dodge or catch the stone.

We're going against gravity, Cara thought. *We would have to be significantly stronger than them to be effective in a battle.* And most of her Wendigos were newly minted from the destruction of Edmonton—too weak to be effective against enemies other than helpless humans.

She tried to ignore the thrown objects as best she could and get distance, but the Sasquatches only grew more aggressive and confident in their defense of their territory. As she saw more and more of the tall figures, she began to think the Wendigos might be outnumbered as well as outclassed in physical power and knowledge of the environment. But it was hard to be sure; the Sasquatches could appear and disappear behind a snow drift in an instant.

A new volley of heavy rocks and ice spears began to thin the number of Wendigos that were still retreating.

The first ice spear that struck Cara took her in the side.

Run, she sent to the other Wendigos. *Do not try to fight. Just ru—*

As Cara tried to sidestep another ice spear, a heavy blow struck her in the head. Black fog began clawing at the edges of her vision.

Where did that come from? she wondered.

The last sight that her brain registered before the darkness took her was the shape of the Great White Hart floating in midair beside her. But that could have been a hallucination. One sometimes sees strange things after a head injury.

Then Cara was falling down the side of the mountain.

CHAPTER THIRTY-TWO

Preparations for Battle, Part 2

After he had announced the establishment of the Fisher Kingdom's first Dungeon, James returned to the apartment via the same route by which he'd left it.

"So that was what you needed some time to yourself for?" Mina asked, raising an eyebrow playfully.

James nodded. "Well, that, and honestly, I just wanted to get away from people asking me for direction for a little while."

"That's going to be your everyday reality, you know," Mina said, furrowing her brow in an expression of slight concern. "You asked for this when you decided to be king."

"I know, and I accept that I'm the decision-maker," James said. "But I need to start giving some of these people more autonomy, have them pick members of their groups to be in charge of the different commissions and projects so they can get things done without having to ask me about them. There's a broad vision, and then there's the nitty gritty detail that I'm not better equipped to handle than the people who have chosen to take up the task."

Mina's face relaxed. "That's good, then. You need to start telling people that. I had a similar thought when I was dealing with commission meetings yesterday, but I didn't want to say anything on your behalf that I couldn't un-say."

"I appreciate that," James said, looking into her eyes and smiling.

"Of course." She shrugged, but the corners of her lips tugged up in an irresistible return smile.

Of course, he thought affectionately. *You always know the right thing to do, don't you?*

"Next on the agenda, I'd like to have lunch with Dave Matsumoto. He can give me more details on our unwanted neighbors, right?"

"He said he told me everything he knew," Mina replied. "But I wouldn't be surprised if you could get more out of him. He seems like a reserved fellow. And people do tend to confide in you."

James prepared a very simple lunch—roasted meat from his hunt with Dave and his friends and roasted potatoes made with canned potatoes he'd found in Carol's Retail—and then he went to where Dave was. One of the advantages of his power as the Fisher King was that he could always find where people were on his land.

Fortunately, Dave had not made other lunch plans, and he agreed to eat what James had brought. They went into the community center, which James saw Mina had already ordered slightly enlarged without changing the fundamental design.

They pulled up a couple of chairs and engaged in small talk for a little while.

James didn't broach the subject he had come to discuss until they were midway through the meal.

"So, I understand that this neighbor we're dealing with right now—speaking realistically, this potential enemy—might have originated in your Orientation." He didn't phrase or pronounce the words in the form of a question, but the sense of an inquiry floated in the air between them, nevertheless.

"That is what I believe, regarding the neighbor located in the forest," Dave said after a long moment.

"I can tell you don't really want to talk about this. And I wouldn't ask so directly if I didn't feel our situation was rather urgent. But the forest sprang up *right there* while I was gone." James pointed a thumb at the wall he had put up to block the forest from view. "What can you tell me?"

"Not much. I didn't actually enter that forest in Orientation. Or not for very long, anyway." He looked into James's eyes and then away.

James just waited. *You're holding something back, Dave. Did you see what I saw?*

"You saw something," Dave said. It wasn't quite a question, though perhaps it should have been.

"I did," James replied. "I think you might have seen something similar. I really wanted to know if this is a problem everyone else would experience if they walked into that forest—or even just looked in its direction."

"Yes. I think that is probably safe to say." Dave's tone was still guarded.

"I can imagine why you wouldn't want to talk more about it," James said. He decided to go first. "I saw my dead father."

Dave stared into his eyes for a few seconds as if gauging his honesty. "Me too," he finally said.

The dam that had slowed their conversation down finally broke then.

"Do you know what the others who have looked into that forest saw?" James asked.

"It's the same," Dave said. "If you see their faces right after they've looked into the place, you don't have to ask to know what they've seen: dead loved ones, same as us. I don't know if they've actually heard the voices of the dead. That was what almost lured me in, beyond the border zone. If my friends hadn't been there . . ."

"Did the apparition sound like your father did in life?"

"Yes. I think so. Or perhaps just like my memory of him." Dave looked disturbed as he pondered the question.

"Not a lot of people would be able to fight well in those circumstances," James said slowly, "so it would render our forces ineffective or at least much less effective as soon as they entered."

"Are you asking me or telling me?" Dave asked.

"Yes." Both men chuckled, but without much humor. "You were a military man, right, Dave?"

"Once. Against my better judgment, probably. The war with China seems so naive now. What a waste of life and time and energy! Fighting China over Taiwan . . . To think, we would be fighting against otherworldly monsters one day."

James could hear trauma in Dave's voice.

"Think of it as preparation," he said. "The world needs you at your best, most-prepared self. Maybe everything you've endured had a meaning, a purpose that we're only going to see right now."

Dave bit his lip, then nodded slightly. "What do you want me to do?"

"Right now, I just want someone to bounce ideas off of," James said. "My colleague, Alan, went to war too. I'll probably have most of the people who've fought in war on a council soon. But before I do that, I wanted your opinion. I want to either engage in diplomacy with or conquer these two neighbors. We can't have a next-door neighbor whose intentions we're not sure about. The question is who to engage first. Do we deal with the swamp creatures or try the forest?"

"What do your instincts tell you?" Dave asked.

"Oh, none of that!" James said, laughing quietly. "Are you going to be one of those people who asks what I think when I've just said I want your opinion?"

Dave smiled dryly. "Fine. Hit the swamp first."

"That was what I was inclined to do. Thank you. What's your reasoning?"

"I imagine that the creatures there are more mobile than whatever dwells in that forest."

James nodded. "So, if we enter the forest and lose ourselves there, the swamp creatures might invade and attack the people we've left behind."

"Exactly. But I suppose you had already thought of that."

"It was a possibility I'd considered. Whatever lives in the forest didn't seem to come out during the duration of your Orientation?"

"No." Dave looked uncomfortable. "We didn't see anything emerge. We only heard them sometimes."

James didn't ask anything else just then. If Dave knew something else that James would need to know, he felt confident the veteran would pass the information on, no matter how painful it might be.

The two sat and ate in silence for a few minutes.

"The other reason why I want to tackle the swamp first," James said finally, "is that I think the forest situation is going to come down to a fight."

"You don't think that the forest dwellers can be negotiated with," Dave said. He was keeping his voice carefully neutral, but James thought he detected the corners of the man's lips turning up slightly.

He approves of the way I'm thinking.

"No, I don't," James said. He allowed a little bit of his anger to show through, relaxing just a little of his control. "Even if they could be negotiated with, would we really want to reach an accommodation with something that dishonors our dead as a distraction?"

Dave nodded his endorsement of James's reasoning, and the silence resumed for a little while.

James was already looking ahead to the fight with whatever lived in the ghastly forest more than he was thinking about fighting the swamp monsters.

Should I take that personally? Roscuro asked, interrupting James's train of thought.

Take what personally? James replied, though he instantly knew what the Soul Eater meant.

That remark about dishonoring the dead.

Ah. No, of course not, James sent. *I would have happily negotiated with you. You just would have had to agree that I was in charge.*

Of course, Master, Roscuro said, in a tone that dripped with irony. *Your diplomacy will surely be legendary for its nuance and sophistication.*

"All right," James said, breaking the silence. "Can you have the hunters gather after lunch? I would like to deal with this alligator problem sooner rather than later."

"Today?" Dave asked.

"Necessary action is only ever delayed to our detriment," James replied.

"What's that? Sun Tzu?"

"A very rough paraphrase of Machiavelli. The quote is about how there's no avoiding war. Postponing only helps others, not us."

"That seems like it couldn't be true in our case," Dave said. "Delaying gives us the chance to train a larger force."

"Honestly, I don't anticipate we'll need a large force," James said. "This is essentially a training exercise for the small elite group that we're taking into the enemy's territory. Assuming it comes to a fight, of course."

"You think you can take them by yourself."

"I think we have a strong enough force that I won't have to, but probably, yes."

That was part of the appeal of dealing with the gators first, honestly. A problem I can just punch my way out of won't be a problem for very long. And, hopefully, this will raise morale for the next situation we have to deal with.

Dave nodded as if he also thought it was plausible that James could defeat the monsters alone.

"If we wait, what's the downside? What additional risks do we face?" Dave asked.

"More hostile neighbors will probably appear on our borders. Even if that doesn't happen, the swamp creatures could take the fight to us, endangering civilians. Or they could form an alliance with whatever lives in the forest."

Dave's eyes widened slightly. It appeared he had not considered some of what James was predicting might happen. "All right. I'll have them ready to go in an hour." He rose from the table.

"I'll get the nonhuman contingent of our forces ready," James said.

Dave stepped away, and James began reaching out telepathically to the leaders he needed: Magnar, of the Mole People, and Luna, of the wolf pack.

The Goblins would, he thought, probably be less than helpful against monsters that were larger than them and armored. Maybe the Goblin Overlord's Illusion Magic would be useful, though, so he sent Duncan a message as well.

There were a couple of humans he wanted to bring into the battle, but he imagined that the monsters could probably do most of the heavy lifting in this fight.

Assuming that there is *a fight*, he reminded himself. It was entirely possible that the swamp monsters would want to be friends, in which case James would consider what he and the monsters could offer each other and, hopefully, hammer out some sort of agreement. But he wouldn't want to count on that seemingly unlikely outcome.

"What are you expecting to happen next, sir?" Hester asked.

"I think we're eating gator meat tonight," he said quietly.

He decided to go over his Status for a few minutes while he waited for his monstrous allies to arrive.

[**Status**
Name: James Robard
Race: Evolver Human, Lv. 22
Class: Predator in Human Skin, Lv. 25
Job: Fisher King, Lv. 20

Health: 22,801/22,801
Mana: 21,920/21,920
Stamina: 21,025/21,025
Wrath Meter: 0%
Stats
Strength: 125
Agility: 134
Stamina: 145
Fortitude: 151
Dexterity: 110
Perception: 155
Will: 160
Intelligence: 137
Charisma: 155
Stealth: 135
Free Points: 0
Skills
Affinity of the Fisher King, Lv. 3
Air Strike, Lv. 5
Aura of the Fisher King, Lv. 5
Basic Elemental Magic: Earth, Lv. 4
Basic Elemental Magic: Gravity, Lv. 3
Basic Elemental Magic: Water, Lv. 4
Basic Non-Elemental Magic, Lv. 2
Berserk Mode, Lv. 0
Blame Avoidance, Lv. 5
Blessing of the Fisher King, Lv. 2
Command Presence, Lv. 0
Command Structure
Compulsion, Lv. 5
Dominion
Dreamwalk, Lv. 4
Empathic Projection, Lv. 12
Enhanced Stem Cell Production, Lv. 8
False Reality, Lv. 6
Fate Resistance
Full Body Control, Lv. 4
Goodwill of the Fisher King, Lv. 4
Hand of Glory, Lv. 2
Identify, Lv. 9
Illusion Magic, Lv. 5

Indeterminate Past, Lv. 0
Intelligence of the Fisher King, Lv. 1
Laying on Hands, Lv. 7
Lightning Strike, Lv. 3
Loyal Following, Lv. 5
Mass Pillage, Lv. 2
Meteor Strike, Lv. 3
Mind of the Predator, Lv. 7
Monster Control, Lv. 8
Monster Generation, Lv. 9
Natural Camouflage, Lv. 3
Omnivore, Lv. 4
Organization, Lv. 6
Pain Resistance, Lv. 9
Perfect Choice of Words, Lv. 6
Pillage, Lv. 12
Predator's Missile, Lv. 3
Predator's Sacred Armor, Lv. 2
Predator's Strike, Lv. 5
Predator's Venomous Armaments, Lv. 1
Rapid Recovery, Lv. 6
Self-Control, Lv. 3
Shed Skin, Lv. 9
Silent Spellcasting
Silk Production, Lv. 9
Skill Fusion
Skill Transfer
Solar Ray, Lv. 2
Solar Recovery, Lv. 4
Soul Bind, Lv. 0
Soul Magic, Lv. 1
Spellbinding Words, Lv. 2
System Interface
System Store Access
Territorial Control, Lv. 1
Threads of Fate, Lv. 1
Universal Language Comprehension
Way of the Predator, Lv. 6
Will of the Fisher King, Lv. 1
Zone of Influence, Lv. 1
Talents

Alpha Presence, Lv. 0
Basic Spellcraft, Lv. 5
Cannibalism, Lv. 6
Cool-Headed, Lv. 8
Earth Affinity
Efficient Magic, Lv. 4
Fisher Land Management, Lv. 4
Fisher Sentient Resources, Lv. 3
Flame Affinity
Genius Loci, Lv. 1
Leadership, Lv. 5
Manipulation, Lv. 9
Marksmanship, Lv. 4
Mass Manipulation, Lv. 3
Monster Patriarch, Lv. 3
Pain Resistance, Lv. 2
Selective Empathy, Lv. 5
Solar Power, Lv. 3
Soul Eater, Lv. 0
Water Affinity
Titles
A Stitch in Time
Chosen One of Anansi
Citizen of the Dead Marsh
Deceiver
Devout Beacon
Dreamweaver
Figure of Destiny
Friend of All Spiders
Living Legend
Pack Leader
Ruler of the Dark Waters
Savior
Spider-King
Storyteller
Sublime Creator
Swiss Army Mage
System Pioneer
Trickster
Usurper
Xenocide II]

Neat. Things are coming along well, I think. Of course, James had no other Ruler to compare himself with, but he could tell he was miles ahead of where he had been in Orientation.

He rose from his seat and walked out to meet the monsters he was bringing with him.

As he opened the community center doors, he saw Luna and the wolfpack and, beside them, Duncan, Magnar, and a contingent of thirty Mole People.

"First things first," he said. "I already bestowed my blessing on Duncan and Magnar, when I appointed them as my leaders of their respective species. Luna, it's your turn."

The leader of the wolves approached James, and he focused on her.

It has been a while, my king, the wolf sent telepathically. *You did not wish for us to accompany you on your adventure to the Goblin lands.* There was a trace of wounded pride in her tone, but James could not tell if she was entirely serious.

I entrusted you and the wolfpack with something much more important to me, he replied. *The protection of my family and my land. Dealing with the Goblins was a distraction from my real purpose here, but I trusted that you and your brothers and sisters could defend what was most precious.*

Luna's ears perked up at that. *Wow. She really was fishing for some reassurance there.*

While you were gone, we patrolled and hunted with great enthusiasm, she sent. *I also chose my mate. I hope that I will bear cubs soon, to better defend our lands and grow in your service. If you are blessing me, I would ask that you also bless my mate.* Her tone turned up slightly at the end of the statement, as if it was a question. A little whine also escaped the back of her throat.

James nodded and smiled. "I would be happy to. Would Luna's mate please join her in front of me?"

A large male wolf with two heads stepped forward from the pack. He must have evolved from his base form while James was away. There were two Command Forest Wolves in the pack now.

I wonder if Luna chose him for that reason. I know she wants her pack to be as strong as she can make it, to better justify her place here.

My king, you honor me by including me beside my mate, the wolf said. *Thank you.* His thoughts came across in a gruff voice with a slight hint of an accent from somewhere up north that James could not specifically place.

Do you have a nickname you go by within the pack? James asked, sending the message to both of them.

No, my king, the male wolf replied instantly.

Are you able to give us true names with this new power of yours? Luna asked.

James nodded. He had done it for Magnar. Luna's tail began to wag excitedly, and she sat up a little straighter. Something important to her future was about to happen.

Please choose a strong name for me, sir, the male sent.

The name was the easiest part for James. There was a good historical precedent that he felt fit. And the proper words for the blessing came to him as he empathized with Luna's excitement for the future.

"As the borders of the Fisher Kingdom expand, so must the defenders of the Fisher Kingdom grow stronger. Their leaders must grow stronger still. Lady Luna and Lord Romulus, as you and your brood will be permanent guardians of this land, may you grow strong and fruitful above and beyond your peers. May you and your children be the foundation for a dynasty."

Power surged through James's body, and he saw the two targeted wolves swell with power in front of him.

In his peripheral vision, he saw Duncan and Magnar fall to their knees, while the rest of the wolf pack bent their front legs and lowered their heads in their version of a bow.

James felt the usual sudden hit of weakness after a blessing, but he was prepared for it this time. He remained standing still, though his vision blurred slightly from the power he had just expended.

The two wolves he had blessed began howling, and soon the pack joined in.

CHAPTER THIRTY-THREE

The Home Front

After the wolves had calmed and ceased their howling, after James had sent an announcement explaining that the wolves' howling was good news rather than some kind of monster attack, and after he had described the situation with the neighbors and his thinking to all the monsters present, James returned to the apartment for a few minutes.

Even if he was certain he would come back either victorious or with a new ally, he wanted to let Mina know he was going somewhere. Otherwise, she'd worry about him—which in this case would be unwarranted.

"We're going to pay a little visit to the swamp," he said as soon as he knew they were the only ones in the apartment besides the children. The kids were down for a post-meal nap, and Yulia had gone out to deal with some Child Rescue Commission business.

As he spoke, James roasted a bit of monster meat from his magic satchel. Mina had finished eating her lunch with Yulia and the children and was about to wash the dishes when he had come in, but James was already hungry again. Thanks to Omnivore, he was confident that eating a meal would restore most of the power he had expended blessing the wolves. And he knew that he would need to be at full strength; he was invading another Ruler's territory.

"By 'a little visit,' you mean you're going to invade and wipe out another species?" She smiled thinly as she spoke. It rang false to James. For a moment, he almost wondered if there was some physical danger present that Mina was worried about. But no. She would certainly have told him. More likely, she was worried about him going.

"Well, not wipe them out, hopefully, but you never know." He gave a little shrug. "The hunters, the wolves, the Mole People, and the Goblin Overlord are all going with me. We'll do our best to make some sort of arrangement for the Kingdom's future security."

"I hope you have fun," she said, clearly trying to affect nonchalance.

"You're not worried?" he asked.

"I know you're in your element. Go kill some big lizards." Again, something about her voice gave away that all was not quite right. "Just have fun with it. Don't forget you are meeting with Yulia later about her commission, and you should probably take a shower after you come back from the swamp. I have a feeling you'll be covered in blood, sweat, and mud. Love you!"

Mina stepped in, went on tiptoe, and kissed him on the cheek. She smiled as she pulled back, but it didn't reach her eyes. She turned away, walked to the sink, silently conjured some water, and began washing dishes. It was a small movement of her shoulders that gave her away. A slight quiver.

James came up behind his wife and wrapped his arms around her. He felt tension running through her body, and he leaned down and pressed his cheek against hers. And confirmed that she was crying. As he felt her tears on his skin, he embraced her more tightly, almost lifting her off her feet. Her body felt so fragile.

Mina leaned back against him and relaxed as completely as she could, allowing him to support almost her full weight. She breathed slowly as she tried to calm herself, but he could still feel the occasional sob mixed in with her normal breathing.

"It's all right that you're not used to this," he said, speaking softly right into her ear. "No one really is—"

"Except you." She turned her head slightly to look at him before continuing. "And all these people who are already finding new ways to help build up your kingdom. I keep thinking about what happened in Orientation. I feel like if I let you or Yulia too far out of my sight, I'll lose you. I know that's not right—at least about you. You can take care of yourself better than anyone. But I still remember the sounds of people screaming when the Wendigos slaughtered buildings full of people. I know it could happen again."

"It's normal to feel that way. You're just being human. You might think other people are okay. But most of them are just trying to pretend that their Orientations never happened. The reason they support us is because they think we can give them back some normalcy. Most of them would be homeless now if we weren't putting up buildings for them. If you take an animal out of its environment, most don't know how to adapt to a new setting. I was just talking to Dave Matsumoto, and he was clearly still rattled thinking about his Orientation. And I think he's stronger than most! You're not doing worse than them or something."

I would read the way they're behaving this way: the more driven people are to make themselves useful, the more desperately they're coping. You're one of the people they're leaning on to give themselves structure. You're part of their sense of security. So, they probably pretend harder when they're around us than they do when they're by themselves."

Mina was nodding as James spoke those last couple of sentences, so he thought she might be starting to calm down.

"What about you?" she asked.

"I'm also part of their sense of security," he replied, deliberately missing the point.

She let out a short laugh. "You know what I mean. Those other people are desperately coping. I'm barely still sane. I tried to protect Yulia as much as I could in our Orientation, so she might be okay. But no one looked out for you and you're moving forward. You're even having fun!"

He spoke cautiously, listening carefully to her breathing to gauge her reactions as he spoke. "Well, I'm a bad example. I'm crazy in a way. Always have been. You know that; you signed up for it. I didn't trick you. And yes, I'm kind of having the time of my life. Not a lot of people are going to be reacting like me. I'm probably psychologically abnormal in some kind of diagnosable way."

There was a moment of silence while she weighed what James said.

"Yeah, you are a little crazy, aren't you?"

They both laughed—quiet shivery laughs from Mina and a low chuckle from James. He felt a little sense of triumph at making her feel just a bit better.

"You know, when you were gone, I dreamed that you died," Mina whispered. "I dreamed that you wound up just like those people the Wendigos killed. A big red-brown bloodstain smeared on a wall . . ."

James's smile dried up. *I should have visited her in her dreams . . .*

"But I can't let that stop me," she continued. "I know you aren't going to die like that. And I won't be left behind and wind up useless."

"You won't," he agreed.

"This swamp battle—I'm guessing it's going to be a physical fight between you and some giant monsters—it probably won't play to my strengths. I'm not as quick as you. I can't hit particularly hard"—she snorted at the idea of her hitting a monster—"so I won't ask you to take me with you. But promise me that when you face the next monster—if you invade the forest and face whatever lives there—you'll take me with you. This mystical stuff is going to be my element. A goddess of magic gave me a blessing, and I'm a Witch. I might make the difference between you living and dying. I'm still developing my understanding, but I won't have you go in there without me and make my nightmare come true."

James took a long moment to think about it. *I would really rather not take her. Even if it increases the odds of victory in the forest, it also increases the odds that we both end up dead.* The image that popped up in his mind first was baby James's tiny face, but the images of Yulia's and Abhi's faces and then the faces of his siblings, Indira and Deepam followed shortly thereafter. Being orphaned—probably orphaned *again* in the case of Abhi, Indira, and Deepam—would be no picnic for anyone.

But there was a values question at play too. What would it mean for Mina to survive and feel like she was useless for the purpose of protecting her family? That was the feeling she was conveying. He imagined there were—and had been and would be—similar conversations taking place in many households both in the Fisher Kingdom and elsewhere. The System had introduced new kinds of disparities between human beings, as well as unique traumas.

And in the event that James died in the forest, how long would Mina and the children live, anyway?

"I won't leave you behind if we hit the forest," he said finally. "But I'm not exactly eager to go in there right now. It is a spooky place. Dave and I both saw images of our dead dads. And the idea of taking you in there with me is even scarier because even if I don't die, I could lose you. Then I—I don't know what I would do. My first resort is going to be trying to figure out ways to deal with that place without going in. Maybe I can have the Mole People tunnel underneath it and collapse the place as a way of indirectly attacking, or we can use some kind of long-range attack to kill whatever lives inside. In the meantime, I'd appreciate it if you could try to figure out some way of dealing with spirit-type monsters. Right now, I've kind of got nothing. Your goddess didn't give you a spell book to study or anything—"

She was shaking her head as he spoke.

"—but if we can find something in the System Store, or you can get something in the new Dungeon that helps, I think that might be the best angle for you to take. Hopefully, one of us comes up with the right answer."

"I'll get to work on it," she said, fixing him with a determined look.

James was happy to see that she seemed more herself. Maybe she just needed a tangible problem to solve to help give her a sense of normalcy; though, he doubted anyone would feel all the way normal again anytime soon. There was no more normal. They shared a long kiss before he left.

He avoided entering the room where the children were sleeping.

I won't say goodbye to anyone else, he thought. *Knowing Abhi, he'd just think I'm never coming back. Mina will know best what to say to Yulia if I'm out all night. And I'll be home soon.*

It was still only midday, and he didn't think that this invasion would keep him out too late.

James rushed out of the apartment, taking the stairs two at a time. The sooner he left, the sooner he would be home again.

And there was a part of him that was looking forward to the possibility of a fight with the residents of this swamp. He remembered his last swamp fight. That had been a good time, and he'd acquired one of his stronger weapons—what could perhaps become his strongest weapon. He tried to keep his smile contained as he thought about this invasion.

He made a quick detour to meet with Harry Luntz, reshape the ground for easier planting, and bless the seeds and potato cuttings that were going to be planted. He had promised to do this, and it seemed this was the only time he was going to have today. Boosting agriculture was not the sort of thing he wanted to put off.

Fortunately, these tasks did not take nearly as much out of him as blessing monsters and humans did. The soil of the Fisher Kingdom responded to his Will with hardly any Mana needed. As if it had a desire to be shaped and molded by him.

James was surprised by how pleasurable working the soil actually was. Before he had magic, he never would have thought of himself as the type to take to farming or even gardening.

Finally, he shook hands with Harry and walked off to meet up with Dave and his hunters in front of the community center. The Goblin Overlord and the wolfpack were waiting there too, while the Mole People were already underground, waiting on the border with the swamp, following James's orders.

Several of the hunters looked a bit apprehensive as he approached, as if they were a little more worried about the swamp trip than James would have expected. He wondered if it was the swamp that was worrying them, or if their minds were really on the forest where they might have to go later.

Most of the hunters had previously killed their share of monsters, both in Orientation and even in the brief period when James had been gone from the Fisher Kingdom. He thought of this as a fairly elite group, and as he recognized that some of them were nervous, he wondered what the effect on Kingdom morale would be if everyone else who lived here could see them right now.

Fortunately, most people have their own tasks they're working on. But I need to do something about this.

"Let's go," James said, projecting confidence through his voice. "Let's make the world just a little bit safer for our people!" He looked to a man he knew was married, Sean McGuire, and he added, "Maybe we'll make a nice purse for your wife, Sean." Then he turned to a woman who James knew was engaged, Veronica Hamilton. "Or we might make a pair of gator-skin boots for your fiancé, eh?"

The hunters began laughing uneasily.

"We're ready to follow you, Your Majesty." Damien's low voice broke through the sound of laughter. His genuine eagerness to fight seemed to finish the shift in the mood that James had started.

"Come on, then," James said. "Let's get this done so we can get back before dinner's cold."

CHAPTER THIRTY-FOUR

Duel, Part 1

James led his mixed team of humans and monsters over the border into the swamp.

Dave and Damien took up the leads to his left and right.

There was an immediately noticeable shift in the terrain. The firm soil of the Fisher Kingdom gave way to soft, moist ground, which eventually turned to a general feeling of mush beneath their feet.

It was increasingly reminiscent of James's visit to the Dead Marsh, though he was glad that whoever the Ruler was, they hadn't flooded this place with mist. It would have been difficult for James's allies to navigate, to the point where he might have ended up having to leave everyone behind except the Mole People who remained far underground, digging cautiously to avoid winding up underwater.

James and his party trudged until James could no longer see the Fisher Kingdom, and they had yet to come upon any enemies. But the ground grew more and more moist. While the wolves managed to find passable places to put their feet and to tread lightly, the humans grew increasingly waterlogged until each forward step was harder than the last.

This place might be bigger than I had imagined, he thought. *Where did we run up against the edge of this swamp last time?* He estimated that point was perhaps half a mile east of where they now stood. *So, if I assume this place expands in all directions just like the Fisher Kingdom, and assuming it's constantly expanding like my territory is—which seems to be a safe assumption since we have a border with them now and we didn't before—it's at least a mile or so wide, with no clear outer limit for how large it might become—except that if it was larger, we would have a bigger border with it.*

But that didn't tell him the shape of the territory, which might not be circular, so he couldn't come close to guessing the dimensions.

As they walked, they came upon a noticeably firmer raised patch of ground, and James led his allies up that elevation. Anything that got them a little further from the mushier ground was better than proceeding further and further into what would undoubtedly become a swamp.

They reached the summit of the small hill and looked down.

James heard muffled gasps from all around him, and he suppressed his desire to roll his eyes. *These are my hunters, and this is their reaction. I guess I shouldn't be surprised. They need some more training to be able to really accomplish an invasion like this. Most of them were never soldiers.*

In the sunken area the hill looked down on, they could see dozens of larger-than-normal alligators, averaging around 50 percent larger than the typical specimen. The creatures were in a large body of marshy water, perhaps a lake; it was difficult to tell the exact size and depth with all the plant life growing up through the water—and the densely packed alligator flesh.

Identify. James picked a random alligator to focus on.

[Mutant Sewer Alligator, Lv. 16]

He quickly Identified a few more.

[Mutant Sewer Alligator, Lv. 17]
[Mutant Sewer Alligator, Lv. 14]
[Mutant Sewer Alligator, Lv. 13]

Hm. That's not good. The average level here is going to be a challenge for most of my group. Not Damien, probably not Dave. Hopefully, this is an opportunity for growth rather than something I'm going to have to save everyone from.

Of course, he had to remind himself, that was assuming that this encounter turned into a fight. So, they should not yield to the temptation of launching a sneak attack. *First, I need to establish what the situation is.*

He sent a message to the Mole People to be prepared to tunnel up near where they were in case the team needed a speedy getaway.

"Hey, you down there!" James called out. He could feel people around him stiffening in surprise as he spoke. The wolves remained steady, though. Ready for anything and calm. James felt his affection for his beasts intensify. When this was over, he promised himself, he would take time to bless every single one of them—after he blessed the rest of his family.

But now the alligators were turning their faces to look at James. A few slow-witted creatures were looking side to side as if wondering where the voice had come from. Their neighbors nudged them and pointed up at the human atop the hill. Gradually, all eyes shifted to stare at James.

"I am looking for the Ruler here," he called down. "We come from the neighboring territory! We're here to talk and establish a relationship."

Some of the alligators began pointing with short, fat, sharp claws. They pointed up at James, it seemed.

No, he realized. They weren't pointing at him. They were pointing at the hill.

Suddenly James felt life signs beneath his feet.

How did something this big hide? he wondered. There was grass growing on the elevated ground he stood on, and it was firm earth, but he could feel something moving now beneath his feet. *It has to have been suppressing its life signs!*

"Everyone, get off the hill!" James ordered.

The wolves and Duncan instantly sprang into action, running back down the way they had come. A few humans followed, but most of them just looked bewildered.

"What's going on?" Dave asked in an urgent tone.

"The Ruler is beneath our feet," James replied loudly.

"Hello!" A jovial, booming voice issued from the area beneath their feet.

James stood in place as the other humans finally began moving down. Fortunately, the creature under the soil wasn't moving its body yet, just talking—and no longer hiding its presence. James could tell from the heartbeat and other vital signs, which he could suddenly hear and feel, that the monster had to be massive.

The size of a T-Rex, maybe. The thought that something so large had been underfoot without him being able to notice shot a chill down James's spine. *The size of this thing, and it's about as stealthy as I am.* He could picture the monster sneaking up on him and his allies. If it had wanted to fight them, he would have certainly lost some people to this creature.

"Hello, Ruler of the swamp!" James said. His mind was quickly shuffling through options, considering what he could do here. Talking seemed like the best choice for now.

"What brings you into my swamp, neighbor?" The voice of the Ruler was almost a rumble. As it spoke, the nearby water seemed to tremble slightly at the sound of its voice. The words echoed through the surrounding trees, and birds began taking flight from their branches.

James could hear a hint of laughter in the monster's tone.

This thing is confident.

"I'm here to decide what sort of relationship you and I are going to have," James replied.

Identify.

[Sewer Alligator Monarch Samuel, Lv. 38]

Based on his level, he's stronger than any monster I've fought before. James's pulse began to quicken with excitement, but he betrayed nothing of his feelings on his face.

"Ah, I thought you were a Ruler!" This response was accompanied by a rolling chuckle that shook the ground beneath James's feet.

He checked to confirm that his people were off the hill, and then James spoke again. "I am the Ruler," he confirmed. "My territory is called the Fisher Kingdom."

"Sounds delicious!" The chuckle turned into full-throated laughter. "I personally find kingfishers very tasty. Some of my little friends down there would tell you that the feathers get caught in their teeth, but I personally don't have that problem."

There was laughter now, coming from the alligator-filled water below James. The residents here all amusing themselves at his expense.

James gritted his teeth. *I won't let this thing mock me.*

"Why don't you show yourself, so we can have this conversation face-to-face?" he asked. "I like to see who I'm talking to."

The ground moved much more radically than it had before, and James leaped off before he could be thrown. He oriented his body to fall and land gracefully. *I can't let myself look bad in front of my own people.*

And as he descended, he saw the monster that he had been speaking to for the first time.

The earth tumbled from his body almost in a sheet as he rose from an apparently prone position to stand upright, revealing an alligator with very dark green, almost black, armor on his head, arms, and legs. On the underside of his body, which faced James, he had noticeably thinner cream-colored armor. James estimated the creature at around forty feet tall.

About the length of a medium-sized whale, with a voice I would expect to come out of a young Godzilla. And he must have used earth magic or a similar Skill to make the soil cling to his body.

"Impressive entrance," James said.

"Thank you," the giant alligator said. His mouth barely moved as he spoke, though James could nevertheless smell his breath even from over thirty feet away. The monster emanated a faint odor of slightly foul chicken. It was easy to imagine that he might really have been eating kingfishers.

I don't know why they gave such a small, unintimidating creature such a noble-sounding name.

"I was even more impressed with your Stealth Skill there," James added.

"I was curious," the monster replied, "what you would do if you believed I was not present. Would you and your little band attack my brethren? Or act as you, in fact, did?"

Well, I'm glad we didn't take the former approach, he considered saying. And rejected the idea. *Can't project weakness to this thing. He undoubtedly already sees me as small.*

"I wouldn't want to annihilate your brethren and leave you all alone," James replied, grinning wolfishly.

Samuel chuckled to himself. "A confident one, aren't you? Even though you're so small I might lose you between my toes."

"Yet, I've fought creatures that could crush you under their feet."

This was technically true—though, only if James counted his "fight" with Anansi's children.

"I thought you might be here to surrender to me," Samuel said, "but now I know you have come to entertain me with silly stories instead." He still sounded amused, but with an edge to his tone. James decided to move directly to business.

"I am far from here to surrender," he said. "I came to establish the nature of the relationship between our two countries. Will we be friends, enemies, or indifferent neighbors who keep out of each other's way?"

"What is this nonsense about two countries?" Samuel replied. There was a distinctly malicious note to his voice now. "Now that you and I have met, there can be only one Ruler. Do not pretend to believe otherwise. I can practically smell the blood on your hands"—he inhaled sharply—"and I know who and what you are: a conqueror. I am the same way. The only question is how we settle which of us is to be supreme over these lands. An all-out war between our respective armies, or a duel between the two of us personally?"

"Well"—James avoided looking down at his allies—"naturally, to minimize bloodshed, I would prefer a duel between the two of us."

I'm pretty sure my group would just get decimated if I had to fight with only the ones I brought. Need Mina, Mitzi, and any Mages I've got to make it a better fight. Or I could throw a tide of Goblins at the enemy.

"The other question to resolve, then," Samuel said. "Do we duel to the death, or would you like me to spare you after I win?"

"In the unlikely event of your victory, I'm only concerned with making sure you don't kill any of my people," James replied. "But I am willing to fight nonlethally. I can imagine you would be a powerful soldier in my army."

"It's agreed, then," the alligator said, chuckling. "We will fight until one of us gives up."

"Any other rules we need to settle?" James asked. *I am a little surprised how rules oriented this big lizard is, honestly.*

"None that I can think of," Samuel replied, shrugging. Clumps of dirt that hadn't quite dislodged themselves before fell from his shoulders with the motion. "You can use any weapons you wish and, of course, magic. And I'll even do you a favor. We can leave my territory and fight in yours. That way, you'll have more of a chance."

As he finished speaking, Samuel finally switched to standing on all fours, the posture James was used to from alligators. Even so, he remained at least a foot taller than James.

James snorted. "Wow. You're so confident you're actually willing to commit suicide. It might be hard for me to fight nonlethally if you give me that big of an advantage."

"You want to fight here?" the monster asked.

"Why don't we find some neutral ground?" James asked.

"How honorable," Samuel replied, in the same tone that someone might say, *How droll*. "I accept. Neither of us will have the terrain advantage that way."

James might have imagined it, but he thought he heard a tinge more respect in the monster's tone now that James had rejected the offered advantage.

I can't win a fight we'd both agreed to on such lopsided conditions, he thought. *It would lose me respect instead of enhancing my authority. The lizard would wonder if I could have beaten him in a fairer fight, and any difficulty I suffered would make me look weak to my citizens.*

"I'll lead the way to an area outside both our territories," James said. He began navigating to the edge of the swamp, near where he, Dave, and the others had gone hunting the other day. Terrain that James knew, but that wasn't infused with his or the Sewer Alligator Monarch's power yet.

He began to assemble his plan for dealing with the giant monster.

CHAPTER THIRTY-FIVE

Mina in the Dungeon

After James was gone, Mina wiped away her tears and waited for Yulia to return.

She planned for her next steps. Soon, the baby would wake again, hungry, and she would be there to feed him. Then Yulia would be back.

After that, Mina thought she could go train. She knew where.

She simmered slightly with impatience. There would only be a small window of time when she could get away for a little while. It would only work if Yulia was there.

We really need electricity, Mina thought. *Then we could get a refrigerator, and I could pump so I wouldn't need to be here every time James gets hungry.* It felt like an ugly thought. If she started pumping instead of feeding the baby directly, she had read during her pregnancy, he might get used to the bottle and stop wanting to feed from the breast. And given how well breastfeeding had been working out, she shouldn't think of taking a chance on giving that up.

Mina had a powerful ability to ruminate and dwell on her own mistakes, but she resisted that tendency here. She would think about her training.

As she managed to shift her mind away from guilt, she heard a small cry coming from where the children were napping. And she went to baby James.

When she came back out, Yulia was there. The timing seemed to line up perfectly.

"I want to go to the new Dungeon that James installed in the warehouse," Mina said, looking down at baby James and rocking him gently as she spoke. "Will you, um—"

"Babysit?" Yulia finished for her. Mina looked up and gauged Yulia's feelings on the subject in a single glance.

It's a good thing she likes kids so much. She did volunteer for the Child Rescue Commission before. When she looks at these situations, does she see it as practice for when she becomes a parent someday? Or does she just enjoy them for what they are?

Yulia had always been transparent in how she felt about children. She had been considering working with them before the System. Either a teaching job or daycare work, probably. She hadn't yet nailed down the details. And now she had her chance, without even having to finish high school first.

I hope you still like it in a year, Mina thought. This logistical challenge wasn't going away anytime soon.

"How are you, um, feeling about this current situation?" Mina asked.

"The babysitting situation?" Yulia asked. "Um, I like it a lot . . ."

"Well, not just that," Mina asked. "I mean, yes, that, but how are you feeling about everything since being back? You've been a blur of activity with the babysitting, helping me with everything else while James was gone, and settling the new children in. Are you okay?"

Yulia avoided Mina's eyes for a moment. Then she said, "I am a little more tired lately. It feels like we came back and suddenly I'm working a full-time job. It's a lot more meaningful than going to school, but it's also definitely harder."

Mina nodded. "It's a lot, isn't it?"

"It is, but I can handle it," Yulia said, nodding with assurance.

"You need a break, though," Mina said. "That's what it sounds like."

"I'm okay—"

But Mina gave her a skeptical look, and Yulia stopped mid-sentence.

"Maybe," Yulia finally agreed.

"Well, you don't have to babysit right now—"

"Oh no, I *want* to take care of the kids," Yulia interrupted. "I'm just struggling with some of the other stuff. This will almost be a break. The kids are great, and Abhi helps out a lot with the younger ones."

"Well, you should make sure you talk to James about ways your life could be easier in the other areas when you meet with him later, then. Just be honest. Don't try to pretend everything is okay. I told him you wanted to discuss the commission. Are you sure you don't want to just take a nap or something? It's not urgent that I go out now."

Yulia reassured her that she was more than happy to take care of the children. And after a little more conversation, Mina handed James off to Yulia and left for the Dungeon.

Even if she hadn't known where the warehouse was, it would have been easy to find the Dungeon. The gaggle of two dozen humans loitering outside was a dead giveaway. There were even a handful of nervous-looking Goblins and a couple of Mole People walking up as Mina made it to the building.

Mina took a moment to appreciate what the Dungeon Core had done with the place before she spoke to anyone. Set down in the unfinished building they had been working on, Carol had actually completed the warehouse and put up a sign on the outside: "Carol's Storage."

It raised all sorts of questions in Mina's mind. *How do Dungeon Cores work? Is this place real? An illusion? A manifestation of Carol's Will? An extension of her body? How much control does she have? What happened to all of the items that were stored in the warehouse?*

"What's going on?" she asked the nearest person. "Is there a line?"

"Um, no, not exactly," the man said.

"Who's next?" asked one of the Goblins who had arrived at the same time as Mina.

The man Mina had spoken to seemed to feel obliged to explain, but also unable to actually do so. "That is—I, um—"

"There's no line," another man said. "I would say a few of us were trying to get our courage up to go in after the last group came out, but everyone who had the guts has already gone in and left."

"That's perfect, then," Mina said. "I'm next."

"You?" the Goblin looked her up and down with narrow, suspicious eyes.

"Hey, do you guys recognize her? I think she's the Queen!" another Goblin pronounced.

Mina couldn't tell the male and female Goblins apart from each other that well yet. Their skin coloration and hair growth were roughly the same across sexes. Only slightly more delicate facial features seemed to distinguish the women from the men. But she was fairly certain that both of the Goblins who had spoken were males.

"That's right," she said.

"Well, I guess we cannot object to our new queen going first," said the first Goblin reluctantly.

"She beat us here anyway," commented another Goblin with a feminine-sounding voice.

"I'll only be an hour at most," Mina promised. *The baby can't be apart from me for too long.*

"Are you going in by yourself?" asked the Goblin who had recognized her.

"That's right," Mina said. She had to live up to the image that James had established in these nonhumans' eyes. "I'm more dangerous than I look."

The Goblins' faces seemed to shift to a more respectful cast immediately.

"Of course you are, Your Majesty," the first Goblin said quietly. "I cannot imagine the King choosing a weak mate."

"Thank you for your willingness to keep it to an hour, Your Majesty," the feminine-sounding Goblin said. "We need to train ourselves thoroughly so that we will not be left behind the next time the King needs fighters to accompany him."

That remark summoned thoughts of James and the peril he might be in even now—images of him bleeding, crying out in pain, enduring broken bones—but Mina forced the images to the back of her mind.

Those thoughts weren't helping her, and they weren't helping James either. The best way she could support him was by finding a way to get stronger. A way to develop new abilities that might assist her in fighting the thing in the forest.

Mina drew her Alder Wood Wand from her Small Bag of Deceptive Dimensions and entered Carol's Storage with her mind firmly focused on what she wanted.

[Dungeon entered! You have arrived in Dungeon: Carol's Storage!]

The room just seemed like a large dark warehouse to Mina's eyes when she entered—almost empty except that there were some generic-looking wooden crates placed in strategic locations around the room.

How does this work? she wondered. *Can the place adapt to what I want? Hey, is this area larger on the inside—*

"Hi, there!" came a woman's voice from above.

Mina almost jumped at the sound of what must be the Dungeon Core speaking to her.

But she forced herself to speak. "Hello back to you, Carol. That's your name, right? Not just the name you put on the sign outside the building?"

"That's right!" Carol's disembodied voice was chipper. "What's your name?"

"I'm Mina," Mina replied.

"Oh, are you James's wife?"

Mina nodded. "I guess he mentioned me?"

"You're almost the only person he mentioned. I had no idea I'd get this much traffic. Welcome to the Dungeon! We've got fun and games." Carol laughed at her own slightly odd joke, and Mina smiled too. "Now, are you here to train or retrieve items from the warehouse?"

"Right now, I'm here to train," Mina said. "I actually had some specific requests in mind. I don't know if that's possible. As for retrieving items from the warehouse, um, I should probably set a password with you or something so that when someone other than me or my husband comes in, you know they have permission to take items out of here. I assume you can keep stored goods pretty secure in this place?"

"Oh, security's getting better all the time, for sure." Carol's voice rang with pride. "Signing on with you guys was, like, the best decision of my life! We can set up a password or something for the stuff in the warehouse. I should mention

I also have prizes for people who clear the Dungeon. And I have some flexibility on the types of threats you face in this place, the environment, et cetera."

Mina started explaining the little information she had on the spooky forest, and Carol listened in silence.

"So, you have some spirit-type enemies waiting for you, and you want to train and study to prepare for those?" Carol summed up at the end. "And you have a little less than an hour in which to do this right now, but you might be able to come back another day. You're especially hoping I could get you a spell book as your prize for winning."

Mina simply nodded.

"I'll go back to my settings and see if I can exchange my current monster type for something more spirit-like. That should be easy enough. You wanted a spell book that would help you deal with a whole forest of spirits, though . . . If I'm being honest, I don't know if I have access to anything like that yet. No, I'm pretty sure I don't. Um, would you prefer more diapers instead? Your husband seemed really interested in those."

Mina scowled.

"Maybe a set of upgraded Mage robes?" Carol asked.

The scowl deepened. "There's really nothing like the spell book I need available? No way to get it through the Dungeon?" Mina asked.

"Oh, I didn't mean to say I can't get it," Carol added hastily. "It's just that there are conditions, and I'm not sure how you're going to feel about them."

"Please tell me what you mean, and hopefully, I can work with you," Mina replied.

"Well, in order for me to get prizes that are that valuable, like decent spell books, I would have to expand this place to a multiple-floor Dungeon. That would allow me to increase the threat level of the Dungeon. If I do that, then you can get better prizes. I was planning to save up for expansion so I can try to present an adequate challenge to anyone who comes in. Obviously, if it's someone like you or your husband, I'm a pretty weak Dungeon . . ." She sounded sad and let her voice trail off before she snapped back to attention. "Anyway, I've already gotten a couple of levels out of the people who tried me earlier, which makes Dungeon expansions cheaper and easier, and I have some System Credits saved, but it's not enough."

"How much do you need?" Mina asked.

"To get a five-floor Dungeon, I would need about ten thousand System Credits unless I get an unexpected jump in levels. I have two thousand saved after my rewards from Orientation and from every group that's been through both the Dungeons I ran. I know it's asking a lot . . ."

Mina thought about it. She didn't have enough System Credits to afford this herself, but when James was back, she thought it might be worthwhile.

"How long would this take you to afford just by leveling up and earning credits?"

"A couple of months? Based on the level of traffic you guys are giving me, even assuming it slows down a little as people get less excited about having the Dungeon, we should be able to get there in three months at the outside."

"All right. I'll see about getting the funding together." Mina would really have preferred to do this without asking James, but she knew that he had been rewarded more for his Orientation victory than probably anyone else in their new nation. And he had saved it. He was careful that way. "For now, could you just get me the most challenging spirit-type monsters you can on this floor?"

"You've got it! One sec . . ."

The Dungeon seemed to grow even darker for a few seconds as if there was an energy source somewhere that was temporarily powering down.

Mina waited, and the darkness settled over her like a warm blanket. It almost made her want to go to sleep.

Then the room half-lit itself again with a soft, ethereal purple glow. The lighting seemed to emanate from the walls—or *almost* from the walls. As if there was a light source reflecting off of the surfaces that came from just out of view.

Spooky. She's definitely getting the mood lighting right.

"I guess the experience is starting," Mina said aloud.

There was no answer.

No verbal answer, anyway.

A timer appeared in the corner of Mina's vision and began counting down.

[00:40:00]

[00:39:59]

Then a glowing, translucent figure appeared, hovering at the border separating the area that Mina could see and the shadowy undefined space beyond.

Investigate.

The species was a Mischievous Phantasm, which seemed to explain the translucent glow.

Mina wasted no time before blasting it with a fireball. Casting with the Alder Wood Wand was both quicker and more impactful than using magic without it had been. The weapon seemed to fit her hand almost perfectly, and it even amplified her precision.

The fireball erased the Mischievous Phantasm in an instant, but the release of tension was brief.

In the back of the room, a column of Mischievous Phantasms appeared and began advancing toward Mina as if they were taking her more seriously than the first one had.

It seems like normal magical attacks work just fine against them, Mina thought. *Maybe there was nothing special to worry about.*

As the spectral creatures drew closer, she took aim and tried to carefully calibrate how much energy she needed for the killing blow, adjusting with each fireball she launched.

She attempted using water projectiles as well, but it didn't seem to work. They passed through the bodies harmlessly.

So, only some types of magic work on them. Maybe because fire emits light or something?

As Mina tried to figure out the best techniques for erasing the Mischievous Phantasms from the Dungeon, a few of them crossed an invisible threshold in the floor. Mina couldn't tell exactly where it was, but they reached a certain proximity to her, and the environment changed. The walls seemed to begin closing in.

Mina felt a sense of discomfort that she hadn't experienced since childhood, when one of her older cousins had locked her in a tiny closet as part of one of her cruel games. Such a dark, confined space . . . It was frightening for reasons she couldn't grasp.

As she froze up, the monsters inched closer. Four of them drew to within six feet of Mina. She blinked, took two deep breaths, and forced herself into action.

She charged several precision fireballs on the end of her wand and shot them almost rapid-fire. The closest monsters shattered on impact with the flames. And she kept going until all those in the room were dead. The sudden sense of claustrophobia faded with the Phantasms' destruction.

For a few seconds there was a silent emptiness.

This threat is not so different from what that forest seems to present after all.

A double column of Mischievous Phantasms appeared in the back of the room, and Mina refocused on getting the most she could out of the situation. Beating the Dungeon's monsters was only part of what she was here for, after all. She wanted to develop her tactics for facing this type of enemy more than anything else.

Mina created another rapid-fire group of fireballs, and she held them suspended around her body with her Will, waiting for the monsters to try some new trick, hoping they would show more of what spirit-type creatures could do.

As she stood waiting, a few of the Mischievous Phantasms began to flicker in and out of view.

So, they can turn invisible for brief periods . . . That definitely upped the threat level.

Mina aimed one of the fireballs toward where the closest Mischievous Phantasm was floating invisibly—or should be, based on its momentum before it had turned invisible. There was an impact! The Mischievous Phantasm flickered back into view and then disintegrated.

The other Mischievous Phantasms accelerated, suddenly moving at the speed of human sprinters. Half of them turned invisible as they did this.

Now this is more like it!

Mina tracked them with her eyes and memory, targeting the invisible creatures before the ones that remained in view. It was great practice in dealing with invisible enemies, at least.

She had to launch her fireballs based on where the phantasms *should be* rather than where she knew they were. But she eventually got into a rhythm where she knew their patterns well. They couldn't become completely intangible, so there was no danger of defeat. The only slightly scary thing, besides the effect they seemed to have on her if she let them get too close, was the occasional unpredictable, jerky movement.

One of the Mischievous Phantasms was particularly difficult to track with her mind's eye. It bobbed and weaved like it wanted desperately to survive and make it to within touch range. Mina ended up just hurling a dozen fireballs at it from multiple angles so that it could not escape. Killing that phantasm required more intense effort than fighting the others, but besides that phantasm, the rest were predictable. She was able to spare her energy.

The minutes passed quickly.

When the timer ran out, Mina was surprised.

The figures vanished from all around, and the room brightened. It was just a warehouse again. She realized her heart was pounding, but as her pulse settled, a smile crept over her face.

I did it!

[Congratulations! You have cleared Dungeon: Carol's Storage!]
[Sufficient experience accrued. Witch of Thessaly leveled up!]

"Congratulations on such a strong performance!" Carol chimed in. "I was a little scared at one point, when they were getting close to you, but then you blew them away!"

"Thank you for the opportunity," Mina said. "You were scared, though? Why?"

"Oh. Well, I guess I never explained to your husband, so you don't know either. When I start the Dungeon working, I don't really have the ability to stop it. I might be able to interfere a little bit, but I don't control the monsters."

Mina swallowed as she considered the implications of this. *In theory, this was as dangerous as anything I could have faced outside, then. I mean, Carol might have tried to avoid sending more dangerous threats than I could handle, but she had no way of knowing what that was, right?*

"Well, I'll have to keep that in mind next time I come," Mina said finally.

Regardless of how dangerous Carol made this place, she would certainly be back. Mina was not going to fall behind.

CHAPTER THIRTY-SIX

Duel, Part 2

James and the giant alligator arrived at the edge of the woods where James had gone hunting with the others days ago, the area that remained unclaimed by any Ruler's aura.

Once they had crossed over into that no-man's-land, they and their respective entourages spent a quarter of an hour clearing a large ring for their fight, flattening the ground with magic and pulling trees up by the roots. The humans did most of the reshaping of the earth, while the alligators used their strong bodies to wrestle the trees free from the soil.

Some of the people who had to work alongside the gators were visibly leery at being so close to the large reptiles, and James could tell the alligators noticed. He again felt slightly embarrassed that his side seemed a bit weaker and more vulnerable than the enemy.

The ground was much firmer here than in the swamp, to James's relief.

Samuel really shouldn't have agreed to fight me in a place like this, he thought. *Arrogance. Or is it honor? I suppose the result is the same either way.*

The audience left a buffer space between themselves and the ring large enough, per James's request, for Sewer Alligator Monarch Samuel to fall down at the ring's edge and not land on any spectators.

"Yes, this should work," James said. "I can't promise we'll keep the fight contained in here, but we'll do our best."

The giant alligator gave a toothy grin and shook his head.

"You're setting some high expectations, human," he said. "You'd better hope you don't disappoint me."

James just snorted, looking Samuel steadily in the eye.

Then Alan arrived, led by a wolf. They were moving faster than James would have expected. *Then again, I guess the situation sounds pretty urgent on paper.*

While Alan caught his breath, the wolf waited expectantly, wagging her tail. After only a moment of hesitation, James rewarded the monster with a physical display of affection, scratching under her chin and petting her on the head.

Just treat them like dogs, he thought. The nameless wolf's tail wagged even more forcefully as she basked in the glow of his affection.

"Thanks so much for fetching Alan, girl," James said as he showed his appreciation.

The wolf rolled onto her back to receive a belly rub, but James kept it short because the rest of the pack was looking on jealously. Alan was also staring wide-eyed at the giant creature that James was preparing to fight, wearing an expression that suggested he wasn't sure it had been a good idea to come.

James decided to get back on his feet and give Alan some reassurance. As he did so, the wolf he'd just been petting went over and started playing with some other wolves. They really were a lot like dogs.

"Thanks for making it, Alan," he said. "How are you feeling?"

"Jesus, James, you're really fighting that thing?" Alan asked, staring at the near kaiju-sized Sewer Alligator Monarch.

"I know, Alan, I know. But you can't blame the big guy for wanting to take on the champ. He thinks he has a shot at the belt. I promise I won't hurt him too badly."

Alan rolled his eyes but looked like he was restraining himself from laughing.

Samuel really is massive, though, James thought. *Could even be stronger than me. I might have to use my brain to win this one. At least I have a plan . . .*

"All the wolf told me was that you're fighting an enormous alligator and you thought you might need a Healer," Alan said. "Any additional information you want to give me?"

"Well, the Sewer Alligator Monarch said he wanted to conquer us, and he gave me the choice between having his army fight ours or having a one-on-one duel to decide who will be in charge," James said. "So, I picked the one-on-one duel. His army isn't very big, as far as I can tell, but I think we'd definitely lose some people in a larger battle. Whereas with you here, I don't think we'll even lose the big fellow."

He gestured at Samuel, and the big alligator bared his teeth in what James imagined was his version of a smile, raised one of his front legs, and waved at Alan.

"He's actually really sporting," James added. "Agreed to a bunch of very fair rules for the fight and waited to start until we had you here."

Alan looked back and forth between James and the giant monster for a moment, then pulled James aside.

"You're really gambling your whole kingdom on this one-on-one fight?" he said. "Level with me. Where is this confidence coming from? Is it just bluster? Arrogance? Or do you know something that backs it up? This monster is high level; I Identified it. Higher than the Goblin King or the Mole Lord. Are you sure you know what you're doing?"

James was quiet for a moment, and his expression sobered.

"Ultimately, the choice was between gambling on a one-on-one fight or having a small war," he said. "I came and tried to talk about building a relationship between our two territories, and Samuel immediately jumped to war. So, there wasn't that much choice. But I do have a reason to feel confident. I'm stronger than any human ought to be. I've fought monsters deadlier and more subtle than this one. And ultimately, he's a relatively smart, high-level lizard. I would rather not kill him if I don't have to, because I think it would be great to have him on our side. But I know at least three ways I could do it reliably. This isn't a question of me losing. My thinking about it has all been on the subject of *how* to win, not *if* I win. So, I had our four-legged friend come and get you because after I tear him apart, I need someone to put him back together alive. A taxidermy Sewer Alligator Monarch wouldn't do me much good, and his head is too big to put on my wall."

Alan looked back at James, and James knew instantly that the old man believed everything he'd said. *Even with the rings, it's always easier when it's true.* James really couldn't imagine himself losing to a big lizard.

"Good luck," Alan said. "You can do this." He squeezed James's shoulder and walked off to join the rest of the spectators.

Everyone that had been working on the ring finally moved back at that point, and the two contestants stepped in to fight. There was no mediator, no referee to say when they should begin or when their fight would end. Just two Rulers with egos that would hardly tolerate a loss.

"You can have the first hit," Samuel said. He looked cocky. And James could actually *smell* the aggression from where he stood at the opposite end of the ring.

He really did get excited for this fight.

James walked toward where the Sewer Alligator Monarch stood on all fours, and Samuel stepped forward to meet him. When they were finally close enough, James defied his instincts, which were telling him to stay away from the giant monster's jaw. He threw a hard, straight punch that struck the left side of Samuel's face.

Although James could feel that he hadn't given it as much power as he had initially intended—mainly because of the strange angle he was punching Samuel at—the hit still jerked the monster's head back. His front feet also staggered backward, though he managed to hold his ground with his back feet.

Samuel smiled again. "Not bad for someone so small."

Then he threw his counter: a swipe with his right front claws. James didn't try to dodge. The Sewer Alligator Monarch had given him a free shot, and James wanted to establish a sense of mutual respect. The blade-like claws caught James across the chest. They tore through the Royal Exoarmor with what appeared to James very little resistance.

He felt the pain a moment later, but it was faint. Barely enough to be perceptible through his high level of resistance. He could tell that the claws had left shallow cuts down his chest.

But James had kept his feet planted firmly on the ground.

"Good shot," he said, grinning.

Samuel gave a frustrated grunt. "Give me your best, then."

James launched himself off the ground with a full-force kick into the underside of Samuel's jaw that threw the alligator's head reeling back.

Samuel's jaw slammed down in the immediate aftermath, snapping wildly, trying to take a bite out of James's toes.

But James had already darted backward out of reach. *He's too slow*, he thought.

Then Samuel lunged forward, and James was diving and rolling under the monster's body. Samuel tried to raise a giant back foot to step on him, but James dodged to the side—and a dark-green blur smashed into the side of his head and sent him skidding across the ground.

The monster's tail seemed to be faster than the rest of him.

Holy shit! I actually felt that. This is great! A real challenge for the first time since I returned to Earth.

Samuel chased after him, but James leaped over the monster's body and landed behind him.

"Nice healing ability," Samuel grunted as he turned and tried to catch James with his jaws.

James kept himself oriented to the monster's tail, just out of sight despite its repeated efforts to twist around and catch him. He had already noticed that his cuts had closed up, but he was glad that Samuel had observed the same thing.

"Let's see how yours is," James said. He grabbed the monster by the tail and pushed up, throwing Samuel off balance so that he was performing an awkward handstand for a moment. Then James threw an Air Strike at the weaker-looking armor of its underbelly.

Samuel let loose a pained grunt.

James saw thick lines appear on the alligator's body and blossom with dark red bursts of blood. But the flow of blood was already slowing before gravity brought the monster back down to Earth.

Good healing, then.

Then Samuel was turning, faster than before, fueled by rage, jaws snapping, claws swinging and grasping. James danced out of reach, keeping only a step or two ahead.

"Cheap shot," Samuel finally grumbled as he slowed and calmed.

James was wheeling slowly to the side now, moving further from the edge of the ring the monster had almost chased him into, and Samuel followed him by turning his body.

"Anything goes, right?" James said.

"Right you are," Samuel breathed. **"Dominion."**

"Dominion," James replied.

The two auras fought a duel that James was certain he would eventually win. Samuel's Strength was at least as high as James's, but James was faster. Given that Samuel wasn't blowing him away in Stats, and that the monster had shown no magic prowess yet, James doubted that he could lose to the Sewer Alligator Monarch in a contest of Mana and Stamina. And those were the energies that combined to form the aura that Dominion emanated.

Samuel seemed to sense the same thing. He launched himself through the air at James—at a speed he hadn't reached before—and James used Lightning Strike to dodge, jumping above Samuel again. He aimed a Meteor Strike at Samuel's back with his foot, but the flaming kick glanced off like he was striking solid steel.

Need to get the underside again. He really didn't like that.

Then Samuel was sinking into the ground with James still balancing on one leg on his back. James realized the monster was using the environmental manipulation component of their shared power to turn the soil swampy.

But two could play at that game. James clenched his fist and exerted his power, and the earth all around them hardened again.

Samuel burst through the sedimentary prison, more annoyed than inconvenienced by the loss of control. As James tumbled from the monster's back, Samuel sprung at him, teeth gnashing, tail thumping against the ground.

The world seemed to slow down, and James took a moment to enjoy the situation he was in.

Honestly, when was the last time I felt this much tension during a fight? Roscuro frankly hadn't given him that. The only times he had really felt worried during that fight were when the Soul Eater was using Soul Magic or trying to kill hostages. Soul Magic was clearly deadly, which was why James wasn't using it now. But besides that, Roscuro had no probable way of killing him.

Here, every one of Samuel's attacks was potentially deadly. He had at least equal Strength to James—no, if James was honest, the alligator's physical brawn was greater than his, if only slightly. If this were just a wrestling match, Samuel would win at least seven or eight times out of ten.

But in fact, superior brain power and versatility are more important than brute Strength here.

As James fell through the air, he decided how to handle Samuel's furiously snapping jaws. His heightened awareness took in the alligator's movements, where Samuel's eyes were looking, the speed at which he was throwing himself forward, the monster's direction of travel, and the speed at which James himself was dropping. James could tell where the teeth would land.

Samuel clearly wasn't trying to kill James anymore than he was trying to kill Samuel. James decided to allow Samuel to land the attack. He began infusing Mana into his left arm—where Samuel's jaws were poised to strike.

The alligator gave himself one final push forward and intercepted James's body before he could touch the ground.

There was a sharp, wrenching agony and the grisly sound of bone separating and tearing away from flesh. Hot blood met dank, moist air and then spilled forward onto the ground.

As time seemed to catch up to him, James's body struck earth, missing one limb.

A searing pain ran through his left shoulder as Samuel roared in triumph.

CHAPTER THIRTY-SEVEN

Duel, Part 3

"You'll heal from that eventually, won't you?" Samuel asked, breathing heavily. There was an unmistakable air of triumph about him now that he had swallowed James's arm, though the monstrous alligator was clearly tiring while James maintained a high level of both Stamina and Mana.

If the struggle continued, it was clear James's aura would overtake Samuel's to dominate the space in which they fought.

"Naturally," James said through gritted teeth. Even with high-level Pain Resistance, it was hard to endure having a limb torn off. His left shoulder bone was visible now, white and jutting through the area where that arm used to be. To the audience, it must have looked a bit like a white flag of surrender. The mood in the crowd was palpable. James took it in through peripheral vision without looking away from his opponent.

Triumph from the alligators. Bitter resignation from the humans and wolves. Even Duncan and a few Mole People were observing the fight with defeated postures.

James's shoulder region gushed a gradually slowing fountain of red. James had ordered his body to diminish the flow of blood to that region, so he knew that soon the blood loss would stop completely.

"Good," the reptile said, looking relieved. "I would hate to think I've crippled you."

"I hope you don't think you've won."

Samuel's narrow reptilian eyes widened. "Isn't it over? You wouldn't fight on with one arm, would you?" As James just stared at him with grim determination, the monster laughed. "Are you *sure* you're human? I feel like you're one of us!"

There was a smattering of laughter from his alligators.

James finally had to grin himself. "I blur the line sometimes. But the fact is, I'm far from giving up. I can absolutely still win this. In fact, it's almost over." His eyes took on a faraway look for a split second. "Yep. You've already lost."

"Wow. That's quite a spirit." Samuel shook his head and stepped forward toward James. "When I conquer this continent, you will be my champion. I love this determination. I—" His jaw dropped in an alarmed expression, and his right forelimb clutched at his chest. "What have you done?" Samuel's voice came out as a painful rasp. Blood began trickling down the corners of his mouth.

"It's something you ate," James said darkly. "You see, I have an ability that allows me to turn my biological material into monsters that share my abilities." He ordered his visible shoulder bone to bend so that Samuel could see one of those abilities in action.

"What ability is that?" The monster spoke through gritted teeth, as if he hoped that might help keep some of the blood inside him, where it belonged. But the trickle intensified.

"Full Body Control," James replied. "Right now, my creature is moving around inside your digestive tract, perforating vital organs. Please give up so that I can stop this." For the first time in the fight, his tone and body language became conciliatory. He knew that if Samuel did not give up now, this would become a battle to the death whether they wanted it to be or not.

"You—*urk*—win." The words came out as a painful croak, but they were loud enough for everyone around to hear, nevertheless. The woods had gone as still and quiet as a cemetery.

Then Samuel's legs collapsed out from under him, and he slumped to the ground.

James immediately began receiving alerts, but he ignored them. First, he ordered his monster to stop killing Samuel. Then he approached the monster and began using Laying on Hands.

"Alan!" he called without looking up. "I need your help, please!"

The old man rushed over, breaking the paralysis that had fallen over the spectators.

Some mixed cheers broke out from James's side, and the wolves began to howl. But James focused his gaze entirely on the fallen Ruler.

"I can see now why you sent for me and not your little sister-in-law," Alan muttered as he arrived.

James nodded without looking up. "We try to spare her from seeing things like this."

Alan began applying Laying on Hands to James's shoulder, but James shook his head. "I don't really need it. I mean, my arm *wants* healing, but he needs it more. My arm would grow back eventually on its own."

"You're certainly something," Alan said. Then he joined James in healing the deadly internal injuries the former Sewer Alligator Monarch had suffered. During their whole interaction, James never looked away from the monster he was healing, the enemy who he intended to make one of his strongest champions.

We really aren't so different, you and I, James thought about Samuel. But even as he used part of his brain to think about Samuel, the main part of his intelligence was already far away, contemplating the next enemy.

The Ruler in the forest would surely be a trickier opponent. James had hoped that Samuel and the other Ruler would have had some tie, perhaps a tacit alliance of some sort, so that he could question the Sewer Alligator Monarch about the other Ruler after this fight was over.

But now that he had spoken and negotiated and fought with Samuel, James thought that was highly unlikely. The extremely direct approach that the Sewer Alligator Monarch brought to their interaction was refreshing and pleasantly surprising in contrast to how the forest Ruler had behaved thus far.

At least I have a swamp now. When Samuel had surrendered to him, James felt an instant change with his Fisher King senses: a doubling of the area of his sovereignty. Though James's aura did not extend over all the land yet, he could still feel his ownership of everything that had belonged to his opponent.

For comparison, when he reached out to touch items in his own Dominion, he felt them almost as if he were simply paying attention to ants crawling on his skin. When he sensed things now in the territory that had belonged to Samuel, it was a bit like touching things with an artificial limb. He could vaguely tell what was there, but the sensation was indirect. A distant awareness.

Samuel, it seemed, had been busy before James defeated him. James imagined he had probably killed another Ruler before to attain his high level and acquire so much territory.

Would the Ruler of the forest be similar in that respect? Bloated with raw power from previous conquests? James doubted that. The reason for the strange apparitions of the dead was probably to lure in the unwary. Which suggested that the Ruler preferred to lie in wait for prey rather than go invading others' territory.

"I think we managed it," Alan said.

"Hm?" James had lost himself in thought about the next battle.

"I think we've saved him," Alan said. "I can pour more Mana in, but I don't think it's doing anything anymore."

James realized that Samuel's breathing had changed—from the frantic, labored breathing of the dying to the more regular respiration of the merely unconscious.

"Well done, Alan," James said, giving him an appreciative smile.

"Let me see about your arm, then," Alan replied. He instantly turned his glowing hands on James's injury, though the shoulder stump had already grown an inch or two of flesh in the time they had been working on the alligator.

James did not resist. Instead, he reached out for the first time to the new population he had just become the Ruler of.

Can you hear me, Mutant Sewer Alligators? James sent. As with the wolves, his Usurper Title had granted him instant access to a telepathic group chat with his new allies. He wondered, as he sent the message, if he was going to encounter Mutant Sewer Turtles later, but did not have time to entertain the absurd thought.

We hear you—uh, new Ruler, sent one of the larger Mutant Sewer Alligators immediately. *Would you mind telling us, um, will former Monarch Samuel be all right?*

He should recover, James replied. *Could a group of you gather around here and prepare to carry Samuel back within what was formerly your territory? I suspect he will recover better in the swamp, which is still bathed in his aura, than outside it. He and I will talk further once he wakes up.*

There were multiple affirmative answers, and James detected a tone of relief. Even though he and Samuel had each promised to spare the other's people, he suspected that might not have been the alligators' actual expectation from him.

He remained pragmatic as always, though. And James thought that an alligator unit within his army would be much more useful than a bunch of alligator meat for the Fisher Kingdom.

The world went dark for Samuel.

It stayed that way for long hours. He had no concept of time while he was unconscious, but as he came to himself, his strong internal clock reasserted itself. He instantly remembered what had happened. He knew he had been beaten.

And badly, I would wager. Samuel reached out experimentally, trying to activate Dominion, but as he expected, the Skill was no longer there. *So, it really wasn't a bad dream. I got my tail kicked.*

The thought was less depressing than he had expected it to be. There was always someone better, after all. This reality, of being someone else's subject rather than the master of his fate and hundreds of others', was one that he knew he would grow accustomed to gradually. He would prove himself useful to this Fisher King—and perhaps rise in his esteem. Eventually be trusted. Be allowed the role of leadership over his own kind.

Samuel began taking a diagnostic of his own body, eyes still closed. Tail was still there. All four legs. Both eyes. Armor over his whole body was intact. He had lost a few teeth in the process of ripping his opponent's arm off as brutally as he had. And, of course, his insides were messed up.

Not as messed up as I remember them being, he dimly realized. *The pain should be sharper, fresher. This isn't exactly agony. It's a dull ache. An injury that's further along in healing than it should be.*

There was the very quiet sound of swimming near him, and his mind was pulled away from the condition of his own body. Samuel still had not opened his eyes, and he did not do so now. He had no need to look to know who was approaching.

"How are my children doing?" the former Ruler asked.

"See, I knew he was awake!" crowed Helga, Samuel's older daughter.

"I said so too!" whined Rowena.

"Girls, could you please ask him if he's okay?" Samuel recognized the voice of Salazar, his boy, from further away.

"If you wanted to check on him, you could've come over yourself!" Rowena called back.

"Children, please stop quarreling," Samuel said evenly.

"You all right, Pop?" Salazar asked.

"I won't say that I've been worse, because that would be a lie," Samuel replied. "I can tell that I'll recover, though. I really wasn't sure about that when I passed out. I guess your old man's still tough as an old boot, huh?"

"Well, the humans did heal you," Helga said quietly.

"Huh. So, I guess the Healer the Fisher King sent for came in handy after all."

"The fisher guy also helped heal you himself," Rowena said.

"Fisher *King*," Helga corrected.

Samuel wanted to stop them from arguing, but he found himself flabbergasted. "What, really? After I ripped his arm off? How was he in any kind of condition to heal anybody but himself?"

"You said he didn't seem human, Dad," Salazar said.

"Yes, son. That I did." Samuel thought about trying to fall back asleep, but the kids were talking again.

"The Fisher *King* said he was going to get in touch with you later, after you woke up," Rowena said.

"Oh, yeah?" Samuel said. "Well, perhaps he will later. I'm sure he is busy with many concerns. He had wolves and some other kind of nonhuman creature with yellowish skin working with him. Running a country with such a diverse population must be challeng—"

A voice rang out in Samuel's head. *I'm glad you survived that beating, Samuel.*

All right, Samuel replied instantly. *Fair.*

Yeah, the Fisher King's voice continued. *I enjoy gloating, but I will admit, you gave me a great fight. I've got to give you that. I think if I'd killed you, that hide of yours would have made some excellent new armor. Is it magic resistant?*

Samuel found himself nodding, then remembered that this conversation was telepathic. *Yes, it is! And you are the winner. You're the Ruler of the Sewage Swamp now. So, I guess if you want my hide, it's yours to take.*

Not at all, the voice replied. *I want you on my council. I just wanted to wish you a speedy recovery and say that, if you're well enough, I'd like to invite you to a meeting of my governing council the day after tomorrow.*

Your council?

Yes. I want you to advise me. If you're not interested, we can revisit that idea of me wearing your skin as armor, though. There are many ways you could contribute to the growth of the Fisher Kingdom.

Samuel snorted with laughter. *I'll be there*, he replied. *I heal pretty quickly, even without help. Thanks for your effort there, though. Meeting in your terri—uh, your preexisting territory, I assume?*

Yes. An image of a human building appeared in Samuel's mind. *We'll be meeting there. I'll warn people to expect a scary giant reptile to walk up. If you don't mind, I would appreciate you leaving the other alligators behind for this visit. People are taking baby steps toward getting used to a world with talking monsters and intelligent animals.*

I'm still getting used to humans being able to talk myself, Samuel sent.

He felt slightly nervous about the idea of treading into the Fisher King's territory alone, but he pushed the feeling away. This was all his territory now. If he meant to ambush and kill his new subject—well, couldn't he have finished him off in the ring already?

Anything else you wanted to ask me before I go to bed? The Fisher King's message carried a slight note of weariness for the first time.

What was your name again?

A moment of silence. Then, in an amused tone, *James.*

King James, one piece of advice before we go. You're a jack-of-all-trades sort of fighter, aren't you? You have magic and physical might. Your Strength is on par with mine, and you're fast too. The trouble with that is that other people will tend to outpace your progress in key areas. You're liable to fall behind. Before you know it, you've lost your edge.

Is that advice? Or a prediction of the future?

That was my post-fight analysis, Samuel replied. *My advice is this: never stop fighting. That's the best way—no, maybe the only way—you can stay ahead.*

I appreciate the wise words, James sent. *Rest well until our in-person meeting.*

Then the connection was broken.

CHAPTER THIRTY-EIGHT

Resignation

After James's arm had fully regenerated, he returned to the Fisher Kingdom. *It's nice to be back*, he thought, though this time he'd only been gone a matter of hours.

He saw his apartment and sighed. Before he continued home, he had another task to accomplish. He went around finding key members of the commissions that reported to him.

He was particularly concerned with speaking to people whose commissions had been lined up outside his door that morning. With security threats increasing over time, James thought it would no longer make sense for everyone to go to him with random problems all the time. Between that and invaders, he would have no rest if things continued that way. And people would start to doubt the efficiency of a monarchical form of government. He believed that most issues could be resolved within the various groups he'd formed, anyway.

So, depending on the commission and its existing dynamics, James either selected a representative or asked for the commission members to do the work of selecting a representative from each. That individual would meet with James and the other commission representatives each week in the community center. And in the meantime, he gave each commission some authority to act on its own behalf.

The Agriculture Commission would have broad authority to make decisions about which crops to farm, when to plant, et cetera.

The Building Commission would get broad approval from James about when and where to build—which, in practice, meant they would indirectly get approval from Mina—and then they would take care of any logistics themselves. James agreed to assign a few Mole People to assist them in choosing building sites that would be stable and not fall in on the underground dwellers' heads.

He made a similar arrangement with the Sewer Commission.

There were parallel discussions. James was very fortunate that he could easily find where people were on his land.

He had a very different conversation with Ari Christopoulos, one of the members of the Child Rescue Commission, in preparation for his meeting with Yulia later.

And he already knew the hunters were competent to act on their own and wouldn't trouble him unless they actually needed his help bringing down some inordinately difficult prey. Dave Matsumoto had already reported to him that their coordination and teamwork were improving.

So, the day wound down, and the Fisher King's responsibilities decreased just a bit. And his kingdom became that extra amount more like a pre-System country. He couldn't be certain yet whether that was a good or bad thing. Right now, it was a no-apparent-choice thing.

He had no particular ideological commitments, so he was simply sticking with what he knew worked.

James returned home, bathed, ate dinner with his family, and played with the children. While he bathed, he sent telepathic messages back and forth with his various nonhuman allies, including Samuel, the former Sewer Alligator Monarch. James's powers indicated that the monster had awoken.

What a monstrous recovery speed, he caught himself thinking. He wondered if he would have recovered as quickly if his internal organs had been similarly brutalized. Then again, he had never suffered injuries quite that desperate himself, as far as he recalled. His Orientation experience had been extremely violent at times, but he had only approached death a few times, and none of them had been quite as violent as what he had done to Samuel. If James had lost any fight that badly, he wouldn't have been given a chance to recover.

During the evening meal, James was only half-awake. He needed rest. But he nevertheless recapped the day's events to the family and tried to be his usual energetic self. When James discussed the duel with the Sewer Alligator Monarch, Mina rolled her eyes.

"I tell him to be careful, so of course he goes out wrestling alligators."

Everyone laughed.

After dinner and play, he put the children to bed and read a bedtime story to them from a book Abhi had picked out—he was the only one old enough to really appreciate the details of a story. *Collected Adventures of King Arthur and His Knights of the Round Table*. James wasn't clear if the book was one that Abhi had brought out of his old home, or if it was something the family had recovered from one of the other ruined buildings, but whatever the origin, he admired the taste. The book was even illustrated by a contemporary member of the Wyeth family in rich colors.

"I used to love these stories," James said. "The name people call me, the Fisher King, is actually from one of these legends originally. Or maybe the System influenced the way these stories were written somehow. Anyway, Abhi, you can pick which story I'll read to you all tonight."

"Okay." Abhi flipped through the pages until he came to an illustration of a man colored all in green. "This one!" he said.

James sat down in a rocking chair that had been salvaged from one of the wrecked apartments, and he began reading them the tale of "Sir Gawain and the Green Knight."

Abhi initially asked him lots of questions, while Indira pointed at the pictures, and Deepam and Junior just made satisfied gurgles and smiled when James looked at them. Gradually, all of them quieted as James's smooth voice soothed them and the story proceeded.

As James got near the end, he realized the children were all breathing fairly steadily.

They're asleep, he thought, slightly surprised. *I would've thought they would want to hear the end of the story.* But he was sleepy himself. He rose and saw one pair of open eyes follow him.

Little Abhi remained half-conscious, his eyes only half-closed.

"What's the end of the story?" he asked, almost slurring his words. "The Green Knight, what happened?"

"I'll finish it," James said, placing a hand on the boy's hair to try to keep him calm.

Then he resumed his seat and read the last few pages of the story. When he rose this time, Abhi was dead asleep. James wasn't certain of whether he had actually heard the ending or not.

It doesn't matter. I'll read it again tomorrow or next week. This is a good book.

Finally, as his last order of business, he sat down for his meeting with Yulia.

They pulled up some comfortable chairs that Mina had brought back from the Dungeon and placed in the living room. Sitting side by side, they each waited silently for the other to speak.

This is so weird, he thought. *Does it feel weird for her too? We're running a government, and our family is at the center of it. It's still so surreal that this is how things are working out.*

"I don't know how to get this started," Yulia finally said, clearly slightly embarrassed.

"Why don't we take stock of where we are?" James said. "We're meeting about the Child Rescue Commission, right?"

She nodded.

"Then we have a lot to be proud of. We've been very successful and done a lot of good. You've helped save the lives of a lot of children."

"Yes, I am very happy about that." Yulia smiled broadly, visibly growing more comfortable.

"I actually sent a message to my flying monsters earlier, and they helped me add up the numbers. A hundred and seventy-nine children. That's the count."

Yulia sucked in a breath. "Wow. That's incredible."

"I hope you're proud. It was your idea."

"That makes me very proud," she said. "But it reminds me that I should get to the reason I wanted to meet with you—what I wanted to discuss."

He waited.

"I—hm. I should update you on how we've been doing so far first. We matched every child with a family or a couple; though, by the end, some of them were unmarried couples. There hasn't been any trouble with that so far."

"I'm sure there will be some eventually, but when that happens, it won't be your job," James said. "I'm thinking about people to constitute a police force when we need that. Which will be soon. We have too many people now to get along without at least a small one."

"Yeah, I figured we would have that eventually." She shook her head as if she was still surprised that they were discussing how to form a government and new society, rather than waiting for the preexisting government to return and bring its version of law and order back into force. "But, um, more in my line of responsibility: I was wondering if—that is, I'm a little worried. If we have more kids coming, we might run out of families to take care of them. A couple of the others and I were discussing if we need a permanent building, or something, and people on rotating shifts looking after children."

"What are people doing about the kids so far when they're working?" James asked. "We don't have schools anymore, right?"

"Since the flow of new children slowed down, some of us have been spending the day taking care of groups of kids sorted by age. People can do that because the hunters distribute food to everyone, so we don't all have to go out foraging for ourselves."

James simply nodded. That was what he had discussed with the hunters when he was laying out responsibilities initially.

"What I'm wondering is—well, a few things. I don't know if we can sustain this with more children. With more kids, this would be very demanding."

"That's not something you have to worry about," James said. "I intend to make Child Rescue a larger group and shift the purpose toward education. And probably change the name. It can't be 'Child Rescue' if that's no longer the main purpose. And 'Child Welfare' has a lot of negative associations for people who interacted with similarly named organizations before the System." He shook his head. "We'll come up with something. Anyway, people will probably take care of their own babies for the most part. But the kids who are old enough should be in school, or at least learning something. The curriculum will naturally start to be different with the world so different, but I don't see any reason why they wouldn't learn reading, writing, and arithmetic at least. We'll probably put a much greater emphasis on physical education than we did when I was in school—but that's something I'm going to work out with some people who are into education: teachers, professors, historians, a lot of professionals. We'll do our best to get a decent system in place for this."

She looked at him curiously. "I thought you were going around earlier trying to give away responsibilities."

"I was, but new ones will present themselves too, whether I like it or not. And until I find out how to displace that responsibility onto someone else—" They both laughed. "Seriously, though, if there's something that we know is important, someone has to do something. Like you, worrying about saving hundreds of children you'd never met before." He smiled at her warmly, and after a moment she smiled back. "I think education is one of those things. It's made a big difference in my life. I think it's been a big deal for you too. I think of it as something that's important whether we want to deal with it or not. People in many different places and times have used it to take control of the youth, to bend their minds one way or the other. If no one does anything with it, someone will slip into that vacuum and offer their services."

Yulia's expression turned slightly suspicious. "And what are you going to be doing with it?"

"Well, don't look at me like that," he said, his expression playful. "Of course, I'm just going to make sure that our schools are teaching true and useful information. Along with trying to establish a sense of community responsibility and respect for other people, whether human or otherwise, and their rights."

"I think, um—I think I'm glad that I'm done with school," she said, eyebrows raised very high.

"Gosh, I guess I'd better sell it better to the public."

They both laughed.

"Yeah, I think so. How is this going to work, though? You're changing the mission, but we'll still need to take care of children who get rescued and match them with families?"

"Not exactly," James said. "There's no easy way of saying this, but I don't think there will be much need for people to look out for future children being rescued."

"What do you mean?"

"The monsters stopped finding new kids. You probably noticed that the flow slowed down to a trickle."

She bobbed her head up and down as he spoke.

"I spoke with one of your commission members just because I had a suspicion about why this was happening—the disaster relief guy who used to work for FEMA?—and he confirmed what I was thinking. It's now been several days since this disaster hit. After an emergency like this, any children are already rescued or dead by now. If they didn't have adults near them when they came back, it's unlikely they'd have survived this long. So—"

"So, we're giving up on any children remaining, then?" Yulia interjected.

"Yes." James nodded. "There's no point in denying it. We are. It's possible more survived, but it's unlikely. We have to be pragmatic. I already have dozens of monsters in the sky, but they aren't finding more kids, and I know there is some limit to the number I can control at once. There's no other practical path forward unless we want to wholly devote ourselves to saving people. And if we did that, then we'd sacrifice ourselves."

"How would we be sacrificing ourselves just by continuing to look?" Yulia's voice didn't sound angry, James noted. Just sad. Resigned.

"There are other projects that these monsters should be taking care of," James said. "I just fought with a potential invader. Fortunately, it became a one-on-one duel. If he had decided to rush at our borders with his army, dozens of people might have died. So, a lot of the monsters will be spying, working to detect invaders before they get so close to the border. Others will be working on gathering valuable resources from the territory that we don't control yet."

These resources included books. James was hoping to establish the world's first post-System library. It would be an especially positive thing for the children. And in a world without Internet or even electricity, who knew when and where else they would even have the opportunity to read?

He didn't want to mention this specific priority to Yulia, though. If she was still imagining finding more lost children, she wouldn't understand why he wanted to start looking for books. James was certain enough for his own satisfaction that he wasn't going to find more surviving children by sending his monsters searching in further random directions, and he wasn't interested in starting an argument or upsetting Yulia any more than he had to.

"I guess I understand," she said, clearly sad.

She fell silent, but he could tell that she still had something she wanted to say, so he simply waited.

"Is it terrible that I'm sort of relieved?" she asked.

"About?"

"I was just starting to imagine what would happen if this place was overflowing with children. More than we could take care of. And I was worrying about the logistical nightmare. I'm kind of relieved that the Child Rescue part is over. Does that make me a bad person?"

James shook his head immediately. "No. You're a great person, Yulia. Most people wouldn't be thinking about strangers' children in the first place. Thanks to you, we rescued hundreds of kids. And I'm going to make sure that everyone here grows up knowing that you did that. What you just told me didn't change what I think of you at all. We all have thoughts like that. What matters in life isn't what you think about doing when you're under pressure. What matters is what you actually do."

Yulia broke out into a smile. "That sounds like a line from a movie. 'What matters is what you actually do.' But it does make me feel better."

"That brings me to my question for you," he said.

She waited.

"I know you have been doing a lot for the Child Rescue Commission. Whenever you're not here with me or Mina and the kids, you're working for them."

Yulia nodded, a slightly weary expression on her face.

"How are you feeling doing all that?" he asked.

"I'm just fi—no, I guess I'm pretty tired. I'm glad I can help, though."

He nodded. "That's about what I'd expect, honestly. I believe it's too much for any one person to be responsible for a leadership role and what you might call a 'frontline role. I didn't intend to give anyone both of those kinds of responsibilities at once, but somehow, I did that to you. You're doing too much, I think. You'll burn yourself out."

She simply sat there, not saying anything, but James read agreement in her facial expression and body language.

"So, I wanted to ask you: do you want to continue being one of the leaders of the group? Or focus on being one of the people who takes care of children? Whether that's daycare, teaching, or whatever. Or do something else? Or possibly none of the above? If you want to try to be a leader and do additional work, we can keep on trying that, but—"

She was shaking her head, so he stopped. "No," she said. "I asked you about this in the first place because I was worried about what was happening to the children out there. And I stayed involved to be responsible"—she hesitated—"and because I like children. I want to work with the kids. Let someone else be the leader."

"Okay," James said, smiling slightly. "I'm pretty sure there will be a few volunteers."

This was what he had expected Yulia to choose.

"You still want to be a teacher, right?"

Yulia had gone back and forth between different professional aspirations pre-System, though all of her preferred jobs involved working with children.

She nodded.

"Now that you've officially resigned from your role as one of the leaders of the Child Rescue Commission, I have a feeling the governing authority is going to approve you for the job."

They both smiled.

The conversation moved on to lighter subjects from there. Yulia and James discussed the children—mainly how Abhi was adjusting. He was still missing his parents, naturally, but he was also behaving more comfortably, in Yulia's opinion. He was coming out of his shell.

Finally, James and Yulia said good night. James joined Mina and Junior in their bedroom, and the entire Robard household went to bed.

All was calm and still for an hour or two.

Then James was awakened by screaming in the night.

CHAPTER THIRTY-NINE

What Dreams May Come, Part 1

James bolted upright in bed.

The sound of screaming echoed in his ears, and he knew in an instant that this wasn't something he had simply dreamed up. He half-turned from lying on his stomach to lie on his side. He was in that half-wakeful state when one wonders if it might be possible to go back to sleep instead of continuing along the path toward full consciousness.

Then he heard a fresh noise of renewed cries in the night. There was no going back. James rose from the bed where Mina and Junior still lay sleeping. He moved slowly and silently so as not to wake her or the baby.

He walked to the door, opened it quickly and delicately—almost soundlessly—and passed into the less private parts of the apartment. And he moved just in time.

No sooner did he have the bedroom door closed behind him than he heard a pounding from downstairs. An urgent fist beating against the front door.

James leaped down to the ground floor and opened the front door in a couple of smooth, brisk motions.

Damien Rousseau and Jeremiah Rotter stood at the doorway. Damien had a hand raised for another knock. Behind them, James noticed a dozen people standing in various states of dress. They looked disheveled, tired, and anxious.

"Good evening," James said. "What's up?"

"We had a bad dream," Damien said.

"We?" James asked. He looked past Damien and Rotter to the gathered individuals.

People nodded in response.

James sighed, stepped outside, and closed the door behind him.

"One of you who feels clearheaded, explain what happened," he said.

There was some hesitation. The gathered men and women looked at each other. No one seemed interested in volunteering. Finally, Rotter let out a long breath and began to explain.

"I assume you know that some of those who have strayed too near the hostile neighboring territory"—he gestured at the wall James had erected—"have experienced unpleasant visions."

James nodded.

"Well, some of us, whether we had actually looked in that direction or not, have had *visitations* in our sleep tonight," Rotter said. "Not just tonight—the last several nights, but it's been escalating every night. Tonight was the worst. None of us could sleep. The dreams were just too terrible. Some of them are the same dream. Most of them are not exactly identical. I—honestly, I would rather not describe my dreams if it's all the same to you."

James shrugged. "I don't need to know the details," he said.

If I do, I'll just enter your dreams.

"Well, it's clear that whatever lives in that forest is reaching out beyond its borders. Showing us things we would rather not see: our deceased loved ones suffering or crying out for us, visions of dark futures. Or the creature in there tells us horrible lies, whispering in our ears slander about the people we see every day." Rotter seemed very reluctant to elaborate any further, and James was surprised Rotter had managed to go into the degree of detail that he had. "Frankly, I hate to ask this of you, but I don't think people are going to be able to sleep unless you do something about this."

Well, of course I'm going to do something about this, James thought irritably. But he didn't let the emotion show through on his face. He assumed Rotter was trying to present it in this way because he was accentuating James's potential heroism in saving them from the threat.

"I'll try what I can," James said, speaking loudly enough for all the gathered people to hear. "And if what I try doesn't work, we might have to invade that fucking forest tonight. Is there anything else I should know before I go and confront the threat?"

"Just one thing," Damien said, speaking in a low voice. "She was asking for you. The thing in our dreams. At least that was what she said in my dream. 'Bring me the Fisher King.'" He shuddered.

"All right," James said quietly. "All right." He was trying to reassure himself almost as much as Damien. There was a little sliver of fear working its way through his brain and into the rest of his body: the beginnings of the notion that perhaps he could not handle this creature. The dark night played into this. The unknown nature of the entity. The fact that she was targeting him specifically.

He banished the fear as best he could. *I am the strongest. It was foolish of this thing to challenge me on my turf. She's invading the Fisher Kingdom, and she's moving in dreamspace.* Perhaps this would mean he could even destroy her without entering her forest.

He gestured brusquely for the gathered individuals to give him a little space; he was acting a little more impatiently than normal. And then he sat cross-legged, back against the exterior wall of the building.

Dreamwalk.

Instantly, he found himself in the dark void he knew as dreamspace. He felt the dreams of everyone in the Fisher Kingdom in an instant. He could identify their locations and even a vague idea of what they were dreaming about more easily than he had ever experienced before, without trying to touch their dreams individually.

The combination of his Fisher King powers with his Dreamweaver powers seemed to be exceptionally potent. He didn't even need to reach out to recognize that he could alter the contents of his citizens' dreams with hardly a thought.

The ultimate brainwashing tool if I wanted to go that route. A dark thought. One he would hopefully never act on.

More to the point, he also immediately sensed another entity dwelling in the same space with him. Self-aware and in control of itself. Malevolent.

James visualized the borders of the Fisher Kingdom, and he recognized where the entity was and the shape it had taken. The thing wasn't near his location within dreamspace, but its glowing, ethereal tendrils were all around him.

It seemed the form of the enemy was squid-like. Long tentacles reached out to scores of dreams, and James sensed the visceral discomfort of the dreamers. Men, women, and children—scores of his citizens were in a state of fear or discomfort. The thing in the forest was sending them disturbing nightmares.

He could not sense the forest thing's mental state, exactly, but he imagined that it must be enjoying this. There was no reason to pick a fight right now, as far as he could see. This *would* weaken the Fisher Kingdom somewhat by undermining the well being of some of its residents. But James felt almost certain that the reason was sadism.

If it wanted to just weaken the Fisher Kingdom for an attack, it would go after me or Mina, or maybe someone else critical to our defense like Damien, but not Rotter or the other random grab bag of people who showed up at my door. It wouldn't attack so many people at once. Instead, the approach was so scattershot that some managed to wake themselves up and escape.

James was glad that none of the tendrils went into his own home. The thing had chosen not to attack any member of his household—though, considering the number of people who now lived with him, that was rather peculiar.

Were you trying to stay under the radar? Hide from me? That might imply that this thing knew what James's abilities were, or at least knew about his Dreamwalking.

Stop psyching yourself out, he chided himself.

He deactivated Dreamwalk and opened his eyes.

Then he rose to address the crowd. Even more people had gathered to watch him in silence while he was sitting on the ground. *At least twenty. No, twenty-five.* But he didn't waste much time counting.

"I found the root of the problem," James said. "I'm going to attack it within the world of dreams. Everyone here, please return to your homes, wait a few minutes, and then go back to sleep. I'll make sure you're not disturbed again. You'll need your rest. Tomorrow, we might need to start planning an invasion of that forest!"

A low cheer went up, but the space quickly turned silent again. Part of the reason for the sudden quiet was undoubtedly the night. People didn't want to wake their neighbors. But James worried that part of it was the subdued mood.

A few words weren't enough to restore their morale. These people had just experienced being attacked in their sleep when they had assumed they were safe. For some of them, it was probably the first time they had felt safe in weeks or months.

I'm responsible for them, he thought. *I'm the only one who can restore the sense of normalcy for everyone. Let them experience the benefits of me being in charge.*

James sat back down. No further words would help the situation. No matter how skillful and charismatic he might think he was, at a certain point, you just had to deliver.

Dreamwalk.

James found himself in the same place again.

This time, rather than simply observing, he leaped into action.

He envisioned a sword in his hand, and the weapon materialized. A black blade. Featureless in the darkness, but, he knew, immeasurably sharp.

Then he set about dealing with the invasion by hacking and slashing at the ethereal tentacles that had wormed their way into people's dreams.

Fortunately, his conjured sword had real physical presence and power in dreamspace. It actually cut through the long supple limbs of the invader, and they recoiled at the touch of the blade.

He was glad he could do the work from the outside. If he had to enter each person's dream and fight the evil there, he wasn't sure he would be done before morning. And he had reassured everyone that he was taking care of the threat.

As he slashed through the fifth tentacle in his territory, James saw the rest of the tendrils beginning to pull away, retreating from the dreamers' bodies.

Giving up, he thought. *Good. I was hoping I wouldn't have to do this all night.*

Then he saw where the tentacles were retreating to. Somehow, without James noticing it, a dark figure had crept up almost to where he had positioned himself in the void. The ethereal tentacles were all pulling back into that body.

James took a good look and tried to understand the nature of his enemy.

It was a towering feminine figure with no legs. The lower body ended in a sort of haze, like the body of a genie or ghost from a cartoon. He finally made out the face through the veil of shadow that concealed most of the figure's features. From the forehead to the chin, it was pale and white as bleached bone. An old woman's face, twisted in an expression of sadistic glee.

He tried to use Identify, but it yielded no result.

Of course. We're not really here, *either of us. I'm still in my body, leaning up against the building. And she's still in the heart of that forest somewhere.*

"You must be the Fisher King," the figure said in a voice that pierced right through him. A mirthless voice that had the rhythm and feel of a cackle.

"Where did you hear that name?" James asked evenly.

"Oh, the birds and the rodents speak it. Also, the wind and the trees. Do you deny that you are the Fisher King?"

"No," he replied. He resisted his ethereal body's desire to shudder. There should be no physical sensations here, no reflexes like that—even if her piercing, half-laughing voice did send cold shooting through his whole body. "Why would I deny who I am in my own kingdom? I'm not the trespasser."

"Oh, how charming." The figure covered her mouth. "I am not truly in your kingdom, though I understand the sense in which you mean that. I have reached out to *touch* some of your subjects."

"Who are you?" James asked, his voice tense. "What do you want?"

"I am a Ruler as well, Your Majesty." She gave a mocking bow. "Before I attained my throne, I was called Sister Strange. Since you and I are of equal stature, feel free to call me by that name."

"And you wanted . . . ?"

"I want nothing more than human suffering." She let loose a horrible laugh along with her words. "*Your* suffering will be especially exquisite."

Suddenly, the tentacles that she had withdrawn from all the dreamers around James reemerged from her body and sprang upon James. He had a fraction of a second in which to react, and he chose to pull his arms in closer to his sides and keep the best hold that he could on his sword.

The tentacles wrapped him tightly from all sides. They did not feel as he would have expected. Rather than sliming their way up and down his body or clinging to him with suckers, they almost caressed his skin—like thousands of feathers. It was uncomfortable but far from unendurable.

"You can't possibly think these can hold me, Sister Strange," he said mockingly. "Sadly, your power is inadequate for that." He flexed the muscles of his ethereal body and pushed the binding limbs away.

Curiously, the monster did not try to bind him again.

"I did not think you would resist," she said thoughtfully, "understanding as you must that it is a choice between your suffering and that of your people."

"Or I could destroy you," James replied. He lashed out with the black sword and sliced through the figure's neck, severing the head from the body.

"You have not faced someone else in this place before, have you?" asked the severed head, almost laughing again as it phrased the question.

CHAPTER FORTY

What Dreams May Come, Part 2

James watched with grim stoicism as the severed head reattached itself to the monster's body.

"I guess that wasn't the right method to destroy you with," James said evenly. He began charging Soul Magic, but then he immediately stopped. He could feel the Mana was concentrating in his physical body, the one leaning up against the wall of the apartment, not the astral form he presented here.

So, I can't use magic here? He had shown Mina some magic in her dream back in Orientation, but that had been a more solid environment—and the magic had not done anything. It was only a demonstration of how magic could be used. *Maybe magic only works in the physical world. Or I haven't figured out the trick for using it here yet . . .*

"I hope you have something better in reserve," Sister Strange said, her voice ringing with mocking laughter. The sound pierced his ethereal form with sharp, chilling vibrations.

"I will destroy you," James said, his voice filled with hate.

"I have four visions of suffering to show you," Sister Strange said, her voice suddenly matter-of-fact, still piercing but no longer infused with her usual ringing echo of near laughter in every syllable. "They are of suffering past that *has been*, suffering present that *is*, suffering future that *must be*, and suffering future that *may be*."

"You should be most concerned about your own future suffering," James said. "When I reach your body in the real world, I'll make sure you die painfully. You shouldn't have invaded my territory."

"That may be," Sister Strange replied, her voice strangely and disturbingly even. "Even so, I have four visions to show you. If you are not capable of destroying me *at this moment*, you must choose."

"Or else?"

A thousand thousand tendrils sprouted from Sister Strange's body in response to his question.

"I am an expert in the realm of dreams," she said, her voice full of that mocking amusement that so infuriated him. "Perhaps I have more practice than you. In any case, I can maneuver in this space better than you can. Either you will suffer my visions or they will." She pointed her hand at the vast emptiness behind James. The space where his people were, with their vulnerable dreams, their bodies tucked into bed safely—or so they thought.

"A sadistic choice," he said.

He lunged across the gap between them and placed his hand on her body, using the other Skill he had gained when he had stolen Roscuro's Soul Eater Talent.

Soul Bind.

Soul Magic and Soul Bind.

Unlike Soul Magic, he had never seen this one used, but it should bind Sister Strange's soul. In practice, what he understood that to mean was that he could freeze her in place—though, he would have to engage in prolonged physical contact first.

Sister Strange whipped at him with her tentacles, but he ignored them and simply kept his grip on her body. Then the tendrils wrapped around his body. She forced his head up with what seemed to be all her strength and locked eyes with him.

"I do not need freedom of motion to share my vision with you," she hissed.

The environment around James faded and shifted.

He found himself in what looked to be a small, musty bedroom. The room was in what appeared, from the furniture and style, to be an old, abandoned mansion. There was a window at one end of the room and four open doors at the other. The open doors seemed to have only darkness on their other sides.

She pulled me into a dream?

"Choose a door or one will be chosen for you," Sister Strange said.

James leaped at the window and beat his fists against it, but his physical power seemed to have no effect. His hands bounced off the surface like it was made of rubber.

And then the room began, impossibly, to contract. The window and the wall it was embedded in pushed against James, then dragged him backward toward the open doors.

Dream logic. Of course the room can contract. Fuck!

James closed his eyes and tried willing the room to reverse and grow instead, but the environment here did not obey him. Perhaps his powers only worked on the dreams of those who did not have dream abilities of their own.

The wall felt simply physical to him, as if this was no mere dream; yet, while his eyes were closed, he felt more aware of his astral body. It seemed that in addition to the self that was in this dream and the self that was slumped on the ground outside of his apartment, the astral form that had been using Soul Bind on Sister Strange was still out there in dreamspace holding her in place.

That was gratifying. *At least she can't torment anyone else while she has me here, unless I'm misunderstanding her powers.*

James turned and faced the doors. Four doors for four visions the specter wished to show him.

He decided not to give in to fear and not to resist this place. Perhaps he would learn something new if he chose the correct door.

Sticks and stones may break my bones, but visions can never hurt me, he thought stubbornly, filled with an almost manic energy. *Even if they show me death and destruction, I have no reason to think it's the end in this universe. There are gods and underworlds aplenty if what Anansi told me is true. The end of life is simply another adventure. Even if I lose everything . . . It's possible that nothing is ever truly gone.*

James's wild thoughts distracted him for a few seconds while the contracting walls pushed him forward. Finally, he leaped ahead into the closest door, the second from the right.

From a dark and disgusting room, James found himself suddenly in a bright white environment. He turned his head just in time to see the door disappearing behind him.

Of course.

Everything that had been dream-like and fuzzy about the mansion environment swam instantly into sharp relief. Now he was in a place that felt completely real. More solid and distinctive than real places, even.

James looked around. He found himself in a land of snow and ice.

Not as cold as it should be based on the way it looks, he assessed.

The air was chilling, but it touched James only at a remove. He stepped forward and saw that his foot had left no indentation in the snow.

That settled it. He was observing this place, but he was only halfway *in* this place. He probably couldn't affect what was supposed to happen here.

Where the hell am I supposed to be, though? Canada? Scandinavia? Siberia?

He heard noise from behind him and turned to look—and saw *himself*.

This version of James wore an unfamiliar armor set and a cape, but Present-James tore his attention away from Vision-James and looked at the other person present in this desolate place.

Vision-James stood opposite a figure who wore green armor that seemed to cover every inch of his skin.

Present-James watched closely as his alternate self attempted to fight the warrior in green with little success.

Vision-James threw punches, Meteor Strikes, Lightning Strikes, and blows with Roscuro—who took the form of an axe in the vision—at the armored figure. The green fighter blocked some blows and simply allowed others to hit him with no apparent effect. He answered some strikes with counterattacks: heavy blows to Vision-James's head, knees, and ribs. The warrior in green had a sword at his hip, but he didn't bother to draw it.

Present-James found that irritating, though he was more preoccupied by how badly Vision-James was losing the fight. His armor was quickly bent or broken in a hundred places, and Present-James began to hear the sounds of cracking ribs and other fractured bones as Vision-James struggled to stay in the fight.

The warrior in green was fighting very efficiently—Present-James found himself reluctantly admiring the fighting technique—but extremely violently.

After one particularly vicious exchange, Vision-James coughed up blood. The warrior in green, by contrast, seemed slightly winded but otherwise completely unhurt.

Vision-James said something, but the sound for dialogue in this vision of the future was apparently turned off, and the armored figure moved so as to block Vision-James's mouth from Present-James's view, preventing him from reading his ostensible future self's lips.

Is this supposed to be the future that will be, *or one that might be?* Present-James wondered.

Vision-James started charging Soul Magic, and only then did the green figure actually take some evasive action. He dodged a blast of magic from Vision-James, then swept Vision-James's legs out from under him.

So that's a weak point, Present-James thought. *He's vulnerable to me attacking his soul, at least.*

At that point, the warrior in green armor seemed to stop holding back. The fight turned into a brutal, one-sided beating. With his gauntleted hands, the figure punched Vision-James in the chest and body over and over. Vision-James raised his arms to defend himself, but they were smashed to bloody broken stubs under the onslaught.

Present-James saw Vision-James's fingers bent and broken, and he winced in sympathy. He saw Vision-James's face and chest cavity smashed and bloody, and he wondered if this was meant to be a vision of how he would die.

Some context would have been nice, unless this is meant to be unavoidable.

By the end of the struggle, Vision-James was embedded in a man-shaped hole in the snow.

I've seen enough now, Present-James thought. But then the vision showed him one more interesting thing.

The man in green walked around and knelt beside the snowy hole. He leaned down and stuck his head into the hole. The best that Present-James could figure, the man seemed to be putting his ear to Vision-James's chest.

As the figure rose from his position, he said something to himself. Present-James saw his lips and was able to read a snippet of what the warrior was saying.

"—still alive."

Then a jeweled armband around the warrior in green's arm glowed a gentle golden color, and suddenly, the figure disappeared completely.

Well, at least I apparently fucking survived. Jesus Christ.

The vision faded, and James was left with countless questions. But before he could even formulate them, he was in a new setting, floating in the air and looking down.

At least this place felt more familiar. James recognized the humidity in the air, the types of trees in the background, the swampy ground in some areas below him, and the style of clothing of some people he saw. He was back in Florida.

And that was the extent of his familiarity with the background. The terrain could be anywhere in the state. Someone had built a new city. It was beautiful.

If I saw a city like this, I would want to copy it, he thought.

A thousand shapes that looked like kites flew over the city, dancing in the wind and sunshine.

There were great towers made from types of metal and stone that he could not recognize by name. There were thousands of multi-story houses and apartment buildings made of stone and painted in a thousand shades of blue-green with red roofs. There were dozens of majestic temples that James knew at a glance were built to honor gods from many different cultures. The city streets were broad avenues laid out in a circular pattern and set with unusually uniform cobblestones. The city's main street was set between what looked to be the rib bones of some massive, dead creature. Long rectangular ponds with lily pads lined the street as well beneath the ribs.

The city was active with a mix of human and nonhuman activity. People and nonhumans he didn't recognize walked around, mingled freely, and seemed friendly and happy to move amongst each other.

There was greenery everywhere in the city. Trees and plants blossomed anywhere where a building did not sit, as if the entire city were a park. When he inhaled, he realized there must be a citrus grove somewhere. The air smelled of lemons and oranges. It reminded him of his grandmother's garden when he was a child.

There was a large doorway set in a hillside, which James guessed led underground.

The city's centerpiece was a massive building, which James could only imagine was a palace, connected to another building that looked like it had been stolen from ancient Athens.

Then James saw a building he recognized, and his jaw dropped.

It was the community center, though much enlarged and now sporting an image of a spider on the exterior.

Which means that either someone in the future stole my building, or this is my city. It had to at least be built where the Fisher Kingdom currently existed.

Then James saw someone he recognized stepping out of the community center.

It was Mina, dressed in a beautiful regal gown and holding a little girl's hand. James didn't recognize the little girl, but he saw a little of himself and his family's traits in her.

So, we have another kid in the future.

James began silently praying without having a particular god in mind.

Don't let this vision be about them . . .

CHAPTER FORTY-ONE

What Dreams May Come, Part 3

Soon James's desperate prayer gave way to an ugly reality.

A mass of people entered the city from several directions, all brandishing weapons and moving with a sense of urgency, heading toward Mina and the little girl she had with her.

The interlopers' faces were covered in a gray haze, but James could see that there were people of all human racial backgrounds, men and women. And they all seemed violently angry with Mina. It seemed unlikely that she was the real object of their fury to James somehow. Mina could be stubborn, sarcastic, and occasionally had dark moods, but she was too lovable for him to imagine anyone sincerely wanting to kill her.

Were these people angry with James? At war with the Fisher Kingdom?

Whatever their motivations, they swarmed into the city by the hundreds.

The Fisher Kingdom seemed to awaken from a slumber of some sort. People rushed out of buildings and moved to fight off the invaders. Goblins, wolves, alligators, and Mole People began joining the human defenders. There were other creatures James did not recognize fighting alongside them: little blue-skinned people, toad-like creatures, and multiple other unfamiliar Races that James couldn't name.

For a brief time, the forces of the Fisher Kingdom countered the unexpected attack effectively. Unexpected sinkholes began appearing beneath some of the attackers. Others got mauled by Mole People, stabbed to death by Goblins, or turned into chew toys by the wolves or alligators. The toad-like creatures spat acid bursts at the enemy, and Mina threw bursts of fire and lightning while levitating above the city.

The tide seemed to be turning. Humans faltered and tried to fall back under the weight of the defenders' power. James let out a breath he hadn't realized he had been holding as he watched.

Then reinforcements arrived.

It seemed the initial onslaught of people might have been just a scouting party because the original group was like a few drops of rain before the deluge. Tens of thousands, perhaps hundreds of thousands, of people flooded the city.

The sheer weight of numbers beat back the forces defending Mina. Monsters like the great three-headed wolves that led the wolfpack in the vision were crushed against buildings by the mass of people and then were stabbed over and over before succumbing to their wounds and falling.

The Goblins and other small Races were killed by the score, but they continued to fight valiantly against the much larger humans who were attacking their home, rushing into close range and striking at any exposed skin with their small daggers, various racial abilities, and even, in some cases, their teeth.

A vast sinkhole opened up to try and swallow the bulk of the enemy force, but they had Mages of their own on the scene, and the enemy warriors were kept from falling by magic.

Where am I in this vision? James couldn't help but wonder. *What's happened to me? Don't I know that my family is in trouble? Don't tell me this takes place at the same time as the last vision . . .*

The invading human force began to prove itself stronger and more numerous. It continued to sweep forward unstoppably, painting the previously beautiful blue-green buildings crimson with blood and gore.

Though James could not make out individual faces in the mass of humans attacking, he could tell that they did so with horrifying glee.

And then the enemy army managed to cut its way through to Mina.

From the way her fire and lightning bolts had begun to subside, James recognized that she must be low on Mana.

Where did the little girl go? One moment, the child had been beside Mina, and the next, James had turned to look over the rest of the battle, and when he turned back, the girl—who he could only assume was his future daughter—had disappeared.

Before he could spend much time considering where she had gone to, though, the enemy were upon Mina.

Three male figures clutched long daggers. James still could not see their faces, but now he saw that these three wore a strange amalgamation of religious symbols on their necklaces: a cross, a Star of David, and a crescent moon all tangled together.

The three men spoke some words that the vision did not allow James to hear.

Mina's eyes narrowed in response. She said something that James likewise could not hear, but since her face was not obscured, he was able to read her lips.

He caught "—kill you for this. You and your families. Your children and your children's children. Your friends and anyone who knows your name."

In his mind, he filled it in as "My husband will kill you for this. You and your families. Your children and your children's children. Your friends and anyone who knows your name."

It clearly wasn't the start of a negotiation. It didn't even constitute a threat.

Simply a prophecy of doom.

There was no further dialogue.

James rushed in, forgetting for a moment that he was intangible, that he could do *nothing* for this future version of his wife and his country. He walked right through the three figures, and, of course, they took no notice of him.

They continued to advance on Mina.

Then the three men attacked and sank their daggers into her chest.

James felt the pain of the blades in his own heart. He clenched his fists and gritted his teeth. He resisted the urge to scream. He would not give Sister Strange the satisfaction.

It's not real, he reminded himself. *It's not real. This will never happen. The monster only wants to torture you.*

But it felt very real as he watched, unable to intervene, while the men cut out Mina's heart and chopped off her head.

As the leaders raised Mina's severed head into the air, their army let out a raucous cheer.

James turned to look away from Mina's bloody body—it was too painful to look, knowing he couldn't even cradle her in his arms—and watched the army. He was caught between seething rage and intense grief, even as he tried to pretend this could never happen.

He tried to distract himself by looking for any face that wasn't blurred out by the vision, any culpable party he could kill to prevent this from happening in some distant future.

Instead, he saw that someone in the enemy army had come up with the bright idea of setting fire to the city. The Fisher Kingdom burned before his eyes.

Compared to what he had just seen, though, the buildings meant very little, beautiful though they were. He felt a bit sad that his other allies were dying, but his heart was too broken at the thought of his wife's death to fully absorb the other fatalities.

Why would this happen? How? I wouldn't leave her undefended . . .

His mind jumped back to the previous scene, when he had been beaten to near death by the man in green armor.

Maybe that was the problem. *I went too far away, to some bloody icy place, to fight that warrior. Now I'm lying helpless, near death somewhere, while these animals kill my wife and my people.*

He wanted to vomit.

Wait, he thought. *Where's the little girl? She might still be alive.*

Out of all the faces the vision allowed him to see, she was the only one he had not seen die.

That pulled his focus back to the vision. No matter how painful it was, he could still get information here.

His eyes scanned the burning city, looking over column after column of blurry-faced foot soldiers, but he could not see the girl. It felt like he was playing a twisted version of the *Where's Waldo?* puzzle, where every potential Waldo candidate had blood on their hands—and frequently on their faces as well as their armor and weapons.

Perhaps the child had an invisibility cloak on or some ability that allowed her to blend in. In any case, no matter how hard he looked, James could not find her.

His heart felt dry and dead as he realized that he believed this was, in fact, a possible future.

If I didn't believe that, I wouldn't be looking for the child.

Before he knew it, the vision was fading.

Fuck, at least it's over . . .

Then the world dissolved and reformed itself. James found himself floating over an ocean.

It's not fucking over. Great.

He was about to wonder what else he could lose when he spotted himself accompanied by a group of flying allies, including giant eagles, winged snakes, and a number of humanoid figures who he did not recognize that floated on the wind. One of them was a man who looked to James like a younger version of himself.

Ah. My son. Of course.

Present-James sat down with crossed legs to watch himself and his adult son die along with all their allies. He imagined they would be eaten by monstrous sharks. It would be as arbitrary and inexplicable as everything else that had happened in these visions.

What actually happened was far stranger than that.

A crack opened in what Present-James guessed was the fabric of reality. Within that opening, James saw what looked like the black void of space.

Then *things* began coming through.

That was all Present-James could think when it came to a description of the invaders. They were horrible, loathsome *things*. Though their appearances did not seem to be obscured in the vision, he could not understand what they were or relate them in any way to earthly creatures, or even to earthly legends or *geometry*.

Their bodies seemed to have one more dimension than those of human beings; that was all Present-James could figure as he watched. And Vision-James seemed to know how to destroy them.

Using a combination of magic that Present-James did not recognize or understand and attacks with a sword that appeared to be made of light, Vision-James split some of the creatures into pieces or forced them back into the fissure in space.

But the others fighting alongside him were much less effective. For every few of the creatures that these fighters destroyed or forced into the void, one of the fighters died. The enemy had a terrible armor-piercing attack that seemed to be irresistible by almost any of the humans whenever the monsters set their eyes on them. A long limb would suddenly extend, and then an ally would fall, a hole visible in their head or chest.

Some of the otherworldly invaders seemed to reform their bodies after being deceased for a certain amount of time, while none of the humans who were killed rose again—at least not as humans. After the battle continued for a little while, some of the fallen humans rose again, their eyes turned black, and they fought alongside the monsters with the same powers they'd had in life.

Vision-James was the only one who seemed to be able to block the monsters' death blow attack, using his sword made of light to deflect it. The sword also allowed him to strike down any of his allies that the monsters raised from the dead. But the enemy's numbers were far greater than those of Vision-James and his forces. Gradually, only he and his son were left.

James's son launched a furious attack and destroyed a dozen of the creatures with just a few blows. But he had left himself vulnerable to one of the invaders that had been standing on the sidelines, waiting. It struck out with an inky-black limb—and Vision-James was there, intercepting.

Wow. My son is a badass.

But he hadn't moved quickly enough to block with the light sword. The blow had penetrated Vision-James through the heart.

Present-James let out a sigh of relief. *Shit. Well, it's only me dying this time. I hope.*

Vision-James was whispering something in his son's ear, but Present-James could not hear the words or read Vision-James's lips. It didn't seem like something he needed to worry about anyway, since whatever it was that he was supposed to say, he would undoubtedly know when the time came.

Probably telling him to run away, if I have any sense left, Present-James thought.

But no. Vision-James reached a hand out to his son, and the younger man reached out and took the sword of light from him. He turned to face the monsters, and Present-James found the vision fading to black. He was in darkness so total that he couldn't even look down and see his own body.

Why end it now? he thought. *Just when I was about to find out what happens to my son . . .*

He felt a shaking and jostling of his body, and he realized he no longer had a sense of where his astral form was. Someone was moving his physical body, and James decided to wake up so that he could find out why. This could be Sister Strange moving their battle from the dream world to the physical one.

He deactivated Dreamwalk and opened his eyes—and saw a pair of familiar eyes.

Mina.

She was holding him in a tight embrace, a look of concern on her face. He didn't need to look around to realize he was back in bed.

Was it all just a strange, elaborate dream? James wondered. *Could my own imagination do that? Be so detailed—and cruel?*

"Are you all right, skapi?" Mina asked. Her eyes were slightly teary, he realized.

James leaned in and kissed the tears away.

"I'm awake now," he said. "Just a bad dream, I think."

"Damien and Jeremiah said you were battling the monster from the evil woods," Mina said.

And James's face fell. His eyes went vacant, staring off into the distance as he went over his nocturnal adventure again.

So, it was all real. At least, it was real that Sister Strange showed me what she calls "visions" . . . But were those the things that she claims must *happen, or those that* may *happen?*

"Tell me what's going on," Mina said. "You were crying out in your sleep. I heard you say my name."

"Oh God," James said slowly, his mind still wrestling with what had happened. "The creature in this forest knows how to make people suffer."

INTERLUDE

The Count in the Catacombs

"Every few nights, the Count emerges from the catacombs beneath the castle and wanders the countryside. He chooses a victim and drinks from their throat." Cassia—who Count Aleph thought of as the tour guide to his castle—paused dramatically, and one of the party of intruders asked a question.

"Excuse me, ma'am, but if the Vampire Count comes out at night and drinks from people, uh, why don't you just leave?"

"Cristian!" One of the other intruders elbowed the first speaker in the ribs. "You're ruining the whole experience with your damn questions, man."

"I just—you have to admit it doesn't make sense, dude. We waited, we let her explain the situation with this place, and she says she's taking us to where the Ruler is. But something's fishy. This isn't a video game, as much as you guys might like to pretend it's *Castlevania* or something. It's the System. Vampires exist, but they don't behave like fictional characters. And if Dracula were real, the peasants would storm the castle or something. They wouldn't wait and get some visiting foreigners to kill the monster—"

"Sir, if you don't trust me, you can go ahead and kill me!" The guide lowered her head as if offering herself up for an executioner's axe. "Just *please* slay the Vampire. For my friends and neighbors."

The full group of intruders seemed to be stunned into silence for a moment. Then they were all talking over each other.

"Don't be ridiculous—"

"Stop—"

"No—"

"—outrageous—"

"—could never—"

"—wouldn't go that far . . ."

"—trust you."

All of them were tripping over themselves to reassure the guide that of course they weren't going to kill her. That they believed her.

She raised her head, and Count Aleph imagined that her eyes dripped with tears as she spoke. No, he more than imagined. He could smell the salt water in the air. Like the salt in her blood. *Intoxicating . . .*

"Then I will lead you into the catacombs. My answer to your question is simple: the Vampire Count does not usually kill the targets of his sick lust. He is the Ruler here, so hardly anyone is foolish enough to fight him. Those who tried were killed quickly. The rest of us understood his rules quickly. Keep your head down, and the worst that can happen to you is losing a bit of blood. We couldn't safely leave, either. The neighboring monsters are even worse than the Count: a race of giants on one side and wyverns on the other." Her voice turned bitter. "Unlike the Count, they would not suffer humans even to live under their rule."

"Then why betray him?" asked a woman whose voice Count Aleph had not heard before now.

"That's a good question," agreed another voice, an unfamiliar male.

"It's personal with me and the Count," Cassia replied. Aleph could hear her gritting her teeth, and he imagined the look on her face. Actually, it would be more accurate to say that he pulled the image of her wearing such an expression from his memory banks. Ever since he had become a vampire, his memory was nearly perfect. Like he was looking at images preserved under glass. *Such emotion*, he thought.

"I'm sorry," said the voice of the skeptic from earlier. "Saying 'it's personal' just isn't quite good enough. *How* exactly is it personal?"

"Remember how I said that he usually does not kill the targets of his sick lust?"

There was silence for a moment. Aleph guessed the skeptic—Cristian, that was his name!—was nodding.

"Well," Cassia continued, "he also normally moves on from a victim after a night or two. Finds new prey. But instead"—Aleph could smell her beginning to tear up again—"he's targeting the same person again! It's my sister, Saskia. She's so sweet and innocent. Beautiful and young. I think the old legends about these creatures are true, and he wants to make her his bride. Saskia didn't ask for this. She doesn't want him. But wherever we move her, whatever we do to try and protect her, she only seems to get weaker. Lately, she flinches away from the touch of daylight. I don't think she has much time left. So, you see, I'm pretty desperate. Ready to try something stupid. Otherwise, my sister might die or become a monster."

"Good enough for me," the other female voice said.

"Yeah," Cristian agreed. "I agree that's a good enough reason. Sorry for doubting you. Let's try and get into those catacombs before sunset, then." There was an edge of nervousness to his voice now.

Good. Pain and fear would make their blood just that little bit tastier.

They walked around for several minutes before Cassia took them to the entrance of the catacombs. Count Aleph was doing some math in his head. It was how he spent most of his time during the day—thinking about the plethora of numbers the System had gifted him with: status numbers, levels and experience, Skills, the number of victims he had consumed over the course of his short life as a Vampire.

After I kill these ones, how long until I hit level forty? I'm at thirty-six now. Assuming the average Race level of this party is around fifteen . . .

Math problems had been Aleph's hobby before the System, back when he was just a human named Alexandru. Perhaps the most wonderful thing about his nearly perfect memory post-System was that he no longer needed any aids to perform complex mathematics. No pencil, paper, abacus, calculator—nothing. He could keep all the numbers and ideas in his head, hold them in place in his mind.

The Vampire Count's current long-term math project was devising a formula to calculate how many victims he still needed before he reached level one hundred. There were still too many variables to make for an easy formulation—in particular, the way in which experience slowly decreased with repeated encounters against enemies of the same type at the same level was proving a difficult element to quantify—but Aleph was getting closer all the time.

As he was whiling away his time working on his formulae, the pipes carried the continued whispers of the adventuring party down to Aleph in his chamber.

"I don't know, man," Cristian was saying. "I still don't quite buy it."

"What are you worrying about?" asked a male voice. Aleph remembered this was the person who had tried to get Cristian to shut up earlier. "Jordan didn't give us the signal for deception. And she has an actual Skill for that. You're going based off of what, instinct?"

"You just don't want to see it because you want to fuck Cassia, Matt. There are probably people who have Skills that counter Deception Resistance. This place is sketchy as hell!"

"Hey, don't get confused, man," Matt said arrogantly. "Just because Cassia is giving me the eye, it doesn't compromise my judgment in the slightest. Remember, we were at the top of our Orientation. You, me, and Arben. We don't have anything to worry about in some dank castle in the middle of nowhere. It's only a matter of time—"

"It's a fucking *Ruler*," Cristian hissed. "We were at the top of our Orientation *except* for the Ruler there, who—"

"Keep your voice down, man," Matt said.

"What, are you worried the bitch will hear us?" Cristian asked, exasperated—but his voice was almost a whisper, the volume back under control. It was even hard for Aleph to hear him, and the Count's hearing was beyond superhuman ever since Race Evolution.

"Look, once we met up with the others, we got ourselves a well-balanced crew—you have to admit that. You said yourself that you thought we could beat the Ruler in that valley now that we have Jordan, Alina, and Florin."

"Yeah, but that—"

"Are the two of you all right?" one of the women asked.

She has a very pleasant voice, Aleph thought. *She must not have spoken up much earlier, or I would have noticed that. Something of a shame that someone with such a pleasant voice has to die . . .*

"We're fine, Alina," Matt said insistently. "Aren't we, man?"

There must have been a nod, based on what came next.

"Okay," Alina said. "You're making the rest of us a little nervous, though. If there's something you're worried about, you'll share with the group?"

"Of *course*," Matt said, again speaking for himself and Cristian.

Cristian didn't say anything to contradict him, and as far as Aleph could hear, the conversation seemed to die out as the adventurers proceeded into the catacombs.

The conflict between these people is interesting. Too bad for them they aren't listening to the suspicious one. If they left now, they might be able to make it to the border safely before I caught up. Though, that would come with its own perils . . .

As he heard them move through the catacombs, Aleph timed his moment carefully. There was a place in the floor they should be walking across where the stone was hollow . . .

He heard the louder sound of movement as they stepped on the hollow stone, and the Vampire Count immediately flicked the lever next to his seat.

"What's that sound?" asked Cristian.

That's the catacomb entrance closing behind you.

"I don't know. Maybe the monster is getting restless," Matt said, trying to play Cristian's question off with humor. But Aleph could hear a note of concern seep through in his tone.

"Maybe we should turn back," the woman who must have been Jordan said.

"What are you saying?" said one of the men—not Cristian or Matt.

"We've come too far now," said another male voice.

"Why would we leave?" Matt said stubbornly.

"I don't think you all could actually make it out of the count's territory before nightfall if you left now," Cassia accurately pointed out.

"Then we press on," Cristian said. Aleph heard the sound of a weapon being drawn.

"Cristian, what are you doing?" Matt said, outraged.

"There's something wrong with our guide," Cristian replied. "I know none of you believe me, and I can't explain it perfectly myself. But if anything happens to us—if we fall for a trap that you walked us into, or if there's actually a hundred vampires down here instead of one, I want you to know that you're going to die first. Before anything happens to any of my friends."

"That's just fine," Cassia said, clearly speaking around a blade pressed to her throat. Her tone was reassuring, tinged with just the right note of fear. "Since I'm not lying, I'm not worried. Let's just keep going."

"This is really beyond the pale, man," Matt grumbled. "After today, I don't think we can work together. This paranoia wasn't so bad in Orientation. But now—"

"My *paranoia* saved both our lives in Orientation," Cristian said. "I—"

"Please, both of you," Alina said, "stay calm. We need to move on. We're losing daylight."

"Your friend is right," Cassia agreed, still gasping slightly around the steel held against her neck. "We should continue. There is still some way to go before we reach the count's chamber, if I recall correctly. If we do not arrive before sunset, your fight will be much more difficult."

Then Aleph heard her lead them away. In the wrong direction.

A smile played across his lips. It was back to his formula-creation efforts.

The group walked for almost an hour before the party skeptic spoke up again.

"How far is it *now*?" he asked, his voice tight.

"Cristian!" Jordan exclaimed.

The rich, salty, sweet smell of blood drifted into Aleph's nostrils, and he frowned. People weren't supposed to be bleeding yet.

And that smells like . . .

"I'm all right," came Cassia's trembling voice.

That little prick cut her. Probably cut her on the neck if his blade was in the same place where he was holding it earlier. Doesn't he know that she's mine? That Cassia's slender neck is only for me to drink from?

A quiet fury began building deep inside Aleph. Where before he had intended to slaughter these visitors as a matter of simple necessity, now it was a bit more personal.

He checked the clock on the wall. Around forty minutes left until sunset.

He weighed his options. Go out and fight them now, and risk them possibly exposing him to sunlight—although he had sealed the entrance to the catacombs, the walls were only stone. Powerful attacks could and would break through them, and direct sunlight would be highly damaging.

Or he could wait and simply hope that Cassia continued her virtuoso performance as the innocent victim, the helpful tour guide.

"I'm sorry," Cassia was saying. "I've only been in here a couple of times, and all before the System. My grandfather worked in the castle, giving tours, but he passed away years ago. I didn't mean to take a wrong turn. We still have time, and I know I can find the room . . ."

Already she was playing for time. Pleading, making promises, negotiating.

Aleph told himself to relax. His Cassia had this under control.

"Just put the dagger down, man," Matt said. "I don't like seeing you like this."

"If you're this freaked out, we can just leave this place," Alina said.

Yes, his friends are on Cassia's side too. He won't be able to do a thing . . .

"I guess we can—" Cristian began speaking, seemingly calming down.

Then there was the sound of a scuffle. Cristian's voice cried out in pain and then issued a low groan.

He started to lower his blade, and then someone disarmed him, the Count guessed. *Maybe one of his friends—or Cassia—kneed him in the groin?*

"Sorry, dude," Matt said. "You're just acting too erratically. Arben and I are going to keep one hand each on you until we're out of here. Sorry, Cassia, I know you wanted our help, but I don't think our group is as functional right now as I assumed we were." He sounded disappointed.

"No, I understand," Cassia said. "Thank you for—thank you for the rescue." She let out a slow, ragged breath. "Let's go, then."

Aleph heard them retracing their steps. They moved as slowly as they had coming down that hallway the first time. Perhaps slower because Cristian's male teammates were insisting on keeping a grip on him as they walked.

So, there should be no way they can get out before sunset, Aleph thought.

He rose and pressed a panel on the wall. A passage opened that led from his chamber up to the main part of the castle. Rather than confront them in the catacombs where he lived, fighting them on the surface would be better. He had been lucky that the last several prey had been too weak to do much damage to his home. Better not to count on that for every encounter.

The enemies would only get stronger from here as word of this castle and its resident spread.

Aleph made it to the surface and walked through the castle, keeping to the shadows as much as he could. As the sun sank below the horizon, he stood in a particularly deep, dark shadow and waited. Finally, just after it had disappeared from sight, he approached the entrance to the catacombs.

The Vampire Count could hear his prey now: tired from hours of walking, still bickering a bit among themselves, disappointed that they had begun a retreat from the object of their quest—and just a little bit afraid of what the night held waiting for them. He could hear that undertone, though none of the adventurers were voicing the specific concern. They could tell by the increased depth of the shadows even in the catacombs that night had fallen.

Their chance to escape had disappeared with the sun. They could not know that, certainly not with any certainty, but Aleph was as sure of their demise as he was that the sun would rise the next morning.

He drew the curved, ruby-hilted sword from his side, and he smiled with grim satisfaction. Aleph loved it when things went to plan.

They began climbing the stairs, and Aleph heard their voices register alarm for the first time.

"Hey, how did this get closed? Who was the last one through here?"

Then Aleph pulled the doors open. The two closest figures—two males—had time to open their mouths wide, as if they were about to scream. Then the Vampire's sword severed their heads just above the lower lips. Instead of screaming, they gurgled as crimson blood gushed forth.

I hope neither of those was Cristian. He had a slower death in mind for that man.

The bodies tumbled back down the stairs, and the first screams issued from one of the women—Alina, he could tell.

That girl has a truly wonderful set of pipes on her.

The Count didn't slow down to appreciate the beautiful smell of human blood. He took in the damage and the group of people left.

Two down. The two who chose to walk up to the entrance were probably planning to brute force their way out. That might mean they were the strongest in the group. But there were four to go, plus Cassia.

The Count drew a dagger from his side and hurled it with superhuman Strength and precision. It flew at incredible speed and plunged into the chest of the woman in the adventurers' party who was not screaming.

Judging from Alina's clothing, she was a Healer, like Cassia. She probably wouldn't have abilities that could harm Aleph, he judged. If she did, it would be that Purification Skill he'd seen once, but that required being in touch range.

Jordan, who had already been gathering Mana around her, crumbled to her knees, her fingers desperately clutching at the dagger between her breasts.

Aleph began chanting his own magic spell, gathering shadow Mana.

Only three left, along with Cassia.

Two men and that Alina girl.

He took a step forward, prepared to descend into the catacombs after them, but one of the men was rushing up the stairs toward him, sword in hand.

"You monster! You killed my friends!"

Aleph would have rolled his eyes. He heard these outraged, defiant shouts almost as often as he heard men beg for their lives. At a certain point, it felt a bit silly.

The Count slashed down with his blade without stopping his chant. He and the human traded several blows.

He's really not bad, Aleph thought distantly. As far as he was concerned, this fight was basically over. The closest that the human came to landing a swing of his sword on Aleph's body was when the Count looked past him to check what was going on in the catacombs.

Cassia was down there using her healing powers on the woman whose chest Aleph had perforated. It was a good performance. Alina, the surviving female member of the band of adventurers, seemed to be too shell-shocked to do anything. The man who wasn't fighting Aleph stared down at his bleeding friends, transfixed.

Aleph hocked a glob of spit right into his opponent's face.

As the man was jumping back and wiping his eyes, Aleph threw his other dagger and struck the off-guard male adventurer who remained in the catacombs right in the neck.

Then he reached out with Shadow Magic, his Mana having charged enough.

A great black hand sprang from the shadows, grabbed Cassia, and pulled her into the darkness.

"Cassia!" the swordsman who had engaged Aleph cried out.

He rushed at the Count, who easily parried his next several sword swings.

Your group might have legitimately been a threat, he thought, *if you hadn't been taken so completely by surprise.*

"Give her back," the swordsman growled. And Aleph recognized his voice.

"That's a pity," he said, speaking in a slow, deep baritone. "You must be Matt."

I had hoped that Cristian would be the last man left alive.

As Matt's eyes widened, Aleph threw a sucker punch that crumpled the front of his armor. Matt fell to his knees, clutching his abdomen and gasping for breath. His sword clattered to the ground, forgotten.

And the massive, shadowy hand reappeared beside Count Aleph. It opened to reveal Cassia, completely unharmed except for the little red line Cristian had cut into her throat earlier.

"Are you all right, my dear?" Aleph asked.

Cassia stepped forward and wrapped her arms around the Vampire's chest.

"I'll be fine, Aleph," she said. She pulled his head down and kissed him roughly on the neck. "How did I do?"

"Oh, no one could have done better," Aleph said.

To his amusement, Matt had a terrible look of shock on his face.

"You bitch," he rasped, still short of breath. "You helped him kill them all!"

He rose, stepped forward, and seemed to realize he had nothing in his hands. He dove for the sword he'd left on the ground, and Aleph threw a kick that hit the man right under the chin.

Matt crumpled to the ground, instantly unconscious. Only Alina was still moving. The count could hear her in the catacombs, haltingly fleeing further underground. There was no way the Healer would be able to escape alone. It was over.

"There, you see?" Aleph said. "We even took a couple of them alive."

CHAPTER FORTY-TWO

Council Meeting, Part 1

Mina ran a gentle hand over James's hair as she waited for him to tell her more.

"I need more information," he said, his body shaking slightly as he spoke. "I don't know how much I can say reliably. I—"

"That's all right," she said soothingly. "You don't have to talk about it now if you're not ready."

What could do this to him? Mina wondered. It was scary to see James rattled. She could count the number of times his emotions had seemed out of control on one hand and still have fingers unused.

"I think I'll need your help," he said, seemingly half to himself. Then he looked back at her, his eyes filled with intensity. *As if he's seeing ghosts*, she thought.

"I'll do whatever I can," she assured him.

He nodded. Then James closed his eyes and took on a focused expression.

[All representatives of Fisher Kingdom commissions, please prepare to meet in the community center this morning in one hour. Though I previously informed you that the meeting would take place tomorrow, urgent circumstances require that the meeting be moved up. I believe it's best that we do it immediately. Any members of the community who have petitions, questions, or comments to share, we will open for a public question and answer session in approximately two hours.]

He managed to sound like everything was normal.

"You mentioned that Carol requires investment in her Dungeon before we can get some spell books that might be useful against our neighbor, right?" James asked.

"That's right," Mina said.

He nodded. "I'll go there before the community center this morning, then. Hopefully, you can train this afternoon."

"Yes," Mina replied. "We'll destroy that forest soon."

James's head moved up and down, but she could see his mind was elsewhere.

Mina rose and placed a hand on his shoulder. "I'll make breakfast today," she said.

"You don't have to," James replied instantly.

"You have a lot on your mind," she said.

"I'll dash on over to Carol for a minute, then. And I'll also drop by Alan and Mitzi to ask them to come to the meeting too."

The way he looked at her before he exited through the window was strange. As though he was memorizing every detail of her face. Like he thought he might never see her again.

James moved through the first hour after waking up from his encounter with Sister Strange in a haze.

You have to decide for yourself if she's some kind of prophet or not.

He definitely didn't *want* to believe there was anything to Sister Strange's power other than the same function that guided his own Illusion Magic. His magic could create an optical illusion that fooled the victim based on what they expected to see. False Reality made the illusions even more convincing by manipulating the victim's sense of reality in general to align with whatever deception James was attempting. The way it seemed to complement his illusions, he had noticed, was by causing the person's other senses to fool them.

Maybe her power could create a vision based on what would cause the person watching to experience the most psychological discomfort. It wouldn't even have to be as effective as James's power, since Sister Strange didn't need to convince James, for instance, that he wasn't dreaming. She only needed an immersive experience. Psychological warfare would do the rest.

James was halfway to convincing himself that Sister Strange's tricks were just that—but he couldn't get past the fact that when he left Mina alone in the apartment, he felt as if she might vanish like a puff of smoke at any moment.

So, it's real enough for me. For now.

He kept that in mind while he handled the morning's business.

James went to the Dungeon.

[Dungeon entered! You have arrived in Dungeon: Carol's Storage!]

Charming. I like the name change.

"Hi, there!" Carol exclaimed from above.

"Hi, Carol!"

"Oh, it's you, James . . ."

After he had transferred her the ten thousand credits, James returned home. Even in the light of day, there was a little trepidation in his step as he walked up the stairs—as if he might not find his family when he reached the top.

But, of course, they were all there, gathered around the table, waiting for him to eat.

James didn't taste any of the food that passed between his lips. He was thinking about his next moves.

"Is James okay?" Yulia asked when James had left the table to use the toilet.

Goodness, Yulia's noticing it too, Mina thought.

But James seemed to have pulled himself back together by the time they sat in the community center with Magnar and Duncan.

He had moved the podium from where it sat on the stage, and he and the commission heads had taken a long dinner table from Carol's Storage and placed it in the podium's place, along with twenty-three accompanying seats for every one of the Fisher King's councilors, except Luna and Samuel, who James said would be sitting at ground level. Luna was tall enough to be seen clearly even when seated on the stage beside the chairs, and Samuel was bigger than her from what James had said.

The former Ruler was running late because he had to make his way from the swamp region of the territory. James said that he had encouraged Samuel to take his time, considering that he was still recovering from their battle.

"It's a miracle he survived," Alan commented drily.

Several people laughed at that, while a few clapped their hands and gave James approving looks.

"I wish I could have seen your victory over the beasts," Jeremiah Rotter said.

Alan, Mitzi, and Rotter occupied seats at the table along with the twenty commission heads, though they didn't head any commissions that Mina was aware of. But James had clearly expected them, so no one asked why they were there.

The seats were slightly crowded together because James wanted everyone to sit so that anyone in the gallery could look them in the eye during question time. Taylor Bunting was almost in Dave Matsumoto's lap. She stuck closer to him out of obvious preference relative to her other neighbor, Lord Magnar.

"We'll need to have a larger table made for next time," James observed.

There were a few dry chuckles.

James had taken the largest chair he could find and placed it at the center of the table for himself, instead of sitting at the head of the table. He kept an open seat at his right hand for Mina, who had watched from the gallery as everyone else set up the furniture and took their seats.

The image of him sitting at the center of the table reminded her of something, though it took a minute for her to place it.

"*The Last Supper*," she murmured.

James clearly heard her even though the words were spoken under her breath. The edges of his lips curled up in a little smile, and she wondered if the imagery, placing James in the role of Christ, had been deliberate.

That would put me in the position of John the Apostle, wouldn't it? The "disciple whom Jesus loved," wasn't he? The longest lived of the twelve apostles. The youngest. The only one of them to die from natural causes. That summed up everything she knew, and James probably knew even less about him; his household hadn't been as religious as hers.

It was a good position to be placed in, as the metaphor went. She wondered again exactly what his dreams had been about.

She shook her head and took her seat by his side. Then she conjured a pitcher made of ice and filled it with water. From her Small Bag of Deceptive Dimensions she drew a package of clear plastic cups the Salvage Commission had liberated from the run-down buildings. She opened the packaging and placed the cups next to the pitcher.

People came around and helped themselves to water and then returned to their seats.

"Let's call this first meeting of the Fisher Kingdom Governance Council into session," James said. "I would have included some additional formalities, but I think we have at least one urgent item to deal with before we'll have the space to think about that sort of thing. Our first order of business is the matter I called you all here to discuss. Who here had unusually bad dreams last night?"

As he spoke, Mina saw that James was silently charging a form of Mana that she didn't recognize. Blue with sparkles. It reminded her of Yulia's pixie friends.

But the rest of the room was more focused on the question itself. Low chattering broke out as people asked each other quiet questions under their breath.

A half dozen hands went up.

"Um, why are you asking, sir?" said Angelina Zuccarini of the Sewer Commission.

"I will explain in just a minute," James said, turning to Angelina and smiling. "I'm trying to get a little more information so my final explanation will be more complete. Now, not counting last night, who had bad dreams over the last few days that felt unusual?" He looked from person to person as he spoke. "They could be night terrors, nightmares, or any kind of bad dream that you don't typically experience."

More than half of the hands in the room went up, including Luna the wolf's right front paw.

"I see," James said quietly.

So, this creature has been targeting us for longer than just last night? Why was last night the first time James heard anything about it, then?

At that point, there was a loud sound of knocking on the door.

"Enter!" James called down.

The double doors pushed open, and Mina saw a monster that looked like it belonged in a scary movie step through the gap.

Oh my gosh, is that the monster James fought yesterday?

"Hail to the Fisher King," the monster said in a voice that rumbled. The sound reminded her of an earthquake.

"Welcome, Samuel, former Ruler of the alligators," James said, beaming down at the monstrous reptile.

Samuel walked through the doors slowly and cautiously. He could barely fit his heavy bulk through the doorway, but he was clearly taking care not to scrape the sides.

"We will have that enlarged," James added.

"Oh, please, not on my account," Samuel said. There was an oddly amused expression on his monstrous face as he spoke. The sight made Mina shudder slightly, reminding her of the last time she had been face-to-face with a predator larger than her—Cara. "I was planning on losing some weight anyway."

James snorted quietly.

The giant reptile closed the doors behind him with a gentle motion of his tail, still moving with care as if he thought he might accidentally take them off of their hinges with any sudden movements.

"I was just discussing the nightmares that appear to be afflicting residents of this kingdom," James said. The Mana around his body had reached a steady, unmoving state, Mina observed. She thought he must be done charging up for whatever he was about to do. "I don't suppose you have any information to share before I tell everyone what I think is going on?"

"I know nothing about this enemy, unfortunately," Samuel said. "I understand they are located on a different side of the Kingdom relative to the swamp, which might explain why I don't know anything about them."

"All right," James said.

The Mana around his body vanished, and an image appeared in the center of the room, at the front of the center aisle of the gallery: a towering feminine figure shrouded in darkness. Her body ended in a haze, like that of a cartoon ghost. Her face was a shriveled, sadistic pale mask.

"This is what we're dealing with," James said. "I encountered her in the world of dreams last night. Who has seen her or something that resembled her in their dreams?"

Most of the hands that had been raised earlier shot back up again. Even one person who hadn't raised her hand earlier held it up now.

Other than that, almost the whole room stood still, waiting for James to explain what was going on. In the silent stillness, Mina noticed the only person still moving was Rotter. He was taking notes silently in the book he always carried with him.

"The fact that almost everyone who had these bad dreams experienced some form of contact with her proves that she really is involved in these dreams," James said. "There is no easy way to say this. We're being targeted. Our neighbor has infiltrated the dreams of a number of people in the Kingdom, not just people in this room."

There was a small outcry at this.

"How can something like this happen?" asked Harry Luntz, of the Agriculture Commission.

"Why us?" asked Zuccarini.

"What are we going to do about this?" asked Taylor Bunting.

Samuel thumped his tail on the ground loudly several times, and the room started to quiet down.

"The King is clearly about to answer your questions," the alligator growled, speaking with an air that said, *If I had won the fight, I wouldn't be putting up with this nonsense.*

Mina smiled thinly.

"The situation isn't very complicated," James said. "We know that the world is full of expansionist foreign powers now. This is one of those. We must defeat her at all costs, of course. As for why us in particular, all she said when I confronted her was that she enjoys human suffering." There was more discontented muttering as the commission heads digested this information, but much more calmly. "Now for my next question. Of those who had strange dreams last night, how did the dream proceed? Is anyone willing to share a general description?"

There was a sharp intake of air, and Mina saw people at the table looking at each other. Waiting to see who would go first. Then three hands went up, almost in unison.

"Dave?" James gestured for the leader of the hunters to speak. "I should add before you start that I don't need any specifics, just the overall course of the dream."

Dave looked slightly confused, but he began to explain his dream anyway. "In my dream, I returned to a certain, um, traumatic experience from my past. Related to the Sino-American War."

"Did you see the being I saw at any point in your dream?" James gestured at the creepy illusion that still stood in the aisle.

"I did," Dave said. "She took a place among the enemy's ranks, and I believe she also occasionally whispered in my ear . . ."

"At any point in the dream, did she stop her activities?" James asked.

Dave blinked several times and looked surprised as he thought about it.

"Yes," he said finally. "There was a point when she wasn't there anymore. I've actually done some experiments with lucid dreaming in the past. At one point I was able to navigate away from my memories. I traveled to some happier places in my past instead . . ." His face took on a faraway look, and a slight smile danced across his lips.

"I'm glad to hear it," James said. He looked extremely pleased with Dave's response. "Does anyone else have any similar *or opposite* experiences to report?"

Zuccarini raised her hand first, and James nodded for her to speak.

"I wasn't asleep at the time all this happened. I was doing some journaling—what I was doing doesn't matter, but what's important is that my wife was asleep next to me. She was tossing and turning and crying out in her sleep for a while. I couldn't wake her up, which was unusual—"

Like James, Mina thought. He had seemed like he was in terrible distress a few times last night.

"—because she's a light sleeper most of the time. I shook her, and I raised my voice and dripped water on her face. Nothing worked! But at a certain point it just *stopped*. Do you—do you know why?" Zuccarini looked at James.

"I think I do," he said slowly. "But before I say what I think, I want to know if anyone had the opposite experience. Is there anyone who had the dream get worse and worse, never changing for the better or stopping until they woke up?"

The room fell completely still and silent for a few seconds.

"Okay," James said quietly. "I guess it actually worked for everyone. So, last night was the first night that I was aware of this thing attacking people in their dreams. I have a power that allows me to visit people's dreams as well, so I entered dreamspace and I started interfering with this thing. I don't seem to be able to kill her there, but it looks like fighting her there was enough. Maybe I can hold her off again tonight."

"Shouldn't—um, and I know these are your decisions and the fighters' decisions more than anything," Zuccarini said, "but shouldn't we go and do something about this evil thing"—she gestured at the illusion of the woman—"before tonight?"

Several people started to talk at once as Zuccarini finished her question.

"Have you looked anywhere near that forest?" asked Steve Luck, of the Construction Commission.

"We need to consider further preparations—" Dave began.

"We have to be cautious—" Alan began at the same time.

"This needs to be resolved *yesterday*," interrupted Luntz. "The effect it's having on our workers is—"

"Is there any way I can help, Your Maj—" Duncan started.

This time it was Luna who let out a strange yelp-like bark to quiet the room down. As people turned to look slightly anxiously at the wolf, who was rising to her feet and looked a bit uncomfortable herself, James cleared his throat. Luna immediately resumed her seated posture.

Was that reaction something he ordered her to do, to get them to shut up? Mina wondered. It was marvelously effective to have a wolf at the table, but she thought they should probably just make sure he had a gavel for the next meeting.

"I have the beginnings of a plan," James said. "I want us to test it out tonight."

CHAPTER FORTY-THREE

Council Meeting, Part 2

Mina waited for James to go into his plan, curious to know what he was thinking.

He had been so reticent about his encounter with the dream-attacking creature last night that she had no sense of what his ideas for dealing with the enemy might be. Clearly, he thought the monster was formidable or, rather than calling a meeting, he would have simply gathered a crew of fighters and invaded her territory in return.

Complete silence fell over the room as James cleared his throat.

"Tonight, I intend to go and seek the monster out in the dream world from which she attacked our territory," he said. "I believe I can hold her in place there. The danger of not going to meet her in dreamspace is obvious. The psychological effects of her nightmares, or the physiological effects of sleepless nights, are her way of undermining our capacity for self-defense. After a few nights of that, we would be softened up for her inevitable invasion in the physical world."

People were nodding along with James as he spoke, and what he said made sense, but Mina sensed something off in his demeanor or perhaps his body language—a reluctance to say something. And why was he bothering to justify going to confront the enemy at all? The entire council—and many outside this room, based on what James had explained—would naturally approve any action he might take against this enemy.

He continued, "When I confront her, I need a brave group of volunteers to attempt an invasion of the enemy's territory, to see if her defenses are still in place while she's preoccupied with me. We don't know for certain if the *visions* that people see when they look into her space are the actions of other creatures or the effect of her power alone. If it's the latter, then this would be an opportunity to attack the enemy's stronghold and perhaps even kill her."

Oh. He's making sure he justifies his plan because he wants other people to risk their physical safety, and he can't go with them.

"I volunteer to lead this group," Dave interjected.

James nodded and offered a slim smile. "I thought you might. If you see anything that disturbs you, please withdraw right away."

Dave nodded his assent.

"We will also need a brave group of volunteers to stand by in case our intrepid explorers are overcome by the power of the enemy, to watch for strange movements that might indicate they're under the control of the enemy. And to be prepared to either forcefully wake me up—using violence if necessary—or to go in after them yourselves."

A silence fell over the room as people thought about what James had just said.

Mina resolved to herself that she would volunteer to lead this second group of volunteers if no one more suitable stepped up. After all, she was certain to be involved in this part of the plan if only because she wanted to be the one to wake James up if that needed to happen. No one else was going to "forcefully" wake her husband up, "using violence if necessary."

"What will we do if the enemy's defenses are still up—I mean, I know our volunteers are instructed to withdraw in that case, but what's our 'Plan B' if invading while you distract the enemy fails?" asked Luntz nervously.

"We'll b—I mean, that sounds like something for everyone to mull over," James said. "If there are ideas, I'm ready to hear them. I have a few thoughts myself. But I'm hoping this works, and we don't have to do anything drastic."

He almost said, "We'll burn that bridge when we come to it," Mina thought, trying not to laugh.

There was a general murmuring as people promised to give the problem some attention after the meeting closed.

At that point, James asked for the individual commission heads to give reports. This was their first meeting. They might as well get a good idea of what was going on in the Kingdom.

Agriculture reported that their efforts were going well.

New building construction was suffering only for lack of suitable land, but they expected that James's steady expansion of the Kingdom would fix that. And he offered to firm up some of the existing land that was not within the swamp but verged on being too *swampy* for construction.

Sewer construction was proceeding quickly thanks to the collaboration between humans and Mole People.

"Frankly, without Lord Magnar and his people, we have no idea how long this project would take," Zuccarini said, laughing nervously as she looked down the table affectionately at Magnar. "As things stand now, the sewer should be large enough for a population ten times our number in a few weeks. Then we're hoping to shift into a general 'Water Commission' that will hook everyone up with running water again."

This provoked a round of applause from the table.

"Well done," James said, smiling broadly and looking back and forth between Zuccarini and Magnar.

To the apparent surprise of everyone but James, Magnar spoke up at that point.

"It is a great honor to be of service to our friends and neighbors," he said in a voice that was surprisingly high and non-threatening for someone as large and scary looking as Magnar.

There was another round of applause at this after the room got over its collective shock.

"What does this gesture mean?" Magnar asked once the noise died down. He pantomimed clapping.

"In our culture, it means that we all approve of you and your actions," James replied.

Magnar nodded. "Thank you all very much," he said in a humble falsetto-sounding voice.

"Ahh," Duncan said quietly. "So that's what it was."

Duncan clapped a couple of times as practice, while Magnar sat up straighter with what looked like a proud bearing.

The status reports continued, but Mina allowed her mind to wander. The most important matters had already been discussed, and she could tell that James was paying attention.

This government is working surprisingly well considering the different Races involved—and the fact that it's composed almost exclusively of people who have never led anything larger than a farm in their lives. Then again, perhaps that was why it was functional. There was no one with a real power base besides James. No rivals. All authority springing from one place, everyone striving to achieve goals laid out or approved by him.

Maybe it wouldn't be as effective once they were beyond the basic subsistence level, but then, monarchies had endured for thousands of years in countries around the world. Longer than any republican form of government. Perhaps there was something to this, beyond simply grabbing for power to ensure one's own family's continued prosperity and security.

There was a silence in the room, and Mina realized the last commission head had finished giving his report.

"All right. Thank you, everyone, for talking and listening. I think our group is going to do great things together. Let's take a quick break, and then we'll admit the public," James said.

People rose from their seats, refilled cups of water, and talked among themselves.

James wrapped an arm around Mina, and she remained seated beside him.

"Skapi?" she asked quietly. *Was there something you wanted to discuss?*

He replied in a low voice, almost a whisper.

"I hate to put more pressure on you," James said, "and I have a lot of faith in our people here. But I also have a bad feeling about this enemy. I think this monster is probably going to be more difficult to destroy than some normal flesh-and-blood creature. I don't know much about what she's capable of. It's just a feeling I have. I'm hoping that sometime in the next few days, we can attack Sister Strange in her own territory. Considering her defense system, I don't know if the hunters and I will be able to destroy her by ordinary means. If it's possible to invade her territory tonight, then that will prove I can at least distract her by confronting her in dreams. But I'd need someone else to help me with actually killing her, since I'm basically powerless to attack enemies in dreamspace. I gave Carol the System Credits for her expansion. So, if it's possible for you to find the method for killing whatever she is, I'd appreciate that."

Sister Strange. So that's her name. James went through his whole explanation and his plan for dealing with her, but he never said what the enemy's name was. What's the source of this aversion?

"Could you tell me more about her?" Mina asked.

And she could see it again: the hesitation, the look of reluctance on James's face that she had noticed when he was explaining the threat to the group as a whole.

"You don't have to tell me about it if you don't want to," she whispered.

"It's nothing I can't discuss, exactly," James said. "It's something I feel"—he searched for words—"uneasy about, I guess." He looked at Mina. "She claimed to be showing me visions of my future suffering, and I've spent the whole day wondering—"

"If it's true," she finished.

And suddenly, Mina found that she didn't want to know. She didn't want to know what the creature's visions had shown James. She felt a horrible sense of foreboding.

They'd had the conversation about whether they would want to know their futures before, years ago, long before either of them really believed that prophecy was possible.

"No," Mina had said, quickly and firmly. "Superstitious people are always trying to find out the future from fortune tellers. It never helps them. Even if I knew, it would only make me miserable. To know how long I was going to live, how I was going to die—why would anyone want that?"

James had been very firm that he wanted to know what would happen in his future if he could somehow acquire that knowledge.

"If you knew what was going to happen to you, it would change the meaning of everything that went before," he had insisted. "I would absolutely want to know. There's no secret that I don't want to know the truth about. Whatever it is, I can handle it. Even if it's painful. Even if it's horrible. Can you imagine knowing how your story ends? The ending of your life is like the punctuation at the end of a sentence." His voice had become passionate. "If it falls in just the right place, it can increase the meaning of everything that came before! Or, if it's wrong, it can ruin the meaning. But if you knew about it in advance, you'd change the sentence. You would write a different sentence so that the people who read it would understand what you wanted them to understand. Even if you're stuck with some shitty punctuation, it's what you do with it that counts."

Mina hadn't known quite how to respond to that. She still felt the same way after his impassioned argument for his position, but she was almost certain that he had been thinking of his own father's untimely death when he had said it would have been better to know ahead of time.

You never had the chance to say a proper goodbye, she remembered thinking.

In the present, James nodded.

"Yes. That's exactly it. I've spent the whole day wondering if that hag is actually showing me real visions of the future."

"That's part of why you wanted to face her again," Mina said the words as she thought them.

"Maybe," James agreed.

"You think she can really show you the future," Mina said. "And it's irresistible to you. You have to see it. You have to know."

She spoke in non-judgmental tones. Her husband's curiosity reminded her of the great hero of the *Odyssey*. Odysseus knew that the sirens' song lured sailors to their deaths, but he had to know what it sounded like. So, he had his sailors tie him to the mast, and while they stuffed their ears with wax, he listened.

James swallowed. "I do have to know," he said. "I also think this is the best path forward to protect our people. But you—you still don't want to know, right? What the future holds?"

She shook her head and gave him a tight smile. "Blissful ignorance for me, thank you."

Even as Mina said those words, the curiosity gnawed at her. She didn't want to know. She was terribly afraid. And she suspected that if these visions of the future pertained to her, they would start to change James's behavior around her. Like when he looked up the ending of a show.

When that happens, I always end up asking him what exactly happens. Half the time, he gave in and told her. But the other half of the time—well, James was good at knowing what to tell and what to withhold.

"I'm glad we had this conversation," James said. He sounded slightly uncomfortable but relieved.

"Me too," Mina said. Her voice softened. "I hope it's a little of the weight off your shoulders, skapi. Sharing your plans with me, I mean. You know, I would never change this about you, any more than I would change the qualities that pushed you to pursue me, or the ones that led you to start your own country."

He smiled and stared deep into her eyes.

"I know," he said. "You always make things easier. Especially the hard ones."

CHAPTER FORTY-FOUR

Reunited

Rotter and Luntz each took a knob in hand, and they pulled the heavy doors of the community center open.

Apparently, quite a few people had been waiting for the meeting to be opened to the public. Members of the community began to stream in, moving in a slow, orderly fashion and filing carefully into the gallery seats.

Mina was impressed by how patiently they had waited. There were a surprising number of them, though Mina realized there were a few faces she hadn't seen around yet.

Damien strode to the front of the group.

"Thank you for opening the meeting to the public," he said, projecting his voice to be heard over the din of moving people and scraping chairs. "If it's all right, we would like to let some new arrivals greet the King and his council members first. There are several dozen new people who arrived this morning. Some of them are very excited to be here. While we were outside, everyone agreed that would be the fairest—uh, the best—thing to do."

There were nods and murmurs of assent from the gallery.

Mina raised an eyebrow. *Really, after they waited all this time, they want to let some new people speak first? And everyone was just okay with this?*

Then Damien took a seat in the front row, and a woman who had seated herself near the back of the room stood. She wore Mage's robes.

Mina suddenly understood exactly why the consensus outside had formed to let the King and his council welcome the new arrivals before handling other business. Her stomach did a little flip as she saw the familiar face.

She's probably the only woman alive in the world who can make me nervous with just her presence, Mina thought.

The older Black woman stepped forward to the front of the center aisle and dipped her head in a slight bow.

"It's good to see you're alive and well, Fisher King," she said in a playful tone, a mischievous smile on her lips.

James rose from his seat. "It's good to see you too, Mom," he said, matching her tone.

He walked around the table to the edge of the stage, then jumped down, took another few steps, and pulled her into a bear hug. The tiny woman looked almost like a child being embraced by an adult in her massive son's arms.

"Not too tight," she rasped breathlessly, almost laughing despite being short of air. "You'll crush me! What, are you part bear now?"

James relaxed his grip but didn't let her go. "I thought—well, I'm just really glad to see you're okay. Do you know if Alice is all right?"

Zora Robard turned her head and tilted it at a woman who sat in the back corner.

And Alice Robard raised a hand and waved, wiggling one finger at a time at James.

James let out a deep breath, then let his mother go and stepped back. He raised his voice so the whole room could hear him.

"I would appreciate it if everyone could give me and my family five minutes," he said.

Mina could feel, and she was certain the whole room could hear, the emotion in his voice.

"Woo!"

A quiet cheer went up in the crowd, along with some applause. Both people in the gallery and those outside began to take it up.

"Woo! Congratulations!"

Mina heard the emotional voices of people who had been separated from their loved ones by the System's advent—many of whom were still not reunited with their families. They seemed to take a vicarious pleasure at James being reunited with his mother and sister.

Mina smiled too. She was happy for James, though she was slightly uncomfortable herself.

There were so many complex emotions at play in Mina's relationship with Zora. On the one hand, Zora was intelligent and sophisticated, significantly more intellectually curious than Mina's own mother. Mina and Zora *should* have a lot in common.

On the other hand, Zora was a very particular person.

For years, I felt like I could never be good enough for her . . . Memories played out behind Mina's unreadable eyes and the mask of her frozen smile.

Then people filed out, still smiling and cheering. The council members followed after them, leaving the room vacant but for Mina, James, Zora, and Alice.

Mina had risen from where she sat and walked around to the edge of the stage, but she stood uncertain for a moment. *Will James want me to stay for this? Should I go down there? Should I go outside and let them have some privacy?*

Then Alice Robard was standing in front of her in her Mage's robes, reaching up to Mina with both hands.

Mina took James's little sister's hands in her own, and then Mina leaned on Alice and climbed down from the stage. The two women embraced.

"It's good to see you guys came out okay," Alice said.

Mina nodded, not yet quite trusting herself to speak.

"You're, um—" Alice gestured at Mina's diminished stomach.

"You gave birth." Zora's voice cut through the awkward, uncertain conversation. She stepped toward Mina, pulled her in close, and kissed her on both cheeks. "Thank you for keeping my son safe," she said. She sounded genuinely grateful. "And I look forward to seeing my grandson." Zora looked into Mina's eyes, and Mina was startled to realize that her mother-in-law was looking for some reassurance.

"Of course," Mina said. "My sister is watching him now, and some other children we rescued."

"Oh, of course," Zora repeated, sighing with relief. "I'm so glad you all made it out okay. How is little Yulia doing?"

"Not as little as last time you saw her," James said, stepping between his mother and sister. "How's my little sister doing?" he asked.

"Oh, just thrilled to come and find my brother in his kingdom," Alice said, speaking with a slight ironic edge. "I survived. Figured I'd look after Mom, but you know Mom."

"Yep," James said. "I hope you didn't let her kill too many of the poor monsters."

They all laughed at that.

"Yes, I *can* look after myself, young man," Zora agreed. "Where do you think you got it from?"

"Definitely you," he said, shaking his head with a faux-exasperated expression on his face. "Again, my sympathies to the poor monsters that had you for Orientation."

"How is, um, Ben?" Mina asked.

"He survived," Zora said, her tone flat.

"He's here with us," Alice said, giving her mother a sideways look and gesturing toward the door. Ben was apparently waiting outside. Giving the family time to reunite.

I guess that's the difference between being a boyfriend and being a wife. I get to be in the room right now.

"Yes, I'm glad he's all right," Zora said. She lowered her voice. "But maybe you can do better? You are a princess now, right? With your brother a king?"

This feels familiar, Mina thought. Zora had pulled back some on the idea of Mina not being good enough for her son after they had become engaged, then even more so when they had married. The insinuations had vanished almost completely when Mina got pregnant, and then the final end to them had occurred when Alice embarked upon her current relationship. Then it was *Ben* who wasn't quite good enough—and look at how well James had married!

"Mom, we're not discussing this right now," Alice said irritably.

"Right, right," Zora said, putting her hands up in surrender. "It's your life."

"How did you guys get back here?" James asked, in a very blatant attempt to change the subject. "You were upstate when this thing started, right? And how did you find us?"

"It's a long story, son," Zora said. "You asked them to leave for five minutes, right?" She gestured to the door.

"Though, you are living in exactly the same place you were before the System appeared," Alice said in an amused tone.

"Later, you guys are going to have to tell me everything about your Orientation—or *Orientations*, as the case may be—and any other news you have about the world outside my borders," James said. "For right now, it's just more than I could have hoped for to see you two again. Alive. In one piece."

"The whole family reunited," Alice agreed.

"Except those who can't be with us," James said. His eyes took on a faraway look that told Mina he was remembering his dead father again. He seemed to be in a very morbid frame of mind today.

I wonder where my other sisters are right now, Mina thought. They might be alive or dead, and she would never know. They wouldn't look for her and Yulia. She knew that. They had their own families to worry about. *I guess that tells you something. Once the phones and the Internet are gone, you only have the strongest ties to connect you. James and I are married, and we have a child together. Yulia is our responsibility. Alice and Zora are his only surviving family. Maybe this says something about which bonds can survive a cataclysm.*

"You know, I knew that you would achieve great things," Zora said. "Didn't I tell you?"

James nodded. "From a young age, I remember. You were asking me when you were going to get your invitation to my inauguration. Filling my head with the crazy notion that I was going to be President, when in fact what you should have led me to expect was that I would replace our representative system of government with a monarchy."

"Naturally," Zora said, chuckling.

"I think our five minutes are up," Alice said quietly. "Why don't we take a seat in the front row here?" She gestured to the chairs behind her. "We'll wait for the meeting to be over."

"Nonsense!" James exclaimed. "You're both going to come and sit at my left side. I'll go and grab another couple chairs."

Zora was nodding, but Alice shook her head.

"I'll sit with Ben in the front row," she said. She looked up at James. "I look forward to seeing how you run things here." There was a slight air of challenge in her tone, as if she couldn't quite believe that her brother had declared, and was really operating, a monarchy.

"And so you shall, Princess," he replied.

They all laughed.

James walked off to find a chair for Zora, and she pulled Mina into a sudden embrace.

"I'm so glad that you're okay," she said, her voice low, directly into Mina's ear. "I know we'll all need to pull together if this *enterprise* is to work. Even if we sometimes have our differences, we all want to stand behind him. And I'm going to stand behind you too, however I can. I just want you to know you have all my support." She spoke warmly, with such apparent sincerity that Mina finally relaxed a tension that she didn't know her body had been holding and sagged into Zora's arms.

"Thank you, Zora," she said with genuine gratitude. The use of her mother-in-law's first name still felt a little awkward to Mina. She had called Zora "Mrs. Robard" through most of her courtship with James, until Zora had finally pointed out that Mina was also about to become a "Mrs. Robard," and them both being called that would be confusing.

"We'll take it one day at a time," Zora said, pulling back and smiling.

If you try, I'll try, Mina thought. That was all there was to it for now.

James was placing Zora's chair up on the stage beside his own, positioning everyone else to that side slightly further away. Mina tried to remember which apostle sat to Jesus's left-hand side in *The Last Supper*, but her mind was spinning, and she didn't want to try to focus on that right now.

We'll work together, she told herself. *Maybe we'll even get along.*

"I'm going to open the doors, bro," Alice said from over by the doorway.

"Sounds good!" James replied.

Then Mina took her seat again, beside James and one away from Zora, and she prepared for whatever was to come next.

As the heavy doors opened, other faces appeared, and again there were those she recognized.

Jose and Paulo. Adelaide and Derek. Alba. Leo!

There were several other faces she knew from her Orientation, but these were the people she was happy to see. Since Mina had spent most of her Orientation sequestered in her rooms, and a couple of members of the group she spent the most time with had turned out to be monsters, there were only a few people she felt she could say she knew and somewhat trusted.

It was so good to see those familiar faces. No, it was more than good. Surreal? Magical?

In some way, it made Mina's Orientation more real; it brought everything back into immediacy. But because Cara wasn't there, the horrors were placed at a remove. Mina was reminded that she herself was heroic, had done great deeds and saved lives—these people's lives. Because that last challenge would have wiped out her whole Orientation if she hadn't beaten it.

And now they were here, alive and safe.

A big, natural smile spread across her face, and Mina felt her eyes watering.

I'm glad you all survived.

There was a man next to Alba, and Mina saw a pair of teenagers beside them. Leo had a woman next to him too: a warrior wearing white armor. The two stood rather close together.

Does Leo have a girlfriend? Wow. He must be ten years older than her...

James was waving at them. *At Leo?*

Then she realized he was actually waving at the woman in armor. *She must have been in James's Orientation.*

Mina looked back at the faces of those she knew. *Are they really all planning to stay here with us?*

She hoped so. But she was surprised these people weren't settling in some other area. How had they all ended up here?

"Once everyone is seated, we'll begin taking questions, comments, and concerns," James said.

Mina happened to be looking at him as he spoke; his eyes took on a distant look for a moment, and then an annoyed expression crossed his face before he quickly smoothed it over for the crowd in front of them.

"What's wrong?" she whispered in his ear.

"Another territory just connected to ours," James said, keeping his voice low. "Another potential headache. No emergencies yet, though. We can continue with the meeting until and unless something crosses the border."

CHAPTER FORTY-FIVE

The Public

The public comment segment of the meeting passed by relatively quickly, at least compared with what Mina had expected. James's commission heads all introduced themselves and what they were responsible for, and then the body took questions and comments—almost entirely questions.

"Um, sir, what can you tell us about the strange dreams so many of us have been having?" the first speaker asked, staring straight at James.

Hearing that out loud feels surreal. I never expected to wake up one day in a world where people would have bad dreams and ask my husband why they had them—and have a reasonable expectation that he would be able to answer them! Next thing I know, they'll be asking him for nicer weather.

"Before I answer that, how many of you are here with a question about the dreams or about the forest behind the wall we recently put up?" James asked.

More than half of the people in attendance raised their hands.

"Okay, I'll give an explanation that conveys everything I know about the situation so we can get those questions addressed all at once."

James discussed the same material he had gone over with the Council in the closed session, even including what the plan was to deal with the monster. He didn't reveal the bit about Sister Strange giving him visions that she asserted represented the future—or even that the monster's name was Sister Strange—but those came across as minor omissions to Mina.

And, of course, no one but her knew there was anything left out at all.

Mina assessed the crowd's response as fairly good. People liked the transparent approach.

Most importantly, it's fitting with James's character as they've come to know him. He's a straight shooter, more or less. I think they expect that he'll solve the problem—or tell him that he's failed if he can't. Probably much better than most of the leaders they've dealt with in their lives.

"Okay," James finished. "Other questions?"

There were other questions, but any sense of urgency around the meeting dissipated with James's explanation of the dream-monster problem. As the more mundane questions—about future food, housing, electricity, and running water plans—continued, Mina found herself wanting to check on baby James.

"Do you mind if I excuse myself?" she whispered into James's ear. "The baby probably wants food."

"Go ahead," he whispered back.

Mina rose, and half the people in the gallery rose with her. That was a little startling.

But I guess I need to get used to it, she thought. *We're royals now.*

It still sounded absurd in her head, but people smiled and parted for her as she made her way down the center aisle and through the front doors.

The meeting went on for almost an hour before James sensed an excuse to end it.

"Sorry to cut this short," he lied, "but there is a minor issue on our border I'd like to deal with."

It is interesting that people don't simply go to the commissions or the commission heads with some of these questions. I need to work on encouraging that more in the future. He thought of Samuel's advice. *If people are looking for me to tell them what's going on all the time, there's no way I'll be able to stay ahead of my rivals in enemy territories.*

He sent the rest of what he wanted to say as an announcement using his powers.

[Citizens of the Fisher Kingdom, a group of flying monsters has entered our airspace. While I do not yet have specific reason to believe that we have cause for alarm, I would appreciate the help of available individuals who have effective ranged attacks or weapons in dissuading the creatures from any possible aggression. We will try to resolve this incursion peacefully if we can, but it's always best to be prepared for violence. If you are willing and able to help, please meet me outside.]

At some point, James would need to give names to landmarks within his territory so he could give more specific directions than "please meet me outside." For now, though, he was confident this would do the trick.

"All new residents," he said aloud, "it's a pleasure to welcome new people into the Fisher Kingdom. Please give your names to the council's secretary, and if you're interested in staying, he'll also be available to coordinate times for you to take the citizenship oath."

Rotter rose from his seat at the end of the table and gave everyone in the gallery a little wave.

James turned to his mother and whispered, "Why don't you grab Alice and go meet the baby? Anyone on the council will be able to tell you which apartment is ours."

She nodded, and a satisfied smile spread across her face.

"I can't wait," she said quietly.

Then James hopped down from the stage, walked through the center aisle, and stepped out into the open air.

There were already dozens of people standing by, ready to assist him, and more followed him out of the community center.

This is, what, a hundred people total? James thought. Most brandished guns. Others, who held staves, appeared to be Mages. *Plus about twenty Goblins, armed with what appear to be homemade slings.*

He was a little hazy about the exact human population of the Fisher Kingdom, mainly because more people were arriving each day, but he knew it was still somewhere under a thousand. Still fewer humans than Goblins. He was surprised there were so many willing to fight, when he'd tried not to sound particularly worried in his announcement.

Then he sensed a change in the movement of the flying enemies he'd sensed. They had turned in their flightpath.

They're heading toward the farming space.

And James could feel that there were a few workers out there at the moment. He had a bad feeling about this.

"Follow me," he shouted. "They're near our crops!"

Then James took off jogging. He would have run faster, but with more than one enemy, and with his opponents airborne, he genuinely thought he might need help dealing with them.

How many is that?

He tried to figure it out as he ran, but when it came to sensing objects in the air, his powers seemed to be relatively weaker than they were on the ground.

Tracking the number of humans on his land was difficult, but only in the sense that counting how many ants were crawling across his skin would be hard if there were more than a few to look at. Trying to narrow down the number of flying enemies was more like trying to count the insects flying through the air while blindfolded, relying only on the sound of buzzing.

James quickly got a better idea of how many they were when the enemy descended to ground level.

Not good!

A dozen monsters landed, setting down close to the farmers who were still out in the fields.

James decided to accelerate. If he left his entourage behind, that was fine.

He turned his head and shouted, "Just keep running in the same direction!"

Then he started running full out, cutting the distance quickly with his superhuman speed. In less than a minute, he was a mile ahead of his allies.

Then he started to make out shapes: creatures moving on air and ground and humans fighting together to defend against them—fighting to protect one man who was tightly held in the beasts' clutches.

James was still too far away to see them clearly, but the outlines of the creatures gave him a good idea of a monster type from a distance. They had massive wings attached to slender bodies.

Looks like bat monsters?

James's eyes focused on the farmers risking their lives to protect their friend. He saw one farmer gushing blood from some sort of wound across his chest. Even as the red liquid poured down, though, the figure threw himself back into the fight. He seemed to try and aim the blood at the bats' heads—*Oh, he's trying to blind them!*

If James wasn't in the midst of a minor emergency, this would have made him feel some strong emotions. This was the humanity that he loved and respected.

His Orientation had made him more jaded toward his fellow man, but this was his reminder. *Humanity is awesome.* Humans might struggle and compete against each other every day of their lives, but when they stood together against a common enemy, no one would be able to break them. James had affection for both of these seemingly contradicting sides of human nature. They were not wolves or Mole People, with their apparently inborn loyalty to their leader. They were no Goblins, to be led purely by fear, or alligators that would follow and respect sheer power. They chose their friends. They chose to follow their leaders—even when that leader was a king, he was still reliant on his human citizens to not try to overthrow him.

Humans would undoubtedly be the biggest pain to govern out of all the Races that James counted within his borders. But he loved his kind, even beyond his own immediate family. It was moments like this that reminded him of why.

Then a slow boiling fury began to overtake him. *How dare they come onto my land and try to eat some of my people?*

That was all he could think. *How dare they. Don't they feel my aura? This land is claimed. Find your own prey somewhere else!*

The more of his citizens' blood he saw, the angrier he became. *How. Dare. YOU.*

James saw red.

He closed his eyes to blink, and when he opened them again, he found himself almost in the midst of the human–bat monster scrum. The distance had turned to nothing.

James was barely aware of his own body as he threw himself into the fight. He grabbed the nearest bat creatures by their heads and instantly crushed them into jelly with his bare hands.

The rest of the bats suddenly turned their attention to him. They dropped the men they were trying to carry off and threw themselves at James.

Good, he thought savagely. *Give yourselves to me! Die!*

The creatures latched onto James's body, shrieking angrily as they did so. James found the sound very unpleasant, but it was as if the noise came to him from somewhere deep underwater. He barely noticed it. He only noticed the vulnerable targets presenting themselves to him. There was a distant sound in the back of his head, and it took James a moment to realize that Hester was trying to suppress a scream.

But James couldn't spare much attention even for Hester's distress.

He punched and kicked with all four limbs as the bats took him to the ground with their momentum. Every strike he threw was potentially lethal, tearing through limb, torso, wing—whatever he touched.

They kept trying to go for his neck with long, sharp fangs. James lunged at the one that was closest and bit into the front of its head with inhumanly strong jaws. It gushed blood and brains into his mouth and then swiftly stopped moving.

James swallowed it down. *I'm an omnivore*, he thought, slightly giddy. *I won't waste any part of these things.*

"Tastes like chicken," he growled through a monstrous smile.

The bat creatures seemed to recognize how outclassed they were at that point. They started to visibly pull their bodies further away from him. James wouldn't let the ones touching him go.

"You asked for this," he hissed, barely aware that he was speaking rather than thinking. "How dare you come into my territory and attack my people . . ."

He began ripping them apart with his hands and teeth.

He could see the fear in each bat's eyes now as they either struggled weakly or waited, almost paralyzed, for him to finish them off.

"Not having fun anymore?" he asked. "Not fun when you're losing? When you're the ones being *eaten*?"

He ripped another bat's head off with his teeth and swallowed the neck flesh down like it was nothing. The meat seemed to make him stronger.

The bat monsters that were out of his immediate reach began taking to the sky, trying to escape.

There were still a dozen of them alive. James wasn't satisfied with the dozen he had ripped to pieces.

"Oh no, you don't," he murmured. "Roscuro."

The Soul Eater Orb responded to James's shapeless Will, his vague but violent intentions. It transformed itself into a hatchet, which James immediately threw at the nearest bat. James could hear the sharpness of the blade as it flew through the air. It almost sang to him.

Then it tore into the bat, chopping its body almost in half.

As the creature fell through the air, it let loose a horrendous scream of agony that James found slightly painful to the ears. Its body began to disintegrate.

Right. Roscuro eats their souls. That's what that looks like. Good. Stay away from my people! Suffer for your mistake . . .

He threw a couple of Air Strikes, but he was too far away to do much damage. He chopped off a foot, slashed a wing, but the enemy were able to remain airborne.

I didn't even manage to kill all of them, he thought angrily; though, even now, only seconds after the enemy had gotten somewhat out of reach, his wrath was fading. He looked down at his hands and noticed, seemingly for the first time, that they were drenched in blood and guts. He raised his arm and wiped off his face. It, too, was gross with monstrous flesh. He looked down at his feet and found that he stood atop a mound of corpses.

Huh. Something really came over me there. I guess it's that Berserk Mode thing. He thought back to the deer he'd fought that he had obtained the Skill from. *If he had a power like that, it's really something that he didn't actually succeed in killing me.*

"Are you okay, Hester?" he asked, his voice ragged.

"I'm fine, thank you," she said in a shaky voice. If she were human, James imagined there would be little tears in her eyes.

He wanted to tell her it was all right, that the fight was over. But it wouldn't be true. He wasn't going to let these invaders escape. He would chase them home. So, he kept silent and watched the enemy, trying to grasp their direction of flight and figure out where they would come to rest—where he would need to go to finish killing them.

James heard rather than saw when his backup arrived. Only a few seconds had passed. Time seemed to have slowed down a great deal for him. There was an incredibly loud noise of guns firing and an intense smell of gunpowder—almost overwhelming to James's senses.

And some of the bats that had been out of range for him began falling from the sky.

CHAPTER FORTY-SIX

The Land of Bats

James looked on in near awe as a half-dozen bats fell from the sky, shot through with bullet holes that, in several cases, had visibly shredded their thin wing membranes. As they fell, fireballs, small bolts of lightning, and even a few carefully aimed rocks, undoubtedly hurled by the Goblins using their slings, struck them.

But he was most impressed by the fact that man-made weapons had brought down creatures he thought were out of his own effective attack range.

How are their rifles more effective than my powers?

Roscuro had returned to him now, floating across the air as smoke. Even if he were to turn back into a hatchet, the bats were outside James's accurate throwing range—though, apparently, not out of bullet range.

Those are quite impressive weapons, Roscuro thought. *I wonder if I can transform into that shape. Could you explain how they work?*

Only vaguely, James replied. *The way it works is that the hollow tube contains something called a bullet.* He sent a mental picture. *Bullets are made of metal. They are tiny projectiles that can sometimes move faster than the speed of sound.*

Oh, like arrows! Roscuro thought.

Yes, but also no. They're so much better than arrows . . . James spent a little time trying to explain gunpowder.

So, the projectiles are propelled by small explosions, Roscuro summarized. *The barrels are shaped the way they are so that you can easily point and aim at a target. In short, they are like arrows if arrows required less skill and were significantly more effective at hitting far-off targets.*

I think that about sums it up, James replied. He felt very dumb, not knowing very well how guns worked when they were such a pivotal technology in world history—and in the history of the former United States in particular.

Well, at least I only look dumb in front of Roscuro, he thought, without sharing that sentiment with the Soul Eater.

Hm. I do not believe I can generate explosive materials with my current capabilities, Roscuro sent. *It may be interesting to see what I could do if you collect some of this gunpowder, though.*

I'll keep it in mind, thank you, James sent.

By now, the sound of gunshots was fading, and James's allies were finally reaching the area where he had made his stand against the creatures. He saw that the monsters the gunmen had shot down lay strewn about the field. They were clearly not all dead. Some wiggled and writhed in noticeable pain. But they weren't going anywhere. Not a single beast had escaped James's territory alive.

We should go spear the wounded, Roscuro suggested gleefully. *Put them out of their misery . . .*

Oh no! James thought suddenly. *The wounded farmers! I was so caught up in killing bats that I didn't check if they were all right.* He turned his head to look around at the people who had been bleeding when he first arrived, but everyone seemed to be fine.

"Is anyone hurt?" James asked.

Then his voice was overwhelmed by the sound of cheering.

"James! James! James!"

There were smaller voices shouting things underneath the general roar of those who'd followed him, but it was harder to hear them.

"How many did he kill?"

"Incredible!"

"That's the King!"

"That's *why* he's the King!"

Several of them surrounded him and made as if to lift him onto their shoulders. James gently pushed their hands away. He had to raise his voice to be heard over the cheers.

"Hey, is anyone hurt? I saw they were attacking some farmers when I got here."

The crowd quieted for a few seconds, long enough for a farmer to shout, "We got potions into them, sir! No one was killed."

Then the cheering went up again.

"James! James! James!"

The crowd seemed infected with James's hatred for the monsters. He suddenly realized it wasn't enough just to kill the bats that had come here. He needed to go into their territory and teach them a lesson they wouldn't soon forget.

"It's not over!" James shouted.

The crowd instantly quieted. "I'm going to go and deal with the monsters in that territory. They're clearly aggressive; they tried to carry off our farmers! I won't ask anyone to follow me except those who are ready to go willingly, who are willing to potentially lay down their lives to destroy this menace."

"Fisher King! Fisher King! Fisher King!" This time the cheering began with the Goblins, suddenly presented with an opportunity to display the valor they had not been able to demonstrate against the bats that had invaded. James had noticed they were the only ones in the crowd who seemed slightly deflated after the bats were killed.

"James! James! James!"

Dave Matsumoto stepped forward from within the crowd and raised his pistol in the air.

"I think I speak for most of them when I say we're ready to follow you!" he shouted.

James had never seen the man so fiery, but Dave looked quite emotional as he spoke. There were tears in his eyes but a strange smile on his face.

"Let's go, then!" James yelled. "Come with me and kill these things!"

He marched toward the border with the bats, and he heard the sound of hundreds of footsteps following after him. As he strode forward, the Goblins ran ahead of him, drawing small knives, and they began killing the bats that remained alive on the ground.

"Sir, you don't want to do any reconnaissance or planning before you launch this invasion?" Hester asked from behind his ear.

"No," James whispered quietly back. "Not when I've got this many people as fired up as I am. We're going to cut through these things like hot knives through butter. Can't risk letting the monsters form an alliance with the thing in the forest or something."

"Oh, yes," Hester said. "That makes sense, then."

But in truth, James would have gone into the land of the bats by himself at this point, completely unarmed. He wanted to do more killing. He wasn't quite satisfied with what little he'd had the chance to do. He wanted to tear out more of the monsters' throats and crush more of their heads. He was still full of wrath, boiling just beneath the surface.

The suddenly formed militia followed James with ferocious energy across the border. Only a few of those who had come out stayed back.

He paid them no mind. His eyes were focused forward as he plunged into enemy territory.

The climate changed as soon as James crossed the border. He felt a wave of hot, moist air hit him. It was as if he'd stepped through a portal from Orlando in autumn straight into the Everglades in summer. The scenery was not swampy like the Everglades, though. There were a number of trees that he imagined he might see in the Everglades, but the soil beneath his feet was firm enough.

James lacked the frame of reference to describe the biome he found himself in, but it featured densely packed trees and vines that looked like they would have been more at home in Central America than in Florida. He was more focused, however, on the abrupt shift in climate.

What the fuck? These things can change the weather? Is the Ruler more powerful than me or something? The thought only made him angrier. *I'll kill him and steal his powers.*

That reminded him that, in his wrath, he had neglected to even Pillage the bodies of the dead bats he'd killed. The thought slightly dampened his fury.

Okay, I'm not going to go that crazy. I can't afford to miss out on gains just because I'm angry.

He took deep breaths and tried to find the calm space inside himself. He felt a wall of ice descend between himself and the anger that had motivated him. It was still there. A cold fury.

He wondered what his Wrath Meter would show if he looked at it now. He was angry, yet he was also now much more in control of himself.

But he didn't want to take the time to stop and look. He needed to move forward. He could feel the squad behind him ready to move. Some part of him suspected that if he paused too long, their courage might falter. He didn't want to find himself forced to rally the troops before they had even encountered the enemy.

And his instincts and superhuman senses seemed to have suddenly sharpened as soon as he tried to get his anger under control. Now he could sense the life all around them and could distinguish the immovable life of the trees and the smaller plants that grew from the other species.

He also had the presence of mind to finally arm himself properly. He reached into his magic satchel and pulled out his Ego Spidersword, Ego Exoshield, and Solar Helm. He was wearing his Royal Exoarmor almost all the time now already, and it had healed its damage from the battle with Samuel over the previous day. Now he felt ready to slaughter the entire population of this land of bats by himself if necessary.

But he knew he wouldn't have to. He had a formidable force of brave soldiers with him.

And just to make sure they would be at their best . . .

Command Presence!

It was the other Skill, besides Zone of Influence, generated by the Alpha Presence Talent he'd taken from the coyote boss back in Orientation.

[Command Presence: Generate a field made from your aura that increases the power and cohesion of allied forces within the aura. Scales with Charisma, Will, and Intelligence. Consumes Stamina and Mana.]

His aura spread out within a limited area, giving a boost to everyone around him. People stood straighter and looked more prepared to back each other up and stand firm. And compared with the time he had used Zone of Influence back in Orientation, the drain on his resources seemed smaller now.

The benefits of continuously getting stronger.

He turned to his soldiers and put a finger to his lips, signaling for quiet. There were nods and murmurs of assent.

"Quiet," people whispered to their neighbors.

Then James led his soldiers further into the enemy's territory, heading straight to the nearest non-plant life that he could sense. He saw them, hanging huddled in a tree: a cluster of a dozen bats, quivering slightly as they tried to hide from the sunlight. For the first time it struck James as slightly odd that the bats were coming out of their territory in the middle of the day.

Aren't they the most famously nocturnal animals in the world?

But he had no time to solve that mystery now.

He used Identify on the closest one.

[Common Bloodsucker Bat, Lv. 12]

They're not exactly weak, but we should have no trouble taking this group. A perfect chance to give my people some experience.

He turned back to his group, who were waiting for him.

"Everyone with quiet projectile attacks, like arrows or magic, prepare to launch whatever you've got on my signal," he said in a stage whisper.

Dozens of heads nodded as people whispered chants or loaded bows, and Goblins loaded slings.

James waited calmly until it looked like almost all of them were poised to attack. It took around a minute.

Then he pointed at the enemy.

Go! he thought.

A wave of magic, stones, and arrows shot forward almost completely silently.

The bats saw the volley of lethal attacks flying through the air, but they had no time to dodge. With the tree at their backs, they only had a moment to scream out as the missiles struck.

"Perfect!" James said loudly as the bats began falling from the tree toward the ground. The tree itself was beginning to burn from being struck with all the balls of fire and lightning, but James did not care much about that now.

Roscuro, javelin form! he sent.

The Soul Eater obediently transformed, and James instantly hurled the javelin into the furthest fallen bat's chest. It let out a horrific shriek and began disintegrating.

James was already moving with the Ego Spidersword as the javelin found its target, decapitating the nearest bats with a single stroke each.

Once they're on the ground, it's like killing fish in a barrel.

Other soldiers from his side flanked him, striking down bats before James could reach them, and he had to hold back his desire to smile. Because this killing business was a serious affair. If it wasn't so serious, he might begin to enjoy it . . .

Roscuro returned to his hand, and James threw the Soul Eater at one of the few bats that was still clinging to the tree for dear life.

The ones with that much vitality left could potentially try to fly away and warn their brethren, he thought. *I can't let them go. I won't lead this expedition into a massacre.* A significant part of why James was leading this invasion, even after his rage had come under control, was his desire to train his forces and strengthen the bonds between them.

The group quickly wiped out the remaining creatures from the tree. As his focus relaxed slightly, some of the System's alerts popped into view.

[You killed White-Furred Bloodsucker Bat, Lv. 14! You gained 650 exp!]

So, there are different species of these things living together, he thought. *Or does the fur color not denote a separate species if they're both bloodsuckers?*

The alerts kept coming.

[. . .]

[Sufficient experience accrued! Predator in Human Skin leveled up!]
[Evolver Human leveled up!]
[Sufficient experience accrued! Fisher King leveled up!]

Nice. It seems like I get Fisher King experience when I lead people into battle.

He Pillaged one of the bats that he knew he'd killed personally and selected Talent as his theft target.

[Common Bloodsucker Bat's body processed.]

[You obtained Common Levitation Cloak, 3x Common Bloodsucker Meat Bundle, and Common Bloodsucker Arrows!]

[Talent obtained: Ultrasonic Pitch!]

The Talent came with the two Skills: Echolocation—which James thought might be a good gift for a blind person, given that he could use Skill Transfer—and Otherworldly Shriek.

I guess that was what those horrendous screeches were, he thought. Though the attack hadn't been particularly effective against James while he was in his enraged state earlier, he remembered the bats he had fought in the Fisher Kingdom shrieking loudly in his face.

Now that he had killed another handful of bats and slaked some of his thirst for blood, the questions that he'd been suppressing to secure a successful ambush came roaring back into focus. James couldn't help wondering why they had sent such a small number of creatures to fight in his territory.

It seemed like a monumental miscalculation; though, perhaps that was the character of the Ruler here. Reckless and rash.

Were they probing for weakness? Was it a rogue group? If I were to stop now and just leave these bodies as a warning—no, that's foolish. No fucking warnings unless I deliver them in person to someone in this place who has power over these things. If I just leave a burned-out husk of a tree where a bunch of bats used to be, all they'll think is that they've been attacked. The bats would just escalate at that point. That's what I'm doing.

"What next, sir?" came a woman's voice—one of the Mages. James did not know her name.

"We advance," he said.

CHAPTER FORTY-SEVEN

Red and Black

James and his war party reached another tree that he sensed was occupied. This time there were more than two dozen creatures huddled together.

We're probably going to have to abandon stealth, he assessed.

"Another volley like the last one," he ordered. "Everyone with firearms, be ready to pick off any creatures that try to fly away. With this many, they're not likely to all fall with the first wave of attacks. The noise doesn't matter as much as not letting any get away."

"Yes, sir," said a chorus of hushed voices from behind him.

The more they do this, the better they're getting at it, he thought. *Are they weirdly good at killing things, or are these just the types of people who have survived Orientation? Humans are predators, after all.*

He smiled. *These are my people. A fierce people, we former Americans. With them, I could build an empire.*

He waited for his comrades to charge their attacks, and then he thrust his arm forward in an overhead chop.

Another wave of attacks launched at his command. The power and fury of it was exhilarating.

Imagine if I had a whole army . . .

He could picture wave upon wave of magical and physical projectiles tearing through monsters, buildings, natural obstacles—anything that might get in his way. And then he thought of the vision Sister Strange had shown him of his future kingdom being overtaken. He had to push that out of his mind to keep from shuddering.

The barrage was highly effective. As James had predicted, a few of the bats managed to survive with little or no damage, but the soldiers in his ranks armed with rifles aimed a concentrated burst of gunfire at them. It was loud, but the previously unharmed bats were dead before they struck the ground. The echoes lasted a little longer.

Well, the element of surprise is broken, but the fact that that last tree burned down will have broken it anyway if the Ruler is like me. Maybe the bat boss just isn't paying much attention.

Then James and his soldiers—especially the Goblins, who seemed to get really into this part—walked around putting the wounded creatures out of their misery. Roscuro absorbed two more souls and the soldiers let out a cheer as the tree burned before they moved on.

I guess I won't get the, um, credit if I pull off a xenocide here, James thought as he marched his troops to the next occupied tree. *I'm not killing off the monsters singlehandedly, although everyone doing damage to these things is acting under my command. Oh well. I probably couldn't do this by myself. There are too many of them, and they can fly.*

As they reached the next tree, James raised a fist to signal his soldiers to stop. He heard a sound almost at the edge of his awareness: subtle, almost silent wings moving through the air.

Only *almost* silent. Nothing in the natural universe could truly move silently, and that seemed to hold true even in the post-System world. So, James could hear the creature approaching them. From the sound of the wings, he thought it was large. A bigger, stronger version of these monstrous bats, maybe.

Probably the Ruler.

"What's up?" asked Dave, who had positioned himself at James's right flank.

"Something big is approaching," James said quietly but distinctly. "Everyone needs to be prepared for a dramatic increase in the amount of resistance we've been dealing with."

Since the invasion thus far had been a one-sided slaughter, *any* resistance would be a dramatic increase compared with what they had experienced. But as James glanced back at the faces of his comrades, he saw that they seemed to understand what he meant.

He reminded himself, *All of these people survived Orientations too. They've all seen things I wouldn't be able to guess. It's not only me. Some of them are also hardened.*

The wing beats abruptly turned and navigated away from James's position.

"What the hell?" James said under his breath. "Where is it going now?"

He couldn't precisely track the position of the apparent Ruler with just sound, but this was definitely a move *away* from him and his troops.

Is it just running away? Abandoning the others of its kind to escape with its life?

He shook his head. It was hard to believe any creature that had risen to become a Ruler would be so cowardly when it hadn't even seen James and his forces yet. Even if the creature had superhuman senses beyond James's, the tree canopy hid them from direct view.

And even James needed to be close to determine from sound alone how many enemies he was facing.

"What should we do?" Dave asked. "Do you want to retreat?"

James shook his head. "No. We haven't even seen the main enemy yet. I won't leave until we at least have some idea of what we're facing."

Actually, this bears telling everyone. Command Presence and their own experiences have made them a more cohesive fighting force than they would be otherwise, but there's only so much I can expect out of untrained soldiers. Hardly any of these people are veterans of real wars like Dave. Even if they were, getting up close and fighting within inches of your enemy isn't the same as shooting someone from a distance. If there's a counterattack, that's what we'll be facing.

He turned to face the rest of the group. "Everyone, we're about to face a stronger enemy," he said, projecting so that everyone could hear him. "All of you who accompanied me here came voluntarily, and I appreciate that. Your efforts have obviously been very successful so far, and you have my gratitude. You have shown that we're a country to be taken seriously!"

A little whoop went up from the crowd.

James's eyes narrowed, and he raised his voice. "But now, I have to remind you that you are all here *voluntarily*. After this next enemy arrives, that changes. If there is anyone who wants to run away before the boss monster gets here, I won't stop them. You will not be punished in any way. I just—I can't have anyone breaking and running once the main enemy is actually here. That kind of display of weakness could cause the enemy to underestimate us, or it could spook others into running, and the end result is that you could end up getting everyone else killed. At the very least, you should expect it to cost some lives. And I know that for all of us, getting one of our friends or one of our neighbors killed would be one person too many. Our community is small, and every life is valuable." He looked from person to person. "If there's anyone here who thinks there's a chance they might run away at the critical moment, please excuse yourself now."

Then he pointedly turned his back on the soldiers.

He could hear people whispering behind him, but he very deliberately ignored them and tried to selectively listen to the distant sounds of flight.

The big monster was moving again, and the situation was worse than he'd imagined. The creature was approaching them quickly, but apparently it had stopped for a good reason. Now it was no longer flying alone. A difficult to estimate number of wings flapped and glided alongside the lead monster.

A hand clapped on James's shoulder, and he had to use all his superhuman reserve of self-control not to jump at the touch. Instead, he simply turned his head and saw Dave was back at his side again.

"Everyone agrees," Dave said loudly. "No one is leaving your side."

Well, I hope you're right, James thought. *And I hope that's not a terrible mistake on their part . . .*

The cheer went up once again from those who had followed him.

"James! James! James!"

And he allowed himself to bask in the glow for a moment.

At least if I die here, it's kind of an awesome way to go out.

Mina's face, James Jr.'s face, Yulia's face, his mom's face, Alice's face, and even Abhi's face all came to mind suddenly. The idea of a beautiful death in battle alongside his soldiers was instantly spoiled.

Can't die here, or what happens to them? His mind returned to Sister Strange's visions. *Maybe that's how Mina dies alone: I'm dead already. Though, that would require that the vision where I'm getting my ass kicked can't happen. Maybe I can't die yet. At least, not if there's anything to that creature's visions . . .*

He swallowed and put on a smile that did not reflect his feelings.

I'll just have to kill *beautifully instead.*

Just then James heard a sound of racing footsteps coming from behind him—coming from the direction of the Fisher Kingdom. It made no sense to him. *Who would follow us?*

Then he saw them. Like the eagles soaring to the rescue in *The Hobbit* and *The Lord of the Rings*, the creatures that were perhaps his most loyal followers would not miss this opportunity to come to his rescue.

We heard that you went into battle, my king, came Luna's voice inside his head. *But you forgot to invite us!*

I didn't forget, James wanted to say. *I just don't know what you guys are supposed to do against a bunch of flying bats! I didn't want to get you killed . . .*

But he didn't respond with that. It would undermine the confidence of his allies to suggest he didn't think they could help.

Thank you for coming, he sent. *We're about to face the main enemy now. You've come just in time!*

And the soldiers who had been cheering for James chanted, "Wolves! Wolves! Wolves!"

Well, maybe we'll all die together, James thought quietly. *Won't that be nice.*

There was one actually useful piece of help that the wolves' arrival brought. Not to be left out, Duncan had joined them, riding into battle atop Luna's mate, Romulus. His illusions might be useful if this became a small-scale war.

"Good to see you're still in good health, Your Majesty," Duncan said as Romulus pulled alongside James. "And I'm very pleased to see a number of brave Goblin fighters accompanied you and your army into this fight."

James nodded. "They've represented your people well," he said. "I'm pleased to be able to count on the loyal support of so many brave soldiers. I was especially impressed that they volunteered. I did not order them."

Duncan looked proud and gave his Goblins a salute, which they returned, drawing themselves up to their full, unimpressive, heights.

Then James ordered his forces into a defensive formation. The fast-moving wolves were to stand at the edges of the mostly human ranged fighting force, ready to sprint or leap at any enemies that touched ground or drew near it. James kept Duncan near himself at the front of the human–Goblin contingent of forces, ready to use his illusions if ordered and close enough for James to easily defend him.

But he ordered all of them to remain peaceful until ordered otherwise, unless first attacked by the enemy.

The combined force stood there waiting in formation for a total of less than thirty seconds, but James imagined they must have made a formidable picture.

The tropical forest ecosystem the bats lived in was relatively densely populated with trees, so the sunlight that came through the canopy was patchy and inconsistent.

The result of that was that when the enemy arrived, the bats' wings almost completely blotted out the sun.

James didn't even allow his expression to change. He maintained his smile. He kept his cool. He let the soldiers see that he wasn't shaken.

As the enemy colony began to land several feet away from him, James counted their numbers.

Around a hundred bats, he estimated. *And—wait, what the hell are those?*

Accompanying the bats were a roughly equal number of gliding, rodent-like creatures. But their faces and body types were distinctly different from the bats'. Whereas the bats looked like they wore grotesque Halloween masks made by a master special-effects artist, these other *things* just looked like giant rats with wings. The flying rat-like creatures and bats were of similar stature, each a bit taller than an average human.

Not quite wings. What are those things between their limbs?

He used Identify on the two lead creatures from both species, which had landed at the heads of their respective forces and which ominously *both* gave off the feeling of being Rulers.

[Red Flying Squirrel Queen Ysabel, Lv. 33]

These are squirrels? Really?

They were by far the creepiest looking squirrels James had ever seen.

[Black Bloodsucking Bat Queen Barbara, Lv. 35]

Crap. They really are two Rulers. I would assume that I could take either of them out alone, but together . . .

A hideous shrieking suddenly filled his ears. James had to exercise some restraint to keep his hands at his sides instead of covering them.

Gradually, it became apparent that the shrieking was actually words. The voice seemed to be speaking English—or at least the shrieks from the Black Bloodsucking Bat Queen were translated into English rather than some other language. James still wasn't quite clear on how *human* the monsters he kept encountering were, and how the System-assisted translations worked.

Queen Barbara was saying, "How dare you pip-squeaks invade my family's home?"

CHAPTER FORTY-EIGHT

Red Queen

Now that the Black Bloodsucking Bat Queen was speaking with him, James was no longer on a hair trigger waiting to learn whether he would have to order an attack or not. He found it possible to retake control of the situation.

"Lower your voice, please!" he barked. "I'm not deaf—yet!"

"You have no grounds to complain about being yelled at, trespasser," she replied. But she did speak at a noticeably much lower volume thereafter. "Why are you here?"

"My territory was invaded," James replied with slight indignation. "Dozens of *your family* invaded and tried to carry off and kill some of my humans."

"Hm." The massive bat scrunched up her already strange wrinkled face and gave James a hard look. Then she closed her eyes.

James thought she must be communicating telepathically with her family members. That, and giving her eyes a rest. He could tell that standing around in the sunlight made all the bats uncomfortable, including their Ruler.

"How do you two manage to get along, exactly?" James asked, looking to the Red Flying Squirrel Queen. "Do you somehow share territory? Are you neighbors? If the Bat Queen wants to borrow a cup of sugar . . ."

James let his voice trail off. The Squirrel Queen tilted her head as if slightly confused by that last question.

"We have different territory," she said in a chirping voice. "She rules the skies. I rule the ground level. We share the trees."

She's speaking Spanish, James realized, though the System was instantly translating it into English. *How does that happen? Do I detect a Cuban accent?*

"How does that work?" James thought aloud. "You guys glide through the air, and her bats have to come to the ground sometime, right?"

"Common courtesy," the Bat Queen interjected. "It's easy to learn, human."

"Did you manage to confirm what I said?" James asked.

The Bat Queen looked at him through slit eyes. "Yes, some of our family were sick, and they were acting strangely, so their cousins kicked them out of the tree. I guess that *might* account for the incursion into your territory."

James nodded. "That makes sense."

Rabies, he thought. *I need to make sure everyone who came into contact with those bats sees a Healer when we get back.*

"Still, what does that have to do with why you're here, *human?*" she spat.

James raised an eyebrow. "I obviously thought it was an invasion by a raiding party of your kind," he said, "so I responded in kind."

"You mean you killed dozens of my family because a little group of them crossed your border," the Bat Queen said. Her beady black eyes stared coldly into his.

"I wanted to ask you about what was going on, but my contact with my neighbors has mostly been hostile," James explained. "It seemed more responsible to prepare for the worst than to hope that there was a simple misunderstanding." He lowered his head and tried to sound humble. "If those bats that invaded my territory were acting alone, then I sincerely apologize for my retaliation. It must seem disproportionate. We are used to being in a state of war."

"Not good enough." The Bat Queen reached out with a long bony claw and jabbed James in the chest. "Show me the bodies of your dead. You never mentioned how many of yours were killed to justify this 'retaliation.' How many did you lose in our *invasion?*"

"Lady, you need to back away from him," interjected Dave from the side. James could hear the sound of metal sliding free from leather as Dave drew his pistol.

James immediately turned to face Dave. "I've got this," he said, giving him a firm look.

Dave made eye contact with James and simply nodded. He didn't put his gun away, but neither did he point it at the Bat Queen. It was simply out, ready to be used. The tension in the air seemed to be increasing. Everyone knew violence could break out at any moment.

Actually, the temperature in the air seemed to be rising quite noticeably. James realized it when he felt long beads of sweat running down his back.

It's hotter here than it was when we entered, and it was already almost a sauna. He looked at the Bat Queen, who was glaring at him hatefully. *She's doing this. She can control the weather. Her territory is the sky; that's what the squirrel said. So, extending your aura into the sky comes with that benefit.*

James wasn't certain whether his own aura could rise into the sky to manipulate the weather. He had never noticed it to extend very far above or below the Earth's surface. Perhaps ten to twenty feet in each direction.

Maybe some Rulers have different domains.

He looked back at his people again and saw the tension on their faces. They hated the Bat Queen reflexively, probably almost as much as she hated them. Part of it was that she was horrifying to look at compared with the monsters they had learned to somewhat accept as part of James's country.

Does she realize how much closer she's pushing this to outright violence by cranking up the heat? Or does she think she's just putting us under pressure, and we're going to fold?

"We didn't lose any," James admitted. "That was only the case because my defense forces and I moved quickly to save the people in danger."

"Not a single loss," the Bat Queen repeated, slowly shaking her head.

"I don't know how I can make this right," James said. "It's my preference to live in peace with other Races. You can see that it's not just humans who are here with me." He gestured behind him, where there were Goblins and wolves standing among the humans.

"I know how we can make this right," the Bat Queen replied. "I could sic my whole family on you right now and wipe out your friends. That could be *my* retaliation. If you live through that, then how about we live in peace from there, *huh*?"

James snorted and shook his head. *How do I get myself into these situations?*

The Bat Queen stared down at him intensely as if it were a serious question worthy of an answer.

"If," James said.

She cocked her head at him.

"If?" she asked.

"You could try something like that," James said. "You're weaker than I am, though. I promise you that. You might 'wipe out' my friends. But *if* you kill them and I live through that, then I'll come back here with ten times their number." He locked eyes with the Bat Queen and let some of his own hatred show through. "If that happens, then I'll kill you."

"Ha! Is that all—"

"You didn't let me finish. If that happens, then I'll kill you. I'll kill your mate. I'll kill *all of your children*. I won't be in a forgiving mood. I've wiped out more than one species already. You're not going to be the first. You're not going to be the last. You're just the second Ruler I'll have beaten this week."

The Bat Queen bared her teeth in a snarl. "You arrogant little—"

She stopped talking as the Squirrel Queen placed a paw on her shoulder.

Then the two walked away, temporarily ignoring their uninvited guests, to talk privately.

James turned back to his people while he waited for them to have their conversation. The soldiers looked nervous but very impressed with his handling of the situation. Some of them gave him confident nods or a thumbs up to signal their approval. Others smiled nervously when he looked in their direction.

Well, at least they're not breaking. Don't worry, guys. I'll keep you out of a fight with this little army—if that's at all possible.

He turned back and saw the hundreds of huddled bats and squirrels looking at him, visibly confused and afraid.

And, of course, James eavesdropped on the all-important conversation happening between the Bat Queen and the Squirrel Queen just fifteen feet away. It was remarkable that they thought they were far enough away not to be heard, even when whispering. Maybe they imagined that all humans were functionally deaf. Perhaps, compared with bats and squirrels, most humans were.

If so, James was an exception.

"I think you'd better let this go," the Squirrel Queen was saying.

"How can I let this go?"

"There was clearly a misunderstanding. He apologized, if you were listening. This is the first time anything like this has happened—"

"Coward!" the Bat Queen snapped. "I knew I couldn't rely on you. Why did I even bother making an alliance with someone whose solution to every problem is running away?"

"It's not like that!"

"How is it not like that?" the Bat Queen asked.

There was silence for several long seconds. Then the Bat Queen stomped back to where James was.

"Are you ready to do this?" she asked.

"Do what?" James asked.

"Fight," she spat. Little flecks of saliva landed on James's left cheek as she spoke the word.

"Are we going to have our armies fight, like two children smashing their toys together, or will it be you and me getting our hands dirty, like two adults?" James asked.

"What's wrong?" the Bat Queen taunted. "Scared these puny worms aren't up to the job?"

"If we're going to war, I could have a thousand more soldiers here in five minutes," James replied. "I'm just establishing the parameters for what we're doing."

"Um, I'm just going to sit this one out," the Squirrel Queen said meekly from behind the Bat Queen.

"What?" The Bat Queen whirled on her and got in the squirrel's face. "What do you think you're doing?"

To her credit, the Squirrel Queen didn't back down. She let the Bat Queen get within an inch of their faces touching.

"Just what I said," the Squirrel Queen said stiffly. "I am not convinced this is in the best interests of my family. None of us died. This guy clearly has no quarrel with me. Me and mine will not be fighting." She looked over at James. "Do you have a problem with that, human?"

James shook his head and just tried not to look smug. *That worked out very well.*

The Bat Queen rounded on James again. "Fine, then. You and me. A duel to the death. Winner gets the loser's territory."

"The winner also has to spare the loser's people," James said.

The Bat Queen narrowed her eyes and stared past James, eyeballing his allies as if she wanted to tear them all to pieces. "You're the one who ordered everything they did, right?" she finally said.

"Yes," James replied instantly.

"Then I guess sparing them is no great sacrifice." She aimed her next words at the soldiers behind him. "Look forward to putting up statues in my honor, you puny creatures!"

This is really perfect, James thought. *Second duel in one week, and I'll acquire a bunch more territory when it's done.*

"Wait, what about me?" the Squirrel Queen asked.

What about you? James wondered.

"What *about* you?" the Bat Queen replied acidly.

"I mean, what happens, um, to me and my people? Um, if the ownership of the territory is being decided by duel."

"As far as I'm concerned, when I win, you cowardly bastards need to clear out of here," the Bat Queen said.

The Squirrel Queen winced at her words, then turned to James. "How about you? Are you up for a peaceful neighbor relationship?"

James raised an eyebrow. "I'll make you the same deal as her. After I recover from my fight with the Bat Queen, you and I fight a duel. It doesn't have to be to the death, since you and I don't hate each other. Winner gets the loser's territory. I haven't had much luck with peaceful neighbor relationships lately. It seems as if I need buffer territory on all sides."

The Squirrel Queen looked slightly downcast. "I see." Then she looked up as if she'd had an idea. "Is that what happened with you and those other nonhumans you have behind you? You fought a duel with their leader and then took over?"

"Um, more or less," James said.

"Do you mind?" She pointed at the fighters behind James. It took him a moment to realize that she wanted to talk to them.

"Oh. Uh, no." James stepped to the side, and the Squirrel Queen breezed past him. She was surprisingly graceful while walking. The tail that James had thought was sort of ugly because it was less bushy than a normal squirrel's tail seemed to be very good for controlling her movements.

Again, there was a private conversation between the Squirrel Queen and someone else that took place so close to James that he couldn't avoid overhearing it unless he put his fingers in his ears.

The Squirrel Queen was asking James's wolves and Goblins if they felt well treated under him. And they were giving him good reviews.

"He is a good pack leader," was a representative comment from the wolves. "Generous with food and skilled at hunting."

"He is a strong yet merciful leader," Duncan said. The other Goblins hastened to agree with him.

"Yes," said one. "I heard that he fought a duel with a giant monster Ruler a couple of days ago, and he even healed him after the fight was over!"

Did he hear that from the wolves? James wondered. *Or maybe the Mole People?* The only Goblin who had actually witnessed that duel was Duncan.

The Squirrel Queen seemed to take their stories very seriously, in any case. She asked question after question. She made certain to clarify how "generous with food" James was, asked if he was constantly starting fights—they claimed that he had been forcibly drawn into fights, which was dubiously true even from his point of view—and if they knew what he thought of squirrels, among other topics.

It's sort of cute, James thought. *She's incredibly naive if this is really part of her decision-making process. If I wanted to be a tyrant, the first thing I'd do is brainwash the people and creatures that are supposed to fight alongside me into fanatical loyalty. This is no more useful than if she just asked me if I was a nice King to my face.*

There was something endearing about it. Even disarming. It raised the question of how this Squirrel Queen had become a Ruler in the first place. Or if she was faking being this naive.

The Squirrel Queen finally turned back from the conversation and faced James. Her tail was standing up weirdly straight, and she looked jittery.

"All right," she said. "I've decided. If King James wins, I want to join him!"

The other squirrels applauded her with their front paws, while the Bat Queen rolled her eyes and spat.

Okay, maybe the squirrel's not faking it.

"We should set some rules for this duel," the Bat Queen said. She had her wings pulled in front of her face like a cape.

Uh oh. Where is this coming from? he wondered.

"What rules?" he asked.

"I don't want you cheating to win. You shouldn't have advantages that I don't have," she said.

"I don't know what you mean," James said slightly impatiently.

"You know, all *that*," the Bat Queen said, pointing at his sword. "I don't have those things. Weapons and armor."

CHAPTER FORTY-NINE

Meet Cute

A knock came at the front door, and Mina sighed to herself.
"Sweet, could you please get that?"

Just when the baby is almost done eating and just about ready to sleep, someone is knocking...

And Mina felt like a nap herself. She knew she would be working hard through the next few days, trying to help James deal with Sister Strange and the forest specters. If she could get some rest now, she'd have an easier time staying awake later in the evening.

She heard Yulia murmur something to Abhi, and then Yulia was descending the stairs.

Mina rose, still carrying Junior, and went to the doorway of the nursery.

From there, she heard Yulia quietly exclaim, "Oh, it's you! Of course it's you. Please, come in. Hi, Alice!"

Oh, it's Zora and Alice, Mina realized. *I guess I'll sleep later. Probably. Plenty of time to sleep when I'm dead, right?*

She went back into the nursery, sat in her rocking chair, and stroked Junior's head while she waited for Zora.

Less than thirty seconds passed before the older woman poked her head into the room.

"Hey!" Zora said in a sing-song voice. She saw the other children besides Junior, all on the verge of succumbing to sleep—Yulia had kept them active through the morning, so they were ready for a nap—and looked surprised for a moment. Then Zora smiled and said, in a lowered voice, "I thought I would come and meet the little angel, but I didn't know you guys had more now."

That was delicate *of her*, Mina thought. She realized she shouldn't be surprised. Zora was never less than a lady. She could be blunt, sarcastic, and, on rare occasions, cruel. But she was always aware of the impact of what she said. *James probably got his social intelligence from her.*

"We are taking care of a few more," Mina said. Because James had been doing it, she added, "Just until their folks come back for them, of course."

Zora raised one eyebrow a millimeter but said nothing to that.

"He's done eating," Mina said, "if you wanted to hold little James."

Zora's face broke out in an impossible-to-fake twinkling smile, and she reached out eagerly for the baby. When she had Junior in her arms, she held him with what Mina thought was incredible tenderness. It reminded her that she had, before all this madness happened, very much wanted Zora to be involved in the baby's life. Whatever qualities might annoy Mina about Zora, her mother-in-law was devoted to family.

"Oh my goodness! You're the cutest baby I've ever met," Zora cooed, holding Junior close to her face. The baby gurgled and patted Zora's short curly hair with his pudgy, uncoordinated baby hand. "Aww."

Is she crying? Mina looked more closely and saw, for the first time since she'd met Zora, that she had a tear running down her cheek.

"I think he likes you," Mina said, smiling.

"He is a very charming baby," Zora said in the same almost sing-song voice she had used when she had come in. "My first grandchild. Oh, but I bet he likes every new face he sees . . ."

Mina thought back and wondered if that was true.

"You're going to be a little lady's man, aren't you?" Zora continued.

Mina just laughed.

"There are a couple of other people waiting to see you, I should let you know," Zora said, nuzzling the baby's thin wispy hair and stroking his back with her thin, deft fingers.

"Not just Alice?" Mina asked.

"No," Zora said, barely restraining herself from laughing. "You and James certainly leave an impression on people. Your other guests are apparently from your Orientations."

Mina rose uncertainly from her seat.

"There's no need to rush," Zora said, keeping her voice low. "Remember, you're the mommy. Let them cater to you. If you want, I'll give you back the baby, and I can go entertain them. Or I could take the baby while I go entertain them, and you could sit here and relax for a bit. I won't let anyone else hold him, but you know people love to look. They can distract themselves with a baby for hours."

That's very considerate.

Mina smiled but shook her head. "I'd better go do this. I want to get rid of these guests, whoever they are. I'll do it as politely as I can. I need to go train once Junior is settled—or if you're willing to watch him, I could go train as soon as the guests are dealt with."

"I would love to watch the little man," Zora said, almost cooing again. She looked up from the baby as Mina moved to the door. "You should tell me about what it is you're training for, though. Maybe it's something I can help with."

Mina looked at Zora thoughtfully. *Well, she is a Mage.*

"All right," Mina said. "I'll give you the details once we deal with our guests."

She emerged from the nursery and saw Leo and that woman who had been with him in the community center. They were standing next to Alice, but the three of them weren't talking. They were just standing around awkwardly, as if no one knew quite what to say.

"Hi, Leo! Good to see you again, Alice!" Mina said. "And nice to meet you, um?"

"Good to see you too," Alice said.

Mina smiled.

"My name is Hilda," the woman in white said.

"I remember James waved at you in the meeting," Mina said, "so I guess you were in his Orientation."

"Yes," Hilda said. She took a deep breath. "I was working with the Moloch cult when we ran into each other the first time."

Mina's face must have registered the shock of that statement. She did remember a few people turned on the cult leader at the end. *I guess she was one of the survivors.*

"I'm, um, just going to go and let you guys talk," Alice said. She sounded uncomfortable, and she walked so quickly toward the nursery that it felt as if she was fleeing the scene.

"I'm so glad to see you again, Mina," Leo said warmly. He stepped past Hilda and embraced Mina. For a moment, she almost forgot what Hilda had just said. It was incredibly reassuring just seeing Leo again. He stepped back, and she smiled at him. "I'm so glad you and your baby are doing well."

"Thank you. It's good to see you too," she said. *I bet James is going to want to recruit you to run the police here.* "Are you planning on staying?"

"That depends—" Leo's eyes shifted to Hilda. "It depends on whether we're welcome."

Mina deflated slightly. *It would be easier if he wasn't tying his answer to hers. I have no idea if* she's *welcome or not.*

"I don't know if there's anything either of you could have done to make yourselves unwelcome," she said quietly. She looked up at Leo. "I know Yulia and I wouldn't have survived Orientation without your police skills. I wish she were here so she could thank you."

Leo scoffed and shook his head. "That's ridiculous. I wouldn't have gotten out alive if it wasn't for you two. I was actually hoping to come here and thank your husband for lending you to our Orientation." He smiled.

"I'm sure he'll want to thank you instead," Mina said. She couldn't help but look at Hilda, who was standing to the side quietly.

"Perhaps it would be better if the Queen and I discussed the situation we're sort of dancing around," Hilda said. "I think I'm ruining your fond reunion."

Both Leo and Mina became silent at that. Then Mina nodded.

"You're not ruining anything," Mina said, "but Leo and I can talk later. Whatever you want to say, Hilda, you should probably tell me now, and James and I will discuss things when he gets back." She spoke in vague terms because she still didn't grasp anything close to the whole picture of the situation.

Leo seemed to understand. "Okay," he said, nodding to Mina with a serious expression. He turned to Hilda and added, "I'll be in the housing the building people showed us, all right?"

Hilda nodded, but her eyes were on Mina as Leo descended the stairs and left the apartment building.

"Why don't you pull up a chair?" Mina suggested once he was gone. "There's no reason this conversation should be awkward."

Any more awkward than it already is, she thought.

Hilda accepted, and soon the two women were sitting across from each other in silence.

Mina was surprised that Hilda didn't jump to speak first, but the other woman seemed to be a very calm, collected person. Calculating, perhaps. Weighing her next move carefully.

Either that, or she's just very confident. I'm not sure where that would be coming from in this situation, though.

"I'm guessing," Mina said, "that you want to talk about switching sides in James's Orientation. I'm imagining, and I'm sure you'll correct me if I'm wrong, that you started out as a Moloch worshipper and ended up helping James kill Moloch's priests."

But Hilda was already shaking her head. "I was never a Moloch worshipper. I was blessed early in Orientation by the God of Light, Baldr. His portfolio of powers includes prophetic dreams. He sees the future that must eventually come." She looked a bit sad. "Even if it's very painful. Sometimes he shares things with me—just bits and pieces, but it is invaluable as I navigate the world." She bowed her head reverently.

"So, how did you come to find yourself with the Moloch worshippers?" Mina asked. Her voice came out more skeptical than she'd intended. But it seemed extraordinarily unlikely to her that she was meeting someone from the Rostov cult for the first time and that person just so happened to have never been a believer.

"I recognize how it sounds," Hilda said, her expression somber. "I will make no excuses. My god told me that if I went with Rostov and his followers, I would survive Orientation and make it here. If I didn't, my situation would be less certain. I'm sure you can imagine that even if they are morally different, a Sun God and a God of Light would have some things in common. They at least would not be likely to show open hostility toward each other. So, it wasn't hard to get them to accept me. I understand that Moloch encouraged his Chosen One to accept me. I never worshiped Moloch, although I did help his followers." She sounded a bit guilty as she said those last words. "I think your husband will confirm that once I was able to, I switched sides and helped him kill Rostov off." Her voice became slightly heated at the end. She seemed concerned that Mina might not believe her. "The end result is that Moloch is weakened, perhaps permanently. He had invested a great deal in Orientation . . ." Her voice trailed off.

"I'll discuss it with James," Mina said, trying to smile at her guest. "I'm sure he is aware of how much you contributed. Are you planning on staying here?"

"More than that," Hilda said. "My god has informed me that a great multiracial empire will be founded under King James. A place where humans and other Races live together in peace. A hub of tolerance and understanding. But there will be many enemies who wish to see this land destroyed!" She raised her voice slightly and sounded genuinely worried as she uttered that last sentence.

"I see," Mina said, not quite understanding. "You want to join the Kingdom even though you predict many enemies will try to destroy it?"

"My god believes that this place is the best hope for lasting peace and stability for Earth," Hilda said. "It may be a flickering candle in the wind, but I must do whatever I can to ensure it does not go out. I want to swear my sword into his service—and yours."

"Well, I know I speak both for myself and for James when I say: we appreciate your confidence. And although I cannot speak to whether he will accept your offer of service, I must admit that it sounds compelling. I will pass on what you've said." Mina gave the other woman a slight smile.

Hilda nodded. "Thank you, Your Majesty. There is no rush, of course. I know that you and the King are still settling this land now. I'm certain there are many things that require your attention. I will take the citizenship oath that others have mentioned when it is convenient for the two of you—or I'll leave if you prefer."

"It is true there are other things we're thinking about," Mina said, slightly relieved. She realized as Hilda was speaking that this *was* a decision that she didn't want to dump on James right now. He was dealing with more than enough.

Hilda rose as if to leave, but she hesitated for a moment.

Mina looked up at her, and for a moment, Hilda reminded her of an older Cara; she was strong and fierce, but where Cara looked like she could be a Viking or a surfer, Hilda was older. Her look was pale and thoughtful. She had muscle, but it felt out of place, like she was unaccustomed to it. As if a bookworm who worked in a library suddenly realized that she needed to train for some terrible ordeal. There was a fierce intensity about her, but she was keeping it under careful control—disciplined power to be applied at the right moment. *Like James. And she's been receiving information about the future like James too . . .* Mina knew suddenly that Hilda was absolutely going to stay—and perhaps be among the most loyal citizens of the Fisher Kingdom.

"Will you let me know if there is anything I can do to be of service?" Hilda asked. "I am eager to prove my loyalty—and I know the nights can be dangerous in this new world. Leo and I already experienced something of this."

Mina had the thought that Hilda might actually know something about the challenges they were dealing with right now.

But if she knew anything useful, she wouldn't be so vague, she thought.

"You should rest," Mina said, "and after that, you should get ready for a late night. We've asked for volunteers to attack the hostile presence in the forest nearby. They'll be going in after dark, while my husband distracts the Ruler in that place. If you're able to go, you just need to follow Dave Matsumoto's lead. He'll be leading the charge, so he's the man to talk to."

Hilda nodded and looked pleased. "I won't let you down," she said.

Mina smiled. "See you tonight."

After Hilda was gone, Zora stepped out of the nursery. Baby James had fallen asleep in her arms. *He really likes her*, Mina thought. That was the ultimate sign. The baby wasn't very finicky, but he only fell asleep for certain people. So far, just her, James, and Yulia.

"I overheard something at the end there about a hostile presence in the forest," Zora said, keeping her voice low so as not to disturb the baby. "Is that place haunted?"

CHAPTER FIFTY

Like the Celts

"I can't believe I agreed to fight naked," James grumbled as he placed the last piece of his equipment into his magic satchel. He now stood in the dense, humid air with no protection from the elements but his boxer briefs.

"Lord Anansi wants you to know that you negotiated well, sir," Hester said. "You preserved what was most important. 'A king must maintain his dignity,' he said."

James wanted to tell Hester to can it, but he could tell that she was genuinely earnest. She—and perhaps even the old Spider God himself—really thought it was good negotiating on his part that he got the Bat Queen to agree that he could keep his underwear, which he had to promise was non-magical.

"More importantly for the actual fight, I got her to agree to fight while the sun is still up," James said, "so my senses will be at their sharpest, while the light makes it harder for her to see."

"That's a good point too," Hester agreed. But James thought she was probably just trying to make him feel better.

Agreeing to unarmed, unarmored combat with a monster, *in her territory*, put him at such an obvious disadvantage that it didn't really bear much discussion.

I guess I can't blame the Bat Queen for being afraid to face me, he thought. He had realized what the root of her change in attitude must have been. The Bat Queen had to have overheard one of the Goblins telling the Squirrel Queen that James had defeated another Ruler that same week. The Bat Queen had convinced herself that it must have been his equipment that allowed James to win the fight.

In fact, that couldn't have been further from the truth. James actually hadn't inflicted *any* damage on Samuel with his weapons. His armor had been almost useless. His insane Stats and ridiculously powerful Skills had done all of the damage. And Samuel was certainly stronger than the Bat Queen.

That was the silver lining in all this. The Bat Queen would realize her mistake soon enough.

Dave approached James now, and he frowned.

I thought they were all going to leave me alone while I prepared.

"What's up, Dave?" James asked.

Dave handed him a slip of paper with something written on it.

The text of the note read, *Do you want us to launch a sneak attack when the duel starts? We could blow the monster away as soon as she steps out into the open to fight you.*

James smiled and shook his head. "Thank you for the offer. I like where your head is at. I'll defeat her with my own power, though. If the opponent were actually scary, I might have considered it."

Dave looked incredulous for a moment, then placed a hand on James's shoulder and silently nodded.

James sent a pair of identical telepathic messages to Duncan and Luna. *Do you detect anything wrong with the space where we are meant to fight?*

I can detect no magical interference, and the Bat Queen has not done anything suspicious, Duncan sent. *Besides posturing as if she believes she can somehow win this fight.*

No, my king, Luna replied. *I've walked up and down the clearing. I can detect nothing wrong. The only thing amiss is the stench of bats.*

The responses made him smile. "Enough delaying," he said finally.

He rose, set Hester down on a branch close enough for her to watch the fight, and stepped out from among the trees into the small clearing the Bat Queen had suggested as the site of their battle. She stood there waiting, tapping her right foot on the ground as if she was getting impatient.

James looked at her and smiled. She responded by twisting her face into an even more hideous version of its usual mask-like appearance.

"Everyone knows to stay back during the fight?" James asked in a loud voice.

There were murmurs of assent from his side.

"All of mine know to keep away from us while I'm killing you," the Bat Queen replied.

James pantomimed a yawn. "Let's get this over with," he said. "I'm starting to get hungry. Some bat flesh might do my body good."

Then the Bat Queen was charging at him on foot.

This soon? he thought. *I could have sworn she would try to make it a long-distance fight to start.*

He braced for impact—and then the Bat Queen kicked off the ground and launched herself into the air above him. Her wings carried her up above him, but the upward movement was slow and awkward.

James whipped his right hand forward and threw an Air Strike, and it instantly unbalanced her. She did not cry out in pain, though James saw a rip had opened in her left wing.

A quiet cheer went up as the soldiers watching below saw a few drops of blood fall from the torn wing.

"James! James! James!"

Unless I'm very much mistaken, the Squirrel Queen is cheering for me too.

James almost wanted to laugh. But he knew he had more to do before the Bat Queen would lie down and die.

He leaped into the air after her, grabbing a tree branch to launch himself further, and finally pulled level with her in midair.

Then she let loose a loud screech. The sound was much more intense than he had experienced from the other bats. His ears erupted in agony. His teeth rattled. Again he almost covered his ears but resisted the impulse.

This was certainly a weakness of his now, but he didn't want to make that too obvious. Higher Perception meant greater vulnerability to these kinds of attacks. It would only get worse over time unless he developed stronger defenses.

His body started to fall, and he threw another Air Strike before he could drop too far. This one struck the other wing. Hitting from such close range, it tore the vulnerable membrane from the bottom edge to almost halfway through the center.

Not bad, he assessed. *If I can just keep her on the ground, the fight's basically over.*

The Bat Queen yowled in pain this time, and James could see her visibly slowing in the air, her wing noticeably less effective. But she continued to rise, albeit more weakly. He tried to throw another Air Strike, but she managed to fly to the side and evade it.

Then he was falling out of reach. He braced himself and took the landing with bent knees while looking up to see where she might strike from next.

His ears were still ringing from her attack, so his detection of the Bat Queen would have to depend on sight and smell more than hearing.

He stood there for a minute in a fighting stance before he realized that the bat was doing something else rather than just preparing a sneak attack. He wiped beads of sweat from his forehead and then realized that the temperature was rising.

"Is that all you've got?" he asked aloud. "You're making the air warmer?" He shook his head and raised his voice even louder. "Don't you know this is Florida? We're all used to the heat!"

James couldn't hear himself talking very clearly, so he also couldn't hear the people around him very well, but he saw some of those in the surrounding area were moving their bodies as if they were laughing.

If this was going to be one of her tactics, she shouldn't have had me strip off my armor. Although his underwear was starting to stick to his body, being naked right now seemed to him much more advantageous than wearing armor and a helmet.

James began gathering water Mana. If he was going to wait for the Bat Queen in a sauna, he might as well keep cool while he waited. Perhaps this would prompt her to show herself sooner.

Almost as soon as he had the thought, he sensed movement in the leaves behind him. He stood still and pretended not to notice.

The black shape launched itself at him—and James instantly spun to face the Bat Queen. He stopped charging water Mana and threw the small amount of conjured water into her face. The Bat Queen blinked, and James leaped right into close range.

He grabbed her head by both ears and yanked her downward. She tried to flap her damaged wings, but they were too weak with their torn membranes to bear his weight as well as her own. She tried to rake his chest with her claws, but she left only shallow cuts.

Then they collided with the ground, the Bat Queen headfirst.

James held the giant bat down by one of her huge fleshy ears and ignored the claws which raked his side and back now that they could no longer reach his front. But he took one hand off her head and began snaking it around toward her throat. If he could just crush her neck, the fight would be over. The bat had shown no great physical prowess, so he thought he could do it.

The Bat Queen managed to turn her head to face him without breaking fully free of his grip. Then she opened her mouth and issued the loudest, most painful screeching sound James had ever heard. It weakened but did not break his grip. She managed to lean her face a little closer to James's and shriek even louder and more painfully.

In his peripheral vision, he saw members of all three armies bending and clutching their ears, experiencing the same sound that he was enduring, albeit less directly.

James felt intense pain in his head as the sound seemed to shatter something inside his ears. He didn't want to take his hands away from the monster he was grappling with, but he felt fluid flowing down the sides of his face from his ears.

Nausea, disorientation, and dizziness hit him all at once alongside the pain—and he tightened his grip on the monster. This had to be the Bat Queen's best move, her best opportunity to weaken him for a killing strike.

All he had to do was hold on and bear through the pain.

He endured. Several seconds passed. He realized his hearing had faded to nothing.

The Bat Queen was still shrieking, but he only knew it because he saw her body moving the same way it had been when she had been screaming in his face.

The pain continued, but he realized that it had peaked.

Well, that was not your best use of that weapon, he thought. *Now you're fucked.*

He shifted his posture slightly to hold her down with one knee. Then he grabbed the Bat Queen's throat with both hands and began crushing the life out of her.

"I was considering so many different ways to kill you," he hissed quietly. "I have so many different abilities I could try. But now that you've flown right into my lap, I'll give you a nice simple death."

The flesh of the Bat Queen's neck burst under James's grip, and blood began to gush onto his almost naked body.

"Time to kickstart the healing process," he said almost to himself.

Still holding the Bat Queen by the neck, he leaned in and bit into the lightly furred flesh of that region. He tore out big chunks of flesh and fur, barely tasting them, and swallowed them down. Then he went back in for more juicy life-giving flesh. He could feel it restoring his Stamina and Health as he consumed it.

The Bat Queen stopped resisting after a few seconds of this. Her only movements were spasms of the body. Uncontrollable death throes. The fight was over, and he continued to eat her flesh to accelerate his own healing process. And to make sure she really wouldn't ever get up again.

As the death throes waned, his ears started to pick up some sounds again. The speed of his healing felt remarkable even to him.

James's soldiers were cheering, chanting his name again.

A few seconds later, the Bat Queen stopped moving entirely. It was finally over.

A series of alerts swam in front of James's eyes, but he ignored them. It was the crowd he wanted to engage with now, not the System.

James stood, thrust his blood-soaked fist into the air, and roared.

The soldiers cheered again, more loudly, while the small army of bats and flying squirrels fell to their knees.

CHAPTER FIFTY-ONE

Eulogy

James allowed himself to bask in the glory of the crowd's approbation for a few long seconds.

He smiled, wiped some gore away from his mouth, and then waited for the cheering to die down.

"Thank you to all the brave fighters who accompanied me here," he said. "There will be other battles, but for now we have won the day and secured peace."

There were further enthusiastic cheers, but James saw the bats staring down at the ground, looking uncomfortable, and he instantly knew he needed to say something conciliatory to them.

"I am also grateful to the late Bat Queen—" he began.

"For dying!" called a voice from James's side.

No, I can't have that, he thought. *We're better than that.*

He allowed his smile to falter and his expression to become stern.

"No," he said loudly. "I am grateful for the Bat Queen's willingness to face me honorably in single combat. She could have chosen otherwise. It would have been a bloodbath *for both sides*—and a tragic one since this conflict was based in part on a misunderstanding. Together, she and I prevented that by putting our lives on the line instead of our people's lives. Thanks to her courage, we will gain new neighbors instead of making a population of fierce and devoted enemies."

The crowd was quiet for a few seconds as people processed what he had said.

Then they began to applaud. Dave was the first one to really grasp what he meant, James noticed, and he nodded wordlessly along with clapping.

James turned to look at the bats and flying squirrels. The bats had lifted their heads and were looking at him uncertainly, as if they expected some trick. The flying squirrels looked happy. Their emotions were very obvious in their body language.

James said his next words both aloud and telepathically, directly into the minds of every bat that was now his subject. "To the bats, I must say that your queen was a fierce opponent." He bent down and used Pillage on the body, selecting a Title to steal.

[Black Bloodsucking Bat Queen Barbara's body processed.]

[You obtained Royal Aeromaster Cloak, 4x Bloodsucking Bat Queen Meat Bundle, and Ego Bloodsucking Arrows!]

[Title obtained: Aeromaster!]

Those all sound quite interesting, he thought to himself. He looked forward to testing them out.

James threw the Royal Aeromaster Cloak—a cape fashioned from the Bat Queen's wings—around his shoulders and continued communicating with the bats.

"Now I will carry her strength with me into the battles to come," he said. "I want you to take a few days to mourn your late Queen and then choose a new strong bat who will serve me directly and represent you within my Kingdom. I intend to treat all of the surviving bats and squirrels as I would have liked the Bat Queen to treat my people in the event that I had lost the fight. I will place you under my protection. Any bat who is unwilling to accept this is welcome to leave, of course, but I will assume that any who remain within this territory after five days' time have accepted the new order."

The creatures bowed low again, and James turned back to his soldiers.

"Thank you again to the soldiers who accompanied me here to ensure peace along our border. With your help, we have once again secured a region of the Kingdom against the possibility of external threat. Soon we will secure all our borders. In time, we will spread peace, order, and security to every corner of central Florida!"

Another cheer went up. This time people were shouting an array of different words.

"Peace!"

"Security!"

"Florida!"

"Fisher King!"

"James!"

"Victory!"

James waited for the cheering to die down, but it took several minutes. People seemed to be very energized.

Well, they did just spend months in a strange place, worrying that they might be killed any day. Of course it makes sense that they would be happy to have some sense of control back.

Eventually, even the bats and squirrels joined in. In their shrill and chirpy voices, respectively, they chanted, "Peace!"

"Fisher King! James!"

"Peace!"

The bats were chanting for peace, while the squirrels were taking their cue from their leader and chanting along similar lines to his soldiers.

Interesting.

He was optimistic that this victory would be another great milestone in the growth of his kingdom. He could feel that it wasn't a vast territory he had inherited from the bats and the squirrels. The combined geographic region was, in fact, smaller than Samuel's massive swamp or the pre-swamp-acquisition Fisher Kingdom.

But there were other gains, and large ones at that. He felt that the power of his aura had changed and enhanced as he absorbed the authority of the two additional Rulers thanks to his Usurper power. He looked through the System alerts until he found what he was looking for.

I took the power of the Ruler of the Tropical Forest and the Ruler of the Humid Skies and merged them into my Ruler of the Dark Waters Title. I guess that explains it. He now felt that his aura extended above the ground further than it had before. He intuited what the change would mean. *I'm guessing I should be able to influence not just the soil and water within my territory now, but also the sky above. I'll have to experiment with it. See if I can change the temperature like the Bat Queen did. Maybe if I practice, I'll be able to make lightning strike my enemies. That would be pretty awesome.*

For now, James put off any experiments. He collected Hester from where she had been watching the battle. He bid the bats and squirrels farewell. He promised to give the former Squirrel Queen a blessing later, but for now he was feeling drained. He didn't want to use more of his energy, especially knowing that he would encounter Sister Strange that evening.

Once he was out of sight of the monsters, he conjured some water to wash off the Bat Queen's blood—it felt somehow disrespectful to do that in front of them and wasteful of his effort in giving her a quasi-eulogy.

Then he clothed himself once more—minus armor this time, simply because it seemed unnecessary in a pacified territory—took Roscuro out of his magic satchel, and led his soldiers back toward the place that had been the border.

Not a single death on our side, he thought. *It is mostly my fault that the Bat Queen had to die, but the results are excellent otherwise. I think we won hearts and minds back there. From my experiences with the Goblins and alligators, nonhumans think differently about these struggles than humans do. They seem to cling to the strong loyally and not take it as personally if they see you beat the tar out of their loved ones.*

And perhaps most importantly, James had seen what his existing citizens could do when the situation called for violence.

He was rather impressed, and the feeling seemed to be mutual.

The soldiers kept coming up to him, clapping him on the back, shaking his hand, and offering him compliments. The ones who had not been present for the fight with Samuel were particularly affected.

"I've never seen you fight, Your Majesty, but you fought like a demon back there! I feel like we're all so much safer with you at the head," said Ardal Byrne, a middle-aged man who spoke with a faint Irish accent.

"Professional wrestling has nothing on you for showmanship, chief," said another man.

"The other Goblins who saw what you did to that bat are all thinking about how they can impress you in the next battle," Duncan said. James wasn't certain if that was a good thing or not.

"I think the next monster that considers invading the Kingdom will give it a second thought," said a young woman who seemed a bit nervous to speak with James.

That seemed to be a common reaction by the female soldiers who had witnessed the fight, James noticed. There hadn't been that many of them in the sudden, informal militia he'd thrown together—he counted eight women out of the nearly one hundred humans—and they seemed slightly less enthusiastic in the aftermath of the battle.

Several of them joined their male colleagues in approaching him, but their expressions as they mentioned the fight were noticeably more squeamish.

The only thing he could figure was that they didn't like how gruesome the fight had become.

I could have ended it much more quickly and easily with Soul Magic, he thought, *but what kind of impression would that have left on the other bats? They'd probably feel as if I had cheated their Queen. Like they were being forced to follow some evil sorcerer.*

He tried to think if there was some way he could have won the battle that would not have looked too grotesque to the female viewers. Then he shrugged.

I guess I'll just have to kiss a lot of babies to remind them that I'm also a dad, he thought. *Completely harmless.*

As the group continued moving forward, James found a chance to pull Dave aside from the group for a private chat.

"How did you feel the invasion went, Dave?" James asked.

"Well, when I got up this morning, an invasion was the last thing I expected to be a feature of my day," Dave said. "However, it was much less horrifying than the last invasion I was a part of."

James had heard some stories about the Sino-American War, so he didn't know quite what to make of that remark. Dave seemed to be forcing himself to put on a brave face, but the two men weren't exactly friends yet, so James didn't want to pry into how he was really feeling.

"I'm thinking about the fact that this might have to happen again at some point," James said. "If you were to review our performance, what would you say?"

"What, do you want me to rate it out of ten?" Dave asked. He sounded slightly needled.

"I want you to tell me if these people are ready to defend our land from the world out there," James replied bluntly. "I'm still not sure what would have happened if we'd had to fight the bats and squirrels together. I have an ability that normally lets me calculate the odds of winning a fight, but I had no data at all on the squirrels, so it wouldn't work in that situation. But I have a bad feeling I know what would have happened."

Dave nodded slowly and spoke quietly as he replied, "You think we would have been slaughtered."

"It was one of the major reasons I was eager to fight alone," James said. "I don't accept it as an inevitable outcome. I want to know what *you* think. And I want to know how you would improve upon the status quo."

Dave shook his head. "I'm not in the military," he said. "Not anymore. I guess what I'm doing for you—well, it's sort of like I'm serving in your military. But this is officer stuff. I'm no general."

"I don't see any other generals around here," James said. "And I don't need a general. I don't have a whole army in the first place. But I could make you a captain."

Dave's facial expression changed, and he stopped moving for a moment. James stopped too, and then the whole group stopped with him. The chatter of the soldiers among themselves died down as they stared at James and Dave.

That finally got Dave moving again. The rest of the column resumed their triumphant march home.

"What is it?" James asked.

"The System just offered me a Job," Dave said, looking and sounding as if he was trying not to laugh—or resisting the impulse to scream. "Captain of the Royal Fisher Army."

"Royal Fisher Army," James muttered. "I guess that has an okay ring to it."

"Do you think I should accept it?" Dave asked. His voice had an edge of anxiety to it.

"I think you have to make that choice for yourself," James asked, putting a steadying arm around Dave. "But if you're asking me, personally, what I would do, the answer is yes. You know I'm going to treat you like you're the captain of my troops anyway. You might as well get the prestige that comes with the rank.

And any boosts to your Stats the System is offering. But there's no pressure to give me or the System an answer now. The offer isn't evaporating."

Dave sagged a bit as if he was slightly less worried.

"While you wrestle with that and consider how our force can become more effective, there's one other task I'd ask you to carry out for me," James added.

"What's that?"

"Select six or so of the most valiant and effective soldiers from this group," James said. "Human, Goblin, Wolf—I don't care, but I need a good handful of heroes to reward for their service today. The seventh one is you, of course. I think seven's a nice number."

Dave looked as if he was about to protest, but James shook his head.

"You're going to want this decoration," James said. "It's not some plastic medal I'm handing out. I'm going to publicly give every one of these people my Blessing. It should accelerate their growth. And you deserve this just as much as anyone else. I relied on you here, and I relied on you when we invaded Samuel's swamp. In fact, it would be pigheaded of you to refuse to be honored in this way, even if you *don't* want to be a captain."

"Oh, would it?" Dave snorted.

"Absolutely," James said in a tone of the utmost seriousness. "You would be diminishing your effectiveness in service of king and country. What could be worse than that?"

Dave shook his head, and both men grinned.

CHAPTER FIFTY-TWO

Necromancer

"Haunted?" Mina repeated. "I don't really know. I think it's something like that. People seeing the dead. James told me about seeing—" She cut herself off.

"My dead husband," Zora finished for her.

"Yes," Mina said.

"You don't have to be so delicate about it," Zora said, smiling softly. "It's been twenty years now. I still miss him, but I can talk about it without feeling sad. We had good times together. Now they're just fond memories."

But you never remarried, Mina thought. *I don't think I would ever marry again if James died, but I also don't know if I would be all right, even twenty years later. I still think about my mom like it was yesterday.*

"I didn't know quite what to say," Mina said. "I wasn't expecting to talk about this with you. Honestly, I didn't even expect to see you here anytime soon. I'm glad you made it." She was relieved to find that she actually meant what she was saying.

"If the forest is haunted, I really might be able to help you," Zora said thoughtfully. "Do you know anything beyond the apparitions?"

"I do," Mina said. "It's all secondhand from James, but . . ." She proceeded to explain everything she knew about the forest.

As Mina was talking, Zora took her Small Bag of Deceptive Dimensions from a pocket of her robe and pulled out a heavy leatherbound book. The characters on the cover looked to be in some ancient language using a non-Phoenician alphabet, which Mina did not immediately recognize, but the text translated itself in her mind: *Book of the Dead*.

"I have a patron god," Zora said. "As I understand James has."

Mina wanted to interject, *Me too!* but this seemed an inappropriate moment.

"This was a gift from him when he gave me his blessing," Zora continued.

"A death god?" Mina couldn't help but ask.

"No," Zora said. "A god of magic. But I was about to go through Class Evolution at the time, and I told him which options most interested me." She smiled mischievously at Mina. "I bet you can't guess what I picked!"

"A witch of some sort?" Mina asked. *Is this going to be like showing up to a party and finding out we're wearing the same dress?*

"No. That sounds like a good option, but no. I decided to become a Necromancer."

"Oh." *Should I be worried about you? I mean, more than I usually am?*

"I know it sounds creepy and unnatural when you first think about it," Zora said. "That's why I didn't walk in here with an army of skeletons or something."

Which implies that you could *have done that . . . You don't have an army of skeletons waiting somewhere* outside *of the Fisher Kingdom, right?*

"But this whole System thing feels pretty unnatural to me," Zora continued. "One day I was counting down the months to retirement. The next, I found myself sucked into another world, fighting mummies in the desert." She laughed, almost a cackle, and then her face became serious again. "I thought very carefully about how to survive in this new world—not the Orientation world, but Earth. And one thing kept coming back to me: death comes for us all, the loved and the hated alike. It's even more unavoidable than taxes. The more I thought about it, the more I wanted to somehow harness that force. In a magical world, anything is possible. I was going to gather as much power as I could to help you guys." Zora smiled sweetly, and Mina forced herself to exhale.

"So, you decided to become a Necromancer," Mina said. "I guess dead allies don't ever get tired." She tried to make it sound funny, but her voice rang slightly hollow as she spoke.

"No, they don't," Zora agreed. "They have their weaknesses, but fatigue isn't one of them. We all eventually succumb to death. It's a tireless force of nature, as enduring as life itself. And the dead will always outnumber the living. More importantly, I think my specialization has given me the knowledge I need to help you with your haunted forest."

"Oh, of course," Mina said. "I'm so happy to hear it!" She was also happy to change the subject from Zora's new Class. Mina had received Necromancer as an option in her own Class Evolution, but she'd quickly dismissed it as too creepy and distasteful.

"I've been studying this book," Zora said, beginning to flip through the *Book of the Dead*, "and I believe what you're dealing with is one of these."

She finally stopped flipping, tapped a page with one bony finger, and turned the book around so that Mina could see. There was an illustration that looked quite a bit like the illusion James had conjured to illustrate the appearance of Sister Strange. The label at the top of the page read, *Dream Wraith*.

Mina read the page. It described what James and the others who had spoken up at the meeting had experienced. It explained where the Dream Wraith came from and described some of its behaviors. A Dream Wraith was apparently a congealed embodiment of energy from unpleasant nightmares and forlorn dreams. It wasn't a particularly fast-moving invader, but it was persistent. The book seemed credible. It described invasions of people's dreams, apparitions of the dead—and the apparent reason *why* Sister Strange was doing all this.

"She feeds on suffering," Mina said slowly. She failed to suppress a shudder at the thought.

"Can't coexist with something like that," Zora agreed. "*Very* icky."

Mina snorted a little at the word "icky."

"I'm glad some of these things still gross you out," she said.

"I am still human," Zora said, chuckling quietly. "For now. And I'm definitely more comfortable in the company of living people than rattling bones. I'm much more interested in the future of this child"—she held baby James up—"than I am in building some kind of undead empire. I just have a certain affinity for death. I've spent—hm. Well, I've spent a lot of time living with it. Thinking about it. How best to die. When will I die? That sort of thing. I never told you guys, but I actually had a cancer scare a couple of years back."

Mina's eyes widened. "A scare? Does that mean you're okay now?"

"There was just a lump. It turned out to be benign, but it really got me thinking." She sighed. "It's not very dignified to admit this, but even at my age, I'm still afraid of dying. I really want to live."

"Well, I don't think that ever goes away," Mina said. She waited for Zora to elaborate more on what the cancer scare had gotten her thinking about, but the silence held for nearly a full minute instead.

"Anyway, I can give you my meditations on death some other time," Zora said. "For now, I think I have an idea about how we can destroy this monster that your kingdom is facing."

"The page doesn't say anything about destroying it," Mina said. "Is there more?" She flipped to the next page, but it had a different header: *Vengeance Wraith*.

"There is more," Zora said. "Not specific to this subtype, but the bit on Dream Wraiths is part of a whole section on Wraiths of various kinds. Useful stuff. I have sort of a half-baked plan already. You mentioned that James is going to distract the monster this evening, right?"

Mina nodded. "Did you happen to overhear that whole conversation?" she asked.

"No, just the parts about the plan to deal with the monster. I didn't hear anything about the Moloch worshippers or Hilda's blessing from the God of Light. I was mostly just paying attention to the baby during that part."

Mina laughed. "Got it."

"He's very talkative," Zora said. "Told me all sorts of things about what you've been up to."

"Sure he did," Mina said.

Both women laughed.

[Citizens of the Fisher Kingdom, the group of flying monsters that entered our airspace earlier was successfully defeated, and the territory they entered from has now surrendered. My thanks go out to all the brave fighters who accompanied me into enemy territory and fought honorably until we subdued the kingdom of the bats! As discussed in our public meeting earlier, we are also seeking some volunteers to enter another territory this evening. This territory is the source of the nightmare-inducing presence that some citizens have experienced in their dreams. Tonight, we will gather more information about that enemy or perhaps destroy it outright. Please see Dave Matsumoto if you wish to volunteer. Glory to the Fisher Kingdom!]

"Glory to the Fisher Kingdom," Mina repeated.

"Glorious indeed," Zora said. She looked energized.

Then they heard the downstairs door opening and firm footsteps treading the stairs.

Mina didn't even need to look to know that it was James. When she did, she saw that he wore a stylish cape made from some dark, semi-translucent material. It reminded her of Count Dracula's opera cape from the old *Dracula* movies.

"Good evening, ladies," he said quietly. "I guess our little one is resting?" He gestured to the baby in Zora's arms.

"He is," Zora said, smiling. "You were a good sleeper when you were his age too. Such a quiet boy. Such a shame you had to grow up."

"I'm hoping he'll be a lot like James," Mina said, looking at her husband with loving eyes.

He smiled softly. "I'm so glad we can all be here together," he said. "How about I get us some dinner, and then we can rest before our evening's activities?"

"That sounds good to me," Zora said. "We took a long route getting here, and I'm famished."

Alice poked her head out of the nursery. "Please make sure you prepare a plate for me too!" she said. "And Ben! If we're eating, I'll call him over."

"Only if the two of you tell me how you've been doing since, um, everything's been happening," James called back.

"That's too long of a story to tell over a meal," Alice replied. "We can have a sleepover, and maybe then I can tell you everything, but you need a pull-out sofa or something. I don't know where we would stay."

"You're going to be living here from now on, I assume," James said. "I asked the Building Commission to throw up a house for the two of you and a cottage for Ben as quickly as they can."

"How thoughtful of you," Zora said.

Alice pursed her lips and said nothing.

She wants to move in with the boyfriend, Mina thought, *and James just made Zora her roommate.* Mina wasn't sure whether she wanted to laugh or console Alice.

"We won't have too much time to swap stories tonight," Mina said. "Your mom has a plan to defeat Sister Strange, and she was just about to get into it before you came in. Since you're going to tangle with Sister Strange again tonight, I think this is a lot more urgent."

"It's really more of an idea than a fully fleshed out plan," Zora said, "but I'm happy to share it. And I agree that sooner is much better than later."

James smiled. "Sounds like all my problems are solved," he said. "I dealt with the small incursion across our border, so the only issue left to wrap up now is Sister Strange."

They spent the next half hour preparing a simple meal together. Alice, Mina, and Zora had all started out as Mages—Alice was still a Mage—so everyone had a command of fire Mana at least sufficient enough to cook with it. They were still a long way from having ovens in the new apartments since the gas and electric infrastructure had been destroyed during the System's transformation of Earth. But magic solved many problems.

This time they ate in two separate groups. Yulia brought food to the children in the nursery, while James and the magic users discussed the threats likely to face them in Sister Strange's forest and formulated their plans over dinner.

"I think this could work," James said as the conversation concluded. "Even if we don't succeed in ending the threat tonight, at least the three of you will gather valuable information."

He opened his Small Bag of Deceptive Dimensions and gave each woman a cloak. Mina examined hers and found that it was called the Royal Aeromaster Cloak.

"With these we'll be able to fly, then," Alice said.

"Well, Mina will be able to fly," James said. "You guys will at least be able to float. I'm not sure how coordinated the other sets of wings are when they're not connected to a bat's body."

"They'll work well enough, I'm sure," Zora said. "They'll have to."

"I have faith you'll at least escape the forest alive," James said. "Bear in mind that if you're somehow still in there when I wake up, I *will* go in after you by myself, and I won't come out until I find you."

"I get it, skapi," Mina said softly. "That's the risk we take by volunteering to go into enemy territory. If we die in there, the family loses you too."

"But you won't die," James said, obviously looking for reassurance.

Mina couldn't find the words to tell James that she would be all right, that she was sure she would survive. She had never lied to him about anything important before. And wouldn't she be lying if she said she was certain she would come out okay?

In the end it was Zora who spoke first.

"No, she won't die," Zora said, taking both Mina's and James's hands from across the table. "Mina will get back to you and your baby no matter what. I'll take care of her. I promise."

INTERLUDE

Once Upon a Time in the Southwest

In a small corner of Mexico, Esmeralda Ortega Cortez knelt in a church.

More than half of the buildings in the village are completely ruined, she thought. *Was there some divine favor that spared this building?* After everything she had seen over the last three months, it seemed completely plausible.

And if that is the case, God, will you help us out of this dilemma we find ourselves in?

As usual, the only answer to her silent plea was the sound of the wind as it pounded against the outside of the church.

Esmeralda rose to her feet, and at the same moment, she heard the door creaking open behind her.

"Is that you, Father?" she asked, hoping against hope that the priest would have returned.

But it was the little girl, Maria Garcia Cervantes, instead. The six-year-old was sniffling with tears in her eyes.

Esmeralda instantly took her into her arms and scooped her off the ground.

"Hey, mama, what's wrong?" Esmeralda asked.

Maria continued sniffling for a moment, and Esmeralda let her cry for those seconds in silence. Finally, Maria seemed ready to share what was wrong. She opened her mouth.

"Contreras is back, and he wants our sacrifice, Esmeralda," she said. "What are we going to do? I'm scared." Her lower lip wobbled as she finished explaining, and Esmeralda thought she would start a renewed round of crying, but Maria managed to hold it in.

"You know, all my friends call me Esmer," Esmeralda said.

VISIONS AND NIGHTMARES

Maria's eyes opened wide. "Am I your friend?" she asked.

"Of course!" *I don't have many, but I'm happy to add you to the list.* "Tell me, why are you so worried, Maria? You know it won't be you. No one could give up someone as cute as you as a sacrifice."

Esmeralda cupped the little girl's cheek, and she was rewarded with a smile and a tiny giggle. Then Maria frowned again.

"I'm not worried about me," she said insistently.

"Then are you worried about me? You know I can hide." Esmeralda said.

"No, not worried about you either," Maria said.

Not even a little bit? Dang, kids are blunt!

"Well, then?" Esmeralda asked.

"I'm worried about Cousin Martin!"

Esmeralda had to keep herself from laughing. She managed to maintain a serious face as the little girl stared at her earnestly. *If I laughed, she'd never forgive me.*

In this little village, everyone knew everyone else's business. Esmeralda, as the teacher, knew more than most about the children's business. She knew that Maria had had a crush on little Martin for the better part of last year until Esmeralda had made sure that someone informed her that he was actually her cousin. Since then, the two had been the best of friends.

"It's sweet of you to worry," Esmeralda said. "Why do you think they want Cousin Martin?"

"I don't think Contreras *wants* Cousin Martin," Maria corrected.

Such a serious young girl, Esmeralda thought, carefully observing the way Maria's facial expressions conveyed her sincerity.

"I think that our neighbors might be willing to give Cousin Martin up," Maria continued. "You know, he's been sick ever since we came back from—from that other place."

Esmeralda nodded. She knew vaguely about the other place Maria meant. The separate space where children had been taken during Orientation.

"Martin has been unwell," Esmeralda said slowly. Her mind raced as she considered this. Despite herself, she was forced to take the wise little girl's thought process very seriously. Being sickly, when the whole village was struggling to survive . . . Would they choose Martin as a sacrifice just for that?

Esmeralda would have liked to simply say, *No, that will never happen.*

But she had reason to believe otherwise.

In Orientation, didn't people abandon the sick? The wounded? The dying? My mother . . .

Esmeralda stopped herself from going back down memory lane. In Orientation, she had learned a lot that she didn't want to know about the people she had grown up with. That was all. What they were willing to do, and what they were not willing to face, in order to survive.

And now they were in a world where real monsters roamed free. Decency might be a thing of the past.

It would make logical sense for the villagers to choose Martin as their sacrifice if Alfonso Contreras was back, looking for human flesh to offer up to his dark god. No one wanted to be carved up and offered to Huitzipochtli.

Esmeralda swallowed. "You might have a point," she told Maria.

"I knew it," the little girl said. Little beads of water started welling up in her eyes again.

"You know what you need to do now?" Esmeralda asked.

"What can I do?" Maria asked.

"Think about how to escape. Can Martin walk?"

Maria nodded.

"All right. Now I need you to be brave and strong. I need you to go into Martin's room and get him out of there. Take him somewhere no one else knows about. Do you have a hiding place like that?"

"I did," Maria said. "Before the Earth moved."

"Do you know if it's still there?" Esmeralda asked.

Maria shook her head.

"Is that a 'no' because it's not still there, or a 'no' because you don't know?"

"I don't know," Maria said.

"Then try taking him there anyway. If Contreras comes after you, I'll find a way to distract him," Esmeralda said.

"Are you going to be all right, Esmeral—Esmer?" Maria asked.

Esmeralda plastered a smile on her face. "Don't you worry about me," she said.

But she was worried.

Esmeralda and Maria emerged from the church together and immediately went their separate ways. Maria headed for one of the few houses that was still basically intact, where Martin lived. Esmeralda looked for where Contreras would be.

She found him in what had once been the village cantina, a building she had never spent any significant time in. Half of the building's roof had caved in. But the bar was still standing.

Of course the bar is still standing. The System couldn't get rid of alcohol, which makes men behave like animals. Then it would be doing us a favor . . .

The proprietor of the establishment, Jose Gomez Vega, was serving Contreras from the meager stock of alcohol that had survived. Beads of sweat stood out on Vega's forehead, and although it was hot and sunny today, Esmeralda didn't think it was the weather that had him sweating.

Contreras was playing with a knife as he drank—a pre-System weapon, not something he'd acquired in Orientation. The shiny metal glinted brightly in the sunlight that streamed through the collapsed ceiling.

"Well, hello, there, Esmer," Contreras said, without turning.

She kept herself from flinching. Esmeralda had hoped he wouldn't spot her so soon. She wasn't certain of what she wanted to say just yet. But now she had to say something.

"Hello, Alfonso," she said quietly. She couldn't keep the sadness from her voice. "I heard you were visiting."

"Oh yeah?" he said, turning his head back to look at her. He smiled. His face was the same, besides the thin mustache, but somehow it was hard for her to see the boy she had thought was cute in school. "I wonder who told you that."

She ignored the question. Contreras got up from the bar stool where he was sitting.

"You know I won't be here long," he said. "We could have some fun before I go. For old times' sake." He stepped closer to her. Almost close enough to kiss her. She smelled the sour odor of cheap whiskey on his breath.

"We don't have any 'old times' to get nostalgic about," she said.

"Just a girl with a crush," Contreras said.

Her face grew hot. *I can't believe I ever liked you.*

"That was when I thought you were smart," she said. She would have gone further, but she had to remind herself that she wanted to keep him in this place for a while. She'd been lucky to find him here.

"Before I fell in with the wrong crowd," he said under his breath.

Understatement of the century. The Azteca Cartel were the worst crowd he could possibly have fallen in with. People around here hated them. But they had looked at Contreras differently after he had joined too, showing him a kind of respect he'd never experienced before. The only real downside, if he cared about it, was that it closed some people off from him forever. People like Esmeralda.

She nodded. "But we don't have to talk about that now."

He raised an eyebrow. "It seems kind of pressing as to why I'm here—ah, but you probably already know that. Esmer the Wise knows everything. Let our friend here get you a drink instead of dwelling on unpleasant things." Contreras gestured at the bartender, and he immediately began rummaging under the counter.

"I don't drink," Esmeralda began. But then she saw Jose was getting her a bottle of water from somewhere.

He gave her a sympathetic smile. A look that said, *I know.*

"Of course you don't drink," Contreras said. "You don't do *anything* fun." He made a lewd gesture.

"If you're going to do that, I'll drink elsewhere," Esmeralda said. "I thought we were just going to talk about our school days and maybe catch up."

"Don't be like that, Esmer," Contreras said. He placed a hand on her arm, and she forced herself not to push it away.

"Then you behave yourself," she said sternly.

He chuckled. "I can believe you became a teacher," he said. "You were always so prim and proper." He turned to Jose. "You know, she considered becoming a nun."

Her face grew hot again. "I told you that in confidence."

"A long time ago, yes," Contreras said. "Since then, I seem to have lost your confidence completely."

"You've done a lot to keep me from giving it to you," she said quietly.

The conversation between them was awkward—by turns mocking and sentimental. Two people who had known each other for years in school, briefly dated, exchanged first kisses, and then gone down very different paths. But she kept him there for an hour.

She thought she might have rekindled some old feelings in Contreras, which was not her intention. *Worth it, though.* The children had to have hidden themselves away by now.

She tried to think about what she would do when the village offered someone else up as a sacrifice. She knew they would accede to the Aztecas' demand. They would give someone up to Contreras. There was no spirit in the village to fight. But she despised them for it.

Once upon a time, I thought the people here were the type to stand up for what was right. She wrestled with what she would do after today was over. *Take the kids with me and get out of here? Go where—south toward the city? North toward the border?* Either way, she would be wandering through the desert with no equipment. She was no Mage who could conjure water. She had thought the Healer path made the most sense—and then had been forced to fight for her life with her stave and anything else that had come to hand.

How would she survive the desert? Let alone keep two children alive with her . . .

This crappy little village was in the middle of nowhere, but in itself, it was technically somewhere. By some miracle, the village well still stood. They still had access to water.

No, she thought. *Have faith.* God had sent her dreams during Orientation. She had heard the voice of an angel. And, most importantly, she had survived. Esmeralda had to keep reminding herself that she had survived when many others had died. There had to be a reason for that.

If God wished for her to try something impossible in order for her to keep faith with Him and honor her convictions, He would give her the tools. She mustn't be afraid.

The cantina had grown quiet, Esmeralda belatedly realized. She turned to face Contreras only to find he was staring at her intensely.

"I always loved the way you look when your mind goes elsewhere," he said. "You were always imagining yourself in a better place—a better life, a higher position, just being somewhere doing more important things than whatever was happening in this shitty little village."

She opened her mouth to reply. "I—"

"Don't deny it," he said, cutting her off. "I know. I'm not so different. I wanted something different too."

And even though she still felt as if they were a world apart, she understood him. She saw things through his eyes for a moment—her mind instantly rebelled at the shift of perspective. The next words she said came out harsher because of it.

"If you wanted to get something higher than this village, then why did you reach so far beneath you to find something different?" She had spoken her knee-jerk reaction aloud before she could take time to consider the wisdom of it.

"Oh, Esmer." He shook his head. His eyes had a glint of sadness in them. "I am no saint, but my family is well provided for." Contreras had moved his mother and little brother out of the village after he had risen high enough in the cartel to take care of them.

"At whose expense?" she asked.

Contreras rose from his seat. "I think the village has had enough time to choose their offering to Huitzipochtli," he said. "If they haven't—well, I'll help them make up their minds." He flashed Esmeralda an ugly grin, and then his expression became more somber. "It's been a pleasure having a drink with a lady. Don't ever change, Esmer. I hope I see you again in fifty years and you've become a nun. Then you can lecture me all you want."

He put on the leather jacket he'd left lying on the bar stool beside him—Contreras seemed to prefer his pre-System clothing over the armor he had acquired in Orientation—and he walked out.

"Phew." The bartender let out a long breath he'd been holding and smiled at Esmeralda. "I think you calmed him some, for what that's worth. And old Felipe's had time to say goodbye to everyone."

Esmeralda's heart sank. She had been contemplating walking away from this insignificant place if people here were really willing to sacrifice one of their friends and neighbors just to keep the village alive. Because Huitzipochtli would undoubtedly be thirsty for blood again soon.

But this was too much to bear. *Felipe. He was such a kind man. Whenever Mama needed a ride into town, or if we were running low on food, he was always there.* It had been a recurring problem after her father died, when Esmeralda was just a little girl.

Now he was going to his death—willingly, if she knew the old man at all—so that others would not have to die in his place. She imagined him saying goodbye to his two adult children, and hot tears welled up in her eyes.

"I'm sure he appreciates the extra hours of life you bought him," Jose said, clearly trying to be comforting.

"Not good enough," Esmeralda said, almost under her breath.

It only takes one person to decide to stand up for what's right, she thought.

"What?" Jose was asking, but she ignored him.

She reached for her Small Bag of Deceptive Dimensions, and she drew out the great bow she had obtained in Orientation. She had decided.

To hell with this village if they want to give up one of their own. I'm not going to let it happen.

"Jose, is there a back way out of this place?" she asked.

His face took on a look of consternation.

"Now, why do you need to know that? What are you going to do with that bow?" he asked.

"Just answer the question, please," she replied firmly.

Finally, Jose led her out the back door. It was hidden by the collapsed roof.

Then Esmeralda ignored his pleas to know what she was going to do. She climbed up a nearby hill until she reached the highest point that she could. She looked out over the dirt road that led out of the village.

This is the road Alfonso will have to ride down to bring Felipe back to his gang, she thought.

Esmeralda looked down and thought about angles and the effect of wind and gravity on even an energy-based projectile like her magic arrows. She would only have one, perhaps two shots at this. If she missed, she might kill Felipe herself.

Finally, she steadied her breath. She heard the sound of Contreras's motorcycle revving.

She drew the bowstring back, a gesture she had needed to perform hundreds of times in Orientation. She focused and materialized her arrow into a glowing shape of pure light and energy.

And he came into view, riding on his motorcycle with Felipe close behind him. Esmeralda would have to be more than precise. She would need to be perfect.

She didn't give herself time to doubt.

Esmeralda loosed the arrow, and she saw the motorcycle instantly spin out of control.

She allowed herself a smile before she rushed down to check on Felipe and Contreras.

Both men were gasping when she reached them. The arrow had taken Felipe through his right lung, and he was extremely short of breath, but he still managed to smile at her.

"Es . . . mer . . . alda." Every syllable was a struggle.

"Hush," she said and began Laying on Hands.

Her eyes strayed to Contreras, who had a hole right through the center of his chest and blood trickling from the corner of his mouth.

Why couldn't you have been different? she thought.

His lips were twitching, and she realized that Contreras was trying to speak. She tried to lean in and listen while still keeping her hands on Felipe's chest.

"You are starting a war," Contreras said.

"I know," she replied.

"You can't win," he rasped, his breath becoming shallower as his body failed him.

"Probably not," she said, "but I couldn't find another way to do things. Better to have the fight now instead of later. We would only be weaker."

"You. You have an answer for everything," he said, almost laughing but running short of breath. "That's why you were top of our class."

I'm just thinking out loud, Esmeralda thought. *I only did what I thought was right. I could not do otherwise.*

"Not much of an achievement in this place," she said.

"Goodbye, Esmer," Contreras rasped.

"Goodbye, Alfonso," she said.

Esmeralda leaned in and kissed him on the forehead as the last gasps left his body.

CHAPTER FIFTY-THREE

The Volunteers

"All right, I've gathered all of the volunteers," Dave said. "We're ready to invade the forest."

The sun was already below the horizon as he spoke, and the whole Fisher Kingdom glowed under a brilliant, quickly fading orange halo—except the part that stood in the shadow of the evil spirit's forest. The darkness there seemed almost impenetrable, as if there had never been the touch of light there. And yet that was where the Fisher Kingdom's eager volunteers stood, armed and armored, eager and ready to do battle.

"There are quite a lot of them," James said, looking surprised. He looked at the crowd of people gathered near the forest around forty feet back from where he and Dave were talking. It was significantly more than the number of those who had attacked the bats with them earlier. A few *hundred* more.

"After your performance in response to the bats earlier," Dave said, lowering his voice, "there has been a surge in enthusiasm for further military adventures." There was a dark irony to his tone as he finished the sentence.

I can't say I'm entirely comfortable with the way people are reacting, myself, but I hope it will serve our purposes well, Dave thought. *We need this kind of fervor right now. We need people psyched up to enter the unknown dangers of that forest . . .*

"Are a lot of the people who invaded the bats' territory signing up for this too?" James asked.

"Most of them," Dave said, "plus anyone who they spoke to about it. A lot of people responded to your announcement."

"Is there anyone still in their beds?" James asked incredulously. He lowered his voice. "Sending this many people feels very risky to me."

"You don't feel that you can distract the boss monster for long enough that we can all get in and out?" Dave asked quietly. "If you think it's too dangerous, you can tell them now, and we'll just go in with a small strike force."

James turned his head and looked over to where his wife, mother, and sister stood, apart from the mass of soldiers ready to invade, wearing their bat capes.

"No," James said after a moment. "We'll go ahead with everyone. I can definitely keep the boss creature's attention. I would just suggest that a few should go in before the rest. An advance party. I just want to make sure whether the creature's apparitions are active or not before we commit the full body of soldiers to that dark forest."

Dave nodded. "That sounds prudent," he said.

I am relieved you're not just blindly ordering everyone in, he thought. *That might work with you there in person, but I'm not certain how well it would work out with you staying behind.* Dave reminded himself for the sixth time that James *would* be in the fight with them because he would be grappling with this "Sister Strange" on the astral plane or something. It was still hard to fully grasp what it meant. *How many planes of existence are there, anyway? There's Earth, all the other universes the System mentions,* other *other places where Orientations happen, plus at least one afterlife . . . and, of course, there's a separate place where dream creatures can move around.*

He sighed to himself. *I have a feeling I'm going to miss normal shooting wars after a few years of this. But I'm in it now.*

James placed a hand on his shoulder. "How are you feeling?" he asked, looking into his eyes.

Right now, I have the strangest feeling that you know *the answer to that question already. You can't also read minds in addition to reshaping the Earth, sensing foreign presences, and communicating with everyone in your territory, can you?* It didn't seem at all out of the realm of possibility.

"I feel okay," Dave said. He could see James looking back at him skeptically but without humor. "Ah, fuck, I'm nervous as hell."

"Yeah, that sounds more like it," James said. "Now you sound like a good captain."

"What are you talking about?" Dave asked. "I have to imbue my troops with confidence."

"Yes, which is why you won't say you're nervous as hell *to them*. But it would be irresponsible not to bring your well-founded concerns to your commander. You're in charge of leading these men and women—wait, are there teenagers over there?"

Dave looked back at the crowd, but they were much too far away for him to tell how old individuals were.

"Probably," he said finally. "I told parents not to let their teenagers come if they asked if they could join, but there were too many people for me to ask them all for ID in the last half hour."

James swallowed. "I really don't want teenagers entering the forest, Dave," he said. "This isn't a game, and it isn't World War One. I want to be better than the governments that came before me, not worse."

"I agree with you," Dave said. "The dark is getting thicker, though. I won't even be able to read IDs in the next ten minutes. If people want to sneak into this fight, we're not going to be able to stop them."

"Yeah," James said. "I know. I could check every ID myself, but soon the first people to go to bed will be falling asleep. I need to be in dreamspace to intercept Sister Strange or she'll start attacking people's dreams." He sighed. "I'll just make an announcement." James closed his eyes.

Dave waited, but he heard nothing. Then there was a small commotion from within the crowd of volunteers. Dave heard raised voices, and then a half-dozen people were shoved out of their ranks. The six individuals looked downcast from their slumped postures, but they headed back to the residential buildings.

"Wait, did you make an announcement?" Dave asked.

"I figured out how to keep them to limited geographic areas," James said. "The more time I spend with these Ruler abilities, the better I'm getting at using them. Absorbing the power of another Ruler also makes mine stronger."

Oh. Well. All right, then. He's just going to keep on getting further ahead of us normal human types, I guess. Cool.

"I'll let you get to your power nap," Dave said. "I'll let the ones going into the forest first know who they are. The rest of us will be on standby, ready to rescue or back them up as the case may be."

James looked surprised at something, though Dave couldn't quite figure out what.

"You just accepted the Captain Job," James finally said.

"I did," Dave said.

"I meant for you to take your time and consider that," James said. "I don't want you to have regrets."

"I meant to take you up on that generosity," Dave said. "Then I realized that the Captain Job comes with bonuses to those under your command. I wasn't about to lead people into battle without giving them every possible advantage. The boost only applies to up to five hundred people. But I think it will just about cover every member of our invading group today."

James had seemed surprised at first, and then pleased. But as Dave spoke, he recognized on James's face a look of respect. He couldn't be sure if he'd ever seen that particular expression on the Fisher King's face before.

"Well considered, Captain," James said. He raised his arm in a salute, which Dave returned crisply.

Just like riding a bicycle, he thought.

"As commander in chief, you know you're supposed to let other people salute you first," Dave said mildly.

"I do know that," James said. "I just felt like saluting you this time. It probably won't happen again. Now, let's go inspire the troops."

Dave smiled, and the two men walked over to where the volunteers stood waiting.

"Volunteer soldiers of the Fisher Kingdom!" James yelled. "Thank you for gathering this evening. Tonight, we take the fight to the enemy who has invaded many citizens' dreams!"

A low cheer went up.

Dave heard them shout, "James!" and "Fight!" and "Rah!"

"I will engage the enemy in the dream world while you attack the forest," James said, continuing in the same raised voice. "Follow the orders of your commanding officer, Captain Dave Matsumoto!"

There were shouts of "Captain Dave!" and Dave felt his heart beginning to race.

This is a bit intoxicating. His mind flashed to moments when he had been ready, eager even, to fight in his last war, and he realized that he was emotionally in a very similar place. *But this time I don't have to lose so many of my friends*, he told himself. *This time we'll win a victory without such devastating losses. This time is different.*

He wasn't sure if he truly believed it or just fervently wanted to believe it, and maybe the difference didn't matter right now. This wasn't a war of choice. This was an enemy who had chosen to attack them. Self-defense was easy to support. He realized James was still talking, and he tuned back in.

"—just the beginning of building up our strength!" James was saying. "We will be taken seriously by all peace-loving countries and feared by all aggressive powers!"

The crowd seemed very energized, and they kept shouting, almost going over James's volume.

"Yes!"

"Victory!"

"James!"

"Fisher Kingdom!"

"Keep control of yourselves!" James shouted. His voice seemed to cut through the noise, as if it was infused with something more than human. The crowd began to calm noticeably. "Follow the orders of your commander. We don't want to lose any people unnecessarily. Before you proceed into the forest, a squad of scouts will move forward to see how active its defenses are. The captain will select those scouts if he hasn't already. Until Dave tells you to advance, everyone else holds tight."

"Yes, sir!" someone in the thick of people shouted.

Then the rest of them joined in, shouting, "Yes, sir!"

James turned back to Dave. He looked satisfied with the effect he had produced. Dave was slightly in awe and couldn't find words for a few seconds.

"Those are some awesome powers you have," Dave said finally. "I've never seen a group of people so eager to fight and kill and *die* before."

"Well, today that's what we need," James said. "A large number of very aggressive humans."

"Yeah," Dave said thoughtfully. "I noticed there aren't a lot of Goblins around. I guess that was your decision?"

James nodded. "Only the ones who can use magic. Humans have a lot of different ways of fighting, but most of the Goblins are only armed with crude physical weapons. Only the Goblin Mages are going to be of any use against the kinds of opponents I'm imagining we'll face."

"I wonder if *I'll* be of any use," Dave said. He looked down at his pistol. It seemed remarkably mundane to face down any kind of supernatural threat, but it had carried him through thus far.

"I think you'll be just fine," James said. "Remember, don't stand and fight against overwhelming odds if you find them. This isn't our last chance to defeat the residents of this forest. If you can withdraw the army in good order, and you think that's quickly going to become difficult to do, you should do that."

"What are they doing?" Dave asked, gesturing to James's wife, sister, and mother.

"They're going to attack from another angle as soon as the scouts give the signal that it's okay for you and your allies to invade," James said. "Apparently, there's a physical location that the boss is tied to, and it might be a point of vulnerability while I have the creature's spirit trapped with me in dreamspace."

"So, we're serving in that time-honored role of barely trained foot soldiers throughout history," Dave said. "As a distraction."

James shook his head but looked slightly uncomfortable. "I wouldn't say that exactly," he said, "but I will admit, I'm hoping that your frontal attack allows them to get further in than they would without it. The reason I wouldn't think of it as a distraction is that any enemies you guys engage with inside are enemies we actually need to defeat. There's not going to be any irrelevant fighting in the forest. Only fighting against Sister Strange and her minions."

"Hm." Dave wasn't sure he was convinced, but he was all right with serving in the role of a distraction if James was lying to him. He knew that real military operations often needed some element of misdirection to succeed. "Well, good luck with your mission," he finally said.

"Thank you," James said. "I think we'll either succeed together or fail together. If you see me appear on the battlefield at any point, you'll know that we've probably already won."

"I will look forward to seeing you, then," Dave replied. He grabbed James's hand and shook it forcefully. And then he spoke in a low voice. "It's all right if you use us as a distraction. I know that sometimes that's necessary in war. But whatever you do, don't disappoint these people by letting them suffer a pointless defeat. If we lose soldiers, it has to *mean something*. Understand?"

James nodded. "Tonight is either the first step toward victory or the whole thing," he said.

This time Dave decided he believed him.

CHAPTER FIFTY-FOUR

Visions and Nightmares, Part 1

James wished Dave luck and then walked away from him and back to Mina, Alice, and his mother.

He was quiet and resolved. He believed this was his best plan, and he allowed himself to mentally detach a bit from the people he was sending into harm's way.

Can't worry about them right now. If I do, I won't make proper use of the risk they're taking.

He looked around as he moved. There were still a few people lurking outside, looking at the forest and the force that was about to invade it. Annoyed, James sent another localized message out.

[All non-deployed personnel, please return to your residences. If the enemy retaliates in response to our advance, indoors is the safest place to be.]

Finally, he reached his family.

"How did that go?" his mother asked.

"I think I instilled Dave with as much confidence as I could," he said. "And as for the rest of them, I think they're ready to tear down the forest with their bare hands."

"Are you going to be all right?" Alice asked.

James smiled. "When did you start worrying about your big brother?" he asked. "I'm the one who's supposed to worry about you, remember?"

"That's how I know everything is fine," Mina said, looking at his mother and sister. "James is still trying to be funny."

"Trying?" he asked. "What do you mean, 'trying'?"

"Mister Comedian," his mother said, rolling his eyes.

Is it possible I'm really not funny?

"You guys don't have to go, you know," he said, becoming serious. "I know you came up with this plan, and I think it's a good one, but it's also risky. We could just use this as an information-gathering trip. You could stick with the volunteers and fight beside them. I think you're going to be in worse danger than they are."

"If we don't follow the plan, the three of us aren't going to get anything useful done," his mother said. "No information, no nothing. Trust me. I'll keep your wife and your sister safe."

"And I'll keep both of them safe," Mina added.

"While Yulia watches the kids and keeps them safe," James said.

"Even though she'd rather be on the expedition with us, keeping me safe," Mina said with a subtle note of sadness in her voice.

"I guess I'll just let these two keep me safe," Alice said, shrugging and offering a small smile.

That made James smile.

"All right," he said, shaking his head. He looked at Mina. "I don't think today is the day any of us die." He looked at Alice and his mother and added, "Have fun, then." The sun was completely out of view now, and the dark was settling in over everything like a thick blanket. "I'll see you on the other side of this."

Mina kissed him, and Alice and his mother embraced him.

Then James sat cross legged on the ground, leaning up against the apartment building as he had the previous night.

Dreamwalk.

And he was in dreamspace, floating weightlessly until he decided which way to move.

There were dreams all around. Even tonight, when hundreds of the residents of the Fisher Kingdom were volunteering to invade Sister Strange's forest, there were dozens of people asleep already.

Probably mostly children, he thought. That only made protecting their dreams from interference all the more critical.

James looked around, seeing little, for a moment.

Where is Sister Strange?

His and his family's plans would be thrown for a complete loop if the Dream Wraith was simply choosing not to come back here tonight. Or perhaps she was trying to hide in one person's dream instead of lurking as a giant tentacled creature and interfering in scores of dreams. She could have him chasing her all night if that was her plan.

He looked carefully around the dreamers in his territory, but he couldn't find a trace of her besides the gross feeling of the energies she had left behind in her last visits. There were those who were beginning dreams infected with the still-raw memories of the bad dreams she had given them last night.

James could feel the seeds of nightmares germinating in a few of the minds around him.

Thanks to that creature contaminating my territory, he thought angrily.

He tried to wipe away the traces with his spectral hands, but there was little he could do from the outside. If he wanted to affect the dreamers, he needed to focus on them more carefully and specifically. It might even be best if he entered their dreams. But that wasn't what he was here for.

James continued to look for the invader as more minds began dreaming.

But there was no sign of Sister Strange.

He began to grow frustrated.

"Where are you?" James said loudly.

Then he saw the shape of her—the tentacled, pale-faced *thing*—coming across the border from the exceptionally dark place that was the representation of her forest within dreamspace.

So she really wasn't here yet, he thought.

"You're here early, human," she said in a curious tone. "Did you decide to sleep at sunset tonight? Were you truly so eager to see me again?"

James rushed toward her, but Sister Strange danced back, keeping her distance, ready at any moment to pull back across the border and into her land again.

"Why so eager?" she asked. "Did you miss my exquisite visions? Are you fond of suffering?"

James already knew what he wanted to say to her. He had anticipated that Sister Strange might be cleverer than the average monster he fought.

"I need answers," James said. "What were those places and times you showed me? Was that the future that's meant to be? The future that *might* be? Or your own invention?"

"I do not know what you saw," Sister Strange snarled, "but my visions are no inventions. They are true representations of suffering that will be, suffering that may be, suffering that is, and suffering that has been. Since you're referring to the future, whatever you saw is either going to happen or is a possible path. If it's the former, then even if some details change, the vision's contents are inevitable."

"Which was it?" James asked. "What did you show me? The future that will be or the future that *might* be?"

"That's for me to know, and you to torture yourself with," Sister Strange said, laughing cruelly. Her face twisted with an unwholesome enjoyment.

"Monster," James growled. His emotion was half feigned and half real. He was afraid that what he had seen represented the inevitable future, and he was almost as afraid of it being a genuine possible future. He had hoped that Sister Strange was simply a liar, or that she was simply conjuring up his worst nightmares. But the more he thought about it, the more he doubted that.

VISIONS AND NIGHTMARES

As much as it would constitute genuine psychological torture to deceive him in this way, she could have shown him worse visions than what he had seen if she was simply trying to torment him. Junior had still been alive when James's last vision had faded out. If she wanted to torture him, why not kill his whole family? Why only show isolated incidents? It felt like there was more to this than the simple desire to inflict suffering.

"I am a monster," Sister Strange agreed, "and you remain merely human. I commend you for returning here, however. You are very brave, despite—" Her facial expression changed, and she turned her head as if to look back at her territory. "What . . ."

James lunged at the tentacled figure and grabbed her center of mass with both hands.

Soul Bind!

"What are you doing?" Her voice was sharp in his ear. Her tentacles whipped at him now, and James thought she must have done something new with them since they'd last encountered each other. They packed a lot more of a punch. They couldn't do any lasting damage to him, but they landed whip-like on his dream body, and each touch felt like a blade's cut.

She optimized them for trying to torture me instead of infiltrating hundreds of people's dreams, he thought.

"Oh, I just wanted to give you a hug," James replied from between clenched teeth. "You seem like you don't get enough of those."

"Release me, human, or I will—"

She stopped. They both felt it. Soul Bind had taken effect. She was locked to his location now.

"What's going on within my territory?" Sister Strange demanded. "Who walks through the Haunted Forest this night? I sense a presence . . ."

"Oh, that's for me to know, and you to torture yourself with," James replied, grinning savagely.

"You will suffer for this impudence!" she shrieked. Then her eyes flashed brightly with supernatural power.

James blinked and found himself in that same room in the ancient-looking mansion he'd visited before.

"Choose your poison." Sister Strange's voice came from the ceiling and the walls.

James found that the doors looked different from the four doors he'd seen last time. Their number was still the same, but they looked subtly different. He couldn't tell if Sister Strange had rearranged them, or if they were simply all completely different doors than the ones he'd chosen from before.

She mixed them up to maximize my confusion.

"I want the future that *will* be," James said aloud. The first time he had encountered Sister Strange, he had gotten the impression she might be willing to accommodate his choice between the four suffering options. Perhaps she might be too angry for that now, but it was worth a try.

I'm glad to be back here again. I'm restraining her from defending her territory, I hope. And if I see the same things again, then I'll know that those—his mind rebelled against where he was going and refused to complete the thought.

"Do you hear me, Sister Strange?" James yelled. "I want the future *that will be!*"

One of the doors began exerting a pull on his body then, almost like it had become the room's center of gravity. James let himself be pulled by that force, hoping it would be the vision he'd requested.

The door dissolved into nothingness as soon as he passed through it. The scenery jumped into view—and almost instantly, he knew that he was in the wrong place.

It was the living room of his parents' home from when he was a kid, before they had had to move into their squalid apartment. Before his father died. He heard his baby sister crying, and the sound pulled him back.

As he watched his mother striding briskly across the room toward Alice's bedroom, James knew what day it was.

"How dare you," he murmured.

The rage boiled up within him, thick and hot.

This was the day his father died. Tears came to the corners of his eyes. For a moment, he was a child again.

He feared what was coming. It was worse than it had been when he was a boy because now he knew what was set to happen in the next hour.

Soon that doorbell will ring. And then . . . Mom and I find out that we've lost him.

The wrathful part of James surged forward and instantly took control of this regression to childhood.

"How dare you?" he said again, loudly this time. He felt his voice rippling through the room. The fabric of the place shook with the sound.

"How dare you waste my time with this bullshit?" James shouted. "This suffering is pointless. *Worthless.* I refuse to do this again. Once was more than enough."

James blocked out the world all around him. He drowned out all sound and light with his mind until he was in a silent, still black box. And he willed the door to reappear.

After a few seconds of this focused state, he saw the door in his mind's eye. He reached out and pulled it open. Then he stepped through, and he felt that he was back in the room. He looked around. The door he had just come through closed, and James felt the distinct sense that Sister Strange would not try to suck him through it again.

It was hard to be certain. Dream logic was no logic at all. Hazy and inconsistent didn't begin to describe it.

But for now, he had won some small part of the struggle for control.

He took deep breaths, trying to brace himself for whatever was to come next.

Three more doors, he thought. *What are the odds that the next one holds something useful?* He considered the question carefully and realized that he could consider the odds quite high if the rest of these rooms were as real as Sister Strange's vision of his past was.

That would mean Mina is either certain to die defending the Kingdom and our child, or that it's a high likelihood. I still don't understand why. I only have the symbols those people wore to go off of. Religious symbolism associated with the three Abrahamic religions . . .

He took one last deep breath and then reached out to his body outside of the room.

He could feel that his astral body continued to keep hold of Sister Strange. Which meant her territory was still a vulnerable target for his soldiers.

It's just a matter of waiting her out now, he thought. *Relax and gather as much information as possible. Time is on my side.*

James chose one of the remaining open doors without much concern for which one was which, and he stepped through.

CHAPTER FIFTY-FIVE

The Haunted Forest, Part 2

Dave exhaled.

"All right," he said. "You, you, and you." He selected three more people. "That completes our scouting party."

A few people groaned, but Dave raised his hand for silence. To their credit, they immediately clammed up.

"Unless something immediately happens to the scouting party, the rest of us will be joining them shortly."

A little hoot of excitement went up, and Dave grimaced. *Whatever. I guess it's better for people to be excited than scared out of their minds.*

"Amalia, you ready?" he asked.

She gave him a crisp salute, which he returned.

"Ready and eager, sir," she said, offering him a slim smile.

He wanted to say, *Don't call me sir. I work for a living!* but he supposed that he was actually an officer now.

"I still feel weird about that," he mumbled.

"Don't," she said. "You've earned it, and everyone here knows. They believe in you, just like they believe in him." She gestured at their commander in chief sitting cross-legged by his apartment.

"Yeah, well, I don't have the power to turn the tide of a battle singlehandedly," Dave said, his words coming out a little harsher than he had intended them to. He softened his tone as he added, "So, please do be careful. If you lead my soldiers into a massacre"—his lips twitched in a perverse smile—"I'll bring you back and kill you again myself."

"Understood, Captain," she said. "We will be the ones doing all the massacring."

"Dismissed."

Amalia strode over to her group. Dave caught her brief words to them.

"Well, we're the ones who got picked, guys. We're the ones who get first crack at the enemy. Hope you're all fucking excited!"

There were hoots from the other members of the scouting party. Among them were those Dave trusted, like Paul Mann and Amalia; those who came recommended by James, like Ramon and Felicia Rodriguez; and those who seemed to have something to prove, like John Carraway, who had apparently once been the landlord here, and Olivar Cruz, who was a former criminal.

"Let's go!" she shouted.

Everyone's infected with your energy tonight, Dave thought, turning back to look at James's sleeping form. *I really hope this isn't an insane miscalculation. Feels kind of crazy that we could be going into battle without you standing beside us.*

But that would all depend on these next few minutes and what the scouts experienced.

Dave followed them closely with his eyes as they walked into the forest, trying to maintain a tightly knit formation. Soon, though, he lost sight of them. The night felt unusually dark, and that darkness seemed even denser in the forest than it was elsewhere.

Perhaps it was just his mind playing tricks on him, but a part of Dave wanted the scouts to run back and tell him and the hundreds with him to abort the mission. He didn't like the thought of leading this large group into such danger and uncertainty.

Time seemed to flow very slowly as he stared into the blank dimness. Time enough for Dave to play out his fears in his mind over and over. He began almost to assume defeat.

How can we stand up to a force whose leader could haunt hundreds of dreams at once?

He shook his head and tried to clear his mind, but the longer he stared into the darkness, the more insistently the negative thoughts asserted themselves.

Even if the King survives, what will become of this country if all his bravest citizens are slaughtered in that forest?

A hand pressed gently on Dave's shoulder, and he emerged from his fog, turned his head semi-consciously around, and blinked twice.

"Oh, Alan, it's you," he said, breathing a sigh of relief.

"Hi, David," Alan said in a hushed voice. "Are you okay? You were looking a little spacey there."

"Yeah," Dave said. "Well, no, you're right. I was kind of out of it."

"It's hard," Alan said, "but there's some sense in which it's just like riding a bicycle, right?"

Dave swallowed. "This bicycle is a rough one," he said.

"You're okay," Alan said. "You can do this. Look at all these people you have ready to follow you into that forest." He gestured at the hundreds of volunteer soldiers just a few feet away from them. "Could all these people be wrong?"

"It's not—I'm not—well. Hm." Dave thought for a minute. *Why am I feeling so pessimistic? Need to stop dragging my baggage into this.* He took a deep breath. "You're right," he said with renewed confidence. "We're going to be fine."

"That's right," Alan said. "We are. And they are." He tilted his head to indicate the other soldiers again. "Because they have you, and you have them. We're all one unit now. Say, is that the signal?" He pointed, and Dave followed his finger.

A red flare lit up the sky. Someone had used fire magic.

"That's the signal!" Dave shouted. "We advance."

The volunteers roared enthusiastically. "Fisher Kingdom! Victory! James! Rahhhh!"

They surged forward, an almost uncontrollable mass now, eager to score kills and win glory.

Dave turned his head to look behind him. It was an afterthought, but he didn't know what James's family members were up to. His mouth gaped. The three women were holding hands as they floated into the air.

Like something out of Peter Pan, he thought. He had never seen a human fly through the air before. *It's those wings that some of us got by defeating the bats . . .*

Then he heard Alan clearing his throat.

"Oh, yes," Dave said. "Let's go. Before we get left behind."

The two men rushed after the troops Dave was meant to be commanding. They moved swiftly, even as the all-encompassing darkness of the forest gave the feeling they were rushing forward into some immense predator's maw.

Dave moved swiftly so that he could try and retake the lead position. Alan was slightly more relaxed; he split off from Dave, and Dave guessed that he was going to go and stand beside his wife, who had also volunteered to join them.

"I feel a little bad about letting them fight without us," Mina said softly as she floated up into the air.

"You shouldn't," Zora said bluntly. "We have the harder job. They might have a higher casualty rate than we do—but if we don't get this right, the mission is a failure. And we might all die."

"You were very reassuring with James," Alice observed. "I guess we don't merit the same treatment?"

"I'm reassuring you now, in a way," Zora said. "Your boyfriend is down there with the other volunteers, right?"

"Please leave him out of this," Alice said, rolling her eyes.

"I'm just saying, he'll probably be okay down there. We might all die, but at least Ben and James will probably live through this."

"Yeah, I'm sorry, Zora, but this isn't really making me feel much better either," Mina said. "Do you have a specific direction I should follow?"

"No, my dear, I don't," Zora said. "I have the book's guidance, but where this Sister Strange's reliquary might be is a matter of educated guesswork. We haven't built any kind of device to track it. We're just using the best information we have available."

"Which is?" Alice asked.

"You know, I explained all of this during dinner," Zora said. "Was I just talking to myself?"

"There's no better time to go over it again than now," Mina said. "Anything you remind us of makes it more likely that we find it."

"All right," Zora said. "We'll start from the beginning. A Wraith, no matter which kind, is a disembodied spirit. It needs to be anchored to the physical world somehow so that it does not pass on to the other side. That anchor has a tangible physical form. Can anyone tell me why this is important?"

"It's like the core of an Elemental," Mina said quickly. "They all have it, and if you destroy it, you kill them."

"Exactly. You win! The reliquary will usually radiate some amount of magical energy, unless the Wraith is exceptionally weak. In the event that the Wraith's ethereal body is damaged or destroyed, she returns to the reliquary to recover—much like the phylactery that a Lich possesses."

"Okay, and what about the how-to-find-it part?" Alice asked.

Zora looked daggers at her for a moment, exhaled, then continued, "The how-to-find-it could start with the magical energy signature. If it's out in the open, we should be able to see it. Mana has a visible appearance, and since it gives off light, I would think it would be extremely visible in this dense darkness. But then there's the typical behavior of the Wraith to consider. They usually want to find some structure to haunt. Broadly, the forest is haunted by the Wraith and her minions, but normally, they'd find some sort of secluded place to make their inner home. They're creatures of darkness—they like the dark—so something that allows for access to the outside world so their prey can get closer to them, like a cave, house, circus tent, or a structure of some sort, is most likely."

"So, we're looking for a dark hidden place in a dark forest," Alice summarized.

"Well, at least we have a bird's-eye view," Mina said.

The three women flew in silence for some time, each keeping their eyes peeled for some visual indicator that they were near the part of the forest where Sister Strange had stored her reliquary.

At a certain point, Mina could hear the distant sound of fighting, but she tried to ignore it. Their mission was more important than whatever was happening to James's troops at the moment. Ultimately, if they defeated Sister Strange, her minions would be weakened, and the conflict would end in the Fisher Kingdom's victory.

So where is it? Mina thought. *If I were an evil spirit, where would I hide my weakness? It's a forest . . .*

"Guys, I think I see something!" Alice exclaimed.

She pointed, and Mina looked and saw a large dark shape below them. The texture of this dark mass was different from the rest of the forest. It was vaguely reddish, not like the brown scrub that covered the ground. It seemed to be a tiled roof.

"Let's drop down," Mina said. She steered them toward the building and began the trio's slow descent.

Dave caught up with the head of the Fisher Kingdom's force at just the moment when they reached the scouts—or what was left of them.

The scouts. *God, the scouts. I sent them here . . .*

Magical light from levitating fireballs illuminated a dozen faces frozen in horrific expressions: mouths open, fixed in expressions of terror; eyes that stared forward, looking up into the vast emptiness of the night sky but seeing nothing; sickening rictus grins.

Every scout's body was intact, but each one's face was contorted in a unique and disturbing way. It almost felt like they had died of fright.

"What the fuck happened here?" Sam Masterson's voice rang through the air beside Dave's head.

"There weren't enough people," Dave said. "They were overrun."

"But by what?" asked another, female, voice.

"Oh, it's you, Mitzi," Dave said. They had briefly interacted as a part of James's council, but Dave had spent more time speaking with Alan.

"I'm still me, yes," Mitzi said drily. "What do you think did this?"

She gestured at the pale, stiff bodies lying on the ground, looking like they had been drained of something even more essential than blood. Some unnameable essence.

Their souls? No, it couldn't be their souls. That thing *James uses for a weapon eats souls, and whenever it does, the bodies full-on disintegrate.* Dave shivered at the thought of what had befallen the men and women laid out on the ground.

No, it's not just my thoughts that are making me shiver, he realized as he saw his breath coming out in visible clouds. *It's suddenly strangely chilly here!*

"Everyone, be prepared to fight!" Dave said. "There's a presence somewhere nearby."

"I wonder why they even signaled us," Sam said. "Like, when did they have time?"

Then Dave noticed it. The scouts' chests—they were still slowly rising and falling.

"Christ," he muttered to himself. "These people are still alive. But they look so *wrong*..." Raising his voice, he called, "I need a Healer up here now. Preferably one who knows the Purification Skill. Our scouts aren't dead, they're just—"

One of the bodies jerked, and Dave found himself gaping as he stared into Amalia's dead eyes.

"I'm sorry, Dave," said Amalia's lips in a voice that was not her own. "I'm afraid I can't let you do that."

"Oh. Oh God." Dave found himself wanting to vomit. The cold, dead eyes. The piercing voice. The obviously unnatural *thing* puppeteering her body, twisting her lips into a horrid mockery of a smile. It was such a horrifying sight that words left him, and it was all he could do to keep from throwing himself to the ground and screaming.

There was a sound of necks and knuckles and knees and ankles cracking, of joints that had grown stiff suddenly coming back into use again.

Then all of the scouts they had thought were dead began rising to their feet.

CHAPTER FIFTY-SIX

The Haunted Forest, Part 3

As the scouts rose to their feet and faced off against Dave and his vanguard, he forced himself to remain steady and not back down.
Identify.
[Amalia Rosario (Possessed), Lv. 8]
Damn it, they really are being controlled—but does that mean we can save them?
The thing wearing Amalia's body leaned in closer to Dave, leering at him, obviously enjoying his discomfort.
"What's wrong, soldier boy?" the thing said in a shrill perversion of Amalia's voice. "*Invasion* not going so well? You want to run home to Daddy?"
Dave felt his stomach churn. This thing knew what Amalia knew. Its remarks were obliquely personal—things Dave had only shared with those who had hunted with him.
He distantly heard the other possessed scouts making similar remarks to figures in the vanguard, but he was ill-equipped to understand some of them. And for the moment, he couldn't look away from the eerie glowing eyes Amalia had affixed to his.
Then her hands were upon his. The skin was soft but ice cold.
Dave felt something being pulled out of him. His body instantly began weakening, but he felt powerless to resist.
Then he heard the sound of a sword singing through the air, and he saw Amalia staggering back. Her hands were still on Dave—he felt their cold grip almost to his bones—but he saw her wrists gushing thick spurts of blood where the hands had been severed from them.

Dave heard Sam's voice in his ear. "Are you all right, Dave? Dave!" The voice became urgent. "Say something to me, man!"

"I'm—I'm—"

Dave felt the cold fingers prying away from his body. He looked down and Sam was ripping the severed hands from his.

He could hear other people shouting.

"Healers to the front!"

"Need Purification! Now! Now, now, now!"

Dave found his voice, and he joined the group of those yelling. "Capture them alive! We have to capture them alive! Don't kill the scouts. They're just possessed!"

There was chaos all around him as some obeyed his orders while others had already begun attacking the scouts with uncertain but devastating movements. Dave saw a Mage's staff crack John Carraway over the head, and the old man went down with an awful grisly smile on his face.

"Are you afraid to kill us, Dave?" the Amalia-thing asked, its voice cruelly mocking in his ears. "It's the only way you'll escape this place alive . . ."

The superior number of Dave's forces began to get hold of the possessed. Except for a few, like Amalia and Olivar, who had maneuvered out of reach, they were caught by the arms and legs and held down, hissing and biting their saviors, to receive Purification from the Healers.

Dave watched anxiously. As the Healers grabbed hold of the first handful of possessed with their glowing green hands, he sent a silent prayer out. The possessed screamed like demons. Then their physical appearances seemed to return to normal as they collapsed to the ground, limp but still alive.

We should have brought more Healers, Dave thought. They had perhaps two dozen Healers among the hundreds of fighters they had brought. Almost all of their fighters had begun as Mages, with the exception of some warriors like Dave, who had specialized in Mana-related attacks. He had been briefed about what these spirit-type enemies were like, and he had repeated the information he was given to his soldiers.

But hearing about it and seeing it were two different things. Dave saw the hope going out of some people's eyes already. This wasn't the harmless adventure some of them had experienced in the bats' forest. There was no one-sided slaughter here, no simple opportunity to gain experience. Many of those here desperately wished they could go home.

He wanted to say something to inspire the troops and renew their hope. His mind started to formulate some generic words about fighting for home and family.

Then Dave saw that the true enemy had arrived. The words died in his throat. Flickering just at the edge of the space illuminated by magical firelight, figures with no legs were floating in the shadows: gently glowing translucent specters.

Dave couldn't hear anything from them or even clearly make out whether the figures had facial expressions, but he somehow had the sense that they were laughing at him.

Mocking all of the Fisher Army's soldiers.

"Be on your guard everyone! They're at the edge of our line of vision!" he shouted.

Dave began charging his pistol with Mana, readying it for the attack. To his surprise, someone flung a large bolt of lightning past his head and destroyed one of the creatures in a single strike. He turned his head and saw Mitzi.

"You're not alone up here," she said, giving him a little nod. "We'll all fight until the end. I can already tell I hate these things."

Dave's first thought was that it was irrelevant how much they hated the creatures because they had a job to do. But then he realized she'd made him smile, and the Mana seemed to be flowing into his pistol just a little more easily after what she'd said.

That's strange, he thought.

When he had briefed Dave earlier, James had said something about the creatures having an effect on the emotions of the humans around them, but he had been vague. *Was this what he meant?*

More figures appeared, but Dave fired Mana bullets and more Mages hurled fire and lightning to destroy them. Still others threw projectiles of water or earth, but it quickly became obvious that those simply passed through the monsters harmlessly.

"Keep up the fire and lightning!" Dave shouted. He used Command Presence, one of the abilities that came with his Job. It allowed everyone under his command within a certain area to hear him. Those who could not see what was happening needed to understand. "The water and earth magic doesn't work on them. If you only have water and earth, save your Mana!"

Even the fire and lightning seemed to be of limited effectiveness, though. For every one of the creatures that silently dispersed, it seemed two or three more appeared. The edges of the firelight began to seem as if they were haunted by an army of specters.

"They're behind us now too!" a voice shouted from the back of the block of soldiers.

Dave's heart sank, but he tried to keep up a brave appearance. It wouldn't help matters to let them know that he was scared.

"That's perfect!" he yelled. "We can fire in any direction and hit enemies!"

They were just distracting us with those first attacks so they could surround us and cut off our retreat.

An air of hopelessness seemed to have settled over the troops like a blanket as they realized they were surrounded. Dave felt it almost as a tangible thing, and he thought he could see the darkness actually creeping closer around them as the number of the enemy hovering at the edges of their field of vision steadily increased. He tried to resist the aura of despair with positive thoughts.

At least we're not seeing the dead, Dave told himself. He realized that if the power that had created those apparitions were still active, the little army's cohesion would have been utterly destroyed. Undoubtedly, his entire group would have succumbed to possession already.

This was only partially effective at raising his spirits.

There was a scream from the side of the group then, and Dave's head jerked back and to the left. He saw a young woman being dragged away from the rest of the block of soldiers. A spectral hand gripped her arm. Three fireballs shredded the figure pulling her away, and the woman stumbled back.

"Be on your guard!" Dave yelled. "Don't let them get close!"

There was a rain of fire and lightning from the Mages in multiple directions as they tried to beat back the attacks from their enemies while the specters sporadically charged them.

Dave heard screams from the right side this time, and he turned and saw three figures being dragged off, two male and one female. The woman began to glow with green aura, and the hand that had grabbed her vanished like morning mist.

Fire and lightning found the specter holding onto one of the two men, and he staggered back, relieved, as the creature dissolved.

But the other man was not so lucky. The lightning bolts missed the specter that held him and struck down a distant tree instead. They came so close that the bolts illuminated the man's face through the encroaching darkness. Dave's eyes widened as he saw it.

Sam! When did Sam get over there?

He took a few steps toward that space and had to stop himself from chasing his friend into the darkness.

Then he heard Sam's voice screaming—followed by a terrible silence.

The darkness seemed to grow just a little denser.

Then Dave saw a half-dozen others armed with sticks and swords rushing toward the edge of the firelight to try and rescue them.

"Stop!" he forced himself to shout. "You're doing what they want!"

Some grabbed for the would-be heroes, but three of them managed to rush out of reach into the darkness. Then their screams joined Sam's tortured cries.

I don't know what to do, Dave thought. *What do I—*

"More light!" yelled a woman in white armor, who had stepped toward the front alongside Dave. "We need more light to keep them back!"

Dave turned his head and saw that the quality of the light around him had dimmed noticeably. He looked back and saw one of the Mages had collapsed to her knees.

"Sorry, everyone," she said, breathing heavily. "Out of Mana."

So soon? Dave thought. It was as if the air around the invaders was sapping their strength.

Mitzi stepped up and filled the air with even more light than there had been before. She conjured a dozen fireballs that she scattered even more widely than the previous flames had been. He heard her breathing heavily as she did this. He guessed she was also starting to get low on Mana.

The creatures seemed annoyed by the light and advanced more aggressively, pressing forward on all sides.

"Everyone, more light!" Dave yelled. "More fire and lightning!"

Mages who had been resting for a moment began chanting again, though there was an air of hopelessness about the whole thing.

Then the monsters rushed toward the band of soldiers.

As Dave fired Mana bullets at the enemies ahead of him, he heard the sounds of more of his allies being grabbed by those to the sides. Dozens of translucent hands began dragging people away from all sides.

"Hold tight, everyone!" Dave yelled. "Grab onto people—"

His words were cut off as a very tangible pair of arms wrapped themselves around his neck and placed him in a headlock. He recognized the pair of arms instantly by the fact that they had no hands attached.

"Amalia!" Dave choked out the name as he tried to fight her. But the body of his comrade seemed to be possessed of strength beyond what she could normally muster. She began dragging him away.

"You're joining us, Dave," she said, her voice full of sadistic glee.

In the corner of his vision, Dave saw Mitzi was being dragged off by another specter.

"No!" he cried.

"Oh yes," Amalia said.

He could only imagine how the group was breaking behind him. This felt like the end.

I can't let this happen.

"I can't go with you," he said sadly. He pointed his pistol at where he knew her heart must be, and he pulled the trigger. Then her grip was broken. Her body tumbled forward, away from Dave's. He didn't allow himself to look down. He knew that she was dead.

Dave started to turn back to his soldiers—still struggling valiantly to keep together and hold off the now hundreds of hands trying to pull them into the darkness—but then Sam lunged for him out of the darkness. Dave moved quickly and pistol-whipped his friend.

Sam went down instantly, and Dave dragged Sam's body with him as he rushed back to the group. He could tell that dozens had been dragged into the darkness, but the solidarity of the group was holding out.

Whenever the pull of enemies on one side grew too strong, Healers would rush over and expel the specters where they were thickest. The bodies of dozens of people lay on the ground. As he rejoined the fight, Dave saw people fall over from sheer exhaustion while others toppled after having been possessed and having the spirits driven from their bodies.

"Keep going!" Dave shouted. "Just keep going!"

The struggle went on for what felt like hours, to the point where Dave couldn't see an end to it.

Every time they pushed the specters and the possessed back on one side, every time they freed someone whose body had been taken over by a spirit, it seemed that on the other side more humans were captured or collapsed. Every minute that passed, another human tired and stepped back or fell.

It felt like the cycle could only conclude in one way.

"Die, vile creatures!" There was the woman in white armor again, yelling and glowing with white light as her sword cut through the heads of a half-dozen specters.

At least that's one person who won't give up, he thought.

Then Mitzi's face leaped at him from out of the dark, expression twisted, a horrifying leer on her face.

She sank her teeth into Dave's right arm, and he screamed and reflexively batted her away with the other arm.

As she staggered back, Dave saw Alan rush into the darkness after her.

"Alan, no!" Dave shouted. But he didn't follow him. He needed to stay where he could be most useful.

He pushed more Mana into his pistol and realized with the sudden onset of weakness that he had just emptied his Mana reserves.

No! I managed them so carefully, he thought.

He fired the Mana bullets he could into key areas where the thickness of the advance meant that he could not miss. Then he stepped back more toward the middle of the group, where he could evaluate the situation in relative safety. Dozens of people knelt, breathing heavily, trying to recover some small fraction of their Mana within the shell created by those who were still fighting.

Dave found himself slightly short of breath too, now that his power had been expended.

Over a hundred other human bodies also littered the ground. Most of them had collapsed from exhaustion. Others were the possessed who had been Purified. There was also a growing pile of those visibly possessed who had simply been knocked out.

We apparently don't have enough spare energy to Purify them anymore, Dave thought grimly. Sam was in that pile, and a few of the warriors stood guarding it.

How can this end? He looked and saw dozens of faces in the darkness: the possessed and the mask-like images of the specters that sought to possess them.

He saw that Ramon Rodriguez had rejoined the ranks of the possessed after having been Purified earlier, and it filled Dave with a sense of exhaustion.

Another pair of Healers stopped glowing and collapsed, and the front line of soldiers on that side began to recede toward Dave and the piles of bodies.

This is the end, Dave thought. He braced himself to hold onto as many people as he could for as long as he could. It was all he could do now that his weapon was useless.

CHAPTER FIFTY-SEVEN

Reliquary

The descent brought Mina, Alice, and Zora down just a few feet from a massive run-down mansion.

"I never knew there was anything like this in the area where we had our apartment," Mina said. "It's strange—" She giggled as she realized what she'd just said. Then she shook her head. "Do you think she built it for herself?"

"Wraiths are pure evil," Zora said, her voice a slightly melancholy whisper. "They create nothing new or good. They only twist and pervert what others have made. It probably came back with her from her Orientation."

"At least we know we're the good guys," Alice said.

"Yes," Mina agreed. *I was never actually uncertain of that, though.* "Let's see if the front door is open."

She began walking toward it, but Zora grabbed hold of her arm.

"Slow down," she said quietly. "There's every chance the Wraith has booby-trapped this place, assuming it really is her hiding spot. We have all night."

Mina had a bad feeling that the Fisher Kingdom's soldiers would not have all night if nothing was done to help them. But she left it unspoken. She already knew what Zora would say to that. *Our mission is more important.* It was true too. There was no argument to be made.

Still. She had an uncomfortable feeling that it was going to be a bad night for the Fisher Kingdom's army.

As she had these thoughts, Zora was quietly chanting a spell, gathering brown-colored Mana around herself.

Earth, just like James, Mina thought. Not for the first time, she wondered if Mana affinities were related to the personality of the person concerned.

Then the glow vanished from around her body, and a massive earthen tendril rippled forth from the ground. It lunged forward and smashed into the mansion's front door, caving it in with a single thrust. Through the now permanently open doorway, Mina could only see darkness.

"Well, there we go," Zora said contentedly. "I guess the front door wasn't rigged."

Mina looked at her mother-in-law in awe. *That thing was so fast! I don't think I've ever moved water at that speed before, and earth is so much heavier. I can't imagine that was easy to learn.*

As she stared at Zora, the older woman crouched low to the ground. Then she ended up sitting down.

"I'm too old for crouching," she said. She began chanting, and another color of Mana slowly came to surround her. This one was a vile shade of green that reminded Mina of radioactivity.

Necromancy. Mina knew it in her bones. Zora was raising the dead. *Is that really wise, in this place?* But Zora knew the enemy best. *If she thinks this is safe . . .*

"Um, Mom, what are you doing now?" Alice asked.

Zora continued chanting and ignored her daughter as best she could.

"Well, she's a Necromancer," Mina said. "I'm guessing she's doing some necromancy."

"Oh, yeah," Alice said. "She did mention that. I've never actually seen her use it. We weren't together for most of Orientation. When we did get together near the end, she already had her blessing and her undead creatures. But then she abandoned them before we got here. It's just really easy to forget that's her power." There was a slight undertone of disgust in her voice.

Finally, the chanting stopped, and the eerie green glow dissipated.

What exactly did she do this time? Mina thought.

And then the ground wriggled and moved beneath her feet.

Mina let out a high-pitched, girlish scream, like she hadn't since she was a teenager, and she ran from whatever was moving below her to hide behind Zora.

Her mother-in-law looked amused. "They're my pets, dear," she said mildly. "You don't have to be afraid of them."

Mina looked where she'd been standing, and she saw rodents crawling from the disturbed earth. Partially decomposed rodents, skeletal rodents, and rodents that were just recently dead with all the fur and flesh still on them all rose from the soil and lined up in a neat row—good little soldiers waiting for orders. Mina counted thirteen of the creatures. And every one of them had a slight green glow in their eyes.

"Mama got a good batch this time," Zora mused. She cackled quietly to herself as she looked over her undead forces.

Alice and Mina exchanged looks. Mina was relieved that she wasn't the only one disgusted by the creatures.

I'm so glad that James didn't become a Necromancer. Though, it feels very in-character for him to want to.

"Go forth, my little ones," Zora said, "one by one into the mansion. Find me the reliqua—or rather, find me something shiny or glowing. Bring it to me if you can, or if you cannot, lead me to where you found it."

I need to start pulling my weight, Mina thought. *If I have to tell James that all I did on this mission was follow his mother around and watch while she solved every problem*—the thought was simply unacceptable.

As she was considering how she might contribute, the first creature in line, a rat with half its fur rotting away in patches, rushed forward into the mansion.

As it got a few feet beyond the threshold, something glowed in the darkness for a moment—Mina saw an outline that resembled the Mischievous Phantasms she had fought in Carol's Dungeon—and there was a distinct otherworldly screech.

"Well, that one's dead for good now," Zora said. She looked down at the other rodents. The next one in line was about to rush forward. "Don't the rest of you go just yet!" she nearly yelled. She turned to Mina. "The one downside of being a Necromancer: they're quite stupid."

"What do we do now?" Alice asked.

Mina was already gathering fire Mana around herself, a smile touching the corners of her lips. "We fight, of course," she said. "We destroy them all."

"We'd better move quickly," Zora said. "It's possible the denizens of this forest will notice all the magic we're using and figure out what our game is." Then she began chanting too. Shortly after, Alice joined her.

But it was Mina who led the way into the mansion—Mina, who had practiced the quick and silent application of her magical power. She quickly finished charging a relatively large share of her available supply of Mana, and dozens of fireballs materialized around her, floating in the air around her body, ready to be hurled.

Then she entered. The hallway came to life with the spectral glow of Phantasms, and as each one appeared, Mina cut its life short. *I'm so glad I spent that time in the Dungeon*, she thought. *I'm so glad I practiced so hard.*

She advanced to the end of the front hallway, and looking by firelight, she found herself in what appeared to be the ill-preserved remains of a stately Victorian mansion. It was just what it had appeared to be on the outside, with the exception that there were several Phantasms floating around. Mina killed them all in a flurry of fireballs. *Magic is the best.*

"Well, that was impressive," Zora said from behind her. She was no longer glowing, but she held a ball of lightning in her hands, and more lightning lay around her shoulders like a scarf.

Alice was still quietly chanting. A pure white light glowed all around her.

"What next?" Mina said.

"Well, my pets are looking around the mansion now, but I imagine they'll run into more trouble in other rooms, away from your protection," Zora said. "And perhaps more intense trouble closer to the goal we're after, so we need to look for ourselves too." She blinked. "Yes, one of my creatures just died again. They're not very strong, and these things seem to have an ability that slowly saps the soul of energy. My rodents barely have souls in them to start with. We might consider burning down this whole building to get to our goal. But there are always pros and cons to that approach."

"What are the cons?" Mina asked.

"You miss out on a lot of loot," Zora said. "This Sister Strange might have some spell book that would save your life someday." She shrugged. "Or something that would come in handy for me, Alice, or James. Fire isn't very discriminating."

Mina shook her head. "I'm not worried about acquiring stuff right now," she said. "This thing is threatening my home." Her voice shook slightly.

"Hm," Zora said, her voice soft and gentle. "Have you been worrying that she might invade the baby's dreams, Mina?"

"A little bit," she admitted. "I didn't want to worry James with the suggestion, especially because he's been fighting her ever since we learned she was a threat. But I do wonder, with how much the baby sleeps, if the idea hasn't crossed her mind. He seems so peaceful, but I really have no way of knowing."

"So that's why the urgency," Zora said empathetically. She placed a soft hand on Mina's back.

"Well, no," Mina said quietly. "Not exactly. Right now I'm worried about James's soldiers getting killed."

"That's fair too," Zora said, shrugging. "Burn the house down, then, my dear, if that's what you want to do. It's of no great value to me. Use your flames, though. I'm going to save my lightning Mana to destroy the reliquary after the fire goes out. If I were the Wraith, I wouldn't make my soul's hiding place something easily damaged by fire. Imagine getting wiped out by a random forest fire."

"Then me torching the house might actually slow us down?" Mina said. "If the reliquary survives that, we'd have to wait for the fire to go out to get it."

Zora nodded. "That's a good point. Then we search. I suggest we start by following where my creatures are dying the fastest."

The three women marched up the central staircase. Alice was still chanting, and the white light around her body only grew stronger, slowly but steadily, until she became hard to look at.

They walked onward, up the stairs. More Phantasms presented themselves, but Mina slew each of them with a single blow to the head.

The women went from door to door in the upstairs hall, with Mina killing

Phantasms wherever they encountered them, until finally they found themselves in front of a door that Mina felt contained an ominous presence. She touched the door handle, and she almost instantly recoiled, as if at the touch of something evil. She had to force herself to grasp the knob again. It felt very cold and somehow clammy. She had to resist the urge to shiver as she touched it.

"I think this is it," Mina said somberly. She saw Zora simply nod in her peripheral vision.

Mina swallowed. She wanted to throw open the door—but another part of her wanted to run from this room, out of this mansion, and back to her own home with her sister and her baby.

There was a sense of intense pressure coming from something behind this door, and Mina felt the fear and self-doubt in her heart multiply with each second her hand remained on the knob.

She gritted her teeth.

By an act of sheer willpower, she forced herself to turn the knob all the way. But she couldn't go that one step further. She couldn't make herself push the door open, though she tried to force herself until her jaw hurt from clenching it too long and her eyes were teary.

Then Zora pulled her to the side and kicked the door open, and the room was exposed to view.

It was a vile little place, filled with cobwebs, rotted out furniture, and the festering corpses of dead animals. All this Mina knew at a glance. But mainly her eyes were drawn to the two vile figures who loomed before them.

They looked just like the illusion James had created to depict Sister Strange in the council meeting that morning.

"There are two of her," Mina murmured, stunned.

And behind them, she could see three glowing rocks that emitted a strange almost black light.

"Well, there are two Dream Wraiths here at least," Zora muttered.

One of the two women let loose a shrill laugh that pierced Mina's heart and made her want to fall to her knees in despair.

"Did you think that someone could be called by the name Sister Strange and be the only one of her family?" the figure asked. "Silly woman, we—"

"Sorry, we're not here for your life story," Zora said. Lightning shot from her fingertips to the glowing rocks in three thick glowing lines, and the rocks shattered instantly on impact.

"You horrible woman!" one of the figures shouted.

"The reliquaries!" the other screamed.

Then they threw themselves forward, hurling their bodies at Zora.

Mina reacted quickly, shooting fireballs at their heads. With all the practice she'd had, they were both perfect bull's-eyes. The ethereal matter of their heads shattered on contact with the fireballs, but then they slowly started to rebuild themselves.

"What are we going to do?" Mina asked. "If headshots don't kill them—"

A blinding light erupted from beside her. Blazing white engulfed the entire room.

Mina was blind for several seconds. She wondered if she should flee, but she didn't hear the sounds of Zora and Alice running, nor did either of them grab her and pull her away.

Finally, she blinked, and she could see again. The two twisted evil spirits were gone. Nothing was left of them. Alice had apparently walked past Mina into the room and was already poking around the enemies' belongings, while Zora was blinking, clearly still waiting for her vision to return too.

"Did we win?" Mina asked.

CHAPTER FIFTY-EIGHT

Visions and Nightmares, Part 2

James looked around and found himself in what appeared to be an isolated desert town.

Some of the houses were ruined, much like the buildings he had seen when he first returned to Earth. But these buildings were completely different than the ones James was used to in central Florida, as if they had been built without access to modern technology. Adobe houses. Dirt paths and roads.

I better not be in another vision of the past, he thought irritably. But he hesitated to jump to that conclusion now, considering that he didn't remember ever seeing buildings like these in real life. *Maybe it's not the past . . . Something tells me I'm not in Florida anymore.*

He couldn't have explained how he knew, but he felt a sense of despair hanging over the tiny town. As if the whole village was waiting for an axe to fall on them.

He saw an old Hispanic man emerge from one of the houses. His expression was sad but calm. A young woman stepped out after him and kissed him on both cheeks.

"Thank you for your sacrifice, Don Felipe." She was speaking Spanish, but the words instantly translated themselves for James as usual.

"It's no sacrifice," Felipe said contentedly. "I've lived a good, long life, and I'm doing it for my friends and my family. I couldn't ask for a better reason to die. Hopefully, it means a longer life for the people here." His face turned dark. "Hopefully, their god will be satisfied with me and whoever else they're giving it for a long damn time." His voice rose with those last words. Then James saw another couple of people, a man and woman who looked like Felipe, come out and embrace him.

And then he watched as Felipe walked to meet a young man who smiled sadly at him and led him to a motorcycle.

The two were riding out of the village, and James found himself floating along with them, shifting through the air as if he was weightless and tethered to the old man—until a fast-moving projectile made of light struck the pair, and they suddenly careened off the road.

The projectile disappeared a second later, and James watched the two men bleed into the sand.

This set of visions must be showing me suffering in the present, he thought. *She wanted to show me this to force me to experience other people's pain, then. Everything feels so pointless. The old man was going to die in some sort of sacrifice to appease the people terrorizing this village. Now both of these people are dying, and what's going to happen to the village?*

The sheer futility of it all was what galled him more than anything. As he saw a woman approaching from a hill overlooking the dirt road, the vision faded.

James suddenly found himself in a stone building. It was dark and torchlit.

A group of people stepped into view. They were following a young woman who was talking about a Vampire Count.

The vision pulled him around after the group of people as they made their way deeper into the stone space James had found himself conjured into. He watched as the group engaged in arguments, in-fighting, and general stupidity, and he found himself thoroughly unimpressed.

So, when is something going to come and eat these fools? he thought.

When the Vampire Count appeared and violently attacked them, James felt embarrassingly inclined to cheer him on.

These people are practically slasher movie victims, he thought. *I guess I don't have enough empathy to worry about a bunch of random strangers whose only salient quality is that they seem to be painfully stupid. Oh, Sister Strange. If you really want me to suffer, you need to show me people I care about . . .*

The scene dissolved suddenly, and almost as if the vision was responding to his thoughts, James saw his soldiers in Sister Strange's forest. Hundreds of ethereal humanoid creatures were crowding in around them, a wave of unstoppable shadowy figures crushing in on the Fisher Kingdom's forces from all sides.

Their only defense, James observed, was a faint and weakening curtain of light from various spells and Healing Auras.

James saw people's faces. They were exhausted, their expressions twisted in looks of despair. The lights they had conjured all around themselves were dwindling. Mages were dropping to the ground from complete expenditure of their Mana. And he saw a general loss of hope in the soldiers' eyes.

James looked around. He saw the numbers of the spectral figures steadily and substantially diminishing over time, but he didn't think any of the people who were actually on the scene could see it. Their eyes were clouded by despair. And the number of humans being possessed by the specters, though small, was slowly but steadily rising, only occasionally interrupted by rescue or use of the Purification Skill.

He felt his own heart waver as he wondered if his friends and supporters would survive their encounter with Sister Strange's army.

And he also felt something else. There was something leaving the soldiers who collapsed to the ground and those who faltered in the attack. Something metaphysical. He couldn't see it, but he could feel the shift in the air. Some element of spirit, perhaps.

Whatever it was, those specters that remained were taking pleasure in consuming it. James couldn't tell if it was making them any stronger or helping them endure enemy attacks—and in terms of numerical losses, Sister Strange's army was clearly doing worse since few of James's troops were actually dying.

But they were also enjoying themselves while those who fought for the Fisher Kingdom were steadily losing power and heart the longer the fight went on. The ranks of the possessed also bulked them up, and occasionally more spirits arrived to fill the dark army's ranks.

It felt calculated to create hopelessness—he saw the same despair on so many faces.

The scene was massively more distressing to James than the rest of what he had seen set in the present day. He could imagine losing so many people whose names and faces he knew. Dave, Mitzi, Alan, Sam Masterson, Amalia . . .

He shocked himself when he searched for them and realized that Alan and Mitzi were both possessed, while Amalia lay on the ground, unmoving. From the bird's-eye view he had, he wasn't certain if she was dead or alive.

Everyone who had fought beside him in the bats' forest was here now. Many of those he had led through Orientation were there.

And this time, you're not there to save them, he said to himself.

If they can't survive this, they weren't made for this world, replied his dark inner voice. *Those who come through on the other side will be stronger for it.*

James was immediately ashamed and angry at himself for even entertaining that thought about people who were putting their lives on the line for him and his cause.

He was trying to think of a way that his army could turn things around before their morale completely disintegrated when the vision faded away. The world turned black for a moment.

No! Damn it, I actually care about those people! Why are you taking this *vision away? Am I not suffering enough? I assure you, this is quite unpleasant.*

He blinked and found himself in the room with the doors once more. Now three of the four doors were closed.

"What is your family doing in my house?" Sister Strange's voice came from the walls and the ceiling of the room all at once, wheedling and insistent.

"Probably killing you off, I figure," James replied, shrugging. If Mina, Alice, and his mother were already there, he knew there was little Sister Strange could do about it. He felt that her ethereal body was still bound to his.

"I deliberately left your family alone, and this is how you repay me?" Sister Strange said, her voice accusing and insinuating.

"We never made any kind of deal," James said, raising an eyebrow. "I didn't even know if you knew who my family were. I assumed you avoided touching the dreams of people who were close to me because you knew I had some connection to dreamspace and you figured that would put you on my radar more quickly. Was I wrong about that?"

There was a long silence, then she spoke again with venom in her voice. "Your loved ones will die screaming, you know. My sisters will tear their souls apart! Look forward to that. I hope your next visions will give you a preview . . ."

Then the last doorway was sucking James in, and he fell toward it so fast that he had little ability to resist.

James found himself standing in front of himself again.

Present-James looked on as Vision-James stepped into a sixty-by-sixty-foot square arena. A crowd looked on, and Present-James saw Mina, Zora, Alice, and Yulia sitting in the front row, watching Vision-James.

Another man entered on the opposite side of the arena. He looked East Asian, with a stoic, composed cast to his expression—and the sorts of chiseled facial features that would be envied by any man who had ever had trouble getting a date.

Go ahead and kick his ass, future me, James thought.

At an unheard command—the whole vision was peculiarly silent—the two combatants sprung into motion. Vision-James threw blades of wind at the other man, and they left cuts on his face and penetrated through gaps in his armor to cut his body as well. But his opponent drew a long straight sword and charged toward Vision-James at full speed.

Vision-James tried to dance back, but it seemed as if the other man was as fast as he was—and perhaps he could even predict his movements before he made them.

As Vision-James dodged the attacks over and over, he didn't let the blade touch a hair on his head or the armor he was wearing. Vision-James continued to inflict the occasional punishing Meteor Strike, Lightning Strike, or Air Strike, but none of those attacks did enough damage to deter the swordsman. At the same time, the amount of ground Vision-James could freely move through shrank as his opponent skillfully pushed him back and cut off his options.

Finally, Vision-James set a foot wrong, and the swordsman swept in with a swift slash to secure the kill. The blade passed through Vision-James's neck, and his head toppled to the ground.

Oh, you found a new way to kill me, Sister Strange, James thought. *How very creative of you.*

Of course, this death was incompatible with his death in the other set of visions meant to depict the future. So, which one was supposedly real, and which one was contingent on his choices and those of others? Was either of these futures truly unavoidable, or was Sister Strange simply trying to force him to accept a fate that was not written in stone? Or tormenting him with visions of things that could conceivably happen?

James looked to the crowd and realized that Mina and the others were weeping. Mina's reaction in particular was violent. Her face had turned dark red, her cheeks were streaked with smeared makeup and tears already, and he could see that there was blood on her hands from clenching her nails tightly. Alice and Yulia were holding her, tears in their eyes. Zora's eyes had gone hollow. The tears flowed down her face, but she seemed to be frozen in a thousand-yard stare in the direction of James's body.

That made the sight of his own death far more disturbing than it had been.

I can't let myself die in front of them.

The vision began to fade, and James saw an image forming of a new setting. He made out a clear blue sky, a swamp, and in the distance, the ruins of a city.

Then a piercing shriek shattered the vision as it was forming. The color and light disappeared, and James found himself surrounded by darkness again.

Jesus, what is it now, Sister?

He reappeared in the room in the run-down mansion, and then that, too, dissolved. He found himself suddenly blinking himself awake, leaning up against the apartment.

What the fuck just happened? How did she throw off my Soul Bind? Are Mina, Alice, and Mom okay?

Then he saw her. The figure of Sister Strange, much reduced, floated in the air several feet to the side of him.

"What have you done to me?" she howled. "How did I get here? Where are my sisters? Where is my reliquary? I cannot feel it!"

James smiled at her genuine distress. *Looks like my family got the job done.*

"It seems we have an *A Nightmare on Elm Street* situation," he said, getting up and dusting himself off.

"What is *A Nightmare on Elm Street*?" Sister Strange asked in her usual eerie voice. But there was a note of fear in it now, James observed. That made him smile.

"An old movie about a demon who liked to invade people's dreams," he said.

"When they brought him into the real world, though, he died. He couldn't handle reality. Only his nightmares."

"You little bastard! You think you can threaten me?" Her voice was the snarl of a wounded predator.

"No, you silly creature," James replied. "I'm going to kill you and absorb your power. And I'm going to enjoy doing it. Threatening you is beneath my concerns. You're just a cobblestone in my path, a little building block in my growth."

He began charging Soul Magic.

"I will not go quietly," Sister Strange growled. Her body glowed with an ethereal power. An odd black light surrounded her as she prepared to face off with him.

James found the desperation in her tone intoxicating, and his smile widened.

CHAPTER FIFTY-NINE

Victory

Standing in the upstairs hallway, Mina spoke almost at the same time as Alice, who was talking from within one of the small rooms.

"So, is this over?" Mina asked.

"Why didn't I get a notification for the other one?" Alice asked. "The System said I killed Sister Odd and Sister Wyrd. Shouldn't it at least say I *helped* kill Sister Strange?"

The building felt different with the sisters gone. Before, it had felt like a haunted place. Creepy, uninviting, inhabited by death. Now it felt sort of cold and lonely but also cozy. Almost as if it wanted someone to inhabit it again.

"I think her questions answer yours," Zora said to Mina. "The System hasn't really lied yet. This isn't over. James said that he was going to be using something called Soul Bind on Sister Strange, right? To keep her with him while we did—" She gestured in the direction of the room they had killed the sisters in.

Mina nodded. "What do you think that means?"

"Well, before now, the reliquaries were the objects keeping these things bound to Earth. But clearly, Wraiths don't just vanish when their home base is destroyed. I think my book mentioned that disembodied spirits can remain on Earth without being anchored, at least in the short term, but they have to avoid light, which becomes more damaging to them without an anchor. That doesn't explain why the other sister didn't just appear back here to try and kill us."

"Do you think she's stuck with him?" Mina asked. "If her soul is bound to him . . ."

"I have a bad feeling," Zora said. She turned toward the room where Alice was searching for loot. "Come on, Alice. Your brother might need our help!"

Alice stepped quickly out of the room she had been searching and, draped with golden necklaces she had just liberated, she moved toward the stairs.

"Well, I'm sure James is fine, but I would like to get back," Mina said slowly as she walked alongside her in-laws down the stairway. "I think he'll need help with backing up our soldiers."

"You're that confident?" Alice asked, raising an eyebrow.

"I am," Mina said, nodding.

"Well, you know his fighting ability best out of all of us," Zora said.

They stepped out into the darkness of the night.

"We'll head toward the battlefield in the forest, then," Zora finished.

The three women took flight once again.

"I disagree," James replied. "I think you will die very quietly."

"Petulant human," Sister Strange said. "I will—"

James locked eyes with her. *Compulsion.*

Their minds instantly created a great battlefield on which their respective forms appeared to do battle. Thousands of copies of James engaged in single combat with thousands of copies of Sister Strange.

It was the most difficult battle of Wills James had encountered in the space that Compulsion created. He did not fully understand Sister Strange's powers. She moved much as she had in dreamspace, freely disobeying the ordinary laws of physics and extending her tentacles to use them as harpoons or whips.

Still, his army had the edge. Every copy of him was armed with Soul Magic, and although it was his most draining form of magic, it was also the most potent. His Soul Magic destroyed any individual soldier of her army instantly upon contact.

The battle was over in minutes, in terms of time within the mental world—it might have been a moment or two in the real world.

James felt his control settle over Sister Strange like an iron collar around her neck.

"Now you will cease this pointless resistance and die silently," he hissed. "Be content that I do not torture you as you wished to torture us. Be grateful. You will become a part of my strength."

Sister Strange's face twisted and writhed in visible discomfort. Then it settled into an expression of forced gratitude. He could feel the rage and hatred beneath the surface, seething with the desire to break free and strike him down.

It made him want to laugh. But best not to tempt fate—especially when his soldiers still needed to be rescued.

He reached out with the small amount of Soul Magic he had gathered around his body, and he used it to grasp the ethereal body of the creature before him. He had to be careful. He had seen how a concentrated burst of Soul Magic could instantly shatter the soul of the target. That would waste the effort he had spent using Compulsion on her and seizing complete control over the situation.

He forced Sister Strange's malleable, ethereal form into a compressed shape, crumpling it into a ball a fraction of its normal size.

He could see her expression as he crushed her. He saw that it caused the malevolent spirit pain. She had a silent scream on her face, and he felt immensely satisfied.

"I hope the suffering is exquisite," he muttered.

Sister Strange ended up being roughly the size of an apple in his hand. She could have been a fruit if there were a tree that produced gray, color-shifting fruits that felt heavier than their appearance. James looked at her a little uncertainly.

This should work, right? I have Omnivore and Soul Eater . . .

Finally, he bit into the condensed ball that he had crushed Sister Strange into and began eating her soul.

It proved chewable, just like ordinary flesh. He crushed it between his teeth and then swallowed. He was pleased that he seemed to be able to consume a bite of it. Yes. This would work. He would take her powers and make them his own. Then he would know if her visions were real or simply sophisticated illusions.

Never mind how bitter the taste was, or how he might be defying some other person's conception of the natural order. He had larger concerns than that.

He took another bite, then another.

Finally, he began wolfing down the condensed soul. There was a degree of urgency to his consumption. One of his monsters floating in the sky told him that his forces in the forest were in trouble.

He was beginning to like the bitter taste.

I could get used to this, he thought.

In the forest, Dave and most of the remaining soldiers linked arms and stood together against the grasping hands of the spirits.

Dave could feel darkness pulling at the edges of his vision now. He was so exhausted now that he almost wanted to pass out or die. At least then this nightmare would be over.

He had no Stamina left with which to raise and aim his pistol, even if his Mana had recovered enough to allow him to charge a shot. He lacked even the power to throw a rock or a punch, and, of course, no physical attacks would do him any good, anyway.

Only the thought of what would happen to the men and women on either side of him kept him on his feet.

All right, so we die, but we'll all go down together, he thought.

Even as that notion occurred to him, a woman to his left fainted on her feet, and Dave found the strength to yank her backward, behind him. Behind the line.

"I can't do this anymore," pronounced the voice of Paul Mann off to his side.

"Just a little bit longer," said a male voice Dave only vaguely recognized as a Healer's. The figure speaking was giving off a green glow, Dave noticed, but the glow was flickering, like a candle about to go out.

Dave looked around and realized the speaker was the only person still giving off the green glow. *Wait, is that guy who sounds like he's about to faint the* last Healer *still standing?*

As the light had weakened, so had the resistance of the hundreds of soldiers; their front had begun to systematically collapse until only a much smaller core of fighters was active.

Only around a hundred and fifty of the soldiers were still fighting now as dozens more crouched or knelt, trying to recover completely depleted Stamina or Mana. Hundreds more lay unconscious, while an unknown number had joined the ranks of the possessed. They mostly tried to drag people away rather than killing them, but the result was that it now felt as if the spirits outnumbered the humans who were fit to fight.

Those people who were left had become easier to drag away, too exhausted to put up meaningful resistance or even scream.

But those who still remained held onto each other. That was all they could do.

Their adrenaline had long ago been used up. It was hard to remember why they were fighting, besides the hope that they would not die.

"Hold firm, all!" Dave shouted. He didn't need to use Command Presence this time. The few people left standing were all close together, standing in a ring formation to try and preserve those who had fallen.

Dave could hear the fear and weakness in his own voice. He anticipated how much he and his comrades would be weakened when even the glow from the last Healer had faded, and his voice shook with the feeling of imminent defeat.

"Stand firm!" The woman in white armor was suddenly back at the forefront of the group, where she had once placed herself earlier in the battle. She began to glow with a bright white light that almost blinded Dave for a moment. "For the Fisher King!"

The darkness was driven back, and Dave felt it: just a small taste of hope.

"For the Fisher King!" he repeated.

Others around him began to rally, and, standing in the glow of the woman in white's aura, they found the power within themselves to summon their own inner lights. Dave saw the light of dozens of auras rekindling themselves in his peripheral vision.

All around, the words were repeated, sometimes in a shout, sometimes in a barely audible whisper.

"For the Fisher King!"

"Fisher King!"

"Humanity!"
"Fight to the last!"
"Fisher King!"
"Fisher Kingdom!"

The blinding light of their forces beat back the darkness.

Soldiers saw human hands that were reaching out to grab them and pull them into the shadows, and they found the strength to pull the possessed humans forward into their ranks instead.

A few more of the specters' victims, rescued. For now. The few Healers who were still on their feet found it in them to use Purification one last time.

Dave and his comrades fought valiantly and with renewed vigor for what felt like a long time but might have been as little as ten minutes.

"I—I'm sorry." It was the woman in white speaking again, but her voice was barely above a whisper. "I can't." The light around her faded almost to nothing in an instant, and the spirits pulled her forward into the darkness.

"No!" Dave gasped. *She was the one who made us believe again, if only for a little while, that we could win.*

Without her, the other lights grew slightly dimmer almost immediately.

The specters in the dark began advancing again, and their human mouthpieces taunted Dave and his allies as they did so.

"So much for the Fisher Kingdom."

"Was that all you had?"

"We could go all night . . ."

Then Dave heard another voice that spoke over them all, even though it wasn't raised above a whisper.

"Dominion."

Dave felt a wave of power course through the air. The specters and the monsters seemed to move back a step.

You're here, Dave thought, relief flooding his body. *We'll survive. I can rest . . .*

He collapsed backward and saw the figure of James floating overhead. The ring James wore on his left hand was glowing bright orange, and his eyes had taken on a strange golden glow.

Then his entire body turned bright yellow, and a massive wave of light shone outward from him in all directions.

Dave felt what seemed to be gentle sunlight striking his skin.

More pleasant still was the sound he heard from all around him: the screaming of specters.

Dave propped himself up on one elbow and looked around him. The whole nearby section of forest had lit up for a moment like it was broad daylight outside, and he could see the aftermath of the apparent solar energy attack James had used. The light of the sun had destroyed every specter that it touched—they had disintegrated with a symphony of horrendous screeches that Dave found beautiful in that moment—and the possessed who were struck by it wiggled, writhed, and screamed before they collapsed to the ground, foaming at the mouth.

As the light faded, Dave allowed himself a smile. Then he lay on his back and closed his eyes.

I'll just lie down and die here, he thought. The smile faded as he thought of Amalia. *I killed one of my own because I wasn't strong enough to stand up to the thing that took over her body.*

All around him, Dave heard the sounds of activity; the soldiers who were still standing did their best to save people who had been wounded in the fight or checked on friends or family members who had been possessed.

He heard the voices of James's family members, who sounded like they were floating in the sky, but Dave was too far gone to make out the details of what they were saying. Even if it was important, he lacked the energy to concern himself. He knew he would feel the pain of this battle when he woke up.

For now, he allowed himself to slip into blessed unconsciousness.

EPILOGUE

"Sir, we may have a problem!" The voice of Cyrus Berberian's lieutenant, Christopher Smith, reached his ears.

Cyrus listened with calm equanimity, even though he felt certain that he knew to whom he should attribute this complaint without needing to hear the details.

He turned, and sure enough, he saw the Galts walking toward him, moving past the 110 or so other members of Cyrus's camp. Christopher Smith led the way, followed by Claudius, Coriolanus, Julia, and their father, the stoic Tiberius.

Claudius was bleeding from one arm, but his sister was already healing him.

Before the little group reached Cyrus, he could tell that the flow of blood had stopped completely. Only the red stain on Claudius's otherwise white sleeve remained as a visual reminder that he had apparently just been attacked.

"What seems to be the problem?" Cyrus asked once they were close enough for him to be heard without shouting. He disliked raising his voice more often than necessary. Almost as much as he disliked the Galts. They were always complaining about some minor issue or another. Except Tiberius. The old man was probably the reason the voices of the angels had guided Cyrus to the family. His temperament was the stuff that new nations could be built from.

"We were, um, set upon by wolves—er, by a wolf," Claudius said.

Cyrus gave Christopher a look, and the tall man raised an eyebrow and gave the slightest shake of his head, which no one seemed to notice but Cyrus and perhaps Tiberius.

"Is there something you wanted me to do about this?" Cyrus asked. "You all seem to be all right now, and frankly—" He looked off to the horizon, where he thought he could see some buildings in the distance. "I think we have a ways to go before we'll want to put down our bedding for the night."

If God wills it, we'll make it out of the woods before nightfall, and the rest of the camp won't have to endure another evening of this family's complaints about sleeping out under the open stars.

But he would not speak in that way to the Galts' faces. He believed they were the only ones in his camp who might doubt the group's divine selection and mission. This was somewhat fair. They were the only members of Cyrus's party who had not seen God perform a miracle through him.

"Would you just have us leave these wild things alone?" Coriolanus asked with thinly veiled hostility in his voice.

"Not that we mean to start a fight," added Julia hastily.

"Do you happen to know why you were attacked by this wolf?" Cyrus asked. "I know a lot has changed since the System appeared, but they're not typically aggressive from what I recall."

Silence fell for a few seconds.

"We tried to take some food from it," Claudius admitted. "It was dragging a thick wild boar haunch, and the food—well, it hasn't been enough for all of us lately, you must admit—"

"God has provided what was needed," interrupted Christopher.

Cyrus raised a hand to signal his right hand man to back off a bit.

"Naturally, we'll exterminate all this blighted world's monsters eventually," he said, "but it's for the best if we establish our base of operations first. I appreciate the initiative you showed in trying to find some more food. The rations we took in Orlando won't last forever." He chuckled. "Fighting a wolf probably was not the best idea, but I appreciate that you were honest about it. Now I understand the situation." He pointed to the shapes on the horizon. "I think I see some buildings ahead, and the faster we get to them, the faster we're safe. Once we've secured our base, we'll come out here and do some hunting." He grinned. "Both boar and wolf. Okay?"

"Yes sir," said Claudius.

"Yes sir," said Coriolanus and Julia in unison.

Tiberius simply nodded, keeping his mouth shut.

When will we see another church? Cyrus wondered. *I need guidance. Should I truly be tolerating these dead weights? Even if Tiberius is a positive contributor, half of all delays and problems are attributable to just three people in my camp. I can't have that!*

If the voices of the angels would just tell him he could rid himself of these burdensome Galts, Cyrus would abandon them in a heartbeat. Even when they were answering him just then, he could hear doubt in their voices.

Are these the men—and woman—with which I am to rebuild America? The shining city on a hill. People of so little faith?

He shook his head and raised his voice so the whole camp could hear him.

"We've stopped to rest for too long, folks. Forward, march!"

It was a testament to the rest of his followers that Cyrus heard no complaints, only the sounds of people getting up and moving.

They walked for some time through the thick branches and increasingly softening soil without being disturbed, only to run across dozens of wild boars like the one that the wolf from earlier had apparently killed.

Once Amina at the front raised the alarm, Cyrus's group formed a tight square knot without him needing to say a word. He found himself quietly grateful that even the Galts remembered their places in the formation.

When the beasts charged, Cyrus's archers, at the center of the formation, feathered them with arrows. His few spearmen stabbed at them with the tips of their long weapons, and the more numerous swordsmen hacked at the creatures that managed to get in closer.

It was a bloody, ugly, dirty business, and the stupid beasts kept at it until the sun had set, but unlike the boars, the humans had Healers. When a creature managed to get through the tangle of blades and actually gore someone, the victim would be dragged into the center of the square to be healed and would eventually get back up to continue the fight. Gradually, Cyrus's group fended them off and Looted the bodies of those they had been forced to kill.

Damned irrational creatures, Cyrus thought. *So territorial that a dozen of you died for no reason! This is why God gave man dominion over the Earth . . .*

He couldn't be too bothered, though. The successful employment of the formation was the smoothest that anything had gone for this group since he began recruiting. And now, they had pork.

As they got on their way again, Christopher set foot on ground that crumbled away beneath his feet. The loose bit of soil tumbled down with a splash, revealing that they had almost stepped into a swamp. The sound of a large creature's movement in the water below suggested to Cyrus that the inhabitants of the swamp were much more dangerous than the pack of wild boars had been.

"Thank God for this," Cyrus proclaimed loudly. "We have avoided stepping into a nest of predators by the grace of our Lord. Everyone, be careful navigating around the swamp's edge!"

It took the rest of the group some time maneuvering around the water in the dim evening light, but Cyrus thought the detour was an absolute necessity.

When he stood next to the patch of swamp and stretched his arm out, he sensed a great and terrible aura pressing upon him. There was a Ruler somewhere in this swamp, something that could easily tear through his group and slaughter them to a single man.

Cyrus was not interested in testing God's protection this evening.

He took the lead then, hoping that by demonstrating his faith, he might keep his group from stumbling into any further environmental dangers. He felt half blind in the increasing darkness that settled over them like a cloak, so he ordered his group to light their torches.

But the light was almost worse than the darkness had been. The flickering flames hid almost as much as they revealed. Every shadow seemed to be pregnant with menace.

Cyrus realized a cold sweat was breaking out all over his body, and he took stock of his situation. He realized that despite navigating away from the swamp's edge and very deliberately taking a different route, he could still feel the aura he had observed before. It was slowly growing more and more intense as he neared the border of this Ruler's territory again.

He looked up, got his bearings, and confirmed he had been moving along a winding path, avoiding the swampland while getting slowly and steadily closer to the landmarks of civilization.

Is there no other way to reach those buildings? He hoped they would not have to fight a Ruler just to reach a place he hoped could become their new home. That would be a true biblical trial. Another thought struck him. *If the aura is growing heavier as I move forward, despite not entering the swamp, could it mean the Ruler resides near the buildings? Or maybe*—he suddenly had to force himself to contain his excitement—*maybe we're moving toward a Ruler of human origins!*

Cyrus took a step forward, almost delirious at the prospect of obtaining the protection of a human Ruler—and stopped in his tracks. He heard a low growling, and let out a quiet whistle. His people moved backward into their square formation again. The concentration of torchlight from so many people standing close together allowed Cyrus to see what he had been missing.

Wolves.

Somehow they had crept up on him, and Cyrus and his people were now surrounded by a pack of wolves.

Gleaming white teeth bared, a furry wall of ferocious beasts suddenly began to growl in unison.

I have to try talking to them, Cyrus thought. *We cannot possibly fight this many.*

Just one of these creatures had probably killed a boar, based on the Galts' statement earlier. They were coordinated, unlike the boars. Their eyes gleamed with bestial intelligence. They would not simply rush into spear points and allow themselves to be carved up.

Cyrus heard the slow sound of tense strings being drawn back, and without turning his head, he raised a hand to tell his archers to hold off. If his group started a fight here, they might win. But this might not be the whole wolf pack. If a Ruler was among them, shooting one of its minions would be suicidal.

VISIONS AND NIGHTMARES

He gathered his courage and tried to form words.

"Excuse me, wise beasts," he said, restraining his teeth from chattering.

He stopped mid-sentence as the wolves parted like a curtain.

From among them, two giants of their kind stalked forward. By some perversion of nature, each of the giants was two-headed.

Cyrus ignored his people letting out nervous gasps and groans at the sight of the monstrous creatures.

Those must be the Ruler's lieutenants, he thought. *If one was the Ruler itself, I would feel its aura more intensely now that we are this close.*

"We come in peace," Cyrus said loudly. "We are merely migrating through this land. We have no intention of disturbing your pack. Please let us through!"

One of the lead wolves made eye contact with Cyrus, and he forced himself to maintain his locked gaze, despite the urge to look away. He had read somewhere that eye contact was actually meaningful to wolves, though the specifics were unfortunately lost to him at this critical moment.

At last, the wolf let out a bark through the head that was not looking Cyrus in the eye, and the monsters began slowly withdrawing, melting back into the trees.

The lead monsters pulled back last. They stepped backward into the brush, keeping their gaze firmly on Cyrus. As those glowing eyes retreated beyond his ability to see them, he finally let out a sigh of relief. Cyrus heard others making similar relieved noises, and several hands clapped him on the back, as those around him realized the danger had passed.

His group continued to advance. At times, he felt that he could still hear or almost see the wolves somewhere in the woods around him. However, he chose to ignore the possibly imagined presence. If they were there, then the wolves were acting as an honor guard. Noble beasts, obeying the will of the master of this place, who Cyrus grew more and more convinced must be human. Why else would a pack of wild monsters choose to spare him and his followers?

As he was contemplating what had happened, Cyrus's group crossed an invisible line. An alert sounded and appeared in the air before them, although the voice this time was not the System voice that Cyrus was familiar with.

[You have entered the territory of the Fisher King uninvited. Surrender to him or his representatives, or prepare for battle.]

I love that name, Cyrus thought. *The figure in Arthurian lore who guards the Holy Grail. A great servant of God. A good sign . . . Whether you know it or not, Fisher King, God has a plan for you.*

"What do we do, sir?" asked Christopher calmly.

"We simply wait," Cyrus replied. "For the Fisher King or his representatives to receive us."

Although he thought it was likely the wolves had been the representatives.

No, that's not quite enough. We can't just wait . . .

"We kneel and pray for God's protection in this critical moment," he added.

He repeated the instruction to the whole group, louder.

"Let us pray for God's protection," Cyrus said, raising his voice.

And the group knelt as a body. Only the Galts were a little slower to move, but even they quickly fell on their knees and turned their faces to heaven.

About the Author

D. J. Rintoul was born and raised in Orlando, Florida. He obtained his law degree from the University of Florida and subsequently returned to Pennsylvania, where he had met his wife and obtained his undergraduate degree. Rintoul now lives with his family in eastern Pennsylvania. He enjoys history, books, board games, Christmas lights, and, occasionally, sunlight.

Podium

DISCOVER MORE
STORIES UNBOUND

PodiumEntertainment.com